WIND RIVER RANCHER

LINDSAY McKENNA

ZEBRA BOOKS
KENSINGTON PUBLISHING CORP.
http://www.kensingtonbooks.com

ZEBRA BOOKS are published by

Kensington Publishing Corp.
119 West 40th Street
New York, NY 10018

All Kensington titles, imprints, and distributed lines are available at special quantity discounts for bulk purchases for sales promotion, premiums, fund-raising, educational, or institutional use.

Special book excerpts or customized printings can also be created to fit specific needs. For details, write or phone the office of the Kensington Sales Manager: Attn.: Sales Department. Kensington Publishing Corp., 119 West 40th Street, New York, NY 10018. Phone: 1-800-221-2647.

Zebra and the Z logo Reg. U.S. Pat. & TM Off.

First Printing: January 2017
ISBN-13: 978-1-4201-4176-4
ISBN-10: 1-4201-4176-7

eISBN-13: 978-1-4201-4177-1
eISBN-10: 1-4201-4177-5

10 9 8 7 6 5 4 3 2 1

Printed in the United States of America

To Rae Noble, one of my wonderful readers
who I met in the early 1980s.
She was with me up until December 2015.
I can't tell you how many conversations we had
over the years, first by letters and later, via emails.
She loved my books and always had wonderful praise
for them. She made MY day, so many times over this
past thirty years. Rae has no idea how many times she
lifted me out of gloom with her enthusiastic praise.

One of the great gifts of being an author is meeting
and really connecting with my readers.
They are like a cosmic family to me.
I always treasured Rae's letters
and emails, knowing she was going to have something
positive and uplifting to say.
Even though she
passed on in December 2015,
I'll always cherish her generous heart,
her caring, and her passion for reading.
I also want to thank her wonderful daughter, who cared
for her as she took one last journey before passing,
Erin Joosten. She's just like her mother, and people
like Rae make this world a better place.

Chapter One

Reese Lockhart's stomach was tight with hunger as he stood at the outskirts of a small Wyoming town called Wind River. The sign indicated a population of two thousand. He'd gone a month without decent food. Six inches of snow stood on the sides of the road where he'd walked the last ten miles on 89A north. It headed toward Jackson Hole, where he was hoping to find work.

The town, for a Monday afternoon, was pretty slow. A couple of pickup trucks came and went, a few people walked along the sidewalks on either side of the highway that ran through the center of town. He halted outside Becker's Hay and Feed Store, an aged redbrick building standing two stories high. The red tin roof was steep and sunlight reflected off it, making Reese squint. Bright lights now hurt his eyes.

Taking a deep breath, feeling the fear of rejection once again, he pushed open the door to the store. Would he get yelled at by the owner? Told to get out? It was early May and snow had fallen the night before. The sleepy town of Wind River still had slush on its streets at midday.

The place was quiet, smelled of leather, and he saw a man in his sixties, tall, lean, and with silver hair, sitting behind the counter. He was sitting on a wooden stool that was probably the same age as he was, an ancient-looking calculator in his work-worn hands as he methodically punched the buttons.

Girding himself, ignoring the fact that he hadn't eaten in two days, Reese's gaze automatically swung around the huge establishment. A hay and feed store was something he was familiar with. Maybe the owner wanted some part-time help. He needed to make enough money to buy a decent meal.

Shoving away the shame he felt over his situation, he saw the man lift his head, wire-rim spectacles halfway down his large nose, his blue eyes squinting at Reese as he approached the long wooden counter.

"Howdy, stranger. Can I help you?" the man asked.

"Maybe," Reese said. "I'm looking for work. I saw you have several big barns out back, and a granary. Do you have any openings?" Automatically, Reese tensed. He knew he looked rough with a month's worth of beard on his face, and his clothes were dirty and shabby. At one time, he'd been a Marine Corps captain commanding a company of 120 Marines. And he'd been damn good at it until—

"I'm Charlie Becker, the owner," the man said, shifting and thrusting his hand across the desk toward him. "Welcome to Wind River. Who might you be?"

"Reese Lockhart," he said, and he gripped the man's strong hand. He liked Charlie's large, watery eyes because he saw kindness in them. Reese was very good at assessing people. He'd kept his Marines safe and helped them through their professional and personal ups and downs over the years he commanded Mike Company in Afghanistan. Charlie was close to six feet tall, lean like a rail, and wore a white cowboy shirt and blue jeans. Reese sensed this older gentleman wouldn't throw him out of here with a curse—

or even worse, call law enforcement and accuse him of trespassing.

The last place where he'd tried to find some work, they'd called him a druggie and told him to get the hell out; he smelled. While walking the last ten miles to Wind River, Reese had stopped when he discovered a stream on the flat, snow-covered land, and tried to clean up the best he could. The temperature was near freezing as he'd gone into the bushes, away from the busy highway, and stripped to his waist. He'd taken handfuls of snow and scrubbed his body, shivering, but hell, that was a small price to pay to try to not smell so bad. He hadn't had a real shower in a month, either.

"You a vet, by any chance?" Charlie asked, his eyes narrowing speculatively upon Reese.

"Yes, sir. Marine Corps." He said it with pride.

"Good to know, Son." Charlie looked toward a table at the rear of the store, which held coffee, cookies, and other goodies offered to patrons. "Why don't you go help yourself to some hot coffee and food over there?" He gestured in that general direction. "My wife, Pixie, made 'em. Right good they are. I usually get a stampede of ranchers comin' in here when word gets 'round that Pixie baked some goodies." He chuckled.

Reese wanted to run to that table, but he stood relaxed as he could be, given anxiety was tunneling through him constantly. "I'd like that, sir. Thank you . . ."

"Don't call me sir," Charlie said. "Americans owe ALL of you men and women who have sacrificed so much for us. Now, go help yourself to all you want. There's plenty more where that came from. Pixie usually drives in mid-afternoon with a new batch of whatever has inspired her in the kitchen each day."

Reese needed something worse than he needed food

right now, so he hesitated. "Do you have any work I might do around here, Mr. Becker?"

"Call me Charlie. And no, I don't need help, but I got a nearby rancher who is looking for a hardworking wrangler-type to hire. You seem like you've worked a little in your life." Grinning, he stood and pointed to Reese's large, calloused hands. "I'll call over there while you grab yourself some grub." He waved, urging Reese to go eat.

Nodding, Reese rasped out a thank-you and felt his stomach growl loudly. He hoped like hell Charlie hadn't heard it. But judging from the man's facial expression, he had heard. Charlie picked up the black, landline phone on the counter to make a call to the ranch.

Halting at the long table against the back wall of the store, Reese's mouth watered. He was chilled to the bone, his combat boots wet, his socks soaked, toes numb. The coffee smelled so damned good, and with shaking hands, he poured it into an awaiting white Styrofoam cup. He took a cautious sip, the heat feeling incredible as it slid down his throat and into his shrunken, knotted gut. God, it tasted so good!

Reese kept one ear cocked toward the phone call Charlie was making. *Let there be an opening for me.* He worried because even though he no longer stank, his clothes were dirty and long past a washing. He knew he looked like a burned-out druggie or a homeless person, his hair long and unkempt, his black beard thick and in dire need of a trim. Reese didn't have a pair of scissors on him to do the job. His scruffy, dark green baseball cap was frayed and old, a holdover from two years ago when he was a Marine.

Eyeing the box of colorfully frosted cupcakes, his mouth watered. He wanted to grab all of them, but his discipline and manners forced him to pick up just one. His fingers trembled again as he peeled the paper from around the pink frosted cupcake.

Reese bit into the concoction, groaning internally as the sweetness hit his tongue and coated the inside of his mouth. For a moment, he was dizzy from the sugar rush, his whole body lighting up with internal celebration as the food hit his gnawing stomach. Standing there, Reese forced himself to take slow sips of the coffee. It tasted heavenly. He heard Charlie finish the call and the man came in his direction.

"Hey, Mr. Lockhart, good news," Charlie said. "The owner of the Bar C Ranch, Shay Crawford, still needs a wrangler. She's coming into town in about two hours, going to be coming by here to pick up some dog food and such. Said she'd meet you at that time."

"That's good to hear," Reese said. "Thank you . . ."

Charlie nodded. "I have a bathroom in the back, with a big shower." He jabbed his index finger toward the rear corner of the store. "It's got some shaving gear in there, as well. On your way there, pick out a pair of jeans, a work shirt, boots, and whatever else you need before she arrives."

"I don't have the money to pay you," Reese said, hating to admit it. But he understood what Charlie was really saying. The woman owner of the Bar C would probably not want to hire him with the way he looked right now. The guy was trying to help him out.

Charlie gripped the arm of Reese's damp, dark olive-green military jacket. "This way. Just consider my offer as grateful thanks from this nation of ours for your sacrifices, Mr. Lockhart. You pick up what you want to wear and anything else you need. It's free to you. It's the least we can do for our vets." Charlie had a look in his eyes that told Reese he wasn't going to budge from his position.

Reese was going to say no, but the man's face turned stubborn. He felt like he was in a dream instead of a nightmare. "Tell you what," Reese said, his voice suddenly thick with emotion, "if I get this job, I'll pay you back every cent. Fair enough?"

Charlie smiled a little. "Fair enough, Mr. Lockhart. Now, eat all you want and once you're filled up, choose your clothes, find a good Stetson, work gloves, and anything else you might need. Bring it to the counter and I'll write it up for you." Charlie studied Reese's sorry-looking boots. "And get a pair of decent work boots to replace these guys." He gave Reese a grin. "They look like they need to be permanently retired."

One corner of Reese's mouth twitched. "Sort of like me," he admitted, more than grateful to the man. He felt like he was being treated like a king.

"Son, you're just having a bad streak of luck. We all go there at some point in our lives. You'll get through it, too." Charlie released his arm and patted it. "I think your streak is gonna end right shortly. Miss Crawford is an angel come to earth. If you present yourself well, I'm sure she'll hire you. She's a good boss to work for. The people she hires, stay, and that says everything."

Reese watched Charlie walk back to the counter. Hot tears pricked the back of his eyes. Reese swallowed hard several times, forcing them away. In the next fifteen minutes, he ate four more cupcakes and had three more cups of hot coffee, and felt damn near human. He found the jeans, work shirts, thick, heavy socks, a couple of pairs of boxer shorts, and two white T-shirts, and carried them up to the counter.

Charlie scowled. "Where's your work gloves? You need a good, heavy Carhartt work jacket. Your Stetson? Get a pair of heavy snow gloves, too. It stays winter until mid-June around here. And don't leave out getting a good, heavy knit sweater you can wear under that winter coat of yours." He pointed in another direction where a rack of men's sweaters hung, with a SPRING SALE sign on top of it.

Chastened, Reese nodded, his throat locked up with shame.

"Oh, and serious work boots, Son." He shook his finger in another direction where the footwear department was located. "Get a darned good pair. Don't skimp on quality because of price."

Reese wished he could nominate Charlie to the powers-that-be at the White House who were in charge of citizen honors, and have Charlie lauded as a hero. There should be a place where civilians who helped out vets who were faltering or who had walked away from society, were recognized for their compassion. Charlie deserved a civilian medal of the highest order. Once Reese located the rest of the gear, he brought it up to the counter.

"Grab your new duds and take a long, hot shower, Mr. Lockhart. There's razors and a pair of scissors in the medicine cabinet, should you want to trim that beard and long hair of yours a bit."

Okay, Reese got it. Charlie was his guardian angel trying to get him spiffed up for this coming interview with Ms. Crawford. Nodding his thanks, Reese took the clothes and headed diagonally across the store. As he entered the men's restroom, he was surprised by how large and sparkling clean it was. Indeed, there was a nice big shower, clean, white towels hanging nearby, a bar of Ivory soap and a soft, thick wash cloth.

Locking the door, Reese gladly got out of his old, filthy clothes. He felt guilty for accepting this man's generosity, but he'd hit the bottom of the barrel a month ago. And it wasn't pride that stopped him from accepting handouts. There weren't any handouts offered until just now. People would take one look at him, turn, and hurry away. Or if they saw him coming, they'd cross the street to avoid him. Women, especially, showed fear of him. He was a dirty, unshaven stranger. Reese didn't blame them, but damn, it hurt to be treated that way. He'd never harm a woman, but they didn't know that by looking at him.

Naked, he tried to ignore how thin he'd become in the two years since leaving the Corps. He'd once been moderately muscled, fifty pounds heavier, and a lot stronger than he was presently. Entering the shower, Reese knew his weakness was directly attributable to not eating for days at a time. Even now, he felt his body responding powerfully to the cupcakes he'd eaten. His stomach growled for more, but as Reese turned on the heavy, warm spray, it was a helluva lot more than he'd ever expected from anyone.

Charlie smiled from behind the counter as Reese approached, holding his old clothes. Reese smelled food. Real food. And then, he spotted two large Styrofoam boxes near Charlie's elbow, where he sat on that aged stool.

"You clean up real good, Mr. Lockhart," Charlie said, rising and taking his clothes. "I'm assuming these are DOA?"

Reese nodded. "Yeah, pretty much. Thanks for your help here." He motioned to the clothes he now wore.

"Like I said," Charlie murmured, dumping the clothes into a huge wastebasket, "our country owes you." He came back and pushed the two Styrofoam boxes toward him. "I called up Kassie Murphy. She owns Kassie's Café down the next block on the plaza. I asked if she'd donate you some vittles. Once she found out you were a vet, Kassie said to tell you it's on the house. You can come and eat at her establishment anytime you want, no questions asked. Folks in these parts? Many of them served, and have sons or daughters in the military. So we have a real soft spot in our heart for military vets like yourself. I hope you like the two hamburgers, coleslaw, and French fries. Julie, one of the waitresses who brought these over here for you, said there's homemade apple pie with three scoops of vanilla ice cream in there, too. Why don't you grab that chair back at the coffee station, sit down, and enjoy your meal? Shay won't be here for another hour."

"Thanks," Reese said. "And thank everyone over at Kassie's Café for me?"

"Oh," Charlie murmured, shrugging, "I've a feeling when Shay gets a gander at how strong and tall you are, she'll hire you on the spot. And then, when it suits you later, you can go over and thank those hardworking gals at Kassie's yourself."

It was all Reese could do to hold it together. He carefully walked to the coffee station, holding the boxes in his hands as if they were the greatest treasure on earth. His feet were warm. He was clean. Really clean. There had been a toothbrush and toothpaste in the cabinet as well. Deodorant. He'd used the scissors to cut his hair the best he could; it was still on his nape, but hopefully he didn't look like the homeless person of before. The beard was gone, thanks to the fact that Charlie had stashed five razors in the medicine cabinet. And he'd used all of them, since his beard was so damned wiry and thick. Emotions swept through him as he sat down and opened up the container with the two huge hamburgers. The scent of the food nearly made him faint. It smelled so good.

Reese had never starved in his life except for the last year. Jobs had been sparse, and then only part-time or they were seasonal and ended in a month or two. Sometimes he was fired because he couldn't handle the stressful demands that forced him to work swiftly and continuously.

His anxiety ran him. He had no control over it and he'd found out quickly, after his discharge, that a stressful job only tripled the monstrous anxiety that was always there, always waiting to leap upon him and scatter his thoughts, his actions.

As he bit into the burger, he closed his eyes, made a low sound of pleasure in the back of his throat, slumping against the metal chair, in Nirvana. Reese knew if he gulped it down, he'd more than likely throw it up, so he tamped down on the animal desire to gulp. He chewed it slowly, savoring every last bite of the lettuce, tomatoes, onion, cheddar cheese, and bacon on it. It took him thirty minutes to clean up everything. The apple pie was melt-in-your mouth, reminding him of his mother's own home-cooked pies.

An old ache centered in his heart. His parents wanted him home, but God, that had been a disaster. Reese wasn't going to make them pay for his PTSD, and they didn't understand why he had to leave. He wasn't the best at talking about his shame over the symptoms that he couldn't control. His father had been in the military, retired, and was now a hardworking mechanic. He had saved all his life for retirement, and Reese wasn't about to take his money that he'd offered to him. He had to stand on his own two feet, pull himself up by his bootstraps, and not accept handouts.

As he rose and placed the chair against the wall, he saw the door open. A young woman with light brown hair, slightly curly around her oval face, walked in. All his acute senses focused on her. She was wearing a black baseball cap, a blue chambray shirt like the one he wore, a heavy Levi's jacket, and a pair of loose-fitting jeans that indicated she had a lush figure hidden beneath them. His heart jolted as their eyes met briefly. She had sky-blue eyes, just this side of turquoise, wide set and intelligent. She was attractive, wore no makeup, but her high cheekbones were flushed, as if she'd been running or working out hard.

His stomach clenched, and suddenly, Reese worried that if she was the owner of the Bar C, he might not get the job. That she'd be afraid of him like so many other women were, once they saw him. In the Corps, wearing his uniform or utilities, women had always given him a pleasing look, scoping him out, their gazes telling him they'd like to know him a lot better. He almost laughed as he struggled to get his anxiety corralled. Since he'd fallen from grace, his scruffy, bearded, homeless look scared the hell out of females. Reese knew he wasn't a bad-looking man, but somehow, no woman could see the real him in his present state of dishevelment. He would *never* hurt a woman or child. But the look in their eyes spoke of exactly that: fear that he was capable of violence against them. It was a bitter pill to swallow to be judged by what he wore on the outside instead of who he really was inside.

"Hey," Charlie called, twisting his head in Reese's direction, "Miss Shay is here. Come on up and meet her, Reese."

God, this was like a firing squad. All his life, he'd drawn straight A's in school and in college. Always a winner. He was first in everything he'd ever tried. And now, he was last. Dead last.

Squaring his shoulders, Reese walked toward the counter and watched as the young woman who was about a head shorter than him, maybe around five foot eight or nine inches tall, assessed him critically. Reese could feel the heat of her blue gaze stripping him from his uncovered head down to his boots as he rounded the corner of the counter.

"Shay, meet Reese Lockhart," Charlie said. "Reese, this is Shay Crawford, owner of the Bar C."

Reese saw a shadow flit across her eyes for just a

moment, and then it was gone. Her mouth was full, lush, just like her breasts and hips. A hum started low in his body, appreciating her purely as a woman. When she extended her slender hand, he engulfed it gently within his. Reese tried to keep the surprise out of his face as he felt the calluses along her palm and the roughness of her fingers, indicating she worked hard.

"Ma'am," he murmured, "nice to meet you. I asked Charlie about a job, and he said you needed a wrangler." Reese released her hand, albeit reluctantly. To his surprise, she stood her ground even though he was a good six inches taller than she was. He didn't scare her, and that made Reese sag inwardly with relief. Those fearless-looking blue eyes of hers were direct and he held her gaze, understanding she was forming an impression of him on an instinctual level. In the kind of black ops work he had done, instinct had saved his life often. Reese sensed strongly she possessed the same powerful intuition herself.

"It's nice to meet you, Mr. Lockhart." She glanced over at the store owner. "Charlie said you were a vet. That you are a Marine?"

"Yes, ma'am. Once a Marine, always a Marine."

Her lips pulled faintly at the corners. "You're right. You're still a Marine even if you're now a civilian. Call me Shay, Mr. Lockhart. I was in the service, too. I'm fine with less protocol."

Reese nodded. "Habits are hard to erase," he noted, a slight, teasing note in his voice. "But I'll try."

She leaned against the counter, hands on the edge of the smooth oak. "What kind of work are you looking for?"

"Anything outdoors, for the most part."

"You're a Marine, so you probably have some skill sets?"

"I ran a company, ma—I mean, Shay, of 120 men and women."

Nodding, she assessed him more closely. "What was your rank?"

"Captain." Reese couldn't translate what he saw in her expression and whether it was good or bad news for him. He wondered if she was enlisted or an officer. Now was not the time to ask.

"I need a wrangler who is good slinging a hammer and nails, Mr. Lockhart. I've got an indoor arena I'm trying to build with too few men to do it, and it has to be roofed before the first snow flies, which is usually mid-September around here." She gauged him for a moment, her voice husky. "I make a point of hiring military vets who are down on their luck. The Bar C is more than just a place to work. Much more."

"Okay," he murmured, "my skill sets are in construction work and also vehicle repair. My father is a mechanic and I grew up learning how to fix anything that had an engine attached to it."

"That's even better news," she murmured, brightening a little. Looking relieved.

"See?" Charlie gloated, preening. "I told you he was a man with a lot of talents."

Reese felt uncomfortable with such enthusiastic praise, but stood as relaxed as he could. Shay Crawford might be attractive as hell, but she was a woman with a lot of confidence and she wore the mantle of leadership well. There was no wedding ring on her left hand, but that didn't mean anything. He was sure she was in a relationship. He didn't see her being snooty, bossy, or power hungry because she was in control. Instead, she seemed pensive, studying him openly and without apology, searching his eyes, looking over his face and body. Reese thought he might as well be a horse she was considering buying. He was waiting for her to ask him to open his mouth so she could look at his teeth.

"I'm dying of hunger," she told Reese. "Would you like to come over to Kassie's Café and have a cup of coffee with me? I can give you a lot more information about the Bar C there. If the place isn't too much for you to handle. I can always find somewhere that is quieter, with fewer distractions."

Reese looked at her and felt his heart stir. The honesty in this woman's eyes held him in thrall. He was shaken over her last comment. Only someone with PTSD would ask that kind of question. He stared at her, trying to decipher more of who she really was. She stared back fearlessly, unafraid of his intense inspection. And if Reese wasn't mistaken, he thought he saw interest in him as a man, in her eyes. Which, he thought, was his imagination because he was clearly drawn to her. In the back of his mind, Reese was sure she was either married, engaged, or had a steady relationship. There was no way a woman like her was single and alone. No freakin' way.

"Kassie's sounds fine. I can handle noise for a while," he said, nodding, settling the gray Stetson on his head. "Lead the way to the café."

Charlie put Reese's purchases beneath the counter, saying he could come by later and pick them up. Reese thanked him and took long strides to the door, where he opened it for Shay and saw her blush. Her glance up at him was appreciative, and something else. But what?

As Reese followed her out to a dark blue Ford three-quarter-ton pickup, he watched the sway of her hips down those six wooden steps to the asphalt parking lot that held spots of melting snow. Several other pickups drove in and parked. Cowboys emerged. Reese decided it was a pretty popular place for ranchers. But given Charlie owned it and he was a good person, Reese could see why he'd get business from the hardworking ranch crews.

He opened the door of the truck for Shay before she could reach for the handle.

Flustered, Shay turned and looked up at him. "Really, I'm not helpless, Mr. Lockhart. I'll open my own doors from now on."

He gave her an apologetic glance. "As I said, habits die hard in me." And he smiled a little, seeing the warmth come to her eyes for a moment as she climbed in.

"Military men are like that," she admitted, a little breathless as she closed her own door.

Reese liked her backbone. She was a strong, self-assured woman. He opened the door and climbed in, his hopes rising. Shay Crawford would not have invited him to coffee if she wasn't going to hire him. His chest swelled with relief that nearly overwhelmed him. Reese had never worked for a woman before, but that didn't grate on him at all. His mother had raised him to always respect women and be courteous toward them. And as she backed the truck expertly out of the dirt parking lot, Reese buckled up, feeling like today was his lucky day.

Chapter Two

Shay sat with Reese Lockhart at Kassie's Café. Midafternoon, there were very few patrons in the small, cozy restaurant. Kassie was behind the counter and waved hello to them. Twenty-nine and single, she had lively green eyes, long black hair that was usually styled in a set of braids, and she and Shay were the same height.

Her father, Marshall, had been in the Marine Corps for twenty years, and she grew up as a military child. He died at age 50 of a heart attack. Two years ago, coming out of her grief, Kassie had taken over running the café, and had continued her father's practice of hiring military vets. Kassie's mother, Jade Murphy, sixty, had a heart condition and remained at home. She was a well-loved woman in Wind River.

Shay sat in a red plastic booth with Reese opposite her. Luckily, the café was very quiet. Kassie never played blaring music, so the patrons could have a quiet, decent conversation with one another, thank goodness. Shay didn't want to be emotionally touched by the Marine captain sitting across from her, his large, spare hands wrapped around a mug of coffee, but she was. It turned her stomach to see him look like so many other homeless vets cast off by the military because of PTSD. He'd never admitted he had PTSD, and she wasn't about to pry. One thing she'd found out from the beginning was a vet with PTSD hated twenty questions: Why are you behaving this way? What's wrong with you? And Shay could provide the litany because it had happened to her. It took one to know one. And because of her own PTSD, she could easily see it in Lockhart.

Reese Lockhart was a tall, well-built man, but he was gaunt looking—familiar symptoms. Shay sipped her coffee, having given her food order to Julie, the waitress. Lockhart had declined to order, saying he wasn't hungry, so Shay figured one of two things had occurred; either the man was too proud to take a handout, or Charlie had fed him already. Pixie provided baked goods for the store's customers nearly every day, so she wouldn't have been surprised to see Charlie urge Lockhart to eat at the table in the rear, where the goodies were kept.

Dear, sweet Charlie had a soft spot in his heart for military vets. He made a point of hiring them when he could. The skin across Lockhart's high cheekbones told the story. That and his red-rimmed eyes. And his pallor. It all summed up to malnutrition or, as Shay well knew, actual starvation. And if she was any judge, even though he wore heavy winter clothing, he'd probably lost fifty or more pounds on his large frame over time. Meals did not come often or easily to this homeless vet.

She compressed her lips. Shay was well aware of Lockhart's tension. Anyone with even a little emotional sensitivity could feel the effects of PTSD on a man or woman, like a bomb ready to detonate suddenly, at any moment. Reese's hands were tense around the white ceramic mug, a sign of his anxiety. And she knew he wanted the job desperately because she saw the need banked in his green eyes, which were cloudy with stress.

"I need to fill you in on the Bar C," she began quietly. Luckily, Shay had been able to grab a booth near the restroom area. It was roomy and out of the normal, busy walkway. This was her favorite place because it was private and quiet when the café was busy. Right now, it was blessedly quiet.

"My father, Ray Crawford, suffered a debilitating stroke a year ago. I had just been released from the Marine Corps and come home to help him run the Bar C, when it happened." She saw him frown, real regret reflected for a moment in his eyes. Lockhart might be dealing with PTSD, but he still had the capacity to feel for others. That was a good sign in her book. So many homeless vets were numbed out to the world around them, kicked around, ignored, abused, and unseen by the rest of society. The only choice they had at that point was to move deep within themselves, going into survival mode.

"I'm sorry," he said. "That had to be tough on you. Unexpected?"

Shay felt warmth flooding her chest as she swallowed her surprise. She hadn't expected Reese to be this aware. But she saw it in the softening of the hard line of his mouth and heard it in the deep, warm tone of his voice. There was real concern in his gaze—for her. Not for himself. So often, vets were self-centered precisely because they were in survival reflex. No one was vulnerable when they scrabbled daily just to keep living. It came with the territory. But for whatever reason, for however long Lockhart had been cut loose from the Corps, he hadn't lost the capacity to have compassion for other people's troubled lives. At least, not yet. Eventually, because society didn't care about these wounded warriors, he might become that way. But he hadn't reached that point and it made her feel hope for him.

"Yes . . . it was, in a way." She hitched one shoulder.

"My father and I never got along, and it's not something I want to discuss much. But yes, a stroke that partially paralyzed him and sent him into a nursing home, did shake me up." She opened her hands around her mug. "It meant I was running the ranch on my own and I wasn't mentally or emotionally prepared to do it." That was barely scratching the surface, but Shay wasn't here to tell her story. She wanted *his* story, to assess him in order to see if he was a good fit for the other three wounded vets she'd taken in over the past year to help them heal, and to help her run the ranch.

"That's a load to continually carry," he agreed.

What was it about this vet that just made her want to spill her guts to him? Shaken, Shay was caught off guard. Maybe it was his low, modulated tone wreathed with understanding? The sudden sharpness coming to his eyes, his realization of her own struggle? Unsure, she smiled a little. "Well, I've pulled the ranch back from foreclosure, so that's the good news, but it's a daily challenge. And we're hanging on by our teeth, if you want the rest of the truth."

"And this indoor arena," Reese asked, "is it part of your plan to expand your ranch so you can bring in more income?"

Her mouth almost dropped open. Shay hadn't expected that kind of clarity and insight from him. "Well . . ." She stumbled. "Yes . . . yes, that's part of the long-range business plan I've tried to put together. Not that I've got a degree in business. My ideas are just that—ideas that I'm sometimes not sure how to fully implement." She cleared her throat and the words rushed out of her mouth. "When I came home, my father was ill and no longer able to run the Bar C, so I decided to change the direction of the ranch. I wanted a place where military vets who had severe PTSD symptoms could come and heal. Find a place where they were valued. To be among their own kind, and be treated with respect. Care . . ." Shay saw his expression change, grow intense, his eyes narrowing upon her, studying her. She'd felt the shift of energy around him and recognized it because she was a warrior herself. She'd struck something deep and important to Reese. Maybe that was good. Shay just didn't know yet.

"That's why you considered hiring me?"

"Charlie called me. He said you were a military vet. He knew I was looking to hire a fourth wrangler." Briefly, Shay saw in his eyes his wounded pride, his crushed state, and then he hid it. Shame and humiliation were the greatest enemies these vets carried within them. That and the constant, gnawing anxiety that dogged them twenty-four hours a day. She suspected by the way his black hair was cut, that he'd lopped it off with a pair of scissors very recently. And Shay knew that Charlie had probably given this vet not only the use of the shower, but had fed him and given him the new clothes he wore. She could smell the fresh scent of Ivory soap around Reese. His hair was combed but pathetically cut, telling her the rest of the story. It broke her heart because these men and women had endured so much, and then to come home and be treated like this shocked her.

"What are the terms of staying on, if you hire me?"

Shay heard the wariness in his voice and saw it in his eyes. "The rules are that you give fifteen percent of any money you earn back to the ranch bank account. I'm feeding you and giving you shelter. I need money to buy food and pay for your room. Another fifteen percent goes into a bank savings account, in your name. It's a way for you to build some equity and have a nest egg when you decide to leave the Bar C and strike out on your own once more. There's a weekly gab fest at the main house that everyone must attend. I try to bring in people from surrounding areas who are knowledgeable about military veterans who are having issues fitting back into society, helping them readjust and return to the mainstream when they're ready. Other than that, I expect you to work eight hours a day, Monday through Friday. You have weekends off."

Shay held her breath. He was thinking over her offer. It was clear that he was an outdoors type of man, had worked damned hard judging from the thick calluses on his large hands.

"Is this gab fest a therapy fest?"

She smiled a little, knowing vets automatically shied away from therapy. But it was one of many healing tools that could help them. "Sort of. I know vets are closed up tighter than a clam. I try to bring tools to your awareness, and you can choose from among them, if you want. There's county services here that might be of use to you, eventually. I just want everyone to be aware of what's out there, is all. What you do with the education and knowledge is up to you. Each of us heals at different speeds." Shay saw relief come to his eyes. For a moment, Lockhart reacted as if he were a bug that was going to be pinned down with needles and minutely examined by a shrink. "It's actually pretty painless. You can ask the other men who work for me about it. Sometimes, we have a lot of laughs and good times, too. It's not uptight or formal."

"I can live with your rules."

"How long were you in the Corps, Mr. Lockhart?"

"I was in ROTC in high school, went to college and got a degree in business administration, and then went through Officer Candidate School. I was pinned a shavetail lieutenant at twenty-two. From there, I worked in infantry, first as an executive officer to a Marine company over in Iraq. Later, after I made captain, I took care of Mike Company in Afghanistan until I was twenty-six."

"That's a lot of responsibility."

"I liked it. I was good at what I did. I'm a good people manager." And then Reese shrugged. "But what you need is a wrangler who is a handyman, to help build that indoor arena for you."

She saw how much he missed being in the Marine Corps, his whole life torn out from beneath him. Shay wasn't going to ask if he'd been discharged from the Corps. It had to be due to the PTSD, and it was either an accumulation of trauma, or one big trauma, that had spun this vet out of his orbit and into homelessness. Her stomach tightened in reaction, because the story was familiar for all of them, including herself. "You said you have a degree in business administration?"

"Yes, ma'—I mean, Shay. Yes, I do."

"By any chance do you have an accounting background?"

He nodded. "I can push numbers around with the best of them." And then he allowed a hint of a smile. "Unlike Charlie, who uses a twenty-year-old calculator, I'm up on the latest software in the business world and proficient with all of it."

She smiled softly. "Charlie hates computers. He won't have anything to do with them. Pixie, his wife, has tried to get him into the twenty-first century, but he's stubborn as the proverbial mule."

Reese smiled a little more and pushed the cup slowly back and forth between his hands. "He's happy that way and it works for him. At least no one is hacking in and stealing his intel."

"You got that right," she agreed. Shay tucked her lower lip, worrying it for a moment, studying the table. Lifting her head, she said, "I'm not good with math or accounting. And I've been hoping to meet a vet who has that kind of background. Would it bother you to take a look at the ranch books? You could work part-time in the office and the rest of it on the indoor arena."

Reese considered her request. "Sure, I'd be happy to support you with my skills in any way I can."

She saw hope burning in his eyes and Shay didn't want to leave him hanging. "I'd like to hire you, Mr. Lockhart. I think you'll fit in fine with the men who are already there. And I think you'll like all of them because they're hard-working, they care, and they're responsible. None of them are addicted to drugs or alcohol. And I'm hoping you don't have those issues either."

His mouth quirked. "No. Thought about it often enough, but it's not my way of dealing with life. We all get thrown curves. It's how we respond to them that counts. I'm clean."

"I like your attitude."

Julie, the waitress, came over with Shay's lunch, a grilled cheese sandwich and French fries. Shay thanked her. The look in Reese's eyes, now filled with hope and something else she couldn't translate, made her happy. Anytime she could help one of these vets, it was a personal high for her. Oh, she knew there would be a period of adjustment for Noah, Harper, and Garret, but they were vets and team minded. Reese seemed quiet, steady, and for sure was a keen observer and listened well. All things that Shay knew would help this man, who was so terribly gaunt, get a hand up and get his life in his control once more.

"Would you like to share the French fries?" she asked, pushing the plate to the center of the table. Vets were proud. They hated handouts. Shay knew they'd rather starve than ask for food. She saw some ruddiness come to his cheeks.

"Charlie fed me earlier. But thanks."

Nodding, Shay liked his ability to be honest. Maybe his pride didn't run him completely. And if it didn't, that was a good sign that he wanted to heal. "Charlie's a good person.

Did you know he was in the Marine Corps for four years? From eighteen to twenty-two. Then he came out of his enlistment and worked with his father at the hay and feed store. Eventually, when his father retired, Charlie took over the operation."

"That explains why he took me under his wing," Reese noted wryly, lifting the cup to his lips.

She grinned. "Yeah, he's a mother hen in disguise. He's got a heart of gold. He couldn't contain his excitement when he told me you were a Marine. After my father had that stroke and Charlie found out I was converting the ranch to help homeless vets, he offered me a forty-percent discount on everything at his store. The guy makes not a dime off me as a result. Talk about taking care of your own. I love Charlie and Pixie."

"He's loyal and he cares," Reese said, moving the cup slowly around between his hands.

"More than most," Shay agreed somberly. "Civilians don't get us. But you can't expect that of them, either. They haven't been in the military. They don't understand our world or the pressures and stresses that are intrinsically part of it."

"Why are you doing this?"

She stopped chewing for a moment, regarding his serious expression. She could feel Reese trying to understand her. Ordinarily, Shay retreated from such questions, but with him, with the sincerity he offered without apology, she swallowed. "It's a calling. A passion."

"Because?"

She moved uncomfortably in the seat beneath his benign inspection. He was a good-looking man, vital, filled with a powerful life force, even though right now, he was nowhere near what she imagined he'd been as an officer in charge of a Marine company. "Because I care." She said it in such

a way that it was all she was going to tell him. Shay could
see his eyes change, darken a little, consideration and respect
in them . . .

"Well," Reese murmured, giving her a look of admiration, "we need more people like you in this world. There's
a lot of vets out there who are hurting. The VA doesn't give
a damn about us, making us wait up to a year or more to get
an appointment in order to get help."

"I know," Shay said sadly. Wiping her mouth with the
paper napkin, she added, "I went through the same process
and never got an appointment because the VA hospital was
so backlogged. It's a national disgrace if you ask me.
Our men and women returning from combat desperately
need medical attention, psychological support as soon as
they step onto our country's soil. But it's not there for any
of them."

"No," Reese agreed, his voice growing quiet, "it's not."

Wincing, Shay heard the pain in his tone. "I know . . . I
hope that you find the Bar C a place where you can heal,
Mr. Lockhart. You'll work hard, but you will be with a
military family of sorts. That will help a lot. I know it has
the other three men. They've blossomed since coming to
the ranch." She felt the full warmth of his look and it gently
enclosed her heart, surprising her.

"Thanks to you. To your vision. Or maybe, I should say,
your passion? You can't do something like this if your heart
isn't invested in it."

His understanding and praise enveloped Shay and she
secretly relished it. There was something different about
this vet, and she couldn't put her finger on it. Maybe Reese
was just very savvy about human nature; it was a part of
who he was. If that was so, then Shay could only imagine
how his PTSD symptoms were tearing him up inwardly. It
was hell on everyone, but a man of his intelligence and

training, a consummate Marine Corps officer, it would be a hundred times worse. To fall from grace? To lose his entire career? She was sure he would have been a twenty- or thirty-year Marine, making military service his life.

"My heart is invested in this," she said, her voice determined. "For as long as I breathe, the Bar C is going to be a haven of healing for our men and women who have served. They deserve no less."

"Can you tell me about the other vets?"

Glad the spotlight was off her, Shay quickly finished her grilled cheese sandwich and ate half the French fries. "Harper Sutton is ex-Navy. He was a combat medic. He was my first hire nine months ago. And a week later, Garret Fleming, Army Special Forces, showed up on Charlie's doorstep. Then, a month after that, Noah Mabry, ex-Army dog handler, applied for a job. They're all between twenty-seven and thirty years old. Good men. Hard workers. They're invested in the Bar C and I'm sure as time goes on and you make friends with them, they'll each tell you their story."

"Yeah," Reese murmured, "we all have a story, don't we?" He studied her.

Squirming inwardly, Shay realized with trepidation that she had no defense against this man's ability to see through her. Did he realize she had PTSD just as badly as he and the other vets did? Most likely, from the way he was assessing her with those clear, dark green eyes of his, he was aware of her plight, too. She noticed as they sat and talked, the cloudiness had left his eyes, and in their place, a hawk-like expression of deep intelligence molded with a lot of human experience was in his gaze. This was a man, Shay guessed, who could tell if someone was bullshitting him or not. He saw a lot, said little, kept his feelings well hidden. But he'd been an officer, and in her experience, most of them were like that. After all, they had the responsibility to manage people. That was their job.

Shay decided not to answer him. Instead, she picked up her purse and put the money along with the bill at the end of the table. "We have a small bunkhouse," she said apologetically as Julie came over and took the payment. "It's only got three rooms. Do you mind, for a while, staying at the main ranch house with me? I've got two spare bedrooms and you can have your pick. I'm hoping to shift Noah, who is doing the grunt work on the indoor arena, to building more rooms in the bunkhouse after that project is completed."

Shrugging, Reese said, "I don't mind, but I'll be underfoot all the time."

She stood and slipped her purse over her left shoulder, pulling on her leather gloves and settling the black baseball cap on her head. "Oh, I think you're intelligent enough to pick up the rhythm of a household and flow with it. I'm not worried."

"I'll give it my best shot," Reese promised, easing out of the booth and pulling the gray Stetson on his head.

Shay didn't want to stare at him, but for a moment, she did. He was a tall man, capable looking, ruggedly handsome, his shoulders squared back with pride, his posture military. Reese might be down, but he was far from out. "How long have you been out of the Corps?"

"Two years."

Nodding, Shay said, "That's a long time . . ." and she was thinking that he'd fallen for two solid years. Most vets were in far worse condition at this point, in her experience. Shay sensed the mental toughness in Reese. She felt he could take more of life's hard blows and still crawl forward instead of letting it pound him into the ground and destroy him, like it had so many others in similar circumstances. Toughness of spirit was the key to whether a vet kept fighting back or surrendered and gave up. Reese had not given up, from what she could tell. And maybe it was in his nature to be a fighter and scrapper. That would serve him well in the end. "Let's go," she murmured, gesturing for him to follow her. "It's time for you to see your new home."

"That has a nice ring to it," he said, opening the door for her.

Shay gave him a glance. "Thanks. I know . . . it's your manners." She saw a partial grin leak out of the corner of his well-shaped mouth.

"Yes, it is," he said. "And not much of that will ever change, so I guess you're going to have to get used to being pampered a little here and there."

A frisson of heat prickled at her nape, went to her breasts, and then flowed hotly down to her lower body. Reese had given her the look of a man appreciating his woman. How could that be? Flummoxed by the mixed signals he was giving her, Shay stepped out on the wooden decking of the plaza. A few brave tourists were ambling from one store to another. She felt him come up behind her, more than a little aware of his blatant masculinity.

Shay would have panicked if he had overtly flirted with her, but Reese hadn't done that. He'd opened doors for her—a gentleman, a throwback to the days when women were treated with far more courtesy than they were today. She smiled to herself, leading him down the walkway to the parking lot behind Kassie's Café. Reese Lockhart moved easily, with the grace of a mountain lion, at her side. And damned if Shay didn't feel protection emanating off him toward her.

She had to remind herself that all military men were protectors and defenders at heart. Why else would they be in the armed forces? They were patriots, too. There was no way to ignore Reese. He walked silently, his boots soft footfalls against the wooden planking. Shay wondered if he had a black ops background. Maybe, with time and space, Reese would share the story of his fall from grace with her. Maybe . . .

Chapter Three

Reese tried to still the quiet joy thrumming through him as Shay drove the truck through Wind River and north on Highway 89A. Damn, he didn't want to be drawn to Shay, but he was and there was nothing he could do about it. She was vulnerable in a way that made him want to reach out and protect her. It took a lot for anyone to be vulnerable nowadays. It told Reese of her internal strength and confidence in herself. And as she shared her transition from Marine to having to suddenly manage a ranch, he'd seen the stress of it all in her eyes. And yet, she was determined in ways he could only admire.

As he looked out the open window, the warmth of the May afternoon air flowing through the cab, he felt a huge load begin to dissolve off his shoulders. He needed this job so badly and was utterly grateful to this woman who he knew had PTSD herself. It wasn't lost on Reese, because for the last two years he'd been involved with men and women vets on the street who had that same energy around them.

"How big is your ranch?"

"Ten thousand acres. My father ran Herefords on it. Actually, he leased a lot of it out to other ranchers during the summer months." Shay shrugged. "The winters are long and hard, up in this area, Mr. Lockhart."

"Can you call me Reese?" He gave her a look, and saw her lips curve a little.

"Of course." She glanced at him. "Everyone is on a first-name basis with one another at the ranch. The guys call me Shay and I'd like you to do the same." Her eyes sparkled. "Stop with the *ma'am?*"

His mouth cracked into a hint of a grin. "Yeah, I got that. I'll work on it, but I might slip sometimes."

"That's okay, I understand. It's hard sloughing off the military cape we wore. And in some ways, I never want to lose it."

Nodding, Reese relaxed a little more. He had a job, he'd eat regularly, and he had a roof over his head. "Thanks for giving me a long leash to run on."

She laughed a little, her hands opening and closing around the wheel. "Speaking of leashes, Noah was a dog trainer in the U.S. Army. I encouraged him to open up a dog training and boarding facility. He and Garret built the kennel area you'll see. Right now, Noah handles twenty dogs that he's training. Plus, he works on the indoor arena and he is also a wizard with training horses. He comes from a ranching family. In fact, he's building that into a full-time business. There's more business in training horses in Wyoming, than the need for trained dogs."

"Sounds like he's got his hands full."

"Yes, but we're always trying to balance our work, vision, and making enough money to keep the ranch solvent." She chewed on her lower lip. "Maybe you can help me with all that? I'm a high school graduate and I've been learning by the seat of my pants how to construct a good budget. I've made a lot of mistakes. I put the ranch in foreclosure once already, and nearly lost it."

"I can support you there," Reese promised. "Looking at your accounting books will give me an idea of what's going on." He saw relief in her features and she stopped worrying that full lower lip of hers.

"That would be so great," she murmured, giving him a smile of relief.

"Do any of the other vets have a business background?"

"No. All three vets are from the enlisted ranks, like me. They all have skills, they're smart as whips, but none of us have ever run a business in our life." She grinned a little. "We were used to taking orders and being told what to do."

"Yeah, that's the way it is in the military."

"Maybe, once you get comfy with your job, Reese, you can sit us all down and give us a picture of the ranch's health? Or lack of it?"

"I'll do more than that, Shay. I learned a long time ago that men and women are a lot more skilled and creative if you give them a chance to have a seat at the table. We're stronger as a team."

She gave him a warm look. "I'd have given anything to have worked in your company. I can tell you were a darned good Marine officer. You cared deeply about your people."

His heart ached for a moment. "It's an officer's duty to care for and protect his people," he said gruffly, wrestling with emotions. "I took my job seriously. I liked handling issues and problems with them and figuring out a way to fix things so they could operate at maximum efficiency."

"I can tell you're astute. You have good psychological skills in place."

He frowned. "I'm not a shrink."

"No, but you seem to have natural insight into the minds of others," Shay said. "I'm sure I can learn a lot from you. We all can."

Reese leaned back, the air scented with pine from the

nearby Salt Mountain Range to the east of them. "People always cross-pollinate one another, I've found. The men and women in my company helped make me a better officer. It's a two-way street."

"I like your humbleness."

He slanted a glance in her direction, watching the wind through the cab move her hair across her shoulders. "Earned it the hard way. I got the officer chip knocked off my shoulders when I was a young shavetail lieutenant. My CO, a captain, made sure I didn't let pride and ego go to my head when it came to managing the people of his company. He was the best thing that ever happened to me."

"Well," Shay said, slowing down and making a right-hand turn onto a muddy dirt road, "you'll get to use all those skills again at the Bar C."

"Are any of the other vets problem makers?" he wondered. Because Reese knew PTSD could make some people nearly unmanageable.

"No, not really. I mean, they all have issues. They've been horribly traumatized. But they're vets, Reese. They are used to working together as a team. And they do." She flashed him a hopeful look. "I think if you just sort of lay back, watch them for a while, you'll grasp their individual situations. And with your officer skills, I believe you'll move gently into the dynamic we've created among us."

Reese hoped so. He saw a lot of barbed wire fence along the rutted dirt road. The grass was thick and lush on his left, peeking up through the latest snow patches here and there.

"Is this the beginning of your ranch?"

"Yes, it is." Shay pointed about half a mile ahead. "There's the main ranch house. You can see the indoor arena being built, out by the two red barns. The horse training area is off to the left of it."

Reese observed the hundreds of acres enclosed next to

the road. "Are you following your father's idea of leasing your good land to other ranchers?"

"Yes, trying to." She gave him a frustrated look. "My father never kept anything on paper. It was all in his head. I'm having to contact these ranchers individually and find out the details. We can keep cattle up here for summer grazing only, and then they have to be trucked south to survive. Most of the ranchers truck their herds to Colorado or Utah, where the winters are less harsh and the cattle don't die like they will up here in Wyoming."

"So, your father left you a mess?"

"You could say that."

"And you're busy, so it's like putting out one fire after another?" Reese gave her an understanding look. Shay's cheeks colored a little.

"That's it in a nutshell. I'm so overworked. I need an office assistant for sure."

"Well, maybe I can help you. I'm pretty good with organizing and getting things lined up." He saw sudden hope come to her expression. His fingers positively itched to thread through her gleaming light brown hair.

"I'd love any help you can give me to get this ranch on more stable ground," she said, slowing and turning into the Bar C.

Reese got his first good look at the huge ranch. There was a two-story log house, probably built of spruce and pine, sitting a quarter mile down the gravel road. It was at least four thousand square feet, huge, and he wondered when it had been built. There were fenced pastures on either side of the road, and they didn't look in good repair. As she drove closer, Reese began to understand that Shay's father had not kept this ranch up. It was broken down. A disaster.

There was a white picket fence surrounding half the ranch house, but the posts were chipped and in dire need of sanding and a new coat of paint. His gaze moved with knowledge over the log structure. The plaster between the long, rounded logs needed a lot of repair work, too. He saw a golden retriever come bounding down the road, pink tongue hanging out, barking as the truck drew near.

"That's Max. He's my dog. Hold on . . . he loves to ride in the back of the pickup."

Reese watched Shay climb out, the dog barking joyously, wagging his thick, yellow tail, licking Shay's hands in welcome. His heart swelled with emotion as he heard Shay laugh, hug the dog, and then walk around to the rear, opening the truck gate. Max leaped up into the bed. Shay shut the gate and came back to the cab.

"He loves to ride in the truck, but I don't let him ride in the back anywhere but here on the ranch. It's too dangerous to put a dog in the rear of a truck out on the highway."

"For sure," Reese agreed. He saw such a change in Shay's face. Maybe she did wear a bit of a mask. Not a game face, but when Max greeted her, he saw her relax completely, vulnerable to her dog. After all, most people let down their shields anytime they were around their pets. He tucked that observation away. In no time, they were parked in front of the log house.

"Welcome home, Reese."

He felt like someone had punched him in the chest as she slid out of the cab. *Home*. He had a home but couldn't go there. At least, not yet. Not until he could get control of his life once more. Reese knew how much it hurt his parents that he'd left, unable to live beneath their roof. He made a point to stay in regular touch with them. When he hit a new town, he'd go to the library and use one of their computers and send them an email so they wouldn't worry about him.

Shay pulled down the tailgate and her dog leaped out. As he emerged from the truck, the playful, happy golden retriever came around, licking his hand with hellos.

Smiling, Reese bent down, caressing the dog's head. His

brown eyes were large, intelligent, and filled with utter joy over meeting him. His tail was wagging with excitement. It made him feel good. He saw Shay walk around to his side of the truck.

"Do you like dogs?"

"Love them." He straightened. "Can I take that dog food in the back somewhere for you?"

"No," Shay said. "Garret will get it. He knows where it goes." She smiled up at him. "First things first. You need to come in and I'll show you the two bedrooms. You can make a choice and we'll get you settled in first."

Reese pulled his sacks out of the back of the truck and followed her up the six wooden steps that had once been painted a bright red. The paint had been worn away by the hard winters in this area. The wraparound porch was enclosed with a railing and he saw a couple of rockers at one end, plus a large swing suspended from the ceiling at the other end. Everything needed maintenance, he realized. Hell, he did too. This ranch reflected him in every way.

Pulling open the screen door, Shay held it for him and gestured for him to go into the mud room. "Come on in, Reese. You can hang your hat there on one of the wooden pegs." She gestured toward the wall composed of spruce boards that glowed in the light from a nearby window. "All hats, gear, muddy boots, go in this area."

Reese looked around. The foyer was large, with a bench in one corner where a cowboy could sit down and pull off his muddy boots and place them on a worn rug. "Nice," he murmured, dropping his Stetson on a peg. His nostrils flared and he picked up the scent of spaghetti sauce cooking. "Something smells good," he told her.

"Garret's making meatballs, spaghetti, and garlic toast for tonight," she said. "Come on. He's probably in the kitchen.

He's our cook, thank God, so I'm free to do other things around the ranch."

Reese followed her into a massive kitchen. The floor was composed of green and white tiles, probably linoleum from another era. The kitchen was huge and U-shaped. He saw a man about his height with a white apron around his waist at the gas stove, stirring something in a large stainless steel pot.

"Hey, Garret," Shay called, "we've got another person for dinner tonight."

Garret, who was once a Special Forces operator, turned, surprise written on his square face. His sandy-colored hair was cut military short, his eyes moving swiftly to Reese. Garret was black ops because the man glanced at him with one hard, assessing look.

"No problem," Garret said. "We have plenty. Welcome."

Shay went over to him, resting her hand on his thick shoulder. "Garret, I've just hired another vet. Meet Reese Lockhart. He was in the Marine Corps. Garret was Special Forces A team operator." She urged Reese to come closer. "Reese, this is Garret Fleming."

"Good," Garret growled, wiping his hands off with a towel hanging off the stove. Turning, he thrust his hand out to Reese. "Nice to meet you, Lockhart. Welcome to the Bar C."

Reese gripped the man's calloused hand. "Same here."

Garret's grip was firm but not crushing. The man was big, broad shouldered, and probably weighed at least 220 pounds. He wore a dark red T-shirt, Levi's, and well-worn cowboy boots. The man's eyes reminded Reese of an eagle searching for its next meal. There was nothing casual about Garret as he released his hand. He definitely possessed the look of an undercover operator.

"Hey," she said, "can you, when you get a chance, take the dog chow back to the kennels?"

"Sure," he murmured, putting the lid on the pot. "I got everything ready. Just going to let the marinara sauce sit and get tasty now."

Shay wrapped her hand around Reese's arm. "Come on, we need to get you a room."

Reese nodded to Garret and allowed Shay to pull him toward the hallway. Max wouldn't leave his side. The pleasant thunk of boots against the floorboards of the wood-paneled hall, which shone gold and caramel in the sunlight, set him further at ease.

"This is my room," Shay said, gesturing to the open door to her right. She halted. "This is one of the empty rooms right across from mine. The other one is down there on the right. Why don't you check them out? Let me know which one you want. I have to go check the calls on the office answering machine." She pointed to the left farther down the long hall.

"Okay," Reese said. He lamented her hand slipping from his arm as she hurried down the hall on the right, disappearing into the office. Turning, he appreciated the sense of hominess that the ranch house exuded. The smells from the kitchen made his stomach clench with anticipation. Now, he'd be getting three square meals a day. It was nearly overwhelming to Reese as he opened the first bedroom door and stepped into it. The dog followed him in and once inside, he sat down, watching him with curiosity, thumping his big, heavy tail.

The room was large and to his surprise, there was a bathroom attached, too. There was an old brass bed with a quilt thrown over the top of it. The decor looked early 1900s to Reese as he moved to the oak dresser opposite the bed. He quickly put his few clothes into the top drawers and pushed them shut. The draperies at the window were patterned in old-fashioned red roses and green leaves on a cream background. They were open, the light from the window spilling into the room. An electric hurricane lamp sat on top of the dresser. In one corner there was a thoughtfully arranged small desk with what looked like an architect's lamp on it, and a wooden chair.

Above him was a large light hidden by a globe of frosted glass and sandblasted with flowers. He wondered if Shay's mother, or perhaps her grandmother, might have once lived here, and had chosen the motif. Everything about the room was from the turn of the twentieth century. It actually made Reese feel more relaxed. He heard a rooster crowing faintly outside the window and it brought back good memories of his own youth. The room smelled fresh and it was spotlessly clean.

What he liked most of all was the huge shower and bathtub. Someone had really thought about the layout of this room and the adjoining one. He wanted to ask Shay who had originally built this house because it was solid, warm, and truly felt like a home where many generations of her family had lived. Now, he could begin to understand why she was battling to save her family ranch. It was important to Reese to help her try to do just that.

"Well?" Shay asked, standing in the doorway, her hands on the jamb. "Do you like this one best?"

Turning, he saw she was worried. "I didn't check out the other one. This one is fine." He gestured around the room. "More than adequate. Amazing, really." Compared to what he had before? Cardboard over a steam grate to keep warm during the winter? He saw her face mirror relief.

"This was my Grandma Inez's room. She loved roses"—Shay pointed to the light above them—"red roses." She walked in, going to the thick, heavy drapes at the only window, fingering the material with fondness. "I remember coming in here when I was a kid, and she had a Singer sewing machine over there, where the desk is now. She taught me to sew starting when I was ten years old. I loved every moment of the time I spent with her."

There was a wistfulness in Shay's voice, her eyes going soft with good memories. Reese felt as if he were trespassing. "Are you sure about this? Me taking her room? It has a lot of good memories for you."

She nodded. "Oh, it's fine, Reese. No worries, okay? I love coming in here, because on bad days, I go sit on the bed and remember all our laughter, the fun we had, and how she'd hug the daylights out of me." She gave him a shy glance. "My grandma always made me feel better."

"What about your mother?" Reese saw pain come to her eyes.

"She died when I was ten years old. Gram Inez lived here and she sort of became my other mother until she died when I was thirteen."

Hearing the loss in her husky voice, Reese wanted to walk over and embrace her for just a moment. It wasn't a sexual thing, it was about one human comforting another. "I'm sorry. Sounds like you had a really rough childhood."

Shrugging, she gave him a wry look. "I've come to realize most children don't have a great time growing up. It just is what it is. Are you ready to look at your new office?"

"More than ready. Lead the way." As Reese absorbed the sense of family history at the ranch, a new feeling of belonging was starting to grow in him. This wasn't his family; he already had one. But the warmth of homecoming was strong here, and he knew it had to do with Shay and how she held her world together. It enclosed him gently, and a little more of the tension he'd carried for two years, started to dissolve. Max happily followed at his heels. Reese decided he had a new furry best friend.

Chapter Four

Shay was excited and a little worried when the four vets sat down to the spaghetti dinner Garret had made for all of them. There was a lot of testosterone at the long maple trestle table. She sat at the head of the table, two vets on either side of her. The kitchen smelled of garlic, marinara sauce, basil, and freshly baked bread. Covertly, she watched Reese. She could tell he was still hungry and wanted to gobble his meal, but he didn't. He ate like the other vets, talking and eating at a much slower pace.

Her heart went out to Reese because he was the only officer in the group. Everyone else at the table had been enlisted in the military. He had to be feeling a lot of shame because of his lost career and fall from grace. If he did, Reese didn't show it. Instead, she saw him relax, as if he were among friends, not enlisted people that he was used to shepherding around as an officer. What touched her heart was Max lying down next to Reese's booted feet, his chin on his paws, watching him with great affection. And sometimes Reese would lean over and place his hand on his head, scratch his fur gently and then resume eating.

"Hey," Noah spoke up, looking toward her. "I got a call from the Lincoln County Sheriff's Department, Shay.

They're interested in purchasing three of our horses. I guess when Sarah and her deputies have to go into the mountains, searching for lost kids and adults, they figured horses might be better than hiking."

Shay brightened. "Wow. Really?" She smiled at Noah, who sat at her left elbow. He was five foot eleven inches tall, well built, with short black hair and gray eyes. Like everyone else at the table, he had cleaned up and changed clothes before sitting down for dinner. Noah liked plaid shirts, and tonight he wore a red, green, and white one, the sleeves rolled up to just below his elbows. She saw the excitement in his intelligent eyes.

"Yeah," he said, giving her a wide grin. "Potentially, that's a lot of money for us. I guess I'm getting a name in the valley for turning out well-trained horses, huh?"

"Could you sell horses to sheriffs' departments in other Wyoming counties?" Reese wondered.

Noah nodded. "Exactly what I was thinking, but I have to pass muster first under Sheriff Sarah Carter."

Shay asked, "What does this all mean, Noah?"

"In the phone call, Sarah said she wanted to buy three well-trained trail mounts for their department. They're getting called out more and more often on searches for children lost in the Salt Mountains east of our valley and the Wilson Range to the west of us," Noah said, pulling open a hot roll and slathering butter on it. "Sarah wants to come here in the next week to look at the stock I've chosen for her department. She's no stranger to horseflesh and she knows a good horse from a bad one. With your permission, I'm going to meet her tomorrow at her office and we'll talk over her specific needs for her department."

"How close is she to actually purchasing them?" Shay wondered. She liked the fact that Reese took part in the conversation and had something of value to contribute to it.

From time to time, he'd look up from eating, but he was listening and saying little. It made her feel protected and it was a strange sensation because none of the other three vets made her feel that way. They treated her like a much beloved kid sister. Reese had her back in a different, more personal way. She gently tucked those realizations away for now.

Noah rolled up another forkful of spaghetti. "When Sarah called, she said she and two of her deputies want to give our three mounts some test rides after they've made their selections. I said that's fine. So, they'll take the horses out in the back country and give them some trial situations. If they pass, she said she had it in her yearly budget to buy them." He waved his fork at all of them, bursting with good news. "Even better, Shay? Sarah asked me if you would consider boarding their horses here at the ranch. I told her I'd talk to you about it. But it would be a huge plus to have the sheriff's horses boarded here. Word gets around fast, and other valley people would jump at the chance to put their horses into a nice place like what we're building."

"That's great, Noah. What kind of money is involved?"

Noah shrugged. "As you know, I train breed and non-breed horses. Sarah wants Appaloosa or quarter horse types. Animals that are real quiet."

"You have two quarters and an App out there," Shay pointed out. "Are they trail trained?"

Giving her a satisfied smile, Noah nodded. "Yes, ma'am, indeed they are. A well-trained horse can cost anywhere from three to eight thousand dollars apiece. Sometimes more. It just depends. The Lincoln County Sheriff's Department is going to cut me a check for these three once they pass their tests." He assessed her for a moment. "That means, I would guestimate, fifteen thousand dollars coming in next week, so cross your fingers."

Her eyes widened enormously. "Really? That much?"

"The horses they specify take a year to train, so they want someone like me, who has a lot of experience, to find the right ones for them. It's not an easy process and it takes time. They're basically buying my knowledge and suggestions on which are best for their needs."

"Of course," Shay said, reaching out, touching his forearm. "This is what it's all about, Noah. You're here to build a business for yourself, and now you're expanding. Look how people are coming to you! Remember? I told you it would happen."

Noah nodded and gave her a warm look. "Yeah, I was pretty down in my cups when I arrived. I was like a tramp dog on your doorstep, wasn't I?"

"You've *never* been a tramp, Noah. Don't you *dare* use that word around here!"

All the men except Reese chuckled and gave one another sly looks of amusement.

Garret looked over at Reese. "We call Shay our cheerleader. She makes us self-correct words we use to describe ourselves. She's hell on wheels if we use words that aren't positive."

Reese nodded and saw how upset Shay had become. She was more than a cheerleader. More like a fierce mother bear with her cubs. The set of her jaw and the flash of fire in her eyes finished the visual for him. "I think it's a good idea." He saw all the men grin, nod, and return to eating.

Shay smiled over at Noah. "You should be so proud of yourself. That's a lot of money."

"Yep, and fifteen percent of whatever it is, will go back to the ranch." Noah lost his joviality and became serious, holding her gaze. "I know we're shaky money-wise, so this is a great break for all of us."

"It sure is," Shay whispered, suddenly emotional. She

gave him a sweet look. "This is just such wonderful news. Congratulations, Noah. It's a breakthrough for you. It means you're on your way up and out. Quit the dog training and focus solely on horse training."

"I can take your place while you work with the folks from the sheriff's department," Reese told him. "I'm experienced with horses. If you want me to take over your chores with them, I'll be happy to do it."

Noah glowed. "That would be great, Reese. I don't expect you to do any training with them, but feeding, watering, and handling them would be great."

Reese nodded. "Consider it done."

Shay felt her heart expand with good feelings as she looked at Reese. He was a team player. He was pitching in where he could to help others. "That would be great, Reese. Thank you."

"Yeah," Garret said, his mouth stuffed, "I ain't gonna clean horse poop out of the box stalls for you, Mabry." He held up his large, wide hands. "I do cooking only."

Harper, who was the medic among them, snickered. "Wouldn't want those soft, lily white hands of yours to get dirty now, would we, Garret?"

The whole table chuckled darkly.

Shay saw Reese following the conversations, lifting his head, studying the men from time to time. He had finished his first plate of spaghetti and meatballs. Only after everyone else had helped themselves, did Reese take a second helping from the steel pot sitting on a trivet in the middle of the table. Garret always made a lot of food for them. There were a lot more baked rolls tonight, and Shay figured Garret had taken one look at how thin Reese was, and made extra. Reese was stuffing those rolls down him, no question. Each vet, as he came to the Bar C, was at least thirty pounds lighter than he should be. Right now, only Reese looked like a scarecrow among the men. In time, he'd regain that lost weight and fill out once more.

"Hey," Garret said, glancing over at Reese, "be sure to take your vitamins." He jabbed his index finger at a small white paper cup sitting in front of his plate. "Shay wants us strong and healthy."

"I see 'em," Reese muttered, eyeing the cup filled to the brim with colorful vitamins and minerals.

"Shay will skin you alive," Garret warned him, giving him an evil grin, "if you don't suck 'em down like a good boy. You'll be getting that little white paper cup in front of your plate three times a day for the next two months. So make friends with 'em. It's part of her plan to get us healthy."

"Yeah," Noah muttered, "highlight of my meals when I first arrived. God, there's so many of them I felt like a horse choking all of them down."

Harper chuckled. "You bunch of wimps. She's right to slug you with nutrition. We *all* were malnourished by the time we arrived here." He looked at Reese, who was at his elbow. "Take 'em and don't bitch."

Reese gave him a sour grin. "I think I can manage a few pills."

"Shay doesn't let you leave the table until they're all gone," Harper promised him smugly. "Just do the duty. She won't give you dessert, either, until that cup is empty."

"Oh, come on, guys," Shay pleaded, "you make me sound like a witch."

Garret snorted. "There are days when I swear I see you with a broom in your hand, Shay."

The whole table burst into chuckles and traded teasing looks with Shay, whose cheeks turned bright red.

"In truth," Harper told Reese in a confidential tone, "we're just teasing Shay. You're going to find that this place isn't a ranch. It's a *home.* And she's the mothering type who thinks all of us are her grown-up children huddled beneath those invisible angel wings of hers." He lifted his chin, smiling over at Shay. "And you aren't a witch. You're an angel to all of us, so relax. For being in the Corps, you sure don't take ribbing very well. Shay."

Her hands fluttered. "Oh, don't worry, Harper, I took a lot of ribbing in the Corps. It's just that here, I'm out of practice."

"Except from us," Garret noted, giving her a gentle glance. "And you know we don't mean it. Right?"

Shay finished her plate of food. She placed her silverware on the empty plate. "Most of the time, but I have my moments when you guys catch me off guard." She felt Reese's gaze upon her and felt too vulnerable at the moment to meet his eyes. That same powerful sense of protection blanketed her once more, like a lover caressing her, holding her close. Holding her safe. The sensation flowed hotly through her and she didn't dare look at him. She might burst into tears, ruining the evening meal. Shay had learned a long time ago not to cry in front of any of the vets. A woman's tears upset them to no end. They were always trying to fix whatever made her cry. Sometimes, Shay just needed to cry and release, it was that simple. But men didn't seem to understand that and it stressed them.

"I've made good progress on the roof of the indoor arena," Harper told her, breaking the thick silence at the table. "Got one more ten-foot section up on the roof."

"That's great," Shay murmured. "I don't know what we'd do without you, Harper."

Reese saw the medic blush and he said nothing, paying attention to his quickly disappearing food. One thing for sure, these men ate hearty and there was plenty for everyone. Reese caught the medic's gaze. "Maybe tomorrow, Harper, you can show me the ropes? I can swing a hammer pretty well if you'll tell me what to do." Reese knew the vets were aware he'd been an officer. And it wouldn't go well if he tried to push his weight around because they were all enlisted men. That would be a disaster. Instead, he was asking for help, direction, and he saw Harper's deeply tanned face grow relaxed.

"Sure. I usually start at 0800." And then he looked over at Garret. "Our chief cook and bottle washer over there don't like any of us to miss one of his spectacular meals. Breakfast is served at 0700 sharp."

"That's because my cooking is five star," Garret said proudly. "And none of you have died from it. All you've done is gained weight, which we all needed."

Chuckling, Noah said, "Haven't had food poisoning yet from you."

More laughter floated around the table.

"Tomorrow afternoon, Harper," Shay said, "I want to steal Reese from you for a while. He's got an accounting background and I want him to look over the ranch books."

Shrugging, Harper said to Reese, "Better you than me. Numbers aren't my gig."

Reese nodded. "You okay with me leaving at that time?"

"Sure. Some help is better than none."

"Great," Shay said, giving Reese a glance. "Garret wants everyone here at noon for the meal. Afterward, you can come down to the office with me and take a look at our accounting books."

"Be happy to," Reese said, using his sixth roll to mop up what was left of the tasty marinara sauce still on his emptied plate. His stomach was full for the first time in a year. He slipped Max a tidbit of the roll, which he slurped down in one gulp his gold-brown eyes shining with thanks.

* * *

The next afternoon after lunch, Reese saw Shay was nervous as they walked into the office. It was a small place compared to the massive bedrooms on the first floor. The top of the rectangular maple desk was overflowing with files. It looked like a disorganized mess to him, but he knew Shay was doing the best she could. There was a large stained-glass lamp on one corner, shedding bright light around the cozy room. Above the desk was a glass chandelier with six hurricane lamps attached, giving the pine room a glowing, golden ambience. There were two windows in the room because it sat in one corner of the log home. The lavender curtains were feminine and frilly; he was sure Shay had chosen the color and style.

Shay gestured for him to sit down. When he did, the chair squeaked mightily.

"I think it needs to be oiled," she offered apologetically. "I just haven't had time." She pulled one of six huge black ledger books from the bookshelf above the front of the desk. Handing it over to him, she said, "This is the daily accounting log. You should probably start there." Their hands met and touched. Shay felt warmth tingle up through her fingers. It was such an unbidden pleasure to connect physically with Reese.

Today, he wore a blue chambray shirt and a red kerchief around his thick neck. She saw dark hair peeking out from beneath the opening of his shirt and swallowed convulsively. Reese was like a sensual, dark, primal animal to her. She'd spent half the night awake, tossing and turning, her mind going to secret places about him as a man. She hoped he couldn't read her mind, because right now she was shaky, nervous, and bothered all at once due to his proximity. Never had a man made her feel more feminine or more aware that she hadn't had sex in a long, long time.

"Thanks," he murmured, taking the heavy book from

her hands. "It's the right place to start. If I find anything, I'll note it as I go along. Then, maybe tonight after dinner we can talk about what I've found."

Rolling her eyes, she said gratefully, "Yes, out of earshot of the guys. They know I'm not good at this, and bless their hearts, they've all tried to help me with it, but I know it's screwed up something terrible, Reese."

He gave her a reassuring look as he opened the ledger. "Relax, okay? Accounting is part art and part dog work. If you don't know the rules, you're bound to make errors, and that's to be expected." He saw her move her fingers nervously through her hair, which fell around her shoulders.

Reese wanted to tell Shay how beautiful the soft pink blouse looked on her. The jeans she wore were loose but didn't hide her curvy figure. She'd been outside working with Noah at the horse training facility until lunchtime. Reese could look from the roof of the indoor arena being built and see in every direction. She was cleaning out the horse stalls while Noah worked with each of the horses he had in training at the nearby oval arena. He admired her work ethic. Shay was humble, and any woman who could shovel horse shit was all right in his world. Just another thing to like about her: She wasn't afraid to get her hands dirty, because ranch work required it.

"Okay . . ." she said, chewing on her lower lip. "I'm so nervous about this. I have horrors of having made terrible errors, and we owe the bank thousands of dollars I didn't know about."

He laughed a little. "I doubt you've done that."

"Oh," she muttered, hesitating at the open door, "you don't know Marston Conroy."

"Who is he?"

"Our banker." She wrinkled her nose in distaste. "He's an evil person. He makes me feel like two cents when I have to go crawling into his bank to ask for a loan or to stretch out a due date for a loan payment."

Rankled, Reese held her anxious blue gaze. "Well, from now on," he growled, "if there's any meetings to be had between us and Conroy, I'll be at your side. I won't let him take a chunk out of you next time. All right?" Reese saw utter relief flood her expression and he wanted to get up, walk around the desk, and slide his arms around her. Shay was terribly vulnerable. More than he'd initially realized. Or maybe accounting was her weakness, and that's where her vulnerability raised its head. It would take a lot of time for him to understand her better.

"Conroy is an arrogant bastard," she breathed in warning. "I hate having to see him. When the ranch went into foreclosure shortly after I got my father to the nursing home, he gloated over it. He told me I would lose it, that I was stupid. He said no woman could run the ranch by herself."

Reese saw the damage from the banker's cruel remarks in her expression. "I'm going to look forward to locking horns with him, then. You've made this ranch solvent. That says everything good about you, Shay."

She folded her arms against her chest. "Now, I have you. You're my big, bad accounting guard dog, Reese."

He smiled a little. "Is that how you see me?" It made him feel good. Did he want to protect Shay? Damn straight. Did he want her in his bed? Hell yes. Reese cautioned himself because he had just arrived at the ranch. Wanting her and getting her were two very different things. But he didn't lie to himself. This woman turned him inside out, and his dreams last night were torrid. For the first time in two years, he'd had a helluva good dream. No nightmares. Shay was magic to him, Reese decided. Hot, beautiful magic. His hands itched, wanting to touch her, explore her, and kiss her until she melted like hot honey into his embrace.

Giving a nervous laugh, Shay said before leaving, "I guess that's how I see you. There's just something very protective about you, Reese. Maybe it's because you were an officer and you took care of your company." She gave a shy shrug. "I don't know. I just feel that way around you."

Nodding, he picked up a piece of paper and a pencil from a cup on the desk. "Hold that thought, okay? I'll make sure the Conroys of the world stop taking chunks out of you." Holding her gaze, he said, "In a symbolic sense you can bet that I'm like a combat assault dog at heart when it comes to protecting children and women from men like that. And I'll protect you." He saw Shay's eyes grow moist and then she swallowed convulsively, resting her hand on the doorjamb. Her cheeks flushed red and on her, it looked becoming.

"I—just never have been protected like that before. I'm going to have to get used to it, and you."

Reese held her gaze. "Do. Because, like my manners, that's just a natural part of who I am. It's not something that's going to change in me . . ."

Shay felt shaky in the best of ways as she hurried down the hall. She had to drive into town, pick up the mail, and buy the food on the grocery list Garret had given her.

She touched her cheek, feeling how flaming hot it was. Reese had given her a look that made her feel like butter running in a hot skillet. She saw desire in his eyes for her. Didn't she? Or was it her imagination? She had been alone for so long, used to doing everything by herself without any help, that it felt odd but nice to have Reese's protective nature surround her. It didn't feel suffocating. Instead, it felt steadying and supportive.

Garret had just come in from his duties outdoors and was tying a blue apron around his waist when she walked into the kitchen. When he wasn't cooking for the crew, he was doing odd jobs on the ranch. Earlier, he'd thrown a leg over Jak, their black quarter horse gelding, and rode fence line. Wyoming winters were rough, and there was a lot of fencing down that needed to be repaired.

"Hey," she called, pulling her leather purse off one of the wooden pegs along the wall, "I've got your list. I'm going into town. Need anything else?"

Garret grinned and pulled a big iron skillet from the stove drawer. "How about fifty pounds of good rib eye steaks?"

"In your dreams, Garret." Shay knew their budget allowed for cuts of only cheap meats like turkey, chicken, mutton, and hamburger. Garret was skilled at making great dishes out of them and it hurt her that she couldn't give these hardworking guys real beef that had more protein in it per ounce than the other meat. She heard him chuckle.

"I got an idea, Shay."

"Okay," she said, halting at the stove, "I'm all ears."

"You know Maud Whitcomb, who owns the Wind River Ranch?"

"Yes, of course."

"She often donates buffalo meat to a local charity in Jackson Hole. She's got a small herd and she culls it yearly." He gave her a softened look. "I'll call her and ask her if she has any leftover meat we might be able to buy cheap. What do you think?"

Feeling shame, Shay kept her face carefully arranged. Why hadn't *she* thought of that? She knew every other charity and country outreach program in Lincoln County for those who had less. "That's a great idea. Maud is one of the most generous people in the valley. I'll call her and ask, Garret. It's my place." She saw his hard face melt a little, his hazel eyes sad. None of them liked begging for hand-outs. She touched his massive shoulder. "I'll do it," she promised firmly.

"You're already doing too much, Shay. I've met Maud many times over at Charlie Becker's hay and feed store. It would be easy enough for me to pick up the phone and call her."

Wincing internally, she kept her game-face in place. "Naw, don't go there. We're all doing too much, and that's the truth. We aren't going to compare who is doing more or less." She wanted to change topics. "What are we having tonight?"

"Roasted Cornish game hens with rice stuffing. Sound good?"

She brightened, giving him a smile. "Does it ever. Well, I've got to run . . ."

Garret got busy with the game hens and making the stuffing out of white rice and veggies, with a bit of his special sauce added to the mixture. Later, he felt someone come into the kitchen, although there was no sound to alert him. It was his sixth sense giving him the warning. Turning, he saw Reese standing uncertainly in the doorway.

"Those accounting books drown you yet?" he asked dryly, pointing to a freshly made pot of coffee on the counter.

Reese smiled a little and sauntered in. "I don't have to worry about being drowned by numbers," he said, pouring himself a cup of coffee. He looked up. "Want a cup?"

"Yeah, sounds good. The mugs are up there." He pointed toward a cupboard to his left.

Reese poured coffee and slid a mug in Garret's direction.

The man had six game hens stuffed and sitting in a large baking dish on the counter. "You would know the most about the food supplies around here, right?"

"Yeah, I'm the one who makes out the lists. Why?" Garret shot him a brief look.

"I'm into the daily ledger and in the last hour I've been analyzing Shay's budget and the food she buys."

Snorting, Garret said, "Listen, Shay does a lot with too little."

Nodding, Reese felt Garret start to get defensive, protecting Shay. "She does a lot for all of us," he agreed quietly. He saw Garret's shoulders start to relax. "I'm trying to grasp how much money goes out monthly on food. Do you have an approximate number for that?"

Mouth thinning, Garret quickly chopped up some celery on the cutting board with swift motions. "Shay will probably never tell you this, but I will. First, those books have to get straightened out. I tried, and it was too much for me." Garret gave him a flat look. "Shay's income varies greatly month-to-month. It all depends upon what the three of us can bring in for her and the ranch. Harper works part-time at a garage in Jackson Hole. Noah trains horses and dogs, and he gives riding lessons. I'm a construction guy, and I get jobs around the valley from time to time."

"And when you're not out working, you're working here?"

"Yeah." He pointed toward the barn area. "That indoor arena is a big deal for her and us. We can start boarding a helluva lot of horses in the valley when it's built. There's no other place in Wind River Valley that has an indoor arena where you can ride and train your horse during the long winters around here. Shay estimates that when it's all done and open for business, we can rent out stalls and box stalls amounting to five thousand dollars a month. But that includes us paying for the horse's hay, too, and that's damned expensive. And don't forget about the grain they'll get daily. Another expense."

"So," Reese murmured, leaning against the counter, "what's the net monthly, do you think?"

"I estimate twenty-five hundred." He smiled a little. "But Shay, being ever the optimist, thinks it's a thousand dollars more. A bale of hay is a hundred bucks. A horse will eat through an eighty-pound bale in ten days—maybe more, maybe less, depending upon how hard he's being worked. Do you have any background in animals or ranching?"

"Enough," Reese answered. "Is there a business plan written up on this project so I can take a look at it?"

Garret gave a short laugh. "You gotta be kidding me. Shay keeps it all in her head. Just like her old man did when he was running this place into the ground. I've tried to get her to write it out. There's an SBA, Small Business Administration, office here in Wind River, but I can't convince her to go talk to those folks. They could help her a lot, plus teach her how to create a business plan." He shrugged. "The truth is she's juggling a whole lotta balls up in the air, Lockhart, and some of them fall. She's doing too much. Her heart's in the right place, but she's one person. She needs help. I tried to help her on the accounting, but her brain is like W. C. Fields's desk—with fifty files piled up on top of one another. Only she knows which file is where." He gave Reese a sour look.

Sipping his coffee, Reese murmured, "She's trusting me to look at the books. Maybe you and I can sit down alone and you can give me the intel I need? Then I can create some business plans, some models, and we can honestly know what the net income monthly liquid cash flow would be on that arena and other areas. And what kind of cash she's really pulling in monthly, right now."

"Damn good idea," Garret growled. He finished with the celery, putting it in a bowl and dragging over a large yellow onion, quickly chopping it up into small, diced pieces. "Shay's strength is her heart, her passion. She doesn't have a head for business, although she's trying damned hard to learn what she needs to do on the fly."

"You seem to have some business background?"

Garret hitched up one thick shoulder. "My dad runs a small construction equipment rental business. I grew up around accounting books and business plans. Some of it rubbed off, but not everything." He gave Reese a hard look. "And you're exactly what she needs. She told me you have a degree in business administration. If anyone is going to help her out, it will be you."

"What about Harper?"

"He's a handyman, not a numbers man. The guy can fix anything. And I mean anything. He's got magic in those hands of his. But he's not gonna be able to help you with those books."

"Okay, how about Noah?"

"Interestingly, Noah's dad runs a big-time construction company in Driggs, Idaho. Right across the border from us. Noah knows how to operate machinery, but always loved working with animals—horses and dogs—more than anything else. He's good at assessing costs of construction projects, though. He'd be a go-to guy for that kind of intel."

"Does Noah see his folks much?"

Garret grimaced. "Do any of us see our parents?"

Raising his brows, Reese nodded and said nothing. "Okay, so you and me? We're going to take an hour and sit down in the office and you can catch me up to speed on the accounting, the budget, and where Shay's at money-wise."

"Be happy to." He wiped his hands, glanced at the clock and said, "Let's get to it. I gotta put those hens in the oven in about two hours."

Pleased, Reese pushed off the counter, carrying his cup with him. He liked Garret's can-do spirit. The man was sharp and communicated well. As they walked down the hall, he asked him, "Where did you serve in the military?"

"Iraq, and then got deployed to that hole, Afghanistan. Real armpit."

Reese couldn't disagree with him as he turned into the office. He was right: Garret Fleming had been deep black-ops. He pulled out the other chair in front of the desk for the wrangler who made the office look small. "Have a seat. Let's get started."

Chapter Five

"Where the hell have you been?"

Shay hesitated at the door to her father's private room at the Haven Nursing Facility in Jackson Hole. Her stomach was tied in knots, as always. And she wished she could shield herself from her father's angry disposition. Forcing a smile, she said lightly, "I had an extra errand to run, Father. Sorry I'm late." Today, he was in his blue pajamas and still in bed.

Ray Crawford's small brown eyes grew slitted as he watched his daughter turn and quietly shut the door. "The least you could do is call and tell me you're runnin' late."

Shay brought over some wildflowers she'd stopped and picked on the way in. They were the first up after the long winter and she had pulled off onto the berm, got out, and picked them for him. Long ago, she'd brought in a small vase and when she could, she brought them if they were in season. "A lot of things suddenly piled up on me, Father." Her fingers trembled as she placed the bright red blooms in the vase on his bed stand. The TV was blaring and she took the nearby remote, muting it. Her father had been a big, muscular man but after a year of being partially paralyzed by the stroke, he had lost a lot of his weight. His triangular face was gaunt, his hawk-like nose more prominent. His thin mouth was pursed, as always.

"What's goin' on at my ranch?" he demanded. Struggling, he grabbed the overhead bar with his left hand, grasping it in order to sit up in bed. His right side was partially paralyzed. Huffing, grunting, he dragged himself by sheer will and sat upright. Breathing hard, he sank wearily against the headboard, glaring at her.

"A lot. I've hired another wrangler."

"What?" Ray snarled. "Another stray dog you found in town? A worthless, broken vet? What the hell for?"

Shay rested her fingers on the brass footboard, wanting to be as far away from her father as she could get. Picking up on the scent of liquor on his breath, she wanted to cry. He was an alcoholic. His doctor told him he had cirrhosis. And yet, she suspected that he was somehow getting someone to bring liquor to him. "He's a good man, Father. His name is Reese Lockhart."

Snorting, Ray muttered, "You always picked up strays, Shaylene. Even as a kid, you rescued little birds that fell outta their nest, found a baby rabbit and fed it until it was old enough to go out on its own. You rescue things. You have too kind a heart. You never hardened it like you shoulda. Your mother was the same way. Look what it got her: breast cancer and she died young."

Wincing internally, Shay kept the pleasant expression on her face even if it killed her. She didn't dare show her real feelings to her father or he'd rage at her, curl his hands into fists, wanting to strike her as he had when she was younger. Ray couldn't get up to do anything to her anymore, but that didn't matter. Shay reacted to what had happened to her too many times in the past.

"Mom worked hard," was all she'd say.

"Hell, we *all* worked hard!" Breathing heavily, he

grappled with his anger and lowered his voice. "What else is going on with my ranch?"

Shay didn't correct him. It didn't matter that the ranch belonged to her. Her mother's family had owned the ranch for generations. The last of the family line, Wanda had agreed to rename the ranch the Bar C in honor of her husband. But she left the ranch to Shay, with the stipulation that Ray run it until he was incapacitated. Then the responsibility to manage her inheritance would be transferred to Shay. She wasn't sure her father remembered that, and she wasn't going to remind him. He had always said it was his ranch and she patiently said, "We've got half the roof on the indoor arena. I have photos on my iPhone. Would you like to see them?"

"No! I think it's a foolish risk, Shaylene. You ought to be putting the money into my cattle leases. They *always* paid well."

It was an old saw to Shay. She wouldn't argue with him. He'd fly into an uncontrollable rage. The doctors had warned her to keep Ray quiet and not to stress him. She wanted to laugh in their faces, but refrained. If they only knew her father's hair-trigger temper. Talk about ongoing, daily stress for the first eighteen years of her life. The tension never went away, as much as she wished she could remove it. Her head knew one thing, but her emotions were trapped when she was eight years old and he started picking on her instead of her sick mother.

"Mr. Lockhart has a degree in business administration," she said, hope in her tone. "He's going to help me keep the accounting books." And she added more softly, "I've never been good with numbers."

"You failed math repeatedly in school," Ray said bitterly, shaking his head. "You came from two smart people. What the hell happened to you?"

Shay gave a weak shrug. "I don't know, Father. I do the best I can."

"Well, those ledgers are fine as is. You keep them. I don't want no one, especially a no-good vet, looking into our private business. You hear me?"

Nodding, Shay pulled the strap of her purse more onto her left shoulder. "How are you doing?"

"What does it look like?"

She was so tired of being his whipping post. The people at the nursing home wouldn't take his tirades and verbal abuse. And then Shay would walk in for her thrice-weekly visit, and he deluged her with his rage. It pulverized her. Rallying, she said, "You have good color. Have they been taking you outside lately? The weather's beautiful, even though it's still chilly out."

"Yeah, they do," he muttered.

Shay saw the regret and grief in her father's eyes. He'd been a vital, hardworking rancher, strong and capable. All except for his drinking habits and his gambling. He was an ugly drunk. Over time, he'd run off every wrangler who'd worked on the Bar C. Which was why it was in a shambles when she'd returned from the Marine Corps. "That's good." She looked around the bright, cheery room. It was a pale blue color; rich blue, gold, and purple drapes were pulled aside from the window, with the sun pouring in. The window had been opened a crack to allow some fresh outside air into his room. "Can I get you anything on my next visit?"

"I'm outta my pretzels. Those bastards won't buy me any more."

She smiled a little. "How about next time I buy two bags? That way you won't run out between visits." She walked over to the bed stand where the flowers sat. "You could put the second bag in here." She pulled open the drawer.

"Good idea," he muttered with a sharp nod. "I'd like that."

Shutting the drawer, Shay straightened. "I have to get going. Call me if you need anything." He never did call her. But this was a litany Shay said to him on every visit.

"Hand me the remote?" He thrust out his left hand.

Shay picked it up off the bed stand and gave it to him. She felt guilty because she had no love for her father, just a feeling of responsibility toward him because she was his daughter. She waved to him and said, "I'll see you in a few days."

"Don't be late next time, dammit!"

Shay got home minutes before dinner. She hurried into the house, inhaling the wonderful smell coming from the kitchen. Poking her head around the corner, she saw all but Reese at the table, and Garret was starting to serve. She knew he hated people to be late for his hot food, and she didn't blame him.

"I'll be right there!" she called with a smile to him, hurrying down the hall.

She practically ran into Reese, who was coming out of his bedroom. He smelled of soap, freshly showered, his hair dark and damp. Instinctively, he reached out, gripping her arms before they collided with one another.

"Oh, sorry," she whispered, stepping back. Her stomach was still tied in knots from visiting her father. Reese's large, warm hands on her bare arms made her melt and relax.

He smiled and released her. "Ramp down, huh?" he

teased, stepping back a pace to give her room. "Is there anything I can carry in for you?"

Grateful, she said breathlessly, "No, thank you. I've got to wash up. Tell Garret I'll be there in a flash."

"You bet," Reese murmured, standing aside as she flew into her bedroom.

He frowned and continued walking down the hall to the kitchen. He heard the men talking in low voices, but his heart was centered on Shay. She looked pale. And her glorious blue eyes looked shadowed. He sensed she was scared. Or tense. Reese knew she'd gone into town to pick up food from the local grocery store. What could have happened there?

Rounding the corner, he saw the other men at their respective places at the long table. Garret was bringing a large pan of steamed green beans, with tiny onions and slivers of almonds on top, to the table.

"She's late," Garret said more to himself than them as he put the pot on a trivet on the table.

Reese sat down. "She said she'd be here in a second. She looks upset."

Noah snorted. "That's because she had to go see that bastard father of hers." And then he looked toward the entrance to make sure Shay wasn't within earshot.

Harper nodded, keeping his voice low. "Yeah, Lockhart, her father's a real piece of work. Hope you never have to talk to her old man."

Shay came hurrying around the corner, wiping her hands on her dark green slacks. She leaned up and hugged Garret, who was twice her size. "I'm sorry I'm late," she said, and then walked toward the table, giving a warm smile to all of the vets.

Reese saw the men put on their game faces. He felt their closeted anger. So, Shay had a father who was less than nice. Was that what accounted for the tension he'd felt from her out in the hall, then? He watched her progress as she took her seat at the head of the table. She'd quickly changed from her white, frilly blouse to a pale pink sweater. She looked flustered. Clearly she was unstrung, because as she nervously moved the silverware around the plate, he saw a slight tremble in her fingers. What the hell kind of father did she have?

Garret brought over her Cornish game hen and with a flourish, he placed it on her plate. "For you, mademoiselle," he teased, giving her a grin.

"It looks wonderful," Shay said, leaning down, inhaling the aromas rising from the steam. There was half a sweet potato, slathered in butter and sprinkled with brown sugar, next to the hen.

"Oh," Harper drawled, "don't tell this Army doggie anything nice. He's already got a swelled head."

Jeering, Garret took off his apron, set it on the counter, and sauntered over, sitting next to Noah. "You squids from the Navy will *never* make up for who we are, so go right ahead and call me a doggie, but I know the truth. Special Forces rock."

Harper gave him a smug look. "Shucks, and here I thought I had it right. It's us squids that risk our butts to save your sorry hides once you've been wounded in a battle and are lying out there bleeding—"

"Guys," Shay said, holding up her hands, "enough, okay? Let's eat in harmony. There are enough battles every day. I don't need it here at the dinner table."

Harper flushed. "Sorry, Shay. You're right."

Garret gave her a soft look. "Peace, Shay. We'll be good."

Reese said nothing, consuming the feast with relish. Shay's cheeks were pale and he saw the darkness remaining in her eyes. The vets quieted, all of them digging hungrily into the food. Garret had made fresh bread, two loaves, sliced them up, and most of it disappeared in ten minutes. He knew the men worked hard, dawn to dusk. None of them were slackers.

"How's the accounting scavenging going?" Shay asked him, trepidation in her eyes.

"Still putting it all together," Reese said, well aware of her concern. He hoped the soothing quality in his voice eased some of her anxiety.

"No surprises?" she asked between bites.

"Not so far." Reese looked up and across at Garret, warning him not to say anything. The operator gave a slight nod. Shay was rattled enough. She didn't need to know anything right now.

While in the office, Reece had heard more about Garret being a Special Forces weapons sergeant. Typical of all operators, he didn't give anything away until Reese had buttonholed him on it. That explained Garret's sharp intelligence. The men in those units were considered the best of the best in the Army, right up there with Delta Force operators.

"I had a good meeting with Sarah and her deputies this morning," Noah told everyone, moving to another topic.

"Tell all," Shay urged, excitement in her voice.

"I had three trail-trained horses saddled and tied out in one of the paddocks when they arrived. Sarah walked around them, checking them out closely. One of the deputies rode each one in the corral. Sarah watched how they moved and handled. They are all five years old, so they're mature and steady for trail work." He smiled a little at Shay. "Sarah liked all of them. I'm gonna trailer them to a Salt Mountain slope east of here on Saturday morning. She and her two deputies will then ride and check them out under actual trail conditions."

Shay sighed. "That's incredible! What a great day, Noah."

Noah gave her a slight smile. "Yeah, it turned out to be max, Shay. I don't think there'll be any problem trailing these horses on Saturday. Sarah asked me what I wanted for each one. I think she's already made up her mind about it, but she wants to give them a test drive, which is fine."

"What are you asking for them?" Reese wanted to know.

"For the App, I'm asking seven thousand. For the two quarter horses, five grand apiece. The color on the App, big black spots on his white rump, will give us more cash. The more colorful the App, the more money it brings."

"Don't you horse-trade a little on prices?" Reese asked.

Noah shrugged. "Well, let's put it this way. I don't quibble about the price of a well-trained horse. I figure-in the hours it took me to get that animal to that degree of skill. Sarah's a smart woman and knows that when I set a price, it's fair and honest."

"Well," Garret said, "it's one thing to horse-trade, but you're training them up to a high level of skill. Most people realize that and there's no bargaining at that point. You get what you pay for, and I'm sure Sarah knows that, too."

"Yeah, she does," Noah said, pleased. "My price on each horse didn't faze her. She comes from a ranching family, so she knows the worth of an animal."

"Wow," Shay whispered, smiling, "this is such *great* news!"

Noah held up his hand. "Don't celebrate yet, Shay. I know you're a giddy idealist by nature, but I'm a pragmatist. I won't celebrate until that check is in my hot little hand."

"Amen to that," Garret said. "I'll bake a pineapple upside-down cake for all of us, to celebrate."

Everyone oohed and aahed. Reese figured that pineapple upside-down cake must be a favorite. He saw the men giving Shay concerned looks. It was clear to him these men loved her like a little sister. The wranglers *wanted* to make her happy. *Wanted* to support her. There was such a team atmosphere at this ranch that Reese felt like a lucky man times ten to have ended up here.

In his own way, Reese would contribute to Shay and her ranch. Accounting wasn't glamorous work; just the opposite. Pushing numbers around was seen as boring to most people, yet to Reese it was the most important job for a business to undertake. He wondered how Shay would react to his news later when they met in the office to go over the accounting information he'd gleaned from the ranch's books.

Shay nervously stood in front of the office desk as Reese wandered in after her. Her hands were damp and cold. They'd left the washing and drying of the dishes to Harper and Noah, whose turn it was tonight. After a dessert of the pineapple upside-down cake, they'd excused themselves.

Reese closed the door and pulled out a chair for Shay. Then, he sat down next to her at the desk.

"Seriously? You haven't found anything yet?" she asked, unable to contain herself. She saw Reese give her a look that didn't do anything to quell her suspicions.

"Nothing yet, Shay. But I do have some questions for you."

She gulped and gave him a wary glance. "Sure."

Reese had three ledgers spread out across the cleaned-up desk. "There's twenty ledgers in total, going back to when your family's ranch was created in 1895. But I was only interested in the books from when your father, Ray, took over the reins of the ranch."

"Okay," she said. "My father drove Ned off about fifteen years before he got that stroke. Ned had taken care of the books since before I was born. It was heartbreaking. Ned was like an uncle to me. I cried when my father suddenly fired him."

"And then your father took over the books at that time?" Reese asked.

Licking her lower lip, she said, "Well, it's a bit more complicated than that. My mom, Wanda, was a self-trained bookkeeper, but it sure didn't rub off on me. She had been taught by Ned. So, he asked her to take over for him. Then she died of breast cancer when I was ten. My father hired Dan, another bookkeeper, but within six months, he fired him and took over the books himself."

Frowning, Reese asked, "Why did he fire Dan? Do you know?"

"No, my mom was gone. My father never communicated much with me, and I was unaware of what was going on at the ranch. I don't know why he fired him. My father tended to drive good people away from the Bar C."

"I see." Reese took a piece of paper and a sharpened pencil, writing down the chronology. "Because," he said, lifting his head and holding her gaze, "there's different types of handwriting making the entries. Maybe you can look at them and tell me whose each is?" He opened the third book. "This must be your mother's writing?" He turned the book around and slid it toward the edge of the desk toward Shay.

"Yes . . . that's my mom's writing."

Reese turned a few pages to a particular date and said, "This one?"

"I think that's Dan's handwriting. I don't know for sure, but if it is, you'll see my father's scrawl after he fired him."

Reese turned until he found the scrawl and showed it to her.

"Yes, that's my father's handwriting."

Reese opened the beginning of the book. "Then this must be Ned's?"

"Yes, it is."

"Was Ray trained in accounting, Shay?"

"No. Why?"

"Well, there's some inconsistencies. I've found that they start here."

Blanching, she stared at the book and then up at Reese, her heart starting to beat harder. "What kind?"

Shrugging, Reese murmured, "Too early to tell. I just stumbled upon them a few hours ago."

Resting her fingers against her throat, Shay swallowed hard. "Well . . . if there are mistakes . . . then I perpetuated them when I took over." Her voice was little more than a strained sound. She saw Reese's eyes grow kind as he looked at her. Instead of feeling blame coming from him, she felt the warmth of his protection, which she was beginning to crave. It always soothed the anxiety that prowled around within her. Tamped it down. Put a leash on it.

"Most likely, but look, the sky is not falling, okay?" He grinned a little to help relieve her anxiety.

Shay whispered unsteadily, barely holding his gaze. "My father's an alcoholic, and that could well play into any mistakes he made."

"You told me that earlier. Is that what landed him in the nursing home?"

"Right. He used to gamble and was a heavy drinker from the time I could remember. He suffered a stroke, and it affected his mind, too." Her mouth quirked. "I don't know how a drunk could keep good books, do you?"

Shaking his head, Reese said gently, "No, I don't, Shay. If the books are in error, this isn't your fault. You know that, don't you?"

She pushed her fingers through her hair, feeling deep anxiety. "God . . ."

"Don't go there," Reese warned her quietly. He shut the books, hands resting over them. "You've got enough on your shoulders already, Shay. Let me carry this load for you, okay? I'll figure it out and we'll fix it."

Giving him an anguished look, she said, "What if Ray screwed things up, though? What if we owe thousands of dollars more to the bank? I know my father has a savings account where he's put money away over the years. I've not touched that bank account because it's his retirement savings." She rubbed her face. "This is so scary."

Reese stood. "Come here," he said gruffly. He wasn't sure Shay would come to him, but the stricken expression on her face was one of utter need and hopelessness. To his surprise, she rose from the chair and stepped into the circle of his arms. It was almost shocking as her soft warmth pressed against his chest, her head coming to rest on his shoulder, her arms wrapping around his waist.

"I need a hug," she whispered, closing her eyes.

Reese knew that Shay hugged the other wranglers from time to time, too. Unable to help his reaction, his whole body went on a five-alarm-fire alert. He'd been without sex for two years. It wasn't that he was a monk. He liked a woman as much as the next man. He recognized though that Shay had only friendship in mind.

Inhaling the scent of apricots as he rested his jaw against her hair, the silky strands tickling his jaw and neck, Reese closed his arms carefully around her shoulders. He wanted to crush her against him, take her mouth hungrily, share his heat with Shay.

He forced himself to do the right thing, felt Shay's weariness, her sagging against him for just a moment. What she needed was a safe harbor. He wanted to press his lips against her hair, temple, trail kisses down to her mouth. Jesus, this was tough to ignore. The fullness of her breasts felt delicious against the hard wall of his chest. He was skin and bone in comparison to her.

Reese relished the momentary hug he gave Shay. And then he opened his arms, allowing her to step away from him. Her cheeks were flushed, and damn, if he didn't see desire in her eyes! That surprised Reese. Was he reading Shay accurately? Or not? He was caught off guard and unsure. Who would want him in his present state? He was a loser. He'd lost everything. There was no way Shay desired him. No friggin' way. He still didn't know if she was in a relationship. No one had mentioned anything about it yet. It was his overactive imagination, that was all.

"Thanks," she murmured, "I needed that."

So did he. Awkward, fighting inside, Reese moved around the desk to protect her from himself. His skin where she had rested felt as if tiny flames were licking across it, exciting him. The last thing he needed right now was an erection. "You need some protection," he told her gruffly, sitting down in the chair that no longer squeaked. He'd found a can of oil and fixed the thing earlier.

She pushed her fingers through her hair. "That isn't going to happen." She turned and walked to the door, opening it. "Thanks for your help on this mess, Reese. Let me know what you eventually find."

"Yes," he said, holding her sad gaze, "I will."

Reese sat there in silence after Shay left the office. Her

voice had been low, filled with surrender, as if she were giving up. Male voices carried down the hallway from the kitchen. He could hear the vets leaving the house to go to the bunkhouse. Finally, they were alone. Reese found that he wanted Shay to himself. Maybe he was more alpha male than he ever believed himself to be, and his mouth curved wryly over that thought. Shay made him want to guard her. Love her.

He wearily rubbed his face, leaning back in the chair, eyes closed, his imagination rampant as his body continued to throb and sense every place she'd lain against him. Reese felt like a thief, shamed by his reaction to Shay's distraught moment. She thought he'd wanted to hug her and that was all. The truth was, if she'd indicated the least little bit that she wanted more than that, Reese would have given it to her. How close he'd come to kissing her.

Something wasn't right, and Reese couldn't ferret out what it was. Garret and he had sat for two hours poring over the books. Garret showed Reese the other books with the entries made by the different accountants. And he'd reinforced what Shay had said about Ray Crawford, that he was a drunk. A mean one.

"Got a minute?"

Surprised, Reese looked up to see Garret lean around the corner of the open door, his hand on the jamb. "Yeah, come on in."

Garret nodded and shut the door, sitting down. "Shay looks really upset. What happened?"

"She asked me if there were any mistakes," Reese said grimly. "I couldn't lie to her, but I tried not to let her know the extent of what we'd discovered, either."

Garret cursed softly, stretching out his long legs. "She's about maxed out."

"I told her to let me help shoulder this load. That it wasn't hers to carry alone."

Garret gave him a narrowed look. "Has she said anything to you about her father, Ray? What he did to her?"

Instantly, Reese's gut clenched. "No," he growled. "What happened to Shay?"

"I managed to drag it out of her over the past six months," Garret groused. "Man, she's tighter than Fort Knox when it comes to giving up personal intel on herself. I pride myself on being black ops, but she puts me to shame. I'd ask her a question and she'd dance around it. I'd time it such that I wasn't pressuring her, and she began to trust me enough to tell me a few things."

"Like what?" Reese closed his hand over the ledger, staring at the scowling vet.

Garret lifted his head. "She's been abused. That much I know. I guess her mother, Wanda, was verbally abused by Ray until she died of breast cancer. When Shay was about eight, her father started picking on her when the mother was too ill to protect her any longer." He sighed and shook his head. "The bastard."

"What kind of abuse?" Reese asked in a low tone.

"Shay wasn't specific. Said Ray was always putting her down. Telling her because she was a girl, she was nothing. He told her he wished she was a boy. He wanted a son, not a daughter."

Clenching his teeth, Reese stared at Garret.

"I asked her once if he'd ever hit her, and she grew real quiet but wouldn't say anything. When you looked in her eyes, you could tell. I can't prove it because she didn't admit to it," Garret said. "One time, when she opened up a little to me, she was in a philosophical mood. Shay said she'd left one war zone for another."

"What did she mean by that?"

Garret shrugged. "That maybe Ray made living under his roof a war zone for her and her mother? And she joined the Marine Corps at eighteen and got sent off to the Middle East, to another war or two." And then he gave a shake of his head. "My old man's an alcoholic, too. Not something I'm proud of, but when I told Shay that, she started being even more open," he muttered. "My old man beat the shit out of me. He'd go after my mother and I'd wave him off, get him to come after me instead."

Reese heard the pain in Garret's deep voice, saw the shame in his eyes. "He still alive?"

"Yeah. So's my mom. You don't know how many times I begged her to leave him. She wouldn't. Blows my mind."

"So when the Army discharged you, did you go home?"

Sneering, Garret said, "Only long enough to hug my mother, pick up my clothes and my gear. My mom is a shadow of herself. There's nothing I could do. So, I left. It's a lousy situation. I don't understand women. I don't understand my parents' marriage, if you could call it that."

Reese gave him a sour grin. "You have a lot of company."

Grunting, Garret muttered, "Well, Shay, in my opinion, has been abused physically and verbally. That's my two cents' worth, based upon my own experience." He flexed his thick-knuckled hand. "I'd like to punch Ray Crawford out, but he's sick and he's not gonna get better. The worst of it is that Shay visits him three times a week. Today was one of those days. You saw how she was when she got back. The old man takes her apart with his mouth and his uncontrollable rages. He blames her for everything that's happened to him and this broken-down excuse of a ranch." He sighed heavily and stared across the desk at Reese. "She does so much for us. She gives us the shirt off her back to make ends meet and to give us a safe place to heal up."

"But she isn't safe," Reese said quietly. "If she has to

see that father of hers, it's like someone opening a wound three times a week. Why hasn't someone gone with her? Protected her?"

"Believe me, the three of us, once we realized what was going on, wanted to. Harper really got into it with Shay. He accused her of enabling her father by letting him continue to verbally abuse her. Told her she should walk away from him and not see him again. Man, she got furious with him. I've never seen her so angry."

"But Harper was right," Reese said darkly.

"Yeah, damn straight. In my book, Harper was dead-on." Garret tilted his head. "You got a decent set of folks, Lockhart?"

"Yes, I do."

"If I coulda been discharged to return to a good home, I'd sure have liked to. As it was, I became a bum walking the railroads, hitching rides on boxcars, living off the land and going deeper and deeper into quicksand by the year." He looked around the small office. "Until Shay found me down-and-out."

"Shay picks up us strays," Reese agreed, his voice low with feeling.

"Why didn't you stay home, Bro?"

"I tried. But all I did was make it hard on my folks."

"What? Nightmares? Flashbacks? PTSD?"

"All of those things. I was causing them to lose sleep. My mom worried a lot about me. My father wanted to fix what was wrong with me." Reese smiled halfheartedly, remembering those emotional conversations with his caring parents. "I couldn't put it all into words. I couldn't tell them what I'd seen, what I'd survived when others didn't . . . You know how it goes."

"Yeah, I do. Ten years in black ops fried my soul." He ran his hands down the arms of the chair. "I was so far down when Shay found me, I didn't think I was going to make it back up to the surface. I'd given up. I wasn't doing drugs or drinking like my old man. I—didn't know where to go. I'd just given up."

Reese heard his pain. "I was heading there myself."

Garret smiled a little mischievously. "Too bad Shay isn't here to hear us talking about this shit. In our Friday-night gabfests, we're supposed to open up and talk, but you know how vets close down. We can't talk about it."

Reese chuckled a little. "Yeah. Been there, done that. She told me about it, but I don't know . . . I couldn't even talk to my parents."

Nodding, Garret stood. "Listen, I'm going to hang my ass out on a long limb that could break off on me, but I think you need a heads-up, Lockhart."

Reese looked up at him, puzzled. "What?" He saw the seriousness in the vet's face, his hazel eyes somber.

"Shay likes you. Do you realize that?"

Stunned, Reese blinked. "What the hell are you talking about?" His heart started to pound in his chest.

"I'm black ops. I'm trained to see little things everyone else misses," Garret said in a low tone. "Shay behaves differently around you."

"I just got here. I'm a stranger to her."

Rubbing his jaw, Garret said, "Doesn't matter. She's not in a relationship, Lockhart. She's alone. The three of us try to be her friends, but she needs something more than what we can supply."

Reese looked away. "I'm a bad bet. You know that."

A grumbling laugh filled Garret's massive chest. "Oh, we're all losers, no question. There ain't a woman who's gonna give us a second look." He waved his hand toward the door. "But there's something in Shay's eyes when she's looking at you. She's interested in you, Bro."

"Christ," Reese said, shaking his head. "I don't need this . . ."

"Hey, she's a damn fine-looking woman. You have to agree with that. And she could do a helluva lot worse than falling for you. If you ask me, she's better off with a vet. At least we'll protect her and stop this shit that's happening to her because of her father. Plus, she deserves a good man." Garret's eyes gleamed. "And you'd make a good partner for her in my estimation."

Chapter Six

Shay couldn't sleep. Tossing and turning was something she was too familiar with, so she got up. Max followed her and took his place near the couch in the living room, watching over her. Out in the kitchen, she put on the kettle to make herself some tea. The clock on the stove read 2:00 A.M.

Rubbing her burning eyes, she kept on the stove light only, and tried to be quiet so she wouldn't disturb Reese. Her faded fuzzy red slippers, which were nearly five years old, shushed across the cedar floor as she put a napkin and spoon on the table. The quiet felt good, embracing her. Max came and lay on his dog bed in the corner, curling up, watching her with large brown-gold eyes.

"Shay?"

Shay jerked around, gasping, her hand flying to her throat. "Oh, God! You scared me!"

Reese gave her a sheepish look, standing uncertainly in the entrance.

Her heart banged away in her throat as she stared at him with wide eyes. He was dressed in a pair of dark blue pajama bottoms, a tan T-shirt covering the expanse of his broad chest. Shay couldn't help but think he looked like a sleepy-eyed young boy in that moment, his hair mussed, eyes puffy from sleep. "I-I must have woke you. I'm sorry, I tried to be quiet."

He shrugged. "I'm a light sleeper by nature," he murmured, wiping his eyes with the heels of his hands. "Are you okay?"

Her heart warmed in her chest. "Yes . . . fine." She gestured toward the stove where the kettle was beginning to whistle. "I get nights like this. Do you want to share a cup of tea with me? Or would you rather go back to bed?" She saw his well-shaped mouth curve faintly as he studied the teakettle.

"Not much of a tea drinker, but I'll give it a try. If I drink coffee now, I'll be up the rest of the night."

"Go on over to the table. I'll fix two cups." Shay was glad he was here with her. Reese took her mind off her worries. She covertly watched him stroll to the table on his large bare feet and sit down, taking the chair he used all the time. Smiling a little, she took down a second mug, placing it on the counter, hearing the scrape of the chair against the floor.

"Do you get nights like this often?" Reese asked, folding his arms on the table. The light from the stove silhouetted Shay's figure, hidden in a fleecy yellow nightgown that fell to her slender ankles. It might be shapeless, but he knew she wasn't. The scruffy-looking red slippers on her feet made Reese smile a little. It was an endearing picture of her and he tucked it away in his heart. Her hair was tangled around her shoulders, but on her, it looked inviting. Sexy.

"Some nights I can't sleep," she murmured. Turning, Shay brought the tea over, placing one mug in front of Reese and sitting down at the head of the table. She felt her anxiety dissolving. It always did when Reese was nearby. "I'm sorry I woke you."

"Any sound out of the normal ones," he told her wryly,

dipping the tea bag into the steaming water, "and I snap awake. Too many years in the Corps and the threat level high and constant."

"Our military sixth sense going online," she muttered, frowning. "I wish I could make it go away. Or reduce it somehow."

"I don't think it ever goes away," Reese murmured. He put the used tea bag on a saucer she'd provided between them. Reaching for the sugar, he poured a spoonful into the mug.

"I try all sorts of things to get to sleep," she groused. "None of them work. Taylor Douglas is the only doctor in Wind River. She's a physician's assistant and says it's my PTSD. I guess I could cave in and take sleeping pills on those nights, but I hate taking anything like that. I know it's necessary sometimes, but I don't want to become dependent upon them. Taylor is doing research on PTSD right now and is studying under a Dr. Sam Cooper, from Jackson Hole. He's teaching a six-month course on how to cure some of the PTSD symptoms, and she's learning a lot. I told Taylor the moment she graduates, I'm going to be on her doorstep for the treatment. She said it is alternative medicine and does not involve taking prescription meds."

Reese gave her an admiring look. "Yeah, I steer away from any kind of drug use, too. Keep me informed on this training she's getting. I'd like to know more about it."

"Oh, don't worry. Once I try it out, and if it works, I'm going to be shouting at the top of my lungs. I'll get the guys to go and get treated by Taylor. I live sleep-deprived, and I'm at my wit's end trying to stop it." Shay gave him a softened glance. "I'm sure you have some sleepless nights, too."

"Yes," he said with a nod. "The very survival mechanisms

that saved us from getting killed over in Iraq or Afghanistan now work against us in peacetime."

Wryly, she nodded. "That's true. My whole system has become wired for survival. Everything over there was a threat. I felt raw at times, but I knew I had to stay alert, stay on guard, or I could be the next person to step on an improvised explosive device."

"I know," Reese agreed fervently, sipping his tea. His brow wrinkled. "What is this brew?"

"Chamomile," Shay said. "It helps calm the nervous system." She lifted her cup and sipped from it. "It's about the only thing that helps me eventually go to sleep."

"Did you have a nightmare?"

"No. I used to get them almost every night, but since being home"—Shay looked around the quiet kitchen— "and with my attention elsewhere, they've slowly been going away. For that, I'm grateful."

Nodding, Reese held the spoon in his hand, moving it between his fingers. "You want us to share our military experiences, but have you ever shared yours?"

"No, not too much."

"Why not?"

"Because this isn't about me, Reese. It's about all of you. Getting you on a more stable, day-to-day routine so you can start healing." Shay pushed strands away from her cheek. "A daily rhythm in a person's life is essential. And I know you haven't been here long, but you're intelligent and you can see how Garret, Noah, and Harper are blooming."

"What kind of shape were they in when they arrived here?"

"A lot worse shape than you're presently in. Just as underweight, and they had malnutrition issues. They all had horrible nightmares and flashbacks. Now"—she sighed, giving him a satisfied look—"not so much. I mean, they still get them, but not as often."

"That's a godsend in itself," Reese agreed.

"They're rebuilding their self-esteem, their confidence and belief in themselves," Shay said quietly, moving her fingers up and down on the warm ceramic mug.

Reese sipped his tea. "They seem pretty solid to me. I've met vets on the street who are in a lot worse shape."

"They've come a long way," Shay said, emotion in her tone. "I'm so proud of them. Noah is building a good horse training business. Harper has skills with electrical and plumbing that bring us in really good money. Right now, he's putting a lot of what he earns by working toward his paramedic degree from the local college. He was a Navy combat corpsman in Afghanistan. He's wanting to get the two-year degree so he can hopefully be hired by the Wind River Fire Department afterward. That would give him a steady income. Garret knows construction and running heavy equipment. He rents himself out to do small jobs around the valley for us."

"And their work contributes financially to the ranch?"

"Yes."

"Garret's one hell of a cook. Maybe he missed his calling."

Shay smiled a little. "He loves to cook, but he'd never want to be hired as one. A restaurant kitchen would be way too enclosed and stressful on him. He can't handle small, confined spaces. But he does well here at the ranch and we're the lucky recipients of his skills."

His mouth crooked. "That enclosed spaces thing. We all have it, more or less."

"To a person," Shay agreed.

"And are you figuring that once you get that indoor arena up, that Noah can start taking on a lot of new clients for horse training?"

"Yep. That arena will serve us in so many different ways."

She sighed. "I worry about getting it up before winter comes, though. Around here, that's early, mid-September. It's been known to snow in August, which I hope doesn't happen this year."

Moving the spoon slowly between his fingers, he asked, "Have you thought about a barn-raising?" He saw her brows move up a bit. "You know? In the old days when a rancher or farmer needed a barn built, the surrounding community would all come together for several days. They'd all work together, bring food and family, camp out, and get the job done."

"No," Shay admitted, "I hadn't thought in that direction."

"Might be worth a shot?"

Sitting back, Shay raised her eyes to the ceiling, thinking. "I have an appointment with Maud Whitcomb tomorrow at noon. We're going to have lunch at Kassie's Café and I'm going to ask her about getting some of her buffalo meat at a wholesale price." Shifting her gaze to him, she said, "Garret said we need more protein-rich food in our diet, and I don't disagree. You guys need that kind of nutrition, but I just don't have enough money to buy beef, which is ungodly expensive. Maud donates her buffalo meat to several local charities, so I'm hoping she'll sell me some. At least I could pay her something, and not ask for a handout."

"You don't like asking her for help?"

Shay sighed. "It's hard for me, Reese, but all I have to do is think about these guys, what they've gone through, how they suffered, and I can easily go ask for help. Maud will give me buffalo meat at a low price, I'm sure. She hires military vets over at her ranch, too, and she's got a heart of gold. She's the maven here in the valley, well liked, respected, and has the richest spread around. Maud is super active in charities and helping other ranchers here in Lincoln County. Her husband, Steve, is a world renowned architect.

She runs the ranch. He creates amazing buildings in many different countries."

"I don't know if I could do what you do," Reese confided gently. "I was never any good at asking for help." He shrugged. "Pride, I guess . . ."

Shay reached out, briefly touching his lower arm. "You don't have to ask for anything. That's my job, Reese. And I don't mind doing it. I'm not asking for myself, but I'm asking for all of you, so it's a lot easier for me to do it. I'm great at fighting on behalf of underdogs."

"Still," Reese murmured, "it's stressful."

"Life is full of stress. So what's new?" Shay gave him a sad smile.

"You mentioned last night your father had a savings account with his retirement in it."

"Yes."

"You've never thought about dipping into that account to help get the ranch on a more stable long-term footing? Then paying it back over time?"

"God, no," she said fervently. "When I came home, the first thing my father told me was that the account was off-limits. And I agreed with him. It took him thirty years to save for his retirement."

"I'm trying to find it in the ledgers. Do you know what the amount is?"

"You won't find it in there. My father insisted on keeping the book for that account with him at the nursing home. I don't think he trusts me with it. He's probably afraid I'll dip into it and steal from the fund, to support the ranch. I would never do that, but he thinks differently. And to answer your question, there's 195,000 dollars in his savings account." She saw Reese's eyes widen a little. "It's a lot of money, but if you consider it took him thirty years to put that away, I think he did pretty good."

"And he keeps the book on that account at the nursing home?"

"Yes, he writes checks from that account. He's not sixty-five yet, so Medicare hasn't kicked in for him. He has to pay the nursing home five thousand dollars every month. He'll give me a check and have me write it out in front of him so he can give it to the manager of the place. And thank God, he's got that stash, Reese." Shay grimaced. "I couldn't raise that kind of money."

"It's a lot of money," Reese agreed.

"I'm so thankful I don't have to take care of him here at the ranch," she admitted hollowly, giving him a glance filled with guilt.

"You seemed upset after seeing him the other day," Reese said quietly, watching her expression.

"We don't have a good relationship. Never did," she said, shrugging. "I wish it were different, but not all families are happily-ever-after ones. Ours was one of the dark ones."

Reaching out, Reese slipped his hand over hers and squeezed it gently and then released it. "You've got a lot on your plate, Shay."

"I know . . ." Her hand tingled where his calloused fingers brushed across her palm. Shay felt her heart leap. Felt that yearning for Reese to touch her. He made her so hotly aware of herself as a woman. It was disconcerting, nice, and frustrating. Shay realized he'd reached out to comfort her. Nothing else. But looking into his shadowed green eyes, Shay swore she could see desire in their depths. For her. The thought was heated. Provocative. Off-limits.

"Tomorrow morning, I'm riding the south fence line," she said. "Garret will start repairing the northern section, and I need to get out and inspect in the south part of the ranch. Would you like to ride along?"

"Yes. Want to repair as we go?"

She nodded. "We have to. I could use a second pair of hands. Repairing barbed wire alone is tough. Another pair of hands always makes it easier and it goes faster."

"Are you going to assign me a horse?"

"We have four quarter horses. All geldings. Just take your pick. I'm going to start riding at 0900."

He smiled a little. "Hard to let go of that military speak, isn't it?"

Shay grinned. "Yeah, it is, but I love using it. It's easier to fall into old habits."

Reese finished off his tea. "It's not a bad habit to keep," he murmured. Rising, he took his cup over to the sink and rinsed it out, placing it on the dish drainer. "I'm going to try to get some sleep now. Thanks for the tea, Shay."

"Anytime. Good night," she murmured, watching him move like a soundless shadow. When Reese left the kitchen, it felt as if the warmth within the room left with him. Shay sat there trying to understand why he affected her so strongly. He was respectful toward her, comforted her when she needed it. Her hand tingled, and Shay could still feel the roughness of his hand briefly around hers. Something told her Reese would be a considerate lover. A man who gave as much as he took. Frowning, Shay wanted to ask Reese so many deeply personal questions, but she refrained. They were still getting to know one another. He'd opened up to her a lot tonight, and she to him. Shay was breaking one of her cardinal rules about not discussing her personal concerns with the healing vets. These men had enough to process and deal with. They didn't need her issues too, but Reese kept asking her more and more personal questions.

Why? Unsure, Shay sipped the last of her tea and pushed the chair away from the table, rising. She heard Reese's bedroom door quietly shut down the hall. Max got up and followed her, alert, near her side as she stood at the kitchen sink. Petting her dog's golden head, she murmured, "What do you make of him, Max?"

Max wagged his tail slowly, watching her.

"You like him. You're biased, big guy. Come on," Shay urged. "Time to go to bed." And as she shut off the stove light and whispered down the hall in her frayed red slippers, Max obediently followed her.

The air was brisk and chilly as Reese rode at Shay's side the next morning. Max trailed them, stopping to sniff a good smell every once in a while. Most of the early May snow had melted, just a few patches to be seen here and there in the pasture. The sunlight was shining brightly on the snow-capped Salt River Mountains to the east of the ranch. It was a beautiful sight, the sky a lapis lazuli color, the cries of a blue jay breaking the companionable silence as they rode side by side. Reese wore his heavy jacket, Stetson, and a pair of thick elkskin work gloves, and his saddle bags were filled with the tools they'd need for repairing fence line.

Shay looked tired this morning, but she put on her game face for everyone at the breakfast table. Reese was beginning to see how she pushed herself beyond her own limits for the men. A person's passion could carry them a long way for quite some time, but Reese knew she was burning herself out. He didn't approach Shay about it because he knew his concern could cause her more stress.

This morning, he liked that she wore her hair down, the brown and gold shining in the sunlight, the thick, slightly curled strands swaying with the movement of the sorrel gelding with four white lower legs named Socks. Like Reese, Shay wore a heavy denim jacket, work gloves, and jeans. Sometimes, as they rode down the five-strand barbed-wire fence line, their boots would occasionally touch . . .

Their breath, along with their horses', was white vapor in the clear, pristine Wyoming morning. There were few trees within the wide, flat pastureland for as far as Reese could see. "This is good land to lease to a cattle herd," he said. "The grass is almost knee-high."

"My father earned his major money doing it that way," Shay agreed.

"And because of all the fence-line repair that's needed, you're not leasing it out yet?"

"Right." Shay spotted a loose wire on a fence down the line. "My father had fifteen wranglers while I was away in the Marine Corps. And it took that many men to keep this place going and repaired. Ten thousand acres of fence line is enough to keep anyone busy full-time."

Nodding, Reese saw the issues. "Is one of your long-range plans to get this fence line fixed so you can lease out sections of land?"

She pulled her horse to a halt and dismounted. "Yes. But I've only been back a year, and my father had let this fence line go for three years before that. When I got home, I saw how badly broken-down the place had become."

Dismounting, Reese said, "That's a real shame." He saw the snapped wire, the lowest strand, and pulled out the tools they'd need to fix it.

"All the guys come out at least twice a week in teams to work on the fences," she said, getting down on her hands and knees. The grass was thickly coated with frost and it instantly soaked her Levi's up to her knees. Reese walked to the other post, ten feet away, and began working on the broken strand. She grasped the rusty wire in her thick leather glove, holding out the end toward him. "They spend half a day at it. That's all we can afford to do right now because they have day jobs, too. It's always a balancing act, and sometimes the fence repair is let go because we need the money the guys pull in from their outside jobs, to keep the ranch solvent."

Reese looped a new piece of wire onto the old one, quickly patching it. "It's all about balancing one need against another," he agreed, taking the end of the wire from her.

"I can't expand the ranch's facilities any more right now," she said unhappily. "I feed you guys, and food isn't cheap. Everyone is pitching in, but it's a slow-growth kind of thing. Not as fast as I'd like."

"Who came up with the indoor arena idea?" he asked, fixing the lowest strand. Now it was taut. If the lowest strand of wire was allowed to hang loose, a cow would try to get down on her knees and shimmy beneath it. Animals weren't stupid.

Shay rose, dusting off strands of grass sticking to her wet knees. "I did."

"You're very astute," Reese praised, standing. He walked over to his horse, Jax, placing the tools back into the saddlebags. "You've got a lot more savvy than you give yourself credit for, Shay." He smiled at her across the saddle. She wore a cowboy hat, a black Stetson, and with her slightly curled hair around her face, her large blue eyes were emphasized. Eyes he could stare at and drown his soul in, if he allowed himself.

"Really?" She mounted. "When I first got home, after I got my father in the nursing facility, I rode for weeks, checking out all the fence line, making notes and realizing it was impossible to lease our pastures this year to ranchers. The cattle would get out all the time."

He smiled over at her after mounting. "So you came up with the idea of the indoor arena, instead. That was a smart move, Shay. It will take a good year and a lot more than four men to get these fences back in shape for leasing once more. That arena will start turning a profit by this fall." He saw her wrinkle her nose as their horses started into a plodding walk.

"If we can get it enclosed before the winter snow hits. I've been giving a lot of thought to your barn-raising idea. When I see Maud for lunch, I'm going to approach her about it."

"Ask for her help. Her expertise," Reese urged. "I'll bet she's done a few barn-raisings in her day. Besides, Steve being an architect? I'll bet he could be a big help in giving you something you can use."

"That's another good idea. I'll ask her about that, too. Maud is in her fifties, but you'd never know it. She's so vital, busy, and bustling around. She's a great manager at the Wind River Ranch."

"How many wranglers does she employ?"

"Well, there's several elements to her ranch. She runs a day tourist facility for families from June through August. And then she has a regular cattle operation, and a very small buffalo one that she utilizes for meat sales to a big national grocery chain."

"She sounds like a good businesswoman," Reese said. "She's assessed her ranch, looked at how to make money with it. With Highway 89A parallel to her ranch, she has a chance to snag a lot of tourists coming through. I'd like to meet her sometime."

"I'll make it happen. Maud has spearheaded ecological changes to ranches in the area. We had a pollution runoff problem and she worked with the state to stop it. She also is eager to bring tourists into this area for all the businesses and ranches. She wants people to stop here for a while on their way north to the Grand Teton and

Yellowstone National Parks about a hundred miles away. She's also actively working with the National Park Service to see if the ranches in this valley can get tourists to stop and consider hiking and camping in the Salt River Mountains. Her hundred thousand acres include the flatland of the valley, as well as the hills and slopes of the Salt Range."

"You remind me of Maud," Reese said, giving her a warm look, seeing the surprise come to her eyes.

"How do you mean?"

"You have vision, too, Shay. You approach your ranch with common sense. You balance the needs of the wrangler vets with your budget, and you're doing a good job."

She laughed a little shyly. "Well, just wait! I know I've messed up the accounting books. I'm expecting you to call me into the office and drop the hammer on me."

"Who told you that you were bad at math?" he wondered.

"Oh, my father."

"What made him say that about you?"

Squirming, Shay said, "I grew up afraid of him, Reese. I always lived in fear of him. When he'd drink, which was often, I'd go hide in my room, afraid he'd come after me. I couldn't study. I couldn't think. My grades were average in school. And math was a hurdle for me anyway, but I was afraid to ask my mom for help. And I sure wasn't going to ask my father. He always says women are stupid. I wasn't going to him and hear him confirm it."

Reese heard the pain in her voice, the tight set of her full lips as they rode. "Why does he think women are stupid?"

Shrugging, Shay said, "His father, my grandfather Hank, believed in punishment. My father was his only son and he was hard on him in every way. He owned a furniture store in town. I never liked my grandfather, either. I stayed away from him as much as I could. Grandfather Hank lived at the house with us when my Grandmother died. I hated when those two got into fights. My grandfather was always berating my father, belittling him, telling him he was a loser."

"Sounds like you had a really rough childhood," Reese said, giving her an understanding look. He could see the loss in Shay's face. "Was your mother able to stand between you and your father?" He knew it was a deeply personal question, but this morning Shay seemed pensive and more available to him. Maybe because she was so sleep-deprived. Reese really didn't know, but he wanted to understand the family dynamic she was raised within. It defined who she was today.

"No . . . my father was horrible toward my mother. Always putting her down, calling her stupid, saying that the only thing she was good for was to cook, clean, and keep things going in the house. Never mind that she was terrific at keeping the accounting and bookkeeping."

"If she couldn't protect you, then who did?" Reese felt his stomach tightening, getting protective of Shay because he saw the anguish in her eyes.

"No one. I made myself a shadow, if you want the truth, Reese. I stayed in my room a lot, or I went and rode my horse away from the main ranch area to escape all the awful anger and arguments in the house. In the winter, it was worse because snowdrifts can pile up to ten feet and I couldn't go ride and escape. I just hid in my room . . . and tried to survive."

Chapter Seven

"Maud? I need your help," Shay said after they'd finished their lunch at Kassie's Café. The place was usually busy, but when the tourists came in from May through August, it was totally packed. They sat in a booth near the corner opposite the swinging double doors to the place.

Maud Whitcomb smiled. "How can I help you, Shay?"

She gave the fifty-five-year-old woman with black and silver hair a slight smile. Dressed in her white cowboy shirt and jeans, Maud always had her frayed red baseball cap nearby, sitting next to her elbow. She was a role model for fifty-somethings, not looking her age at all. Most people thought she was around forty. Giving Maud a shrug, she said, "You know the struggles I've had since coming home."

"Indeed I do." Maud folded her hands, her coffee mug to the right. "I keep telling you to let us help you, Shay. You're such a fighter but you think you have to do everything alone, and you don't." Maud gave her a kindly look. "You're young, you're passionate, but now, you've got four vets you're trying to help."

"I know." Shay sighed, looking down at her hands folded on the table. "Reese Lockhart, my newest vet, said the same thing."

"I like this vet already." Maud chuckled and sipped her coffee.

"You would like him. He was a Marine Corps captain and ran a company over in Afghanistan. That's a pretty important and responsible position for an officer in the military."

"Indeed it is."

"And Garret, the vet who does all the cooking for us, mentioned the other day that maybe we could buy some beef for the guys to eat." She opened her hands, holding Maud's warm stare. "You already know my budget-balancing woes. I just can't afford beef, unless it's hamburger."

"Then," Maud said gently, "let's get some of our buffalo meat over to you from our warehouse in Jackson Hole. I don't mind supporting your efforts, Shay. You know that. Pay me what you can. And if you can't pay anything? Consider it an ongoing gift between ranching friends. That's how we survive in this tough place called Wyoming. We need to do everything we can to help our struggling vets. This is just another way to do that in my mind."

Compressing her lips, Shay said softly, "I know that, Maud. It's . . . just so hard to ask for help."

Reaching over, Maud put her hand over Shay's clasped hands. "We *all* need help every now and then, Shay. There isn't one human being on this earth who hasn't needed a hand up, some support or help from time to time." Her fingers tightened for a moment. "You're so young and you're doing so much with so little. I've watched you struggle hard, for so long by yourself." She released Shay's hands, giving her a stern look. "And you've never asked me for help of any kind. This is the first time. I'm glad to see you're being more flexible about it."

Feeling guilty, Shay gave her an apologetic look. "You do so much for so many already, Maud . . ."

"Because I have a lot, I can give a lot. That's the purpose of having money. Not hoarding it, but sending it out to good people who are doing good things for others. You're one of those people. Our two ranches hire nothing but returning military vets. I'm working with a number of other ranches here in the valley to get them to see how smart it is to hire these men and women. I've wanted to support you for a long time, but you had to ask. If you don't ask, Shay, you don't get. So let this be a lesson for you. And another thing?"

"Yes."

"You're not asking for yourself." She planted an index finger down on the Formica table. "You're asking for *them*. You want to help these vets. But you have to get out of your own way. You think it's bad to ask others for help, but it isn't. Your father, Ray, taught you that. He was an isolationist personality and antagonized every rancher in the valley."

Grimacing, Shay looked away for a moment. Her voice trembled when she turned and held Maud's warm stare. "I-I grew up knowing there was never any help coming, Maud."

"I know, I know," Maud murmured, patting Shay's hands gently. "You were in a rough family situation. I wanted to help more, but your mother, Wanda, never asked for outside help either. She never reached out to me, or to our community as a whole, either. Your father is a very wounded man and he took it out on her and then you. But don't be your mother, Shay. You need to ask. Okay?"

Tears burned in Shay's eyes and she quickly wiped them away, embarrassed. Maud was kind and gentle with everyone. She was firm, though, and she always spoke her mind. And Shay knew just how much Maud helped others.

"Okay," she whispered, taking a deep breath, "then I'm going to ask two things of you."

"Fire away," Maud murmured.

"Reese Lockhart, the newest vet, wanted me to discuss a barn-raising of sorts with you."

"I'm liking him more and more," Maud said, grinning and leaning forward, focused. "But you already have two barns. Gossip is that you're building an indoor arena right now?"

"Yes, we are. Reese has a four-year degree in business administration. I was telling him I'm worried that if the snow starts flying early, and we don't have the arena completely closed in, it will be damaged. He suggested a barn-raising, only the objective would be to get the other half of the arena built. The shell is already in place. It's the roof I'm worried about. What do you think? I really need help and ideas on this, Maud, because I'm not familiar with barn-raising, and Reese thought you might be."

Maud grinned a little more. "Just a bit. Did he say I was old as dirt and would know?"

Shay laughed. "No . . . He'd never say something like that to you or anyone. He's a real gentleman."

"Hmmm," Maud said, giving her a wicked look. "That's because he was an officer in the military. They give them a nice set of social skills. You know, every time you mention that vet's name, your eyes change." She gestured toward Shay's face. "They go soft."

Startled, Shay sat back. "Really?" She felt heat sweeping into her face.

"I think you like this new hombre a bit. Eh?"

Maud's prodding made Shay feel suddenly nervous. "Well . . . he *is* nice. Reese is pathetically thin—at least fifty pounds underweight—tall and broad shouldered."

Maud gave her a wry look but said nothing more. "Then, all the more reason to start putting you on our weekly list of buffalo-meat deliveries. I'll have our truck driver stop by every Monday and drop off twenty pounds of meat to you. That ought to start pumping heavy protein into your hard-working vets. I'll charge you forty cents a pound until you can pay me more. And there's no rush on that, okay?"

"That would be wonderful, Maud. This won't be forever. Reese thinks that if we can get the arena roof on, we can start bringing in more money late this fall. Then, I can pay you full price for your buffalo meat."

"Fair enough," Maud said, nodding. "Reese ought to get together with my husband, Steve. You know Steve has an MBA from Princeton? The man is a brilliant financial strategist, which is why our ranch is doing so well when so many others in the valley are not. Steve handles the books and I'm the chief visionary, figuring out how to make money for us. I'm not bad at it, either. They could meet here at Kassie's. It sounds like they'd get along like two peas that came from the same accounting pod." She grinned.

"I was thinking about that," Shay said, smiling a little. She had met Steve, a vibrant, robust rancher, at a local square dance that was held weekly at Charlie Becker's hay and feed store, from June through September. Every Saturday night, the people of Wind River Valley drove their families to the popular dance in one of Charlie and Pixie's barns. Everyone was welcome, and it was free. Those who attended always brought a casserole or drinks, and it was where all the ranchers and townsfolk gathered to talk, find out what was going on with their neighbors and their families. Business was discussed as well. Shay had attended her first one last year, shortly after returning home from the service, and loved it. Her father hated such gatherings and made a point of never going. He'd forbade her mother and herself from going, as well.

"See? You keep puttin' yourself down that you're bad at

math and business, Shay, but you're really not. The indoor arena is a brilliant idea. I don't know why we didn't think of it, but I'm fully supporting you doing this for the Bar C. It will be a steady source of income. You'll need that to keep pulling the Bar C out of debt."

Giving an embarrassed shrug, Shay said, "Thanks, Maud. It feels good to hear from you that the indoor arena is a solid idea. I just see something and think of ways to fix it or make it work."

"Such a typical rancher's kid," Maud said, smiling. "A lot of your lack of confidence in your own ideas is because Ray beat you down as a kid." Maud shook her finger at Shay. "Your father didn't do you any favors. You need to listen to this Reese fella. He sounds reliable and smart."

"I'm trying, Maud. I really am." Shay saw the woman nod and give her a look of pride. It felt good to be with the older woman because she always built her up. Shay wished she had her formidable confidence. Maud and Steve were at the forefront of ideas to move Wind River Valley into a tourist hot spot. They were great role models and she was desperately trying to learn from them and emulate them.

"Okay, this arena-raising?" Maud said.

"Yes?"

"Let me call a few of the ranchers around here. Between us, we can do the hard work of coordinating a two-day arena roof-raising. If we have twenty men and women, all good, hardworking ranchers, I'm sure we can get the other half of that roof completed in one weekend."

Shay gasped. "That would be incredible. Really? It could be done in two days?"

"Of course. Twenty men and women working on it? I'm gonna go to Red's Machine Rental here in town. Red will donate his heavy equipment and be happy to help.

He'll truck out a crane, and you're going to need it to lift those joists into place for the roof."

"Ugh," Shay said, nodding. "It takes us three days to lift one section of joists into place, the building is so tall. I can't afford to rent a crane. Harper, who knows about them, said that's what we needed. But the rental fee is horribly high."

"Well," Maud said, "I know Red Grant personally. We used his cranes when we built a new barn on our ranch. He's ex-military, Army Delta Force. I'll put in a call to him when I get back to the ranch. I'll tell him this is gratis, that it's for the military vets at your ranch. I'm sure he'll donate his time and equipment to you. He hires vets, too. And this job will be close to his heart."

"I met Red and his wife, Melba, at the barn dance last year. They were very nice to me and said if I ever needed anything to just let them know. Vets helping vets," Shay murmured, nodding. "That's the way it always goes."

"Yes, and if Red offers you help like that, young lady, you take him at his word. If you had gotten up the gumption to tell him about your indoor arena, I'm sure he'd have either donated a crane for your use, or charged you a low fee for it. But you have to ask, Shay."

Glumly, Shay nodded. "I get it, Maud. I really do. And you're right. I'll go ask him about it."

"This valley holds a lot of fine civilians who respect what women and men in the military do for them, too. And they're the ones donating to fine charity organizations like Operation Gratitude out of Van Nuys, California. Those folks send out boxes to the military folks overseas. They do a great job. And it was created by a civilian woman whose heart is in the right place. She's an awesome and passionate gal. And you're a lot like her in some ways. But instead of sending boxes of goods to our folks in the military, you've opened up your ranch as a place of healing for vets who are really down-and-out and need a hand up. We have Delos charity here as well, who have a food kitchen they man for a lot of the poor who struggle to make ends meet here. We're lucky to have them, too."

"You're right," Shay murmured. "And we couldn't do what we do without their help, either."

"When you consider only one percent of the men and women in the U.S. volunteer for military service, it's a very tiny amount compared to our country's population. And I'm grateful our nation does support our men and women who are sacrificing so much, even giving their lives, for our country. Which is why I want to coordinate with Red Grant, and we'll get this arena-raising planned for you, Shay."

Tears fell from Shay's eyes and she gave her a smile, wiping them away. "You're such a guardian angel to everyone in this valley, Maud," she whispered, her voice trembling. "Thanks . . . thanks so much . . ."

"I'm sure that man of yours, Reese Lockhart, will be very happy to hear this. You tell him to call me. I want to put some of the organization for this arena-raising on his shoulders. If he led a company of Marines, he can certainly help Red and me get this thing coordinated. We'll meet at your ranch house in the coming week and get the details hammered out."

"I'm sure Reese would jump at a chance to help, Maud. He keeps grousing at me that I'm carrying too much on my shoulders. That I should share it with all of the vets."

Giving her a pleased look, Maud said, "This man is smart and he has a lot of good insight into people. Steve and I need to meet him sooner, not later. Okay?" She rubbed her hands together, smiling. "Between us, we'll get that arena roof on in no time."

Shay sat back, feeling as if a ton of weight was miraculously dissolving off her shoulders. "That would be so wonderful, Maud. Thank you." She reached out, gripping the woman's strong, roughened hand.

There was something special about Maud Whitcomb. And secretly, the times that Shay had met her as a child growing up, which hadn't been often, she had always imagined that Maud was the other grandmother she never knew but had always wanted. And like a fairy tale grandmother, she was playing an important role in Shay's life right now. Not only that, Maud was changing the face of Wind River Valley, one idea at a time. She knew that many of the ranchers in the valley were eagerly supporting her ideas to get new money into the area.

If tourism took root, it would be because Maud and Steve were at the helm of the great idea. Ranchers led hardscrabble lives in this valley. Shay was no stranger to that fact. Most ranches were a mortgage payment or two from default. The reasons were many, and a lot had to do with the short sixty-day growing season. Plus, cattle could not be wintered in this part of Wyoming.

"The best time to put that roof on is mid-July," Maud said, thinking out loud after squeezing Shay's hand and releasing it. "We're gonna need at least a month of lead time on this. Ranchers have a lot going on in the summer because it's such a short season around here. Everyone is working their hardest at that time. Usually, the hay bailing is done mid-July. That's when the ranchers will have time to help us with this project. Plus, we'll get the wives together and plan a huge buffet. Each family will bring their kids, dogs, and food. I love a barn-raising! It's a great time for the community to get together, chat, and have fun. You'll see," Maud said, pleased. "So let me, Red Grant, and this Reese Lockhart do the heavy lifting on this mission. All you have to do is show up, smile, enjoy all the good food, and take photos of the arena roof going up. Fair enough?"

Reese was in the office when Shay returned. He heard the screen door open and close. Coming out of his office, he walked down the hall. meeting her as she entered the kitchen. "Well? How did it go with Maud?" he asked, watching her hang her hat and purse on a peg.

"Unbelievable," she said, turning to him. "I wish I'd talked to Maud a long time before this." Shay gave him a warm look and gestured to the table. "Sit down? I'll tell you everything."

Nodding, Reese walked over to the table, pulling out Shay's chair. "You look happy." But he also saw redness in her eyes, as if she'd been crying. He wasn't sure what that was about. Going to the sink. he poured them glasses of water and brought them over to the table. Earlier, Garret had made a mulligan stew with chicken, and the spicy aroma was permeating the kitchen, making his mouth water. Tonight, the vet was going to make sourdough biscuits that were presently rising in a huge bowl covered with a cloth on the counter.

"Thanks," Shay said, taking the glass from him.

Reese sat down at her elbow, his fingers tingling. Damn, he wanted any excuse to touch Shay. "Tell me what happened." He sat and listened to her bubble excitedly about her lunch and discussion with Maud Whitcomb. When she was done, he smiled a little.

"No question, Maud Whitcomb is a dynamo," he said. "And I'm glad I'll get to meet her and Steve."

"Maud is going to call you in a few days," Shay said.

"She wants to get you and Steve together. Wants to meet here to organize the arena-raising—a planning session is what she called it."

"Good," Reese said, seeing the excitement burning in her blue eyes. His chest flooded with warm feelings. He wanted to always see that hope in Shay's eyes. Reese had to tear his gaze from her eyes, and from the lips that he swore he could feel beneath his own. He coveted her in the worst of ways. And a part of him felt guilty because Shay wasn't even aware of his interest in her. Maybe, in time, when he'd proven himself as a person she could rely upon, he could let her know in small, subtle ways, that he wanted to know her better on a purely personal level. Everything was so tentative. How could she be interested in *him* at all? Now or later? He was not successful. Just the opposite. That cold wash of reality flowed through Reese and he gently tucked his yearning for Shay away.

"Do you want to help in the planning, Reese?"

He smiled, forcing himself not to reach out and touch her hand. "Absolutely. Anything that can get that arena enclosed is money just waiting to come into your bank account." He saw her glow, a flush coming to her cheeks.

Shay reached out, gripping his hand, squeezing it. "I owe this all to you, Reese. It was *such* a great idea! I'm so glad you pushed me into talking with Maud." Reluctantly, she released his hand.

Reese felt his body respond to her unbidden touch. Did she realize what she did to him? No, she didn't. She was a spontaneous wild child of sorts, and he liked her that way, but it was playing hell on his hungry body. He grinned. "Well, give yourself a little credit. You took the idea and ran with it."

"Oh!" Shay touched her cheeks. "I forgot to tell you! Maud is going to have twenty pounds of buffalo meat dropped off at the ranch every Monday! She's only charging us forty cents a pound. Can we afford that?"

Chuckling, Reese said, "Yeah, Garret will stop bitching about having no beef to cook with. And I'm far enough into the ranch books to see you can afford to pay Maud that amount for the meat."

She laughed huskily and smiled at him.

His heart flew open. The look in Shay's blue eyes went straight into his heart and he held it gently. In that moment, Reese realized he was seeing the unfettered Shay Crawford, not the woman who had been told by her father she was stupid and of no importance. His heart ached for her, and Reese desperately wanted to love this woman who was chained to her past with her truculent father. As long as Ray was alive, she was going to be under his influence. Reese wanted to change that dynamic, but he wasn't sure how he could do it. Silently, he admitted Shay triggered every protective instinct he owned. She deserved to be held, loved, and kept safe.

"Garret will do a dance when he hears buffalo meat is going to be delivered," Reese said with a chuckle, finishing off his glass of water.

"Yes, we'll never hear the end of it." Shay laughed softly, scooting the chair back and rising. "I need to get to work."

"Me too." As he stood, he said, "You told me your father keeps the accounting book for his savings account at the nursing home?"

"Yes. Why?"

Shrugging, Reese walked over to the sink with her. "It would be nice to see it. It's part of the ranch's financial health and history. Part of the moving pieces that help me understand the financial ups and downs a ranch goes through. I know it's his money and he's not loaning any of it to you."

"Oh," Shay murmured, rinsing out her glass and putting it on the drain board, "I would never ask him for a loan. He's made it *very* clear I don't get a penny of it."

"But legally," Reese said, leaning against the counter, folding his arms against his chest, studying her, "you own the ranch because your mother left it to you. It was her family's legacy."

"That's true," Shay said, giving him a confused look.

"Did Ray Crawford make out a will?"

"Yes."

"Would you mind if I took a look at it?"

"Well," she murmured, frowning, "sure you can. But what do you hope to find, Reese?"

"From an accounting perspective, I need to know the legal boundaries of your ranch finances," he assured her. "It's helpful because it will draw a bigger picture of the ranch and its financial health. Wills often impose, modify, or change things. I'd just like to understand what those changes might be."

"Okay," she said, gesturing toward the office. "It's in the top file drawer. It's a copy. I have the original document in a safe deposit box at the bank."

"As it should be," Reese agreed. He allowed his hands to drop to his sides. "Okay, thanks for letting me look at it."

"If you see anything, would you clue me in?"

Reese gave her a warm smile. "Shay, you're my client, in a sense. Accountants work for a business or a person. You'll always be the first to know after I know." He saw her cheeks color a little. When she tucked her lower lip between her teeth for a moment, she looked endearing. Now, he was beginning to see a larger picture of Shay. To the world, she put on a game face that was confident, can-do, take-charge, and that showed she was a tough ranch woman running her business. But at home, with him and the vets,

Shay was another person. The mask dropped away and they got a woman who wasn't all that confident. But one thing Shay did unerringly, and that was to follow her heart's passion. And the four of them were better off for it.

Shay didn't realize her effect on people, how good and kind a person she really was. Her father had drilled into her that she was unimportant to him and to the world. That she was stupid and couldn't do math. Reese found himself wanting to have a talk with Ray Crawford about how he was treating his daughter. Reese knew it wouldn't happen. He couldn't get in-between a father-daughter relationship. If Shay asked him to, that would be a different story. Then, he could. But if she didn't reach out for his help . . . his protection . . . Reese could do nothing but step back and watch the damage the man was doing to his only daughter continue.

"Good," Shay murmured. She touched his upper arm. "Gotta go. I'll see you and everyone else tonight at 1700."

Grinning, Reese nodded and watched her grab her Stetson, her work gloves, and hurry out the screen door, off on another project. He stood there for a moment, feeling his flesh warm from her unexpected touch. And damn, had he been imagining what he saw in Shay's eyes for a split second? When she'd touched his arm, he saw yearning in her eyes. For him. No . . . that couldn't be. What woman wanted to get involved with a man who had lost everything? Who was wounded emotionally and mentally? Who was scrambling to just try to act normal when normal didn't exist anymore in his life?

Wandering down the hall to the office, Reese thought about Shay. She was no less wounded than any of the rest of them. Shay did not realize her own formidable strength; she saw herself as weak and sometimes incapable. Damn, he wanted to fix that for her. To help her realize what an amazing woman and human being she really was. Her own PTSD had set her on this passionate course to help other vets. And for that, Reese felt such fierce gratitude that it choked him up.

Halting at the four-drawer file in the office, he pulled open the top drawer. He'd give Shay this, she was good at organizing. All the files were in neat, alphabetical order. Toward the rear of the drawer there was a file marked WILL, and he opened it up, pulling out the document.

Closing the file drawer, his heart still on Shay, he sat down. It was eating at Reese that he wanted to start rebuilding Shay's confidence in herself. He'd done it before with the men and women in his Marine company. As the commanding officer, his job was to take care of those who reported to him. And Reese was damned good at judging a person's weaknesses and strengths. And where they were weak, he helped to guide them toward success. Often, he was able to show the young Marine how to turn a weakness into a strength. He prided himself on being able to help, and his company as a whole had been better off.

Lifting his head, Reese stared at the open door for a moment, knowing that he could help Shay change her perception of herself. It would take time, no question. Often, Reese would spend a year, off and on, with a Marine, to help him or her recognize their issues and then adopt a healthier path. Reese knew that many of the Marines he'd helped came from dysfunctional families. Shay had come from one herself.

As he turned on a lamp and focused on the will, Reese silently promised Shay that he was going to help change her negative vision of herself. Her father had promoted a dark self-image, encouraged her to feel she didn't measure up.

It wasn't so, and Reese knew it. He felt blessed to have two terrific parents who hadn't screwed him over like so many other kids had been. They'd loved him fiercely, allowed him a lot of latitude to find out who he was and what he wanted to do with his life. They were firm with him, punished him upon occasion, but never lifted a hand to hurt him in any way. And that was why now, Reese ached inwardly that he'd had to leave his parents after being discharged from the Marine Corps. They loved him so much, but were confused by the PTSD that controlled his life right now. One day, he hoped that he could return to them, explain his condition simply so that they finally understood what had taken him so far down. God, he hoped he had an opportunity to do that. He loved them.

And then, an image of Shay's face gently came into his mind, and Reese felt a helluva lot more than just gratefulness toward her. His heart was in the mix, whether he wanted it to be or not. And it made it hard on him in many ways because Reese had never expected, in his condition, to be drawn to a woman. The last two years of his life, women had been an unreachable dream. No one looked positively at a down-and-out vet sleeping on a sidewalk near a grate. No one.

He'd lost his marriage to Leslie at twenty-seven because when he came home after the year-long deployments, his PTSD symptoms chased her away. Reese didn't blame her for divorcing him. He was a hot mess. And he was too proud to ask for help, thinking he could handle his symptoms on his own. But the truth of the matter was his stiff-necked pride had destroyed his marriage. And then, because he refused to get help, the Marine Corps had released him from a career that he loved.

So much for pride . . .

Chapter Eight

At the dinner table that night, Reese watched as Shay excitedly shared the news of her lunch with Maud Whitcomb. Her face was flushed, her blue eyes dancing with joy. The vets responded with big smiles, relief in their expressions, and they heartily and sincerely congratulated Shay.

When Shay was thrilled about something, her hands were never still. And she was so damned graceful. Reese had to curb his desire for her because he imagined those long, slender fingers of hers slowly moving across his body, inciting fire, and turning him on. Shay didn't deserve those kinds of thoughts from him, and Reese shoved them down deep.

"A barn-raising," Garret said, nodding. "Great idea, Reese."

"Thanks."

Noah sighed. "Just because we get the arena enclosed, we still will have a lot of work on the interior to do, Shay."

"I know," she said, enjoying the mulligan stew. She opened another sourdough roll, steam rising from it. Sliding a pat of butter in between the halves, she said, "That arena will need pipe fencing erected within it. Sand will have to be brought in. The lockers have to be installed. A huge tack room built. There's a lot left to accomplish."

Harper said, "We should get those dump-truck loads of sand from the quarry south of Jackson Hole lined up soon, Shay. The sand will have to be brought in first before we start on pipe railing. We'll have the equipment here to haul it and lay it out where the arena is going to be built."

Shay nodded. "I totally agree with you, Harper."

"That's on my list of things to talk to Maud and Steve about," Reese assured them. "I want to get as much done in those two days as possible. We'll need to develop a time line for all the work."

"Good," Garret said, spooning two huge ladles of the stew from the pot in the center of the table, "because equipment rental is charged by the day and it's damned expensive. When you're creating that timetable of arrivals and departures of everything and everyone, don't let the equipment sit around for hours at a time, unused. Time is money when it comes to renting what we need."

Reese agreed wholeheartedly with Garret. "I got a call from Maud Whitcomb," he told Shay. "About four thirty this afternoon." He saw Shay's eyes light up with expectation.

"And?"

"She talked earlier to her husband, Steve. He's coming over here tomorrow at 1:00 P.M. for a meeting with us. If it's okay with you, Shay, we'll just sit out here at your kitchen table and hammer out the plans and lists."

"Sure. I'd like to be there for it, too."

"Of course."

She gave him a happy grin, rubbing her hands together. "This is just so overwhelming and wonderful," she murmured. "I feel like I'm in a dream of some kind."

Harper said, "About time. You've deserved a break like this, Shay."

Shay laughed a little. "Well, I'm not one to normally get a break, but I'll sure take this one, Harper."

Reese said nothing, thinking that Shay deserved a helluva lot more breaks. He lifted his chin and looked at the vets. "What I'd like from each of you by tomorrow morning. You all have experience with construction, one way or another. Give me your list of what you think is important to do regarding the arena. No detail is too small. If you were going to handle this job, what would you do first, second, and third? What would your priorities be? What order should they be done in?" He saw the vets give him thoughtful looks as they ate.

"Yes," Shay added, giving Reese a warm smile, "let's use our own experience. It can help Reese and Steve set up an agenda to make this project a success."

Reese saw that his request made the vets feel good about themselves. They were included in the process, not left out or ignored. The feelings at the table right now had never been more positive and upbeat. A strong sense of purpose threaded through all of them, and it reminded Reese of the years he had command over his company of Marines.

There was a delicate balance in the managing of people. And although he knew these vets were autonomous and he was no longer a commanding officer, the feeling of doing something good for the team, soared through Reese. For once in the last two years, he felt like he was turning a corner. He was believing once more that he had what it took to manage people and do it well. The proof, however, would be in that meeting tomorrow afternoon with Steve Whitcomb.

"I can't sleep," Shay mumbled to Reese as she walked out into the kitchen. It was near one o'clock in the morning, and he was sitting at the huge table, a lot of paper and files spread out around him. Shay had gone to bed at ten, exhausted.

Reese looked up and his heart swelled. Shay was in an ankle-length lavender flannel gown tonight, and wore those ratty-looking red slippers on her feet. There had to be a story to those slippers because from the looks of them they needed to be thrown away. Her hair was mussed, eyes drowsy as she walked to the sink and poured herself a glass of water.

"Want some, Reese?" She held up the glass.

"No . . . thanks." He liked the sense of peace in the kitchen. "Why can't you sleep?"

Making a muffled, unhappy sound, Shay turned and shuffled over to the table. "My mind is going a thousand miles an hour." Looking down at his work, she added, "My brain looks like the stuff you have spread all over the table."

Chuckling, Reese stood and pulled out the chair for her.

Shay rolled her eyes at him. "I can pull a chair out from the table just fine."

"I know," he answered patiently, his hand on the back of the chair. "You can blame it on my manners. Have a seat?"

Grumbling under her breath, she sat down. "Thanks . . ."

His mouth curved a little more as he sat down, picking up his pencil. "Are you always this grumpy when you get up?"

She rolled her eyes. "You have such a dry sense of humor, Reese. Who knew?"

"Well," he said as she sipped the water, "if we keep meeting like this at night, we'll know a whole lot more about one another over time. Won't we?"

Rubbing her face sleepily, she set the glass down. "The other vets don't know about my insomnia," she muttered.

"And the only reason you do is because there's no room in that bunkhouse for you. Don't tell them. Okay?"

He wrote down a few items on his list that he was going to present to Steve. "All your secrets are safe with me." He hesitated, searching her drowsy face. "Are you sorry that you let me stay here?"

"No, not at all." She reached out, touching his shoulder briefly. "I like your manners, Reese. You're a throwback to another age and time. It just catches me off guard because no one, except the vets here, pulls out my chair for me. It's nice and I appreciate it."

"I'm not *that* old, Shay."

She giggled and ran her fingers distractedly through her hair, trying her best to tame it behind her shoulders. "I didn't mean it quite like that."

"Nothing wrong with manners," Reese said lightly, writing down some figures on another piece of paper. "The world seems to have forgotten a lot of them over the past three decades."

"Military men tend to go the other direction. And it is nice, but as a Marine, I wasn't treated like a woman. I was treated like a Marine."

"Rightly so, but this is different. We're in the civilian world now." He gave her a quick glance before transferring more numbers to a third list, his brow scrunched.

"You had women Marines in your company?"

"I did. In the motor pool. Mechanics. Drivers. Good at what they did. The men gave me more problems than the thirty women in my company ever did. They were squared away, responsible, and displayed great teamwork. And they could shoot straight." He smiled over at her, watching her cloudy blue eyes slowly begin to clear. Shay wasn't someone who woke up very fast, he was discovering.

"I shot expert while in the Marine Corps."

"Something to be proud of."

"My CO wanted me to go to Marine sniper school. They were just opening it up to women."

"That's quite a coup," Reese said, pushing the papers aside. "Did you take him up on it?"

Shaking her head, she said, "No. First off, I couldn't kill like that. I could defend myself and my team and kill to protect them, but I don't have a sniper's mentality. I also knew I didn't have the patience it required." Her lips curved. "You've lived with me long enough to see I can't stand still for more than a minute or two."

"Were you always like that?" He saw her eyes grow pained and then she hid the reaction from him.

"Sort of . . ."

Reese didn't want to drag up a lot of bad memories for Shay. "Hey, I went through all the ledgers and there's nothing on your father's savings and retirement accounts in any of them. Not a trace."

"Right. Remember, I told you he kept the ledger? He has his own set of checks for the nursing home."

"Yes, I remember. Why wouldn't he trust you to do that?" Reese saw sadness come to her expression. He wished he could dig deeper to get more information on what Crawford was up to, but every time he asked about her dad, it hurt her. Reese didn't like doing that to her, but he had no choice.

"Because of the amount of money, I guess," she said. "He thinks I'm stupid when it comes to math. Why would he ever entrust me with his personal savings account or the ledger?"

Rubbing his stubbled jaw, Reese said, "He's like that even after the stroke?"

Her lips thinned. "Worse. He's more angry now than ever before because he can't get out of bed and walk. He won't use a wheelchair. He's so nasty to the nurses that even when he rings the buzzer for someone to help him, they won't come."

His gut tightened. "It has to be hard on you." He searched her eyes, which were shadowed with so many unspoken emotions.

"It's never easy with my father, Reese. He's . . . well . . . he's just who he is. If anything, as he's gotten older, he's gotten angrier and more bitter."

There was so much he wanted to say, but Reese clenched his jaw instead. "What's the possibility of me sitting down with him to discuss the savings ledger in relation to the ranch finances?"

"I don't think he would. He'd be angry because you're a stranger and he wouldn't trust you with anything financial."

"And then he'd take it out on you?" The words were spoken before he could stop them. Cursing to himself, Reese saw her shift in the chair, look away for a moment, touching her throat with her fingers. Finally, her hand dropped and she looked at him.

"Most likely."

"Can you ask him, then? I could write you a list of questions."

"I could try. No promises, though. I've tried to get him to help me with the accounting books before, but he refuses. He thinks he owns the Bar C and that he's still in charge. When he had the stroke, it reset his memory to a single time in his life when he ran the Bar C. He has no memory of my mother's family owning the ranch, her leaving the ranch to me, or of me going into the Marine Corps at eighteen. I haven't had the nerve to remind him of all that. He'd fly into a rage that would probably kill him, and I've got enough guilt about him, without him dying on me.

I let him think he still owns the ranch, Reese. I just don't have the personal strength to go there with him right now."

Reese sat up and dragged in a deep breath. Releasing it, he said, "I understand, Shay. Life's been hard and un-relenting on you since you had to come home to take over the running of the ranch. I looked over your parents' will. Now, I'm not a lawyer, but from what I read, that savings account does *not* belong to him. It belongs as part of the ranch finances." He saw her eyes widen.

"Are you serious?"

"Yes. Is the lawyer who wrote up this will here in Wind River?"

"Yes. Eddy Dobbins has a small office in town. He's been the family lawyer forever. He wrote up the will for them."

"Would Eddy see me so I can ask him some questions about the will?"

"I don't see why not. Going to my father isn't going to get you anything but a temper tantrum. Eddy's a nice guy and easy to get along with. I'll call him and tell him that I gave you permission to speak to him about all ranch business. I'll let him know you're our ranch accountant now. He'll want me to put the permission in writing, and that's fine. You can give him the signed paper when you see him."

"Sounds good. Thanks. When you came home from the Marine Corps, did you read the will?"

"I went to Eddy and asked him what the will meant."

"Did he tell you that all the monies regarding this ranch were in your hands?"

"Yes." Shay sighed and gave him a frustrated look. "When I couldn't find the savings ledger, I asked my father if he knew where it was. He blew up at me. He insisted the savings account was his and his alone. That it didn't belong to me or the ranch. He told me he would always keep it in

his possession." She pressed her fingers against her brow.
"I let it go, to tell you the truth. I just didn't want him
screaming at me anymore. I couldn't take it . . . I was too
raw from my own PTSD symptoms. It hurt too much to
take him on and press for more information."

Reaching over, Reese didn't give a damn anymore. He
needed to touch her, soothe her. "I'm sorry, Shay. Is there
any way I can help you with this situation?" He slid his
fingers gently across the back of her hand. Her flesh was
warm and firm. His body reacted. Reese couldn't be
around her and not become aroused. It wasn't Shay's fault.
It was his. His fault for lack of control over his own emotions, but then, PTSD had a way of dismantling his feelings
in ways that always took him off guard. Reese wouldn't use
that as an excuse, however. It was up to him to control himself around Shay. Period. Lifting his hand away, he saw her
eyes widen slightly, shift to a hazy blue. Reese fought what
he thought he saw. There was no way in hell that she was
attracted to him! He was half the man, or less, that he used
to be.

Shay managed a strangled laugh. "Yes, be my shield,
Reese. When I have to see my father three times a week,
come and stand between me and him."

"I'd be more than willing to do that, Shay." He tried to
bite back all he wanted to say and ended up growling, "No
woman deserves to be verbally abused by a man. And especially not by her father."

"I'm used to it," Shay muttered, shaking her head. "I
don't like it. I find myself dreading seeing him. If I'm late,
he screams at me. I can't do anything right."

The kitchen hung thick with tension.

Reese struggled not to ask obvious questions such as:
Did Shay ever stand up for herself? Tell her father to stop
how he was treating her? Sadly, Reese knew those answers

because over the years he'd counseled so many young Marines who had come from dysfunctional families. Some had been mentally and emotionally abused. Others, physically abused by their father or a boyfriend. Sometimes, a few had been abused in all three ways.

Reese had learned the hard way not to ask questions like that. It only served to make the Marine defensive and even more ashamed because they hadn't fought back and stood up for themselves. Abuse survivors were branded with low self-esteem as young children. Fortunately it could be cured with the right help and support. Reese had worked to help rebuild that broken confidence and give it back to the Marine in question.

"That's why I left the Bar C at eighteen," Shay said, running her finger slowly down the outside of the glass in her hand. "I couldn't stand what he did to me. I knew it was wrong. I didn't know where to turn, where to go for help."

"Most children growing up in a home like yours don't realize there is help out there. But it means going to law enforcement, or telling a teacher or a trusted peer, about what's going on at home."

"Right," Shay agreed, her voice low. She glanced over at him. "I figured it out when I was in the Corps. I never thought I'd be coming back here. I was in for twenty. I loved what I did as a truck driver in the motor pool, and I was good at it. Until the PTSD caught up with me . . ."

"And then your father had that stroke and you came home again?"

"Yeah," she muttered. She shook her head and pushed back on the chair, standing up. "It caught me off guard. I was given an honorable hardship discharge to return and take over the running of the Bar C. I knew what I was walking back into and I felt like a lamb going to slaughter. I was just too overwhelmed with anxiety, paranoia, and terror to think clearly."

She gave him a sad smile. "My father's behavior just ratcheted up my symptoms. When he had the stroke—I hate to say this—I felt nothing but relief because it was going to get him out of this house and away from me." Her mouth turned in at the corners. "I know that was wrong of me. He's my father." She pushed her fingers through her hair. "I'm not proud of what I thought."

Reese held her guilt-laden gaze. "When you're in a survival reflex, Shay, you can't judge yourself like that. You came from an abusive home. Your father continued to injure you verbally and probably emotionally. And if I'd been in your shoes, I think I'd have felt nothing but relief after he had that stroke."

She studied him, the quiet embracing her. "Because I was in survival mode? Doing what I had to do to survive rather than die?"

"Exactly." Reese gave her a sympathetic look. "When I left the Corps, I agreed to go see a shrink. I lasted with her for three sessions. But it wasn't wasted time. The woman was a civilian and hadn't a clue about what it was like to be in the military or battle situations, but she did help me see myself and where I was at. For that, I'll always be grateful to her."

"She explained that you were in a survival reflex?"

"Exactly. Like you were when you were forced to come home and take over running the ranch."

"It was hell," she muttered. Shay paced the length of the kitchen. "I wanted to run away from all this responsibility, but how could I walk away from taking care of my father? Our family home? We've been in this valley for over 120 years." She halted and made a choking sound. "I felt like I was dying all over again by living under this roof with my father. And yet, the fear of giving up on the ranch and letting it rot was ten times worse than what I was putting up with daily."

"The devil you know versus the devil you don't know," Reese agreed. "We all choose the devil we know. It's the fear of the great unknown that makes us freeze. We're paralyzed because we don't know what will happen if we strike out on our own. Been there, done that."

She tilted her head, studying him intently. "You don't seem like a man who'd run from anything, Reese. I know you have PTSD, but there's something so solid and secure about you." She opened her hands. "When I'm around you? All my anxiety goes away. That's pretty amazing, and it has never happened to me before. You help me. Am I making sense?"

"A little," he said. "That's the old part of me that didn't get wounded by the PTSD. I've always been like that." Reese smiled a little. "My mother would tell you that I'm the Rock of Gibraltar." His smile faded. "But that's no longer true. The PTSD . . . well, it destabilized me. Like it does everyone, sooner or later."

"Mmm," Shay said, sitting back down. "Tonight at dinner?"

"Yes?"

"The guys are really starting to naturally gravitate to you, Reese. It's not because you were a captain in the Marine Corps, either. It's that steadiness you have; you exude leadership energy. I look so forward to meals with you. I'm not as good at assessing people as you are, but even I can see that Garret, Noah, and Harper all respect you. When you talk, they really listen and listen hard."

Shrugging, Reese said, "I honestly hadn't noticed." And he hadn't, too wrapped up in his own internal processes, his confidence having taken such a hit two years ago. "And don't sell yourself short: You see people very clearly. You picked us." He let a grin curve the side of his mouth.

"You know how to make me feel good," she whispered, giving him a soft smile, gratefulness shining in her eyes. She opened her hands. "Just being around you, Reese, you make me feel more confident about myself."

"Well," he drawled, teasing her, "maybe we'll just rub off on one another a little at a time. In a good way."

"It is good," she said, her voice filled with sudden emotion. "Living with you"—she gestured toward the ceiling— "you never raise your voice. You always respect a person talking to you and you don't interrupt them. That's so refreshing to me."

Anything would be, Reese thought. Her father probably interrupted her all the time and discounted anything she said or suggested. There was no respect given from father to daughter. He felt Shay's pain because she felt responsible for Ray Crawford. And it was that push-pull between them, blood ties that would never be broken. Shay was suffering deeply from it and now Reese understood better why she had chronic insomnia and shadows beneath her eyes. It wasn't the amount of work she was doing around the ranch. No, it was dealing with her father on an emotional battlefield three days a week that she had no control over. But maybe, she did.

Reese felt a fierceness to protect her rise in his chest. It took everything not to reach out and haul her into his arms and allow her to feel a bit of safety for a while. Not all men were like Crawford.

"My dad taught me a long time ago that everyone was my teacher. They had something to give me," Reese told her. "It might be an awareness. Maybe an idea. Or a way to fix something. All I had to do was listen and not interrupt."

Shay sighed and finished off her glass of water. "I'd so

like to meet your parents." She gave him an ironic look. "You're going to think I'm a horrible person, but as a kid, I used to lie in my bed at night creating a father that I could love. A man who loved me. Who never yelled at me or made me feel bad about myself . . ."

"No shame in that. I've seen my share of young Marines who've come out of homes like yours and they think and wish the same things. It's normal."

She gave him a relieved look. "Truly?"

"Scout's honor."

She grinned. "I'll bet you were one!"

Reese felt heat tunnel through him as her blue eyes danced with sudden joy. There was a heated, yearning connection alive and throbbing between them. He could feel it and he knew Shay sensed it as well. He smiled. "Guilty as charged. My dad is still a Boy Scout leader to this day. I'd like to think I watched and learned a lot from him."

"You're a natural-born leader," Shay said, smoothing down the front of her rumpled lavender granny gown. "I knew that the moment I met you."

"It's pretty much trampled and gone," Reese warned, leveling with her. Talking to Shay felt like a gift to him. To be able to speak openly to her, knowing there would be no confusion, no recrimination or misunderstandings, was like fresh air circulating through his entire being. Shay freed him in ways that he never thought possible.

Snorting softly, Shay walked over to the sink and rinsed out the glass. "It's not destroyed, Reese." She turned and smiled warmly at him. "Your ability to lead is underground and, I'm sure, just waiting to be tapped and used again."

"You do hold out hope for the hopeless, don't you?" he teased, falling beneath her radiant smile. She had an arresting mouth, well defined, her lower lip a bit fuller than her upper lip. How Reese wanted to drown in that smile of hers by taking her to his bed and loving her. His dreams were torrid. Realizing he was seeing the real and spontaneous Shay Crawford, he felt himself melting into his tortured and fractured soul, that smile of hers so damned healing and beguiling. He saw her smile deepen.

"Always."

"Well," Reese murmured, holding her gaze, "you need to take that heartfelt passion and apply it to yourself, Shay. No one deserves support and encouragement more than you do." He saw his huskily spoken words touch her deeply, sudden moisture brimming in her large blue eyes. She was trapped with a parent who was always striking the frightened young girl that still lived within her. Everywhere else, Reese saw the woman living out her passionate vision for all of them. If only he could somehow release her from Ray Crawford's talons. If only . . .

Chapter Nine

Shay could barely contain herself as she served coffee and cookies to the gathering at the kitchen table the next afternoon. At the head of the table was Maud Whitcomb. Next to her, Steve, her husband. Reese sat next to Steve. She took the seat across from the wrangler, her heart pounding with excitement.

"Shay, we've had a few conversations before about your ranch and your dream of makin' it a place for military vets to heal," Maud said.

"That's right," Shay said, giving her a warm look. "And you've been instrumental in helping me to make it happen because you've been helping them years before I arrived back home."

"So now we're taking on a new project. Steve and I see it as a positive evolution of your vision for the Bar C."

Steve, who had already met Reese, said, "We're having an arena-raising instead of a barn-raising."

Reese opened his portfolio and lifted his head. "Is everyone ready to get started?"

Steve opened his binder. "Let's get to it."

Shay followed along as the two men hammered out the time line and the details on the raising of the roof on the arena. They were all business, and she liked that they got along well with one another. Maud followed along and occasionally made comments or asked a question. Mostly, it was the two men creating the plan. At a certain point, Shay stood and brought over fresh coffee, filling everyone's mug. She was excited and felt such pride over how Reese adroitly led the conversation and guided Steve into the areas that needed to be discussed and resolved. He was a true leader—quiet, listening fully, and able to incorporate good suggestions from Maud and Steve.

"Okay," Steve said with a smile over at Reese. "We've nailed this down. Nice work, Reese. You're a man who has an eye for detail and that's what a project like this takes."

Maud nodded, giving Reese a pleased look. "You're everything and more than what Shay told me the other day at Kassie's. Obviously, far more than an accountant."

"Thanks, Maud. I enjoy working on big projects like this."

Maud rubbed her chin. "Shay? Have you thought about enlarging this project a bit? We know that you have a three-room bunkhouse. Word is out that you're wantin' to expand and build on more rooms." She gave her husband a warm look. "That got Steve and I to thinkin' about this other project of yours."

"In what way?" Shay asked, interested.

Her eyes sparkled as she looked at Shay. "Young lady, you don't need extra rooms on that bunkhouse of yours, from where I stand. What you need is what we've been doing: building two-bedroom, single-story homes nearby for the vets you're hiring and helping. We buy a log home package of their choice, but they do the building of it on their own, free time. We'd like you to consider something along this line, but a little different: If each vet had his own home, it would go a long way toward helping them reclaim themselves. It would help them acclimate, get used to having a *home*, not a room in the bunkhouse. It would instill responsibility in them, give them something to be proud of, to work toward paying a monthly mortgage. It's a psychological thing. Having a home raises a person's confidence, makes them proud, and they grow because of it. In a good way."

Steve added, "All our vet wranglers who have worked two years or more for us, now have their own log home on our ranch. We're constantly expanding and building. It gives them something money can't buy: hope, pride in ownership, and a future. Have you thought about this angle, Shay?"

She shook her head. "No, I haven't." She opened her hands. "I love the idea, but we can't afford to build a house for one vet, never mind the four who are here with me right now."

"But what if you had the funds?" Maud prodded. "Would you consider it as a possible option?"

Shay smiled a little. "Of course I would. If I had millions of dollars, there's so much I'd love to do around here for them." She saw Maud give her a smile. The maven of the valley was up to something. But what?

Maud sipped her coffee, took a bite of her cookie, giving them all a thoughtful look. "Okay then. What's to stop us, on that same weekend for the arena roof completion, from building four houses as well? Steve has been calling the ranchers around the valley with the date and what your needs are. Right now, he has seventy-five volunteers. That's a lot of muscle, and they can't all be working on the arena roof-raising. Just not enough room. Why don't we put them to work on something else?"

"But," Shay broke in worriedly, "I don't have the funds for that. I mean, I wish I did."

"What if you did have 'em, Shay?"

She turned to Maud, feeling her heart beat harder in her chest. "Well . . . of course, it would be a great time to do something like that. If I won the lottery."

Steve smiled over at his wife. "Shay, we'd like to donate the money it will take to build your four houses. I figured this all out the other night. We'll provide you the funds up front. Once the homes are built, the vets who live in them can then send us a monthly mortgage payment on the house. We don't want to loan you the money with interest attached to it. Rather, a friend-to-friend money advance. You all right with that?"

Shay gasped, her hand flying to her mouth. Her eyes went wide as she stared at Maud, who was smiling at her. "I-I don't know what to say." She gave Reese a stricken look, unsure. "That's so much money . . ."

"We can't take it with us, Shay. Steve and I want to see good things happen to good people here in this valley. You've worked hard and I see the changes in the Bar C coming to life here because of the wranglers you hired. You're trying your hardest to give them a fair shake."

Tears ran down Shay's cheeks. "Oh . . . Maud . . . this is just overwhelming." She wiped the tears off her face, giving the older woman a grateful look. "Th-thank you . . ."

"It's for them"—Maud pointed at Reese—"these men and women have been sacrificing their souls for this country. It's about darned-good-and-well time that this country did something for them!"

Reese looked into Maud's angry-looking eyes. "Maybe you should run for president? We can use someone like you to go to D.C. and stir that political vat. Get something done."

Maud snorted. "I wouldn't run, Reese. I'm too blunt and honest for most folks. What I can do is help locally, and that's why Steve and you are gonna handle all the details and finances so that Shay can also, on that same weekend, have four new homes built on her ranch."

Reese managed a grin. "Your heart's in the right place." He gave them both a grateful look. "Thank you."

"I think it's a grand idea," Maud said, smiling and reaching over and patting Shay's shoulder. "So we need to enlarge the scope of this mid-July weekend to not only finishing the roof of the arena, but building four houses for Shay."

"Looks like," Reese agreed.

Steve said, "Shay? Just to be clear about this, if it's all right with you, I'm going to handle the financial side of this, but we'd like Reese to handle the construction side of things."

Shaken, Shay said, "Th-that's doable, isn't it Reese?"

He nodded. "Garret and Harper have a construction background. We'll handle it together. And I can work with the time sheets and other details with them."

Maud rubbed her hands together. "Sounds like military-style teamwork, don't it, Steve?"

Steve gave his wife a pleased look. "That's why you and I, when we can, hire military people. We know they're organized, disciplined, and have the can-do spirit that we need."

Shay felt her heart bloom fiercely with such joy that she thought she'd explode on the spot. Everyone was so positive, and it lifted her. Money was such a monster in her life that she could never have done something like this alone. She felt such love and gratitude for Maud and Steve. If only the world realized how powerful, wise, and caring they were to the struggling people of this valley. She knew that the younger generation paid no attention to them, and that was their loss. She had always found that these two ranchers provided the life experience she didn't have. And now, they were helping her to help her vets.

Reese smiled over at Shay. Her cheeks were flushed, eyes bright with moisture, vulnerable and happy. The shock over this unexpected development had swept her away. It would anyone. He was still catching his breath.

Steve opened up his briefcase and handed Shay and Reese another folder that read HOUSES on the tab.

"Study all the finances and requirements," he said to them. "I think you'll find our donation to Shay is all in order. Maud and I would like to spend a bit more time with you this afternoon going over these items."

Shay nodded, barely skimming her fingers over the folder that meant so much to her. "Of course we can."

Slipping the folder on top of his others, Reese said, "I can hang around. Let's do it."

"Good," Steve said, handing Maud a folder and opening up the last one in front of him. "We might need more fresh coffee in a bit," he added, and he grinned at all of them.

Shay nodded. "For sure. I'm so shocked by all of this, if I drank I'd want a shot right now." But she didn't drink because of her father. She saw Steve smile; he understood.

Reese couldn't believe the generosity of these two people, his throat tightening with emotion.

For the next two hours, they pounded out a lot of necessary details. He was glad to have Garret and Harper waiting in the breach. Those two knew construction from different angles, but together, they created the whole package.

"Reese? You and me need to make out not only a budget for each of these projects, but a revised time line," Steve said.

"Already there," he agreed. "I'd like to get Garret and Harper in on that side of the planning. They're very familiar with what it's going to take out in the field so we can refine these budgets."

Steve agreed. "Good. We have a lot to do in a short amount of time. We need to get volunteers to come in a week early to first put in a septic tank for each house, lay out the foundation, put in the plumbing, and then pour the concrete for the foundation. It has to cure for seven days. After that, it's ready for the house to be built on top of it. I can get a group of them together a week early to get that done for you."

Reese happened to glance across the table at Shay and saw her expression, soft with gratitude, aimed at him. He would be contributing heavily on this project, and it felt so damned good. Shay was finally getting some support. Long overdue and so well deserved. The look of admiration for him in her blue eyes made his heart do funny things in his chest. Made him feel hope. And maybe, something else that he'd thought was out of his reach.

Reese didn't even smile a little as he heard Shay's bedroom door open and close quietly. It was 3:00 A.M. and he was out in the kitchen making some more of that tasty chamomile tea, unable to sleep. The scrape of her slippers stopped, so he lifted his head in that direction. He heard the clacking of Max's claws against the cedar floor, following his mistress down the hall. That dog didn't get much sleep, either, but didn't seem any worse for wear.

"Not you, too?" Shay croaked, rubbing her eyes.

Max walked around Shay, looked up at Reese, and slowly wagged his tail in a hello to him. Reese smiled down at the golden retriever and ruffled the fur on his neck.

"It's an epidemic, I guess."

Shay gave a short laugh and then shook her head, straining to see what he was making. "Tea? You said you didn't like drinking it."

"Well, the chamomile tasted good when you gave it to me the other night." And then he added with an amused tone, "Don't tell the other guys, who are coffee hounds, that you've turned me into a tea drinker." He saw her lips curve, a glint in her drowsy eyes.

"Yeah, they'll never let you live that down, will they? A Marine who is a tea drinker. Your secret's safe with me, Lockhart."

"They wouldn't take any prisoners if they found out," Reese agreed with a chuckle. "Want some tea, too?"

"Yes, please."

"Go sit at the table. I'll bring it over."

"Thanks . . ."

Reese liked the shuffling of those slippers whispering across the cedar floor. It was a sound that gave him a sense of home. It was a crazy reaction, of course. His heart yearned for a home once again. This wasn't his home, but Shay made him feel like it was. He wished for the hundredth time that she realized the positive and healing effect she had on him and the other vets.

Max made himself comfortable in his doggie bed in the warm corner of the kitchen, curling up and going back to sleep.

As he brought over the mugs and set one in front of Shay, he said, "Your mind must be going a million miles an hour over that bombshell Maud and Steve dropped on you this afternoon."

She wrinkled her nose. "No kidding. My brain is doing Mach 3 with my hair on fire."

He chuckled and sat down at her elbow, sipping the chamomile tea. He'd worn his blue pajamas and a white T-shirt, his feet bare. All Reese wanted to do was stare at Shay. Her hair was loose and mussed around her face, her eyes still filled with drowsiness. He knew that when a person was sleep deprived, it took them longer to wake up. It bothered him that the dark smudges were still beneath her eyes. When she licked her lips, he felt his groin tighten. The woman was positively sensual with every movement she made. It put him through a special kind of hell.

"Is that why you're awake?" she asked.

"Yeah, better reason than a nightmare or flashback. Right?"

Grimacing, Shay nodded, hands around the mug as she sipped her hot tea. "I still can't believe the Whitcombs are doing this for us, Reese. I feel like I'm in a dream and I'm afraid I'll wake up and that's all it was."

"Maybe," Reese said, leaning back in the chair, "we're so used to being kicked, ignored, and cursed at that it's tough for us to believe when something good happens, it really is good."

She held his somber gaze. "You're right," she said softly. "Especially me."

Reese heard the emotion behind her words. He wanted to keep the tone positive tonight. "I like Steve Whitcomb. He's sharp and he has a lot of good ideas."

"He's a cowboy at heart, never mind he's a world famous architect. They're all like that, men of their word. A handshake still works in the West. Nowhere else anymore, though, unfortunately."

"He's not a vet?"

"No. He was a twin at one time. Barkley, his brother, went into the Army when he was eighteen. Steve went to Princeton. It was so sad because Barkley was killed in Afghanistan. It tore the Whitcombs up something terrible, from what Kassie told me at the café one time." She shook her head, sad over their loss.

"Do you know the source of their money?"

"The Whitcombs came into this valley about five years before my family did. Half their family stayed here in Wind River and the other half went on to Jackson Hole, where they claimed a lot of land. In the 1930s that part of the Whitcomb family sold it off. They died shortly after that and all the money went to the family living here in the valley. I've heard a lot of talk around town that they're worth fifty million or more. But it doesn't matter. Steve, because of his MBA, also has a lot of funds in the stock market. Kassie once told me that they're probably worth a hundred million dollars at this point." She shrugged. "I love Maud and Steve with or without their money. They're so kind and generous to so many in this struggling valley. And because Steve's twin was in the military, after he died, he made a promise to always help vets. And they make good on that promise every day. The past decade, they've given every wrangler a log home package for free, plus five acres to build it on. They recognize the importance of owning a home and they're giving away acreage. It's a wonderful program. When I heard about it, I wished I could do the same thing, but I didn't have the money. I could help a few vets, though, and they could live out in the bunkhouse."

Reese remained somber, sipping the fragrant tea. "That explains a lot then, of what they just did to help you. They're giving you the money interest-free. It's not going to hurt your ranch's financial standing at all. The wranglers will send that mortgage payment, free of any interest charge, to them and you won't pay out a dime. Except that fifteen percent you were collecting from them."

"Yes. But I won't keep making them pay that to me monthly."

"You should," Reese said. "They owe you for where they're at now. These homes are on your land. Although the land the homes are built on will belong to the owner of that house. I don't think any of them will kick one bit over giving you a monthly fifteen percent from what they make."

"Really?"

Nodding, Reese said, "The Whitcombs have discovered the most important thing to a military vet who is homeless—and that's a home. That's everything, Shay. All of us should pay rent for the home being on your property. I was looking at the costs, and the mortgage on such a house, without any interest attached to it, is going to be like three hundred dollars a month. They will be able to take fifteen percent out of their pay to give to you, no problem at all."

Shaking her head, she whispered, "I just can't believe their goodwill. No interest. They won't make anything back on the money they're loaning us, Reese."

"They don't want to," he told her quietly, holding the look of disbelief in her eyes. "They know they can't take money with them when they die. What they can do is begin parceling it out now and making a positive impact in a lot of people's lives. They're in their fifties now. If Kassie is right about their finances, they should probably start distributing their wealth at about this age. Do they have any children?"

"No, unfortunately. Maud could never conceive. Over the years, they were foster parents when they were younger, and they do have lots of kids, but they haven't adopted them. At one time, when I was growing up, they had ten foster kids under their wing at the ranch." She gave him a fond look. "Maud loves children. It seems horrible that she could never get pregnant. That's heartbreaking to me."

"Yes, but look at how many other children they've helped. She's a mother, there's no question. A gruff, kind of no-nonsense one, but you don't have ten kids under foot in your home if you don't love them."

"Oh, she's a big softy, Reese. Sometimes she gets gruff, but in a loving kind of way. I've never heard Maud raise her voice or her hand to anyone. And I would hope they are going to give their foster children some of that money."

Reese shrugged. "I don't know. Unless they tell us, we can't ask because that's a deeply personal and private question."

"Right," Shay agreed. "But knowing them, I'm sure they'll take care of every one of them."

"I agree with you. They're kind, generous people."

"I have no money to put in the stock market like Steve does."

"That's true. If you did, would you?" Reese wondered.

"Absolutely. There's a way to protect your investments."

"There's a lot of pitfalls to stocks," he warned her. "Steve is brilliant and he knows how to work the market to his advantage."

"You're not a risk taker, Lockhart," she teased, smiling at him.

He gave her a wry look. "Bean counters tend not to go in that direction."

She laughed and then became serious, searching his eyes. "I'm glad I got up, Reese. Honestly, I was hoping you'd be out here."

"Yeah?"

"I like our early morning time together. It's . . . nice." Her voice softened as Shay gave him a shy look. "I always found it tough to talk to guys. I don't know why. But you're easy to talk to."

"Maybe because I'm a bean counter by nature?"

She laughed outright. "I love that you're showing me your humorous side. A lot of vets fighting to get back on their feet, lose their sense of humor in the process. I mean, it's understandable."

"Oh," Reese murmured, "we always have black humor in our back pocket."

"That's a given."

"You communicate fine with everyone around here. I don't know why you say you have difficulty talking with men."

"I just get shy and I overthink what I'm going to say."

"Well, I don't see it," he said more firmly, giving her a steady look. Shay needed to stop second-guessing herself. She seemed only to do it on a personal level. Or did this have to do with her father, and she was projecting it on everyone around her? Reese couldn't blame her. If her father was cutting her off, interrupting her all the time, it was a big signal to Shay that she wasn't worth listening to. That, or if whatever she said to her father, Ray Crawford took it the wrong way. Shay would certainly begin to question that she didn't have the ability to communicate accurately or clearly with him. He saw relief in her eyes.

"If I start to do it, stop me? Tell me I'm not making sense?"

His lips twitched. "You sell yourself short, Shay. Since I've been here, you've been clear as clean water. There's no having to guess where you stand."

Lips thinning, Shay said, "I hope so . . ."

"Tomorrow afternoon," he said, "Garret, Harper, and I are driving down to see Steve at his office on their ranch. It will probably take a few hours. We'll be home by five."

"Garret already made us dinner." She hooked her thumb toward the refrigerator. "He didn't want me messing in his kitchen." She grinned.

"Territorial, isn't he?"

"Yeah, but he was black ops, Reese. Those men and women are alpha wolves. That's their nature."

"Can you cook?"

"Oh, come on!" she said, laughing. "Of course I can."

"Do you ever want to?"

"Sometimes I'd like to bake," Shay said, giving the kitchen a look of yearning. "But I'm usually so busy and Garret is so good at cooking that I just let him take it over."

"When we get the homes built, he'll have his own kitchen and you can have yours back."

"I was thinking about that. Among a hundred other things," she admitted.

"What do you like to bake?"

"I love making bread. My mom taught me and I love the process, the hands on, the smell of the yeast, the bread or rolls rising. And then baking—" She rubbed her stomach. "It's making me hungry just thinking about it."

Silence fell softly around them.

"What about you, Reese? Were you ever married? You seem like a man who would be married." She gave him an apologetic look. "If I'm getting too personal, tell me to butt out."

He pushed the mug away from him and studied it for a moment. "I was married once. Her name was Leslie, and she's a good woman. I chased her away by being, among other things, a jerk, too full of pride and too scared to admit I had a problem." He saw Shay's expression turn sad. Just the way she looked made Reese reluctantly go on. He'd never told anyone about his divorce. "I was too full of myself at that age. I thought I knew what I was doing. Told her I could handle it," he went on gruffly.

"The PTSD symptoms?"

"Yeah." He pushed his fingers through his hair that desperately needed to be cut well. "She begged me to get help. Instead of agreeing, I told her I'd change. Of course, I didn't see my symptoms, but Leslie did. My parents did. I just didn't want to address them because if my superiors knew I was going for any kind of therapy, I could kiss my career good-bye." He shot her a grimace. "You know how it goes in the military. If you ask for therapy, they get rid of you."

"I certainly do," she whispered. "For officer or enlisted. The military doesn't care. They want to sweep us and our PTSD under the rug."

"Turning a blind eye for damned sure."

"You didn't go, then? And your symptoms spiraled?"

His lips tightened and he looked away. "I'd been on four deployments to Iraq and Afghanistan, maybe three or four months back to the States, and then redeployed back over there again. I was waking up screaming at night . . ." He felt his stomach churn with grief. So many mistakes he'd made with Leslie. Rubbing his stubbled jaw, he barely got out, "I was in the middle of a flashback. She turned over to wake me up and I hit her." Reese glanced up to see her reaction. Shay had tears in her eyes. Unable to hold her gaze, he looked away.

"Long story short," he went on in a clipped tone, "is that I never wanted to hit her again. She was so shaken by it. Confused. Les didn't understand about flashbacks, how you get caught up in them. I didn't help the situation by explaining what was going on, either." Reese flexed his fist on the table, staring down at it. "Two days later, after a lot of arguing, anger, and hurt, she asked me for a divorce. Said she couldn't continue to live that way." His voice lowered with regret. "And I agreed with her. I loved her. I never wanted to hurt her ever again. I don't believe a woman or child should ever have a hand lifted toward them."

"God, I'm so sorry, Reese. So sorry." Shay reached across the table, stretching her fingers out to grip his momentarily. She blinked back the tears. Reese wouldn't want to see her crying for him. It would just make him feel worse. His eyes were moist. His mouth was thin and tight, forcing back emotions. Shay was sure he was battling grief and anguish over the divorce. Over how it happened.

Reese pulled his hand out of hers. "It was my fault. All of it."

"Did you go back over to Afghanistan after that?"

"Yeah, received the divorce papers four months later over there." He snorted. "It made a bad month even worse."

Hearing the agony in his lowered voice, Shay sat there feeling so bad for Reese. "How long were you married?"

"Not long enough. Five years."

"As I said, you look like you're the type to be married." She saw him give her a look of disbelief. Shrugging, she said, "Some guys just look marriageable, Reese. To me, you're one of them."

"Leslie was a civilian paralegal at Camp Pendleton. I met her in the legal office one day." Reese swallowed hard, unable to meet Shay's eyes. "She's a good person. Always will be."

"Is there any chance you'll get together again with her?"

"No. She remarried two years ago. Has a baby girl now. And a husband who is good to her. She's happy and I'm happy for her. For all of them."

Her stomach clenched. There was such grief in Reese's face, no matter how much he tried to hide it or make it go away. "At least, she had a happy ending," Shay said gently.

"She deserves a lot more than I ever gave her."

"Were you able to tell your parents what happened?"

Giving a shake of his head, he said, "No. The divorce was my path to hell. I went down hard after that. I stopped being a good leader, an officer. The Marine Corps told me to suck it up, but I couldn't. Eventually, they told me I needed to resign my commission. To leave . . . They never said it was because of my PTSD, but it was. They didn't want it diagnosed so I could get financial benefits to help me get back on my feet."

Wincing, Shay saw the utter devastation in his eyes, in his low, rough voice.

"And that's when you went into this two-year spiral?"

"Yes."

"I hate that vets have to pay twice for serving their country. We go into combat, come out with PTSD and memories we'll never forget. And then we come home and no one cares. It's a kick in the teeth," Shay muttered defiantly.

Dragging in a ragged breath, Reese gazed at her disgruntled expression. "If it's any consolation, coming here has helped me more than you'll ever know, Shay." He looked around the quiet kitchen and then held her gaze. "You have no idea how much you're helping me and the others. I wish I had the words to share it with you."

She gave him a slight nod. "I see you changing daily, Reese. All the guys growing . . . blooming . . . starting to take their lives back. You have no idea how good that makes *me* feel." She touched the area where her heart lay. "It's healing to me, too. All of you give me hope, actually."

She saw Reese's confused look. "Over the past year since I returned, the other three guys have been so helpful to me. I might have to deal with an abusive father, but when I come home here"—she gestured around the kitchen—"Garret, Noah, and Harper love me like long-lost brothers, each in his own way. They're always respectful, and caring. It's great to be treated with warmth and respect."

"That's good," Reese said, his voice thick with emotion. "You're like Leslie. You deserve nothing but good to happen to you."

Chapter Ten

Reese rode Smoke the gray gelding along the fence line on the late June morning. It was barely sunrise, the golden sun slanting across the valley while a robin chirped from a nearby fence post as he rode toward it.

Low-hanging fog twisted here and there across the flat grasslands. The peace and quiet were a salve to his broken soul. His gloved hand rested on the leather chaps across his thigh as his gaze continued down the line of rusted barbed wire. It, too, should be replaced, but he knew that wouldn't happen for a long, long time. The barbed wire had originally been strung seventy years ago, from what Shay had told him.

Shay. Every time he got around her, his body took off with yearning. His heart. Hell, his heart was fully involved with her and he'd never kissed her! They'd established a good, close friendship and Reese now looked forward to getting up at night, meeting her out in the kitchen to have tea and talk with her from time to time. For whatever reason, they were good for one another and he ached to do something more about it. But what? Every day, he was proving his self-worth to her, to the ranch, and to the other vets. He had a better feeling about himself because he and

Steve Whitcomb were hammering out a complex schedule for the arena-raising that was taking place in two weeks. Steve had embraced him like a brother.

It felt good to be wanted. Respected. He was slowly showing everyone that he could be responsible and reliable. That he could work and finish what he started. Even his symptoms were not bothering him as much.

As Shay had recommended, he'd gone to see Dr. Taylor Douglas, the physician's assistant who was working on a study of PTSD with another physician. She had him on an adaptogen for thirty days, which halted the leaking of the hormone cortisol into his bloodstream. The anxiety had stopped in its tracks and it had shaken him. The doctor had laughed and said it was supposed to happen that way. Said he wouldn't have that anxiety ever come back unless he was in some kind of high stress trauma again. And if he was, he could take the adaptogen once more and stop the cortisol from leaking into his bloodstream 24/7.

Reese hadn't felt so good in such a long time that he couldn't remember feeling quite like this. The sway of the gelding beneath him, the cool Wyoming morning, the hush of nature surrounding him, all served the new sense of peacefulness that resided within him.

He missed having Shay come with him. Usually she did, but today she had to go see her father. Scowling, Reese dropped the reins on Smoke's neck, lifted the Stetson off his head, and pushed his fingers through his freshly cut hair. He worried about Shay every time she saw that mean bastard. She always came home pale, her eyes looking wounded, moist, and sometimes reddened. It meant she'd cried by herself in the truck.

Aching to hold her during those times, Reese's mouth flattened. He pulled the Stetson down across his brow, picked up the reins in his left hand and allowed the quarter horse to follow the fence. Up ahead, he saw wire was down. His horse automatically slowed, seeing it too. Reese grinned and as Smoke came to a stop, he dismounted and drew the tools from the saddlebags. The horse was trained to remain where he was once Reese dropped the reins to the ground.

As he worked to repair the three strands of barbed wire that were broken, he worried about Shay. She hadn't told her father yet about the arena-raising, or the four homes that would be built at the same time. She had worried he'd be angry, but for the life of him, Reese couldn't see why. She'd just shrugged and said it didn't take much for him to get angry. He didn't like what she'd done, taking the ranch in a different direction, helping fellow vets. For the past week, Reese had seen her trying to work up to telling her father. Shay knew that gossip about it would eventually get back to Ray, and she didn't want him to be surprised by it. Damn. Reese's protectiveness toward her was building powerfully within him and he'd almost asked if she wanted him to come along for that confrontation. But he hadn't.

His leather chaps darkened with the dew on the grass as he knelt down and began to cut out the old, frayed wire. Shay was going to be seeing her father shortly after breakfast, and Reese had let Garret know he was going to ride instead of eat. Planning the arena-raising was taking up all his time, and his other work was falling behind. The only way he could continue to repair fence was to get up earlier, at sunrise, and make it happen.

Shay girded herself as she peeked in the open door of her father's room. His empty breakfast dishes were on a rolling tray that he'd pushed away from his bed. He was in a pair of pale green pajamas that hung on his once powerful, muscular frame. Over the year, he'd lost a lot of weight. His black hair was thinning across his skull. She remembered when it was rich and thick. His brown-eyed gaze snapped up at her as she entered.

"You're early," he muttered, scowling.

Shay shut the door. She hated when his yelling at her drifted down the hall. Even the staff at the desk always gave her a sad look, knowing she was going into the lion's den, as they referred to her father's room. She forced a smile and placed her leather purse on the nearby dresser. "I had to get an early start, Father. There's a lot going on and I have to keep ahead of it all. How are you feeling?" She wiped her damp palms on her jeans as she approached his bed. The sunlight was pouring into the large room, making it feel good and positive. But one look into her father's eyes, and her stomach knotted.

"The same. Why the hell should I feel any different?"

"Just hoping." She reached out to touch his hand that had cuffed her so many times growing up. Only now, the veins on the back of it were prominent, the skin shiny and thin, like the rest of him. She wrapped her fingers around his, squeezed them gently. He pulled his hand away, bringing it onto his lap, frowning.

Her heart sank. She wished he could love her. She wished he could say the words to her. But he never had. Shay had grown up knowing she was always underfoot. Her father hadn't wanted any children, she'd found out. But her mother had insisted. She was the result. Her father had never been demonstrative. She'd never seen him kiss her mother, embrace her, or even hold her hand. She'd grown up calling him the Ice Man because she didn't think he had a heart in his chest.

"What's going on that you're so busy?" he demanded.

Shay swallowed and tried to prepare herself. Launching into the plans for the arena-raising, how it came about, her words streamed rapidly out of her mouth. As they did, she saw her father's thinning black brows go lower and lower. When she finished, breathless, she placed her hands on the side of the bed, fingers digging into the mattress.

"You're taking handouts from strangers!" he yelled at her. "What the HELL were you thinking, Shaylene?"

Wincing, she felt the full power of his rage striking invisibly at her. She stepped away from the bed, fighting tears that always wanted to come when he yelled at her. "It's not a handout, Father. Maud and Steve have given other ranchers desperately needed money to make ends meet. She has the finances to do that. She *wants* to do it for us."

Curling his lip, he glared at her. "It's SHAMING to us as a family. I NEVER took a dime from anyone!" He jabbed a finger down at the bed. "That ranch grew and was damned prosperous when I ran it! It's humiliating to take money that don't belong to you, girl! Just plain, damned wrong! What's the matter with you?"

It felt as if her gut were on fire. Shay held her father's gaze, felt the anger like barbs going through her. Fingers curving into her palms, she whispered in a hurt tone, "I'm trying the best I know how—"

Ray slammed his fist down on the bed with all his strength. "It's not good enough!" he screamed.

Tears burned in her eyes. She blinked several times, forcing herself to try to relax. Shay remembered him when he was vital and would cock that fist at her. She always felt terror so deeply, as if she were going to die if he struck her.

Mouth dry, her throat aching with unshed tears, her voice wobbled as she said, "I'm sorry I'm such a huge disappointment to you, Father. I'm not doing this to upset you."

His breathing was harsh and raspy as he glared silently over at her. "You make us look weak. Like we're beggars,

Shaylene. I'm going to go to my grave humiliated, knowing the people of this valley will think little more of us than scum."

"I-I don't think they will. You are still respected—"

"Get out."

"But—"

"You shame me, girl." He dismissed her with a weak wave of his hand.

Turning, blindly heading for the door, Shay pulled it open and walked out. Choking, she shut the door, pressing her hand against her eyes. Making a muffled sound, she quickly walked down the waxed floor toward the bathroom.

Pushing open the door, Shay found the restroom empty. And then, she let go of the sob that had become a huge lump in her throat. Leaning against one of the wash basins, she struggled to stop crying. She knew someone would hear her and she was embarrassed enough without that, too. Grabbing several paper towels, she wet them and pressed them against her hot face, her eyes red rimmed as she glanced in the mirror. God, she couldn't go home just yet. Shay wanted none of the vets to see her like this. She *had* to get ahold of herself. She just had to.

"Hey, Reese?" Noah called, ambling into the barn where Reese was unsaddling Smoke in the cross ties.

Reese looked over the back of the gelding. "Yeah? What's up?" He had already hauled the saddle and blanket off Smoke and was currying him with a soft brush. Reese saw darkness in Noah's face. He wasn't a man to give much away, still suffering from PTSD. Now, Reese saw concern in the vet's eyes as he walked toward him, hands stuffed in the pockets of his jeans.

"I just saw Shay drive in." He hitched a thumb across his broad shoulder. "I was out at the picket fence painting it when she came home." Halting on the other side of the horse, he said, "Something's wrong."

Reese's hand stilled on the rump of the horse. "What kind of wrong?"

Shrugging, Noah said, "Red eyes. She's been crying. Bet it's that old man of hers. Every time she goes there, she comes back tore up. This is getting old."

Gut clenching, Reese's mouth thinned. "What do you want me to do about it?" He studied the vet. The last couple of weeks, the three men were turning to him more and more for advice or counsel. Reese wondered if it was a natural response to the fact that he'd been an officer. He didn't know, and he wasn't comfortable with the change, but had said nothing. He was still trying to get his own life in order, and was not ready to be a manager of others. He saw Noah look steadily at him.

"She likes you. You know that, right?"

Reese froze inwardly. He swallowed hard, staring at the vet. "No . . . I didn't know." And he didn't. What the hell did Noah see that he couldn't? The news elated him in one way, but scared the hell out of him in another. Never had Reese thought Shay could like him as he liked her. Never.

Noah rubbed his square jaw. "I just know it," he said stubbornly. "I feel it. Things change when you come into the kitchen. There's a softening in her eyes and voice when you're with us. I see her look at you sometimes when you don't realize she's staring at you . . ."

"Is this your horse intuition talking?" Reese said, trying to tease, hoping against hope that Noah was right. The vet had damn good intuition and used it training his animals. Why hadn't he seen her signals if Noah saw them so clearly? It told Reese how numb he was to those around him. When in the military, he'd had a sixth sense about his Marines. He could always tell when one was hurting or in trouble. Just the same way Noah was picking up on Shay and how she felt toward Reece. He saw Noah's mouth curve sourly.

"Could say that, Reese. Didn't you pick up on it? I'm surprised. When a woman looks at you like she does, her heart is involved in the mix. I honestly thought you'd caught on."

Reese felt heat in his cheeks. He avoided Noah's glance and began to brush the horse down. "I didn't pick up on anything." And he wasn't about to tell Noah about their middle-of-the night talks.

"God," Noah said, his mouth lifting, "you live under the same roof with this lady. I'd think you'd have figured it out."

Frowning, Reese growled, "I'm not aware of her liking me any more than any of you."

Noah chortled and lifted the Stetson off his head, then settled it back on. "You've been without a woman too long, Lockhart."

Snorting, Reese said, "Have any of us had a woman in the last two or three years?"

"No, sucks doesn't it?"

It did, but Reese wasn't going to admit it. Right now, he was protective of what he shared with Shay. There was no way he was going to give it up to anyone.

"When you get done with the horse, why don't you mosey in and see if she needs some help? She looks a lot more upset than usual. That old bastard probably tore into her good this time," Noah suggested before turning around and walking down the concrete aisle.

Reese stared after him for a minute. *Damn.* He finished brushing the horse's legs and unsnapped the cross ties. He led Smoke out to a large paddock where he could join the other horses. Glancing to his left, Reese saw that Noah was back in the horse training area. Looking up, he saw Shay's pickup parked at the front of the house. Every cell in his body screamed at him to go immediately to Shay. But Noah was nearby and would see it.

So what was he afraid of?

Himself.

Reese was at a point with Shay that he wasn't sure he could keep his hands off her any longer. His dreams had been torrid and scalding. If someone would have told him he'd feel desire again, he'd have scoffed at them. He hadn't felt like this in two years.

Flexing his gloved hand, he hesitated at the corral, watching the gray gelding walk toward the other three horses munching grass. A greater part of him wanted to be at Shay's side, to protect her. But hell, he couldn't protect himself, much less anyone else, at present.

Life had been so damned black and white when he was well. When PTSD hadn't run his life. Being without anxiety the last week had been a miracle, and for that, Reese was grateful to his soul. With the anxiety gone, and the paranoia and jumpiness that came with it, he was finding himself thinking normally again. And because of that, it pushed him to go to the main house and find Shay. His protectiveness was clamoring in every cell of his body to go and find out if he could help her.

It was 10:00 A.M. as Reese pulled back his glove to look at the watch on his wrist. He knew that Shay had gone over to see her father early because there was so much to do today. He pushed open the back door to the house and stepped in, wiping his boots on the mat, getting off the dirt. Looking down the long, polished hall, he heard Shay moving around in the kitchen. Dragging in a deep breath, Reese made some noise walking down the hall so she would hear him coming. The last thing he wanted to do was startle her.

He rounded the entrance to the kitchen and saw Shay at the counter making bread from scratch. She had a huge slab of dough on the counter, gently kneading it with her hands. Her hair was piled on top of her head and held with a tortoiseshell comb. Around her waist she wore a red apron. Shay looked beautiful in the tan slacks and feminine pink short-sleeved blouse she wore. She turned, twisted a look across her shoulder at him. His heart dropped. Noah was right; her eyes were red rimmed. And there were spots of flour on her brow and cheek. It made her look hauntingly vulnerable.

"Hey," he murmured, taking off his Stetson and hanging it on the peg. "I just got back from riding fence line and was coming in to make some coffee."

"Go ahead," she said, returning to kneading the dough.

Reese heard the low huskiness in her voice. He knew she'd been crying earlier. He floundered around inwardly, unsure what to do. She looked happy to see him, though. How blind had he been? "I'll stay outta your way," he said, going to the other end of the counter. "Looks like you're tapping into your inner baker?" he asked, quickly setting up the coffeepot and flipping on the switch.

"Yes . . . I wanted . . . needed to do something positive for a while."

He heard the hesitation in her voice and noted Shay refused to look at him, her eyes on the bread she was gently folding between her hands. "What kind of bread will we have tonight?" he asked, leaning against the sink, watching her profile.

"Whole wheat and honey. My mom"—she stopped to push some hanging tendrils of hair off her brow with her forearm—"created the recipe when I was a kid. I remember coming out here when I was only seven years old. I loved the smell of the bread being mixed with the local honey."

Reese heard a tremble in her low voice. "Those kinds of

good memories are the ones we always want to keep close in our heart."

Shay took some more flour from a bowl, smoothing it over the huge lump before her. "My mom brought over a stool and had me help her. I don't know, there's just something life affirming about making it. We had so many wonderful times when she'd make us bread. She had such a great sense of humor and I can remember standing on that stool and she'd give me part of the dough, dip my hands in flour, and then show me how to knead it. Said that it really was the staff of life."

Reese could feel the tension in Shay, although it wasn't transferring to the dough she kneaded with her slender hands. She wasn't pounding the hell out of the dough; she was kneading it with great gentleness, almost as if the bread was sacred. "You miss her a lot." He saw her hands freeze for a split second and then she continued to fold the bread.

"Anyone who loves you," she choked out, "you miss . . ."

His heart twinged as he saw the silvery path of a tear streaking down her cheek. Ah hell, he was such a goner when it came to Shay. He pushed off the counter, unlocking his arms, walking up to her. "It sounds like you could use someone to listen." He gently placed his hand on her shoulder. Instantly, he saw Shay's mouth tuck, as if to stop from crying out. The tension in her shoulders was real beneath his fingertips. She stopped kneading, her hands stilling over the dough.

"Let me get this done?"

Lifting his hand, he said, "Sure." Shay felt brittle, as if she were going to snap. Amazed that his old intuition was back and working once more, the cortisol hormone no longer running his life and desensitizing him to others, he stepped away. "Coffee's almost done," he managed, trying to keep his voice light. Reese was smart enough not to push it with Shay. He was going to give her an opportunity to tell him what was bothering her if she wanted.

"I-I'll take a cup. Please?"

"Sure," he rumbled, pulling down two mugs from the cabinet. Reese watched as she pulled out six aluminum loaf pans, greased them and then divided the dough into them. When she was done, she placed a small terry cloth towel over each one to allow them to rise. He went over to the table, set the mugs of coffee down, and pulled out her chair for her. She wouldn't look at him after she washed her hands in the sink, wiping them off on her apron as she came over to the table.

"Thanks," she whispered, sliding her hands around the white mug.

Reese settled into a chair, worried that Shay was going to explode. Lips tight, she stared down at the coffee between her hands. The tendrils of hair were soft around her pale face and he stopped the urge to reach out and touch them. God knew, he wanted to. But he didn't trust himself with her any longer, the drive to touch her . . . kiss her . . . was powerful.

"What inspired you to make bread?" he asked, giving her an amused look. "Our talk about not having your kitchen because Garret took it over?" He saw her lift her chin, her blue eyes marred with darkness. Now, he could see how much she'd been crying. His heart lurched. Reese put a clamp on his anger toward Ray Crawford. Only he could do this much damage. Reese's fingers itched to touch Shay, comfort her, hold her. What would she do if he tried to embrace her? Was Noah right? God, he was so screwed up inside, unable to honestly figure out how she felt toward him.

"I needed to do something I loved doing. Bread always

makes me focus on the good things in my life." She took a sip of coffee, unable to look at him.

"It's nice to see you back in your kitchen." Shay reminded him of all the good things a marriage brought to a man. He wasn't a slouch in the kitchen either, but there was just something heartwarming about her making bread in her kitchen. Reese couldn't explain it, only feel it. "After the arena-raising, you'll be that much closer to reclaiming your house from all of us," he teased. He saw Shay give him a sad look, her fingers moving restlessly around the cup she clung to.

"In one way, yes, but I will miss us being a family, eating together at night . . . the conversations, the laughter and fun we've all shared at this table."

"It does get rank every once in a while, though," he agreed with a slight smile. Her eyes were downcast on the cup again and he saw her lower lip tremble. It broke Reese that Shay was trying so damned hard to not talk about what was bothering her.

He tried to steel himself when he asked gently, "You saw your father this morning?" Instantly, he saw Shay stiffen, her mouth compress. Worse, the pain in her eyes tore at him. He had to bring it up. Reese knew what it was like to hold an emotional bomb within and not release it. The damage it did was untold and it was as good as receiving a physical wound. He braced himself for what was to come because it was clear Shay wasn't going to be able to control the hurt in her expression, in her eyes.

Chapter Eleven

Shay abruptly stood, releasing the cup and nearly knocking over the chair as she pushed it back. Walking to the sink, she gripped the counter, head down, shoulders hunched.

Reese slowly rose and walked over to her. The moment he grazed her shoulder, a strangled sound came out of her. She tried to pull away from his touch.

"Shay . . ." he rasped. *To hell with it.* Reese took the biggest risk he had taken in the last two years. Reaching out, he gripped her shoulder and turned her gently toward him. The look on Shay's face pulverized him as she pressed her hand to her lips, looking up at him. He felt gutted.

"Come here," he said roughly, hauling her into his arms, holding her tightly against him.

Nothing had ever felt so good as Shay pressed against him, her face buried in his shirt as she sobbed. The sounds of hurt scored his heart and Reese closed his eyes, holding her, feeling her entire body tremble with weeping. He felt his shirt dampen where her tears fell.

When her arms went around his waist, he groaned, sliding one hand into her soft, thick hair, holding her tenderly. His other hand came to rest against the small of her back.

Mouth thin, Reese closed his eyes as he rested his chin against her hair, inhaling the scent of oranges from the shampoo she had used that morning.

"Just let it all out, Shay," he whispered raggedly against her ear. Her hair was silky against his nose and cheek as her arms tightened even more around him. The warmth of Shay, her softness, her woman's strength, all conspired heavily against Reese. She was crying so hard, shaking in his arms, that his chest imploded with grief, care, and something he never thought he'd ever feel again. It scared the hell out of him, feeling love so vibrant, so real, that it made him freeze for a moment. No! It couldn't be. What was going on?

Assailed by the violent flood of shocking emotions tunneling through him as Shay cried, her face buried against his chest, Reese felt his entire world shifting. The sensation was real. The emotions . . . oh, God, they were too real, too needy, too hungry. He felt guilt and shame overwhelm him.

He buried his face in her hair, absorbing the contact, her feminine scent, her arms around him. The urge to kiss her, to comfort her even more, seized him.

Gently, he slid his hand from her hair and down across her back, and up again. What he wanted to do—and what he *should* do—were two different things. Shay needed comfort. Not a kiss from him. He wanted to make love to her and he knew it was the wrong thing to be thinking about at that moment. He was so starved for a woman's touch, a beggar greedily taking from Shay, when he should be giving back to her, instead. How little he had to give her. Reese felt terrible that he'd sunk so far down he didn't have the compassion he'd had before starting his slide into oblivion.

It didn't matter. He would summon everything left in him that still had a shred of integrity, and give it to Shay.

Reese drew her solidly against him, whispering low, gruff words of comfort against her ear, hoping she'd hear them through her sobs. Each time he grazed her hair with his hand, her sobs lessened a little bit more. He was helping her. Reese was grateful . . .

Her arms began to loosen a little around his waist, so he eased up on how tightly he was holding her. When she nuzzled her cheek against his chest, he groaned. He couldn't stop the pleasurable sound. Just the softness of her cheek against his hard-muscled chest, sent frissons of fire licking down through his body and settling hotly in his groin. The woman didn't realize how she affected him and Reese couldn't blame her. Shay's actions were innocent, seeking solace, not sex, from him. And he damn well knew the difference, placing a choke chain on his own sexual hunger. He forced himself to translate those needs into something far more compassionate, for Shay's sake.

"There," he murmured, holding his hand on her sagging shoulders, "that's better . . ." To his surprise, his thick words had an effect upon her. Shay made a muffled sound against his chest, eyes closed, as if needing his continued nearness. That, Reese could give her honestly without thoughts of sex. It tore him up to think of her savaged by her father. But this time, her reaction was the worst one he'd seen following a visit to Ray Crawford. Shay was devastated. And so was he, but in a different way, because Reese wanted to protect her. How could Shay stand to be torn up like this so often? So continually? Her strength was more than Reese had ever realized.

To whisper to her that everything would be all right, Reese knew would be an outright lie. A child and parent relationship lasted forever, even after the parent died. The emotions, the branding by her parents on Shay as a child, lasted forever. He felt so damned helpless, wanting desperately to comfort her but knowing his platitudes would be empty words.

So he continued doing the only thing he knew that would help her, and that was to slide his hand slowly up and down her back, caressing her, caring for her. Shay's sobs finally ended and the silence gently embraced them as they stood together in the kitchen.

Shay clung to him as if to be torn out of his arms would mean she would die. Her unspoken feelings struck him fully. And truth be told? Reese wanted to keep holding her, because she completed him in a way no woman ever had. The realization was as shocking and stark as it was heated with blazing promise. Closing his eyes, he rested his chin lightly against the top of her head, knowing that was an impossibility. He was so damaged. Beyond repair. Shay deserved someone who was whole. Someone who could give her what she so richly deserved. He'd come to realize he was only half a man. Never again would he be whole.

It didn't stop Reese from dreaming. But that's all it would ever be: a dream. Noah had been right, however. There was something good and clean and wonderful that they shared. With the bitterness of his destroyed marriage, and his two-year spiral into hell, Reese had become a pragmatist about his fall. The reality was that Shay wasn't nearly as damaged as he or the other vets. She, at least, had a hope of recovery. And he wanted to be the man to help her do just that: support her in her efforts to heal. She deserved it more than any person he knew. She'd done so much for so many others without a thought for herself. She'd given her heart to the vets, her home, her food, and care.

And what could Reese give her in return?

The bitter reality, the harsh answer, tamped down all the hope crying out to be heard in his heavily scarred heart. He was afraid if he ever slept with Shay, if caught in one of those flashback nightmares, he would strike out, hitting her as he'd once struck Leslie. Only this time, he might do even worse injury. Reese had killed with his hands in combat. He knew what it was like. A lump formed painfully in his throat and he kept swallowing, wanting to howl with anger over the unfairness of life. He wanted so desperately to give back to Shay. But he was beneath her. Broken.

Reese felt Shay lift her head. He opened his arms so she could stand and move away from him if she wanted. He felt her hands easing from around his waist but hovering over his hips as she looked up at him, her eyes filled with grief as she studied him in silence. Without thinking, Reese smoothed damp hair from her pale, wet cheek and eased the strands behind her ear. He saw her eyes change, pupils enlarge, her lips part slightly in response to his butterfly-light touch.

And then, the impossible happened.

Shay leaned up, her hand resting lightly against his jaw, her lips finding his. She kissed him.

Reese's world halted, as if tethered by an anchor, as her soft, trembling mouth slid so tentatively, so shyly against the compressed line of his lips. Shocking heat bolted down through him. And as her lashes, damp with tears, fell against her cheeks and she nudged open the seam of his lips, asking him to kiss her in return, his heartbeat pounded out of control.

Taking her mouth gently, Reese heard a low sound in her throat telling him she liked what he was doing. Never had Reese thought he'd be kissing Shay. It had been a dream. That's all. Just a dream.

Until right now. He slid his mouth across hers, letting her know he wanted to kiss her, too. His mind spun. Was she kissing him out of neediness? Or was she kissing him because she wanted him as much as he wanted her? Reese didn't know, feeling the moist warmth of her breath feathering across his nose and cheek, sinking deeper into the softness of her open lips against his.

It had been two years since he'd felt the heat and joy of connecting with a woman's mouth. Reese's body went giddy inwardly, so many suppressed feelings flooding brightly and powerfully through him. All he could do was focus on Shay's mouth, her tenderness as she explored him a little more with each breath she took. He felt her fingers tighten against his cheek, felt her leaning into him, her breasts pressed fully against his chest. His one hand cupped the back of her head, the other coming to rest on the small of her back. Reese angled her head just enough to take full advantage of what she was offering him.

The moment her mouth blossomed in scalding invitation to his, he shuddered—the pleasure, the heat of her lips fully against his. Flooded with dormant sensations he thought he'd never feel again, a deep, rumbling groan rose in his chest. Reese felt Shay's other hand slide firmly against his spine, desperately blending them against one another until he was melting into her like hot, sweet honey.

Her mouth was beguiling, her arms sweetly strong, holding his broken spirit, mending him back together with her courageous heart. It drove tears into the back of Reese's eyes as he completely gave himself to her. He felt Shay respond in kind. The world centered only on their mouths clinging hungrily to one another, searching one another with an eagerness that shocked him. Shay was just as starved as he was! That realization struck Reese deeply. It told him how wounded she really was, that Shay hid her own injuries from all of them. That he'd been wrong: She wasn't light years ahead of them when it came to her PTSD.

He brought her completely into his arms, caring for her, loving her, glorying in something so beautiful and right between them, that they celebrated it together. They understood one another completely because they had walked in the same shoes.

Reese became aware of so many things about Shay, about himself, that it overwhelmed him emotionally. More than anything, he felt her fragility on a level he'd never plumbed before. Despite Shay's strength, she was so terribly, mortally wounded, that it scared the hell out of him. Only when she'd dropped those walls she'd held so well in place, with this one kiss, did he honestly realize how much she was struggling. It broke his heart in one way, and in another, his protective nature reared up like a dragon within him and he swore silently he would do something to shield her. Reese didn't know what. Only that he would. Shay had the courage to not only open up to him, but trust him enough to fully reveal her wounds to him. Shaken to his core, Reese gently eased from her mouth, their ragged breaths mingling.

Slowly opening his eyes, he stared down into her deep blue eyes that were flecked with what he swore was joy in their depths. Shay still held him, had not released him, silently wanting the connection they'd forged with one another earlier. Her cheeks were flushed, and his gaze dropped to her wet lips, swollen from the power of his kiss. Instantly, Reese regretted it, had not even realized he'd kissed her so urgently, a starved beggar.

Looking into her dazed eyes, Reese hunted for signs that Shay regretted kissing him. He found none. Instead, he felt happiness begin to infuse his heart, a simmering hope that scared him. Could he hope? Did he dare? Ruthlessly, Reese drank in her softened expression, the tender way the corners of her mouth curved slightly up. He couldn't believe what he saw. Shay had wanted to kiss *him*. This wasn't about being comforted; she'd wanted him woman to man.

Could he be reading her expression correctly? God, he was afraid to translate any of it in that direction.

The woman in his arms right now was sweet, vulnerable, hurting, and joyous all at the same time. How could that be? Reese walked in a minefield of confusion. He didn't trust himself to read a person accurately anymore. But Shay felt so damned good in his arms, made him feel like a whole man once more, that he just couldn't begin to go there and believe all that he was feeling and sensing.

Reluctantly, he released her, his throat tight with so many words, so many things he wanted to say to her and her alone. He managed to gruffly ask, "Are you sorry?"

Shay blinked slowly, easing out of his arms, her hands on his lower arms, as if she didn't trust herself quite yet. "Sorry?" she whispered, tilting her head, drowning in his gaze. "About what?"

Reese felt terror combined with such violent hope that he stood awkwardly, not wanting to lose contact with Shay. He could feel her fingers gripping his arms, saw her dazed expression. She was excruciatingly open to him right now. Feeling like a jerk, he swallowed hard. "About kissing me?" It had been painful to ask, but Reese had to know. To hope against hope. He found himself trying to protect himself inwardly from what her answer might be.

Shay made a sound in her throat, her voice husky. "No . . . I needed to kiss you, Reese." Her voice grew wispy. "It . . . was wonderful. You were wonderful . . ."

Never had any words melted him more than hers in those moments. His mind refused to believe her, but his heart was hammering with elation. Reese felt her release his one arm, her fingers coming to rest against his chest. Lifting his hand, he wiped the last of the dampness from her cheek.

Just then, the screen door opened.

Shay released him and, giving him a look of apology, moved toward the sink. The thunk of boots echoed down the hall toward the kitchen.

Reese turned, heading to the table, picking up the cups.

Garret rounded the corner. He looked first at Shay and then over at Reese.

"Am I interrupting something?"

Reese shook his head, "No, we're done with our coffee. Kitchen's all yours."

Shay looked at her watch, her voice oddly husky. "Time for lunch."

Garret moved to the hook near the stove where he pulled the apron off the hook, wrapping it around his waist. "It's that time," he agreed, giving them questioning looks.

Reese could feel Garret's stare on his back as he walked to the sink to wash out the cups. He saw Shay leave and hurry down the hall to her bedroom. His heart was still trip-hammering. Garret knew something had happened. The vet didn't say a word, but he didn't have to as he came to the sink to wash his hands.

"Everything all right?" Garret demanded.

"Yeah."

"Noah told me earlier Shay looked really upset."

Nodding, Reese put the cups in the dishwasher. "Her father," was all he said. Straightening, he walked out of the kitchen and out of the house, needing time to think and clear his head.

Shay sat on the edge of her bed, bent over, hands pressed against her face. She reveled in the power of Reese's kiss, her mouth still tingling. The terrible ripped-up feeling in her heart stopped the instant he'd returned her daring kiss. What had driven her to do that? It was crazy! What must he think of her now? She'd screwed this up so badly. She wasn't supposed to fall for one of the vets.

Dragging in a jerky breath, she sat up, wiping her cheeks with trembling fingers. Never had a kiss felt so healing, so grounding and wonderful. He'd been so tender and gentle with her and God knew, that's exactly what she'd needed after being run over by her father's scarring words this morning. Something told her Reese would understand. She'd always felt protected when he was nearby. The sensation rolled off him like sunlight against a granite rock. It radiated off him. And just now, she'd lapped it up like she was dying. And if he hadn't given back to her, she didn't know if she would survive or not; it was that vulnerable a feeling deep in her soul.

But Reese had sensed her, knew her needs without her saying a word. She had just been so desperate for the least little bit of human kindness, a little love, that she'd taken the bold step to lean up and kiss him. And his response shook her universe. The man was incredibly tender, as if realizing she felt so destroyed and in need of healing, in need of love. And he had loved her with a man's gentleness toward his woman. In those sweet moments, Shay had felt him pulling her back together, gluing her ragged, torn, and frayed emotional edges, salvaging them, soothing them, bringing her back home to herself. Lifting her chin, she stared blankly out the curtained window, thunderstruck by Reese's innate sensitivity. Rubbing her brow, eyes closed, Shay felt tears beginning to fall down her cheeks again.

She'd been so raw from this morning. Walking into Reese's arms was like turning from death's grip and embracing life instead. It was that dramatic. That stark. That hauntingly, soul-beautiful to her. My God, the man could kiss! Every movement of his mouth against hers, Shay could feel herself knitting back together again. She could feel her injured heart respond and then gallop to the utter joy as his mouth slid confidently against hers.

Shay felt so different right now, she could barely think, much less comprehend what had happened when Reese had returned her kiss. He was pure magic! She sat there feeling the heat continuing to nudge her lower body, coals of fire coming back to glowing life, reminding her she was a woman.

Slipping her fingers across her abdomen, she closed her eyes and absorbed all the flames licking hungrily through her, reminding her of how long it had been that she'd gone without love. It was more than just about sex. Shay wasn't built for one-night stands. She needed a deep, serious relationship for a long time before she would commit her body, because when she did, her heart was fully involved.

As she sat there, slowly running her hands up and down her thighs, Shay still felt enveloped within Reese's strong, caring arms. His kiss had been so healing. She was afraid to say it was love, but it *felt* like love.

Real love.

And her mind spun and rejected that thought instantly because she hadn't known him long enough. No man had held her heart like Reese did. As his mouth moved against hers, inviting her, cajoling, asking for entrance, Shay had felt her world move. It was the strangest sensation and yet, the most incredible feeling. She could still picture opening her eyes and looking up into his burning, narrowed gaze. There was no mistaking the look in them: Reese wanted to take her to bed and love her until she melted in his arms. Oh! Shay knew that if Garret hadn't walked into the house, she would have done anything Reese had asked. He'd been so healing to her; she'd been vulnerable in a way she'd never been with another man. And it had allowed her to unveil herself, all of herself, her terrible lack of self-confidence, her fears, her hopes and dreams. Reese had held all of her and she could feel his warm, masculine protection dissolving anything bad within her and replacing it with lightness, joy, and most of all, hope. Shay had given up on herself. Her father had driven her so far down, she had nowhere else to go. Reese kissing her was like an invisible hand being held out for her to grasp and get pulled back on her feet. How much stronger she felt right now in comparison to before the kiss.

Reese had been gentle at first, testing her, asking her how far she wanted this to go. When she opened her lips to his, there was a powerful surge of need flowing out of him and into her. His kiss had deepened, become hungry, taking but also giving equally in return.

Reese knew how to love a woman thoroughly, there was no question. And as Shay dropped her hand to her lap, watching the play of sunlight through the lacy curtains, the soft breeze lightly moving the thin fabric, Shay knew. Knew that Reese would be a man who would pleasure her as much as himself.

What was Reese thinking right now? He'd asked her if she was sorry. Sorry for the kiss? Kissing him? The question had stunned her, but then, she was so wrapped up in the explosions going off in her body, lost in the male heat of his searching mouth, that her brain was still in park. What a question to ask! She rubbed her brow, trying to understand why he had asked it. It wasn't one she was expecting, that was for sure. Frustrated, Shay warred between wondering if she'd made an utter fool of herself with Reese or had, in some way, embarrassed him by being so bold. He'd seemed surprised. As if it were the last thing on earth he'd ever expect from her.

Making a growling sound of unhappiness, Shay launched to her feet, pacing around her bedroom, emotion running rife in her. Now, she was questioning herself and what she'd done. The kiss, the act, had been so beautiful! Nothing had ever healed her so much as Reese wrapping his arms around her, making her feel safe, loved, and cared for all at the same time. Shay hadn't expected that. What had driven her to kiss Reese was her own selfish need to feel loved. To feel wanted by someone. And deep within her heart, she knew Reese would be the man who would step up and do the right thing for the right reasons.

And then her heart dropped. Did he think her wanton? That she was just flirting with him? Terror seized her for a moment. Is that why he asked the question he did? *Oh, God.* Shay stood at the window, feeling the breeze, smelling the scent of grass. Heart plummeting, she swayed and caught herself. No! Reese couldn't think that of her. Could he? It was possible, given his question.

Shay nibbled on her lower lip. All the hope she felt was dashed. What if Reese thought she was some kind of woman who toyed with a man to get what she wanted?

She needed to talk to him. To try to explain. Would he understand, without her talking about the morning with her father? How it had driven an icy stake through her heart? Her bleeding soul? That she needed someone . . . not just anyone . . . but Reese, to run to. Somehow, Shay knew Reese was the only man who could help her.

She had to find a time and place to sit down and talk to him alone. Without interruption. To try to explain her actions. Now, Shay felt like she was the defendant pleading her case. Only this time, Reese was the judge and the jury.

Chapter Twelve

"Where's Shay?" Garret asked, bringing over the lasagna he'd made, placing it in the center of the table.

Reese was getting the buttered garlic bread out of the oven. "She's in her room," he said.

Glancing up, he saw the three wranglers looking at him. He placed the bread in a basket and brought it over to the table. The kitchen was filled with the smell of the Italian food Garret had made for them.

Garret studied Reese for a moment. He kept his voice low. "You had a talk with her earlier?"

Reese nodded. He wasn't about to go into what happened. It bothered him that Shay hadn't come out for the meal, but he knew she was upset. And probably about their kiss, too. *Damn.* He felt anxiety rise in him. And his protectiveness toward Shay increased. Garret was staring hard at him, as if trying to read his mind. Reese knew the black ops vet well enough that if he didn't do or say something, Garret would go marching off to Shay's bedroom to find out why she wasn't at the dinner table.

"I'll go check in on her," Reese told them, his voice firm, his gaze sweeping over the vets.

Harper scowled. "She needs to eat. She's losing weight."

Garret snorted and sat down. "No shit."

"My guess is she's had a bad day with her father," Noah offered. "Probably got a headache and doesn't feel like eating. This has happened before."

Reese walked away, heading down the hall. His gut was tight. Shay needed to be left alone. And he wasn't sure how she was going to receive him, coming to her bedroom. Girding himself, he halted and knocked gently on the door, unconsciously holding his breath.

The door opened.

Reese looked in Shay's eyes. "The guys are worried about you. Are you coming out to dinner?" His heart wrenched because he saw darkness in her blue eyes, the corners of her mouth drawn inward.

"Uh . . . no . . ." Shay touched her wrinkled brow. "I've got a headache. Can you tell them that? I just need to sleep it off."

His mouth went dry and all Reese wanted to do was step forward, pull Shay into his arms and hold her. That's what she needed. "Of course," he said.

"Wait." She reached forward, touching his hand briefly. "I-I need to talk with you later, Reese."

His heart thudded as her cool fingers grazed his hand. "Sure . . . whenever you want, Shay. You're looking stressed out. Can I get you some aspirin?" Because he wanted to do something . . . anything . . . to take the anguish out of her eyes. He saw her lift one corner of her lush mouth. A mouth he'd kissed earlier. Even now, Reese could taste her on his lips.

"I just took a couple of tablets. I'll be okay. The guys know that sometimes I get headaches and I just need to rest, is all."

Taking a step away, he nodded. "Okay . . ." It wasn't okay, but there was nothing Reese could do right now.

He didn't want the other vets to know what had happened between them. It was sacred. Private. And he wanted to keep it that way. He saw her nod and she quietly closed the door. Mouth tightening, he turned and walked into the warm, fragrant kitchen. All the vets were seated and waiting for him.

"Chow down," Reese said as he joined them. "Shay has a headache and told all of us to go ahead and eat without her."

Garret gave him a dark look from across the table as he spooned huge squares of lasagna onto each man's plate. "It's her father, isn't it?"

"Most likely," Reese agreed, taking the basket of bread and putting four pieces of garlic bread on his plate. "But she didn't tell me that."

"Some days are better than others for Shay when she visits her old man," Noah muttered, frowning. "She looked like hell when she drove up earlier." And then he turned to his right to glance at Reese.

Reese nodded, saying nothing.

Harper shrugged. "The guy is a mean rattler. Shay's never said anything, but I think the dude takes it out on her on some days."

Garret snorted. "Shay protects him, but dammit, we all see how upset she is when she comes home from those visits to the nursing home."

Reese said little. His stomach was tight and he'd lost his appetite, but he forced himself to eat. Little by little, he was regaining that lost fifty pounds. The pleasant clink of forks and knives against the plates filled the kitchen as the men hungrily dug into their meal. Reese began to relax a little. The men seemed to have dropped this topic of conversation, much to his relief. Was Shay's headache because of their kiss? Or seeing her father? Or both? He hoped Shay would tell him what had happened on that visit earlier this morning. The other vets seemed well informed that the tension between Shay and her father was an ongoing, torturous route she had to walk.

Later, Garret brought over dessert, butterscotch pudding with walnuts sprinkled over the top, plus whipped cream. Noah had gotten up and cleared the table, rinsed the plates and flatware, putting them into the dishwasher. Reese sat because it was his turn to clean up the kitchen after they were finished with their meal. There was no official schedule. It was assumed everyone would pitch in, and they did. It reminded him of the military, the training that still was very much a part of their lives even now.

Noah wiped his hands on a towel, hanging it up and heading to the table. "Did you get to talk to Shay after I saw you in the barn, Reese?"

Reese felt anxiety flood him. *Damn.* He was hoping this was a dead issue. He pulled over his bowl of pudding. "Yes."

Noah sat down next to him. "And? Did you find out what upset her?"

"No," Reese said. He picked up the can of whipped cream. "You were right. She was upset. But I couldn't pull answers out of her."

"Shit," Garret growled unhappily. "Shay is always telling us we should open up, but when it comes to her old man and herself, she's buttoned up and never says nothing."

"She's a caregiver," Harper reminded them. "She's dividing time between us and her father. He's a miserable son of a bitch to be around. And we're not exactly whole, either. There's a lot of stress coming at her from different angles. You shouldn't be pissed at her, Garret."

Garret glared at Noah. "I'm not angry at her. I'm angry at the situation, dude."

"She won't let us help her," Harper told Reese.

"Yeah," Noah said, shaking his head. "What's wrong with this picture? It's okay if she helps us, but when she clearly needs some support, she won't allow us to do anything for her."

Reese compressed his mouth. "Look, Shay has PTSD, too. She's in the same place we are. She's doing the best she can. No one said she was perfect."

The men quieted. They focused on their dessert.

Reese felt the tension amp up at the table. Garret was upset, but it was because he was protective of Shay, too, and wanted to help her. And they were all looking at him to do or say something. It wasn't spoken, but Reese could feel the pressure weighing on his shoulders.

"Well," Garret muttered darkly, "she's doing way too much. I've said that all along. She's one woman and she does a helluva job, but she needs some serious help."

"And she can't hire an assistant because the ranch is this close to foreclosure"—Noah held up his thumb and index finger—"and we can't do it because the three of us have odd jobs that bring in the money to cover that monthly mortgage payment."

"We're all busting our humps to the max," Harper agreed quietly. "Reese? You're about the only one she can lean on right now. We know you've taken over the daily accounting and other things that need to be done for the ranch. You've sort of become her assistant, and that's a good thing."

Reese quirked his mouth. "What Shay needs is a full-time office assistant. I'm pinch-hitting here and there. The rest of my day is spent out riding fences and repairing them."

"We need more help," Garret agreed, finishing off his pudding and pushing the bowl away from him. "But Shay can't afford to hire more wranglers."

"Hell," Harper said, "she wouldn't if she could. She wants vets like us."

"Well," Noah added, "Shay doesn't have two nickels to rub together. Never mind having extra money to hire anyone else, vet or not."

"She's stretched too thin," Garret growled. "I've been here the longest and I've watched her rescue this ranch from foreclosure, watched her trying to care for her father, Ray. She's got one foot in her father's issues and the other foot in trying to save the ranch."

"And don't forget, save our sorry asses, too," Noah reminded them dryly.

"Yeah," Garret grumped, sitting back, running his fingers through his hair in frustration. "That too."

"We need to clone ourselves," Harper said in jest.

"We work weekends on that damn fence line," Noah muttered. "Ray Crawford let this ranch fall into a three-year spiral of disrepair before Shay arrived home from the Corps. She stepped into a mess. Her old man was a mean drunk and Charlie from the hay and feed store told me one time that Ray drove off all the wranglers who worked for him. That's why the fences are in such bad shape."

Garret looked across the table at Reese. "If Shay could get those pasture fences fixed, posts replaced, she could once more lease pasture to the ranchers around here. Ray Crawford made a tidy little sum every year with those leases. That's what has kept this ranch on its feet. But he's an alcoholic, and hasn't leased any of those five pastures out for three years. That's why this ranch was in foreclosure when she got here."

Reese nodded. "I've been able to go over most of the accounting books and see the issues."

"That bastard, Marston Conroy, is the one you want to watch your six with," Garret warned.

"He's the banker, right?" Reese asked.

"Yes. The First Wyoming Bank in Jackson Hole. They

have the mortgage on this ranch," Garret said. He flexed his huge fist. "Has Shay told you about him?"

Reese shook his head. "Just that she considers him evil. I've been trying to straighten out the books before I go see him. I need to have a firm understanding of what's going on financially, and then talk with the guy."

"Good luck with that. The Bar C is teetering on the edge of disaster," Noah said, giving him a sad look. "When Crawford drank and gambled the ranch's lease money away, he drove the wranglers off with his abuse and anger, and the fence lines crashed and burned. No lease money, no way for Crawford to pay the monthly mortgage on the ranch. You need to know that Marston is in cahoots with Visions Corporation out of Idaho Falls, Idaho. They want to buy this ranch and build a condo resort on it." He waved his hand around the kitchen. "Visions has already done a fancy media presentation on what they're going to do when they snap up this property."

"How can they do that?" Reese demanded, secretly alarmed.

Snorting, Garret snarled, "Because Marston is just waiting for one month's mortgage payment missed, and he will be swooping in like a vulture to take this ranch away from Shay." He held up his finger. "One fuckin' month, Lockhart. Shay has been scrambling for all she's worth to ensure that the payment is always made. It's a sword hanging over her head every day."

"Yeah," Harper added, "and if we weren't producing, working to bring in that monthly amount, we wouldn't have a home to go to, either. We've got a big stake in seeing she makes that mortgage payment."

Reese heard the passion, the frustration, and the worry from the vets. The kitchen felt like a dog with its hackles up and he couldn't blame the men for their anxiety. Shay had not told him any of this. He was starting to put the financial picture together, but these new revelations impacted him heavily. One month's mortgage payment that was past due and the four of them would be out on the street again. And Shay would lose a family legacy. God, this was an unending nightmare for all of them.

Garret stared at him. "Obviously, Shay wasn't forthcoming about all of this when you started digging into those books."

"You could say that," Reese said. "I was asking her questions as I went, and she answered them."

Noah shook his head. "Hey, you know how people with PTSD hate to open up? They hate being asked questions, too."

Rubbing his jaw, Reese said quietly, "Shay is as bad off as we are, only she hides it a lot better than we do."

"Got that right," Garret said grimly. "We've all gone into the 'reading mode' with Shay. She won't open up and spill what's bothering her, what's hurt her, or what she's worried about. We've all learned by Braille, of a sort, how to read her on a daily basis. You haven't been here long enough to realize that."

"You're right," Reese agreed.

"Which is why I came to you this morning," Noah told him. "I saw her face. It was a bad day for Shay. Like she'd run into a buzz saw or something with her father." He shrugged. "I was hoping you'd have a better connection with her, Reese, than we do. You're living under her roof."

Reese grimaced. "I wish I did have a stronger connection, but I don't. All of you know a lot more about what's going on here than I do."

"Let's not get down on Shay," Garret warned them. "She's overwhelmed, and we all know how that feels because we've been there far too many times ourselves. The question we want to ask is what can each of us do to relieve that load she's carrying?"

Reese liked Garret's insight. But then, Garret was black ops, and those men and women had the ability to look deeply into a person or a situation. They had a fix-it mindset. "That's where we need to focus our energy," he agreed.

Harper finished his dessert and looked toward the doorway. "Look, we need to have this discussion, but not here. What if Shay comes out of her room and hears us talking like this? We need to table this topic, just in case. Can we meet somewhere else at another time?" He looked at all of them.

"You're right," Reese acknowledged.

Garret cracked his knuckles. "What about tomorrow? It's Saturday. Though Shay gives us the weekends off, we still work anyway. We usually break up into two teams and ride fence line and repair it. We could ride together. I don't think Shay would notice or care if we did. I just don't want her overhearing us. It would hurt her feelings and the woman has enough to handle with her sick father."

"I'm in," Reese told them. He heard Noah and Harper quietly agree to the idea.

"Okay," Garret said, looking at the watch on his thick wrist, "we'll meet in the barn at 0700 after breakfast tomorrow morning. Maybe we can figure out some other creative ways to help Shay."

They all rose and left, leaving Reese in the silence of the kitchen. He wanted to see how Shay was, but stopped himself. He knew what headaches felt like and he hoped she was sleeping it off. Still, her mouth on his, that womanly warmth of hers, had him shaken up and wanting more. Wanting Shay.

Reese forced himself to clean up the kitchen, trying to remain as quiet as he could, not wanting the noise to drift down the hall toward Shay's room.

He finished loading the dishwasher, cleaned off the table and counter. His mind was spinning with the added information the vets had supplied. In hindsight, he should have gone to them and asked what they knew about the ranch and its financial standing. It was a mistake he'd made and he wasn't happy about it.

Reese realized it was the PTSD overcoming the meds he'd been taking, warping his normal vision, flooding his brain with cortisol, screwing up his thinking, and he hated it. The frustration curdled in his throat as he cleaned off the stove. Now, he could go back and take another look at the declining lease money coming into the ranch. And since Garret had been at the ranch the longest, he was the man to talk with. Garret wasn't black ops for nothing, and he'd obviously snooped around, figured things out, probably talked to Charlie Becker or others. It would be a good idea to talk to Charlie himself. Right now, with Shay unable to communicate, Reese had to reach out to her friends to take the temperature of not only the ranch, but her as well.

"Reese?"

He turned, hearing Shay's husky, sleepy voice. His heart turned in his chest. She stood uncertainly in her voluminous ankle-length granny gown, white flannel sprinkled with a pattern of pink roses. Her hair was mussed and he saw puffiness around her eyes. She reminded Reese of a lost waif, the haunted look in her expression tearing at every cell in his body. He put a hold on himself. That kiss lingered between them and Reese didn't know what Shay had made of it all. Oh, she had initiated it, no question, but he wasn't laying the bulk of the responsibility on her shoulders. After all, he'd responded. He'd kissed the hell out of her.

"Hey," he murmured, "how are you feeling?"

Wrinkling her nose, she said, "I don't even want to look

at myself in the mirror. I'm afraid of what I'll see." She managed a halfhearted smile. "I slept hard and just woke up. The guys must have come and gone. Did dinner go okay?"

"Slow down," Reese murmured, slipping his hand beneath her elbow. The endearing red slippers stood out on her feet and he wanted to do more than cup her elbow as he led her to her seat at the table. Pulling out the chair, he guided her into it. "Are you hungry?"

"My stomach's growling, so I must be," she admitted, wiping her eyes.

Keeping his hands to himself, Reese wanted to smooth her mussed hair around her face. He didn't dare. Right now, Shay was utterly fragile. He had no wish to startle her, make her feel defensive or otherwise. "How about we start with some chamomile tea?"

She looked up. "That sounds good. Thanks . . ."

He turned and walked to the counter, busying himself. Reese swore he could feel her warm gaze lingering on his back, but he didn't turn around. "The guys left about an hour ago," he told her over his shoulder. "Went back to ride a few hours on the fence line before it turns dark."

"They're good men," she whispered. "Honorable."

Reese brought the teapot, teabags on the side, and the mug she used, placing them before her. "They are good men," he agreed. "How about something to eat?" He searched her features. His body tightened as he watched her hands gracefully move around the porcelain teapot that was painted with bright, colorful flowers, placing the bags inside it. Hands that he wanted skimming his body. Hands that could love him. And now, Reese knew, unequivocally, that Shay would be a wonderful lover, thoughtful and sensitive. The vision rose in front of him and he struggled to gently turn it away. Right now, Shay needed some TLC.

"Garret was making lasagna."

"Yes. Want some?"

She shook her head. "No . . . my stomach's been on the fritz. Let me start with the tea."

"Sure."

"Garret's been after me the last two months," she muttered, pulling over the mug. "Said I'm losing a lot of weight."

Reese walked to the cupboard and pulled down a mug. "Are you?"

"A little, I suppose."

He heard the mild defensiveness in her smoky voice as he came and sat down by her elbow. She poured him and herself tea, setting the teapot aside. Reese knew why now. There was no way he was approaching Shay about her weight loss tonight. "How can we help you, then?" He held her soft blue gaze that was exhausted-looking.

She managed a sound in her throat. "I don't know, Reese. Maybe a different life? No," she said, holding up her hand, "nix that. I didn't really mean that."

"On bad days, we all wish for a different life, Shay."

Sobering, she held his gaze. "Yes . . . that's true."

"I call those days, hitting the wall." Reese studied her as silence swirled around them. "I think you had one of those days today." He saw the corners of her mouth draw in, as if to hold back so many emotions that wanted to flood out of her. He wasn't going to talk about their kiss unless Shay brought it up. Reese had to let her take the lead, let her decide what she wanted to talk about, or not. Her fingers were wrapped gently around her cup, reminding him of her fragility.

He had no idea of the kind of weight she was carrying silently by herself. Anger rose up in him over the PTSD symptoms. Those symptoms savaged a person emotionally, mentally, and physically. Depression stalked many PTSD sufferers. He wondered if it hadn't taken Shay down, too.

Given the responsibility she had, her father's stroke, her mother dead, he couldn't begin to comprehend the personal pressure on her. His parents were alive. They loved him. They wanted him back in their lives. Shay had no one. Except the vets. The wounded carrying the wounded.

"Yes," she whispered, "it was one of those days." Looking into the golden tea in the mug, she added haltingly, "my father was having a really bad day. Maybe it's in the air."

"I imagine he has quite a few of those."

"He gets very bad headaches and no amount of pain meds can relieve them. So, they put him on a low dose of morphine, which knocks him out. At least then he doesn't feel the pain. The next day, he'll be free of the headache, but he has a nasty reaction to the morphine. He gets cranky. And of course, PTSD squirrels around with me, too. When I'm having a bad day and he's also having one, it's generally an emotional train wreck for both of us."

"Like today was?"

She licked her lips and dragged in a deep breath. "Yes. Like today."

"The guys were worried about you."

"They've always been big worrywarts," she grumbled, her expression growing soft.

"They care about you, Shay." She closed her eyes and her brow wrinkled. Reese saw tears in her eyes, but she wasn't going to let them fall. If she could use that strength differently, it would help her heal. But Reese understood what she was doing and why. Shay was afraid if she let go of all those dark, violent emotions she struggled to control, they would howl out of her and destroy her. He felt similarly about his own demons. Afraid he'd lose control.

And then what?

Chapter Thirteen

It was all about timing.

Four days had passed since the kiss with Shay, and they had yet to discuss it. In fairness, the last four days had been hectic as hell. Reese felt like he was the little Dutch boy plugging holes in a badly leaking dike, and he didn't have enough fingers to stop all the leaks.

He sat in his office going over the last of the accounting information. Now, he had something to bring to Shay's attention. As well as to her father, Ray Crawford. He wasn't sure how either of them would take the news. But it had to be broached now, not later. There was a continuing feeling of upset among the other vets as well. Everyone was on edge because of Shay's predicament.

Their agreed-upon morning ride to repair the fence line on Saturday yielded nothing of consequence. It all came down to getting at least one of the five massive pastures repaired so it could be leased for part of the season. The four of them had worked until dark. They were exhausted when they arrived back at the ranch. Luckily, Shay had done the cooking for them and everyone had been grateful.

Now, gathering the pages of his report on the results of his scrutiny of the accounting books, Reese slowly rose.

He could hear Shay puttering out in the kitchen, cleaning up after all of the vets left after breakfast. There wasn't a lack of work around here, that was for sure. On a ranch, there was always something that needed attention, large and small.

He walked into the kitchen, finding it sparkling once again. Shay had gone out and picked some flowers, placing them in a cobalt vase in the center of the table. Reese was struck by her woman's sense of making a sterile place come alive and feel nurturing. None of the vets had thought about picking wildflowers to set in a vase. Warmth flooded his chest as he halted at the entrance, watching her work with quick efficiency, wiping down the long, L-shaped counter. He tried to ignore her rounded hips and long legs encased in the jeans she wore. Today, he knew Shay would be visiting her father. It was Wednesday and he knew she'd be leaving shortly after lunch.

"Got a minute?" he asked her.

Shay turned. "Oh . . . Reese. Yes . . . hold on." She quickly finished wiping down the two aluminum sinks. Grabbing a towel, she turned. "What's in your hand?"

"Just some information I think you need to know about," he said, keeping his tone neutral.

"Want some coffee?"

"Sure, thanks." Reese made himself comfortable at the table, watching her pour the coffee. There was an economy to Shay's motions. He found himself wondering how she had survived in the Marine Corps. At one time, she might have been a lot stronger, before the PTSD hit. When she turned, he admired the pale yellow, short-sleeved T she wore. It lovingly outlined her breasts and long torso. The way her hips moved, that female fluidity, he felt himself responding whether he wanted to or not.

"Okay," Shay said, sliding the mug into his hands and sitting down at his elbow, "What did you find?"

"Things that I need to go over with you in some detail." He gave her a slight smile. "You're the only one who knows all the ins and outs of this ranch." He saw Shay frown.

"What's wrong?"

He heard the trepidation in her low tone. He slid one paper in her direction so she could look at it. "I know you told me the savings account belonged to your father, but it doesn't, Shay. And you knew that too, because Eddy, the lawyer, discussed it with you right after you got home. I talked to Eddy yesterday and he agreed the savings account belongs to the ranch, so it's a legally binding amendment that can stand a court test, if necessary." He tapped the SAVINGS line. "Legally, that money is yours, as you know, and not his."

"I know," she muttered, pulling the paper closer to look at the numbers. "But it doesn't matter. I'm not touching his money, Reese."

"I understand." he soothed. "But here's the problem." He brought out two more papers and ran his finger down one column of numbers. "I'm beginning to understand the pressure you're under. If you fail to make one mortgage payment, the bank will immediately foreclose, take the ranch and every asset attached to the property."

Grimly, Shay nodded. "I'm very well aware of the possibility."

"Okay," Reese murmured, "then we need to do something to protect your father's savings, because the bank would take all of it." He saw her eyes widen.

"But that's his savings!"

"Doesn't matter," Reese said apologetically, watching the stress come to her eyes. "When I gave this hypothetical to Eddy, he said that the bank has a right to take everything.

Even the savings account money." He saw her shock, and without thinking, Reese reached out, and enclosed her hand. "I don't want you upset over this. There's a fix for it, Shay. Just listen to me." Forcing himself, he removed his hand from hers. "We can legally remove the savings account money from the ranch property. All your father and you have to do is sign a paper making it so. I'm not saying we'll default on a mortgage payment, but just in case it does happen, we need to protect your father's hard-earned money."

"There's a way to protect it?" She leaned forward, looking at the numbers. "Really?"

Reese saw her expression become less tense. "Yes. Eddy gave me the instructions on how to do it, but I need to talk to your father directly. Can that be done? I know you're going in today to see him." Reese saw her lean back, confusion in her eyes for a moment.

"He's not a pleasant person to be around, Reese."

Hearing the warning in her tone, he nodded. "That's okay. I'll get along with him."

"Good luck." She pushed her fingers through her hair. "I never realized if I missed a payment on the mortgage that his savings would be gone! He'd be out in the street."

"Don't go there," Reese urged her gently. "You couldn't have known this. And we're catching it now. If I can explain it to your father, I'm sure he'll be happy to sign a document that will remove his savings from the ranch assets."

"He doesn't trust anyone," she muttered, shaking her head. "He doesn't know you, Reese."

"No, but you'll be with me. Vouch for me so I can explain this issue to him. Eddy has emailed me with all the information to draw up the document. He does trust Eddy." He saw such worry in her face that it tore him up. "Why are you so nervous about us meeting?"

"Because he *hates* that I've turned the ranch into a place for helping vets with PTSD," she whispered. "And once he knows you're one of the vets . . ." Shay opened her hands, giving him a helpless look. "He's almost always in a bad mood, Reese. Some of it's because of the pain in his head. The rest of it"—she sighed—"is not being able to drink alcohol anymore, though I suspect he has someone sneaking it in. He's gone through detox, but he's always angry . . ."

"Then," Reese said quietly, holding her anxious gaze, "we'll just persevere. He needs to understand what's going on and the measures we can take to protect his nest egg. He is of sound mind—right?"

"Yes, he's got his mind," Shay said bitterly, the corners of her mouth pulling inward. "He's legally competent."

"Good," Reese said, gathering up the papers. Taking a sip of his coffee, he rose and said, "I'll get the document drawn up so you and he can sign it. I'll take it to Eddy tomorrow and he'll do his legal magic on it. Then, your father's money is protected from the bank should we default on a payment."

The look in her eyes ripped his heart up. Reese saw uncertainty, anxiety, and fear. Would Ray Crawford savage him as he did Shay? Shay was struggling to hold her feelings and words within her. "You okay with me going with you this afternoon?"

"Yes . . . but it's not going to be easy," Shay warned him in a low voice.

"Nothing ever is. We'll get through this together." Reese saw some of her anxiety recede. "I've got to think that even if your father is cranky, he'll see the logic in my request. We're there to protect his money."

"I think he will, too," Shay said, sipping her coffee. "But he's cranky all the time."

"Duly noted," Reese said, giving her a warm look. Was she ever going to bring up that kiss? Or would she continue to pretend it didn't happen? Reese wished life wasn't so pressured for Shay. For him to broach the topic would most likely be seen as one more brick in her load.

Shay tried to prepare herself as she walked into her father's room. Wisely, she had called ahead to warn him that Reese was coming along with her, saying that he had a degree in business and was helping her out with the accounting at the ranch. She omitted the fact that Reese was a vet, staying at the Bar C. She knew her father might remember her bringing up his name in a previous conversation. With his stroke, he often forgot what she'd said, and she hoped he had forgotten that. She prayed that her father wouldn't grill Reese or refuse to talk to him. Wiping her damp hands on her jeans, she knocked lightly on the open door.

"Come in," Ray called.

She smiled hello to her father, who was sitting up in bed. The lunch tray was pushed away, his meal partly eaten. "Hi, Father. I've brought Reese Lockhart, the accountant I called you about, with me." She stood aside as Reese entered.

"Mr. Crawford, I'm Reese Lockhart," he said, extending his hand to the man in the bed.

Ray sized him up. He raised his hand and shook it. "What's this about my savings being in trouble?"

Reese pulled up a chair and sat down next to Crawford's bed. He handed some documents to the rancher. In as few words as possible, he explained the situation. Glancing up, he saw Shay standing on the other side of the bed, hands clasped in front of her, tense and pale.

Ray's left hand shook as he scrutinized the papers and

then intently studied the document he had to sign. "So," he said in a growly tone, "this will keep my money safe? Right, Mr. Lockhart?"

"Yes, sir, according to Eddy, who is your lawyer, it will." Reese handed him the document to sign after placing it on a clipboard. He handed him an ink pen.

"Well," Crawford said, giving Shay a hard look, "under the circumstances it was a good thing you found this. My daughter is not good with math."

Reese felt Shay's reaction. Her lips compressed. He saw shame in her eyes. After Crawford scrawled his nearly illegible signature with his left hand, Reese took the proffered clipboard and pen. "Your daughter, Mr. Crawford, has done a near miraculous job of meeting the bank's mortgage payment every month since she arrived home." He nailed Crawford with a chastising look. "Her math is just fine."

Crawford snorted, moving his hands restlessly across the white blankets on his bed. "It's not one of her strong points."

Shay signed the document next and handed it back to Reese. She tried to quell her nervousness and asked, "Do you need anything while we're here, Father?"

He glared over at her. "Yes. Don't lose my ranch."

Reese saw how her father's angry words struck her. She blanched. He slid the signed document into his briefcase and closed it. Rising, he held the man's gaze and said, "She has been saving that ranch one day at a time, Mr. Crawford. She came home with nothing in the bank account and made the payments you had neglected to send into the bank for nearly six months before that. She's the reason the Bar C exists right now, and I think you know that."

Reese glanced at Shay. Her lips parted briefly as he stood up for her. Obviously, Crawford's stroke made him forget it was he who had put the ranch into its present state.

However, Crawford struck him as a manipulator who'd lie if it suited his purpose. Reese wasn't going to let him get away with blaming the ranch's condition on Shay.

"No one asked you," Ray snapped at him. "You mind your own business, Lockhart."

Reese moved over next to Shay, keeping her somewhat behind and to the side of him, becoming a human shield of sorts against her angry father. "Accounting ledgers tell a story, Mr. Crawford," he told the man. "Your daughter has kept the ranch in the black since the day she stepped foot back on the Bar C. You should be proud of her. She's worked hard to keep it solvent."

"Never liked bean counters," Ray muttered irritably, waving them away with his hand. His scowl was dark and he refused to look at Shay. "I'm tired. Leave me alone."

Shay gulped and quickly left, Reese on her heels. She slowed her pace once she was in the hall, her heart pounding. Placing her hand against her chest, she waited until they were up near the front doors before she spoke to Reese in a low tone that couldn't be overheard by the personnel who worked at the home. "That went better than I ever expected. I don't believe it."

Reese opened the door for her. The sun was bright and warm as they emerged from the building. "You okay?" he asked, slowing his stride for her sake. Shay's face was pale, her eyes darting, like an animal that had been cornered. Her hand was pressed against her heart and he could only imagine how she was feeling.

"I am now. I thought he was going to start in on you like he does me. But he didn't, thank God."

Reese couldn't stop himself from cupping her elbow, guiding her off the walk and into the large parking lot. He needed to touch her, and instantly, he saw the effect of his contact. Shay's tense shoulders dropped and relaxed. There was even a hint of flush to her cheeks as he walked her to the truck. "Can't say he's the most politically correct person I've met," he said, teasing her. He saw her lips soften. Maybe their kiss was working a subtle magic that he'd not realized. In his heart, Reese desperately wanted time with Shay, just to talk with her.

"Being PC isn't his style," Shay said wearily. "I'm just glad he went along with it and didn't ask where you worked. He may have forgotten I told him who you are the other day. Maybe the stroke has some benefits."

"I would have handled it."

"Well, he was respectful to you. I was amazed. I thought for sure he'd light into you like he does me."

His heart ached for her. "Maybe in time, that will change," Reese said soothingly, opening the passenger-side door for her. "He knew what I was talking about in there. That he'd put the ranch into foreclosure. He knew the truth."

Shay sat down and gave him a warm smile. "I haven't seen my father so nice with anyone."

Reese nodded and shut the door. Ray Crawford was a son of a bitch, in his estimation. He had a lifetime of alcoholism, so Reese doubted he got much nicer than he was today. Besides, they were there on his behalf, protecting his money. So why wouldn't he be less cranky than usual? Right?

Climbing into the truck, Reese drove them over to Becker's Hay and Feed because Shay needed some supplies for the ranch. Charlie greeting them warmly, invited them to the back, where Pixie had just brought her latest goodies for their customers. She'd made donuts.

Shay grinned after hugging Charlie. "Oh, I love them!" she told him. "But I'll be good. I'll take only one."

Charlie patted her shoulder. "Miss Shay, you take as many as you want."

"Would you mind if I took one for each of the guys back at the ranch?"

"Heck no! Go right ahead." Charlie opened the door beneath the table and pulled out a sack for her to use.

Reese felt a fierce emotion move through him as he watched Shay come alive beneath Charlie's fatherlike care. It was obvious he doted on Shay, and she needed this kind of love from someone. He just wished it was him, but tucked his desire deep down inside himself. The fact that she'd thought of the vets spoke volumes.

"I'll get the list of stuff ready for you," Reese told her. "You stay here, eat your donut, drink some coffee, and keep Charlie company."

"But—"

Reese held up his hand. "Relax. You've earned a break. I can take care of this." There was such a difference in Shay now versus being with her father. The paleness had left her face. Her blue eyes sparkled as Charlie teased her and told her a couple of jokes as they stood at the food table munching donuts.

Reese's skin riffled when he heard her laughter, and he smiled as he walked toward one section of the store. Reese knew Charlie gave Shay a 40 percent discount on everything in his store, so that she was able to afford the small items necessary for any working ranch. The leather reins on one bridle needed to be replaced. Instead of buying expensive leather replacements, Reese bought a much cheaper but equally good set of nylon reins.

He quickly got everything on her list. Shay's change was remarkable and served to tell Reese that she wasn't always under pressure and stress. Truth be told, Charlie's cajoling, constantly touching her arm or shoulder, seemed to help

Shay stabilize. Why wouldn't it? Her father had made no move to kiss her good-bye or hug her. Charlie gave her what her father did not: love, attention, and genuine care. Hurting for her, Reese put the items on the counter as Charlie walked up.

"Hey," Charlie chided. "Go get your donut while I ring these up."

"Okay," Reese murmured, "just as soon as we get this bill settled."

Charlie took the items. "You're looking good, Mr. Lockhart."

"Call me Reese?"

Charlie nodded, writing down the items on a separate bill. "You're lookin' like you're gaining back some of that lost weight. Garret's food must agree with you."

Reese said, "I've gained about twenty pounds and you're right, Garret ought to open up a café. I think everyone would come to eat his chow."

Chuckling, Charlie grabbed a paper sack and put everything into it. "I hear you're an accountant?"

"Yes, sir, among other things." Reese took the proffered sack. Charlie had put a copy of the bill in the bag. And then he turned around and dropped the original one into the wastebasket. He wasn't charging Shay anything, and Reese felt a lump form in his throat for the man's incredible generosity.

"Shay said you're real good with numbers." Charlie leaned forward, hands on his counter, voice lowered. "I can pay you fifteen dollars an hour to come and help me with my books. My accountant just retired and I'm terrible at this. What do you say? It will put some cash in your hands."

"Sure," Reese said, "but let me talk to Shay about it first. If she gives me the go-ahead, we'll discuss it." Reese was sure that she would, because he needed to have some kind of outside work that paid him regularly. This was exactly what he needed in order to contribute to the Bar C.

"Good. I'm sure she'll be fine with it." Charlie straightened, rubbing his hands together. "After she says it's okay for you to take on a part-time accounting job for us, what's a convenient time for you to drop by, Reese?"

"Mornings from nine to eleven are fine for me."

Charlie stuck out his hand. "Good! Can you possibly drop by tomorrow morning?"

Reese nodded and shook the older man's hand. "Sure thing, Charlie. I'll call you later today to confirm it. Thanks for the job offer."

At dinner that night, there was a remarkable difference in Shay, and Reese saw it in every vet's expression. She was laughing, eating well, and even telling some of Charlie's jokes. The warmth at the table felt good, and even Garret, who he could see was intently listening to Shay, seemed happy.

It was Shay who told everyone that Charlie had hired Reese to be the accountant for his store. Reese saw the relief in their faces because it meant another income flowing into the ranch. One more step away from foreclosure.

Reese knew that Harper had a steady mechanic's job. Noah's income relied on training horses and dogs. It was Garret who did a lot of construction work, whose income rose and fell with jobs sporadically coming his way. One nice thing about any business: They'd always need an accountant to keep the books straight.

Everyone at the table was uplifted by the good news. Especially Shay. She seemed almost giddy and girlish, and it sent a deep desire in Reese's heart to always give her days like this one.

Later, after dinner, the men went out to the barn to saddle horses and ride fence line until dark. That was when Reese was surrounded by the other vets.

"You saw Shay's old man," Noah said in the main aisle. "What was he like with you?"

Reese saw Garret and Harper draw near so their voices wouldn't carry far.

"He's an unhappy person."

"Was he mean to Shay?" Garret demanded.

"Somewhat," Reese said, and he told them what had transpired. He saw Garret give him a pleased look afterward.

"You put the bastard in his place." Garret clapped him on the shoulder. "Well done."

"You said Shay was pretty nervous?" Noah asked.

"Yes, like she was expecting her father to blow up at me or something." Reese shrugged. "I didn't feel it, but she did."

"The fact," Harper pointed out, "that Shay said he was respectful toward you when he isn't with anyone else, says a helluva lot."

Garret's eyes gleamed. "That's because he saved the old man money."

Reese smiled a little. "Most likely so."

"I've never seen Shay this happy," Harper said.

Shaking his head, Noah said, "Me either. Have you, Garret?"

"Never."

"It's gotta be you," Harper said, pointing a finger in Reese's direction.

"Yeah," Noah chimed in.

Garret gave him a long, hard look. "What did you do, Reese? Kiss her?"

* * *

Shay stumbled out of her bedroom, her red slippers whispering down the cedar hall to the kitchen. Rubbing her eyes, she saw Reese in his pajamas and tan T-shirt sitting at the table, a cup of tea in one hand. "You too?" she mumbled, going to the kitchen counter. The clock read 2:00 A.M.

"I beat you out here."

She grinned lopsidedly, placing the teakettle on the stove. "By how much?" She turned to see his mouth curve faintly. Right now, Reese looked so incredibly handsome. His beard stubble made him look dangerous, in a good kind of way. And his hair, recently cut and now carefully combed, was mussed, giving him a boyish look. Reese was always so mature, so courtly toward her. That kiss they shared had told her that beneath his officer's decorum, there was a primal man who made her heart race and her lower body ache for him.

It had been a week since they'd kissed and she still hadn't discussed it with him. Shay knew they were both avoiding it. Probably for different reasons. It was the elephant in the room neither was willing to talk about.

"Probably half an hour."

"Hmmm," she said, pulling down a mug from the cupboard. The chamomile tea was open on the counter. "What's your excuse this time?"

"Can the excuse be that I ate my donut at bedtime and it caused indigestion and woke me up?"

She laughed outright. "Like Pixie's baked goods would cause anyone indigestion? I don't think so."

"I've learned I shouldn't eat anything a couple of hours before bedtime, but it was there on the dresser staring at me and I couldn't say no."

"Somehow," she teased, turning, watching him, "I think you're telling a big fib, Reese Lockhart."

Chuckling, he held up his hands. "Guilty as charged."

Absorbing his smile, drowning in his eyes, which danced with merriment, her heart lifted and hope infused her. The teakettle started to whistle and Shay turned, picking it up and pouring the hot water into the mug. "Busted," she called to Reese over her shoulder. Setting the teakettle down on the stove, she picked up her mug and a tea bag, turning toward him. "I was wondering if you were ever a kid. Now, I know you have that side to you."

Reese felt his face go hot as she wandered over in a pale yellow granny gown. This time, because of the light from over the sink, he could see the silhouette of her body through the thin cotton material. He was sure Shay wasn't aware of it, and he sure as hell wasn't going to point it out to her. "I do have a playful side."

"Hmm," she said, sitting down, smoothing the ankle-length gown over her lap. "Well, you sure fooled me until just now."

"I might say the same of you," Reese murmured, looking at her over his cup as he sipped his cooling tea. He saw her cheeks deepen in color. And this time, there was no mistaking the interest in her eyes. It was a clear, undiluted message.

Chapter Fourteen

Shay wanted so desperately to have alone time with Reese. His kiss . . . She would never forget that kiss. The responsibilities of the ranch had to come first, not her personal life. Not her dreams, which were many, but only that.

"Tell me about your growing-up years." She was eager to know more about Reese. The demands of the ranch hovered over them, and personal time alone with him was rare. Shay saw his mouth pull into a faint smile as he moved his fingers up and down on the mug of tea in front of him. Max had come over, laying between them, his head on his paws.

"I was born when my father, Joe, was in the Marine Corps," he began, holding her gaze. "He stayed in ten years, made sergeant and then got out, coming home to Caspar, Wyoming, to set up a small garage and fix cars. My mother, Maggie, started a day care center. She loves kids, and both their small businesses took off. That's what they do to this day."

"Where were you born?"

"Camp Pendleton, the big Marine base in Southern California. My father had just returned home from his third deployment overseas. He was home in time to coach my mom through the birth process. I was a home birth." He smiled a little. "My dad fainted afterward."

Shay laughed and nodded. "Yeah, birthing isn't for the faint of heart, for sure."

"My mom soldiered on. Said I was a ten-pound bowling ball she gave birth to." Reese chuckled fondly.

"How long had your dad been in when you were born?"

"Five years." Reese's mouth tightened. "My mom pleaded with him to get out after I was born. He'd been wounded once already. She feared he'd be killed, leaving her and me without support. But he'd just re-upped at four years for another six, so he was stuck in the Corps until he hit that ten-year mark. They sent him and his team back to the Middle East."

Groaning, Shay shook her head. "Do you have any memories of those times, Reese?"

Shrugging, he murmured, "Not too much, really. My dad got wounded once more. Shrapnel, nothing serious enough to take him out of the fight, but I remember my mother crying her heart out. She was so fearful he was going to die."

"I can't even begin to imagine what she went through." Giving him a tender look, Shay said, "At least you were young and couldn't grasp all of it."

"My mom protected me from it, too," Reese said with a nod. "The only time I heard her crying was after she got the phone call that my dad had been wounded again. I didn't understand why she was crying. She held me and lied to me about it."

"Did you buy it?"

"Yes, I did. I found out much later, when I was a young,

green lieutenant, that she cried all the time. Just at night, after I was in bed, so I couldn't hear it."

"It's so hard on the families of service people," Shay agreed quietly. She saw the pensive expression on Reese's face. "So he got out when you were five years old?"

"Yep, and my mom's sense of relief told me a lot. We moved back to Caspar, where they'd both been born, and they went to work."

"Did you grow up in the city?"

"No. My dad was born in a rural area just outside Caspar. He bought a home on the outskirts. He'd take me fishing and hunting with him every chance he got. Mom loved being in nature, too. She always had a huge garden every year, but because of the short summer, she lost a lot of what she'd planted. Most of the time I was out with our dog, Blackie, hiking, fishing, or just exploring the area."

"Did you always have a dog growing up?"

"Always. Mom loves cats. She's got two calico females right now." He smiled a little. "She always told me women were like cats and men were like dogs. I understood what she meant after I went into the Marine Corps." He laughed over those fond memories.

"And your dad still has his garage?"

"Yes. It's grown a lot, though. He's got five garages around Caspar and runs a pretty large business at this point. They're doing well financially, and I'm glad for them."

"Did car mechanics rub off on you?" she wondered.

"It did. My dad started teaching me how to fix cars and anything else that had wheels on it when I was eight years old. He's enlarged his business and now has a group of men who also work on farm machinery and small engines."

Shay gave him a teasing look. "So if I need my truck fixed, you can do it?"

"I could. But I think Harper has that area pretty well covered. He's a good mechanic, too. And Garret's no slouch, either."

"We're lucky to have all of you here. Each of you has a number of overlapping skills."

Reese gave her a sincere look. "We're lucky to have you, Shay. You're giving all of us a chance to reclaim our lives. Make something of ourselves even though we struggle with PTSD."

Shay saw his vulnerable expression, his eyes narrowing as he stared at the cup between his hands. She felt as if there was a raw, open wound still bleeding within Reese. Whatever he was carrying around within him was dark and toxic, because she could see it in his shadowed green eyes. Shay sensed a fine, subtle tension racing through Reese, as if he were remembering an event she'd triggered with her questions. She said, "I'm sorry. I didn't mean to upset you."

Reese shrugged, and put down his mug. "It's not something I've ever talked about to anyone. Not even to my dad, who I'm pretty sure would understand."

Treading lightly, she asked, "But your dad? Was he aware of what happened to you?" She saw pain come to Reese's mouth, which flexed down as the corners drew inward.

"When I was released from the Corps, I did go home." He opened his hands. "I tried to regain some kind of life for myself, but I couldn't do it. I'd already lost Leslie. I couldn't handle the people, the pressure, and demands on me. I was a failure. I couldn't do any job in my dad's garage without getting stressed out to the point where I walked off and disappeared. I'd get in the car he loaned me and go back to my old haunts near our home. I just needed the quiet. The peace. I couldn't handle stress anymore."

"I understand," she said gently, reaching out, laying her fingers on his arm. Shay saw some of the tension decrease as she touched him. No one knew the importance of him talking this out more than she did.

Curving her fingers a little more firmly around his forearm, she said, "What happened next?" Inwardly, Shay held her breath because so many vets resisted going any deeper than what they were able to give voice to. She saw Reese struggling with her question. Felt it around him. Shay knew he trusted her and the only question was, how much? If Reese trusted her enough, he'd divulge more of his painful past.

"My dad and I had a talk out at a trout stream we always fished, about a week after I got home." Reese's voice grew strained. "I told him that after I came home from deployment, I took it out on Leslie. She was the innocent in all of this. I trashed our marriage because I couldn't handle the symptoms ripping through me. I projected them on her. I verbally used her as a daily whipping post."

Moving her fingers lightly up and down his arm, Shay held his grim gaze. "What did your dad suggest you do?"

"Get help. Therapy. Said he'd pay for it. So I tried it. The therapist was a civilian who'd never been in the military. Never saw combat. I lasted three sessions and told my dad I couldn't do it. I'd failed him again . . ."

Heart aching for Reese, she soothed, "No, you didn't. PTSD plays out differently in everyone. It's never the same in two people. And I've seen you up front and close for two months, Reese, and if I didn't know you had PTSD, I'd never have guessed. So you are internalizing a lot of it, whether you realize it or not." Her fingers grew firm on his hand. She saw the amount of suffering in his green eyes.

"I've had two years of different kinds of therapy to work

on my symptoms," he replied wryly. "Over time, some of them have dulled or turned down in volume. And that adaptogen that your doctor, Taylor Douglas, gave me a while back, has stopped my anxiety completely. That's been a huge turnaround for me. I'm not irritable, jumpy, or see everything around me as a potential threat. There's peace inside me, not the monster that used to prowl around making me ready to overreact to the slightest setback."

"Yes, that usually happens when you take the adaptogen. It did the same for me, thank goodness," Shay said.

"They say time heals everything," Reese said, "and since taking the adaptogen, all my hypervigilance, paranoia, and anxiety have gone."

Nodding, Shay said, "Yes. And I've never been so grateful as I am for her help. Taylor Douglas has done a lot of time in grade working with vets who have PTSD. The adaptogen isn't widely known about, but because she did an awful lot of research on it, she started devoting part of her practice to it. She discovered a small company in Washington that was manufacturing it. They didn't make any claims about what it could do, but she did some trials with it and found it made a remarkable difference in vets' lives when it came to high levels of cortisol in their bloodstream, which causes that horrible anxiety feeling."

"Well," he murmured, "those particular symptoms have stopped. It's a miracle."

She didn't want to release his arm. She saw desire replace the grief in his eyes. Her mind told her to let go, but her heart clamored to remain in contact with Reese, that it was healing for him. *Important.*

In her dream last night, Reese was holding her. Kissing her. And he'd made love to her. She'd awakened at 2:00 A.M., shaky, needy, and realizing that her body was no longer dormant because of her own PTSD symptoms. She was starting to come alive once more after being numb for so long. Being around Reese triggered that part of her, a vital part, blossoming to life within her. Searching his eyes, Shay felt that wonderful cloak of protection and desire settle around her shoulders.

"Tell me more about yourself, Reese. Please?" She saw his cheeks grow a dull red. It was an endearing reaction, telling Shay that he was far more reachable than she first thought. So many vets were armored up like an Abrams tank. But Reese wasn't. Or at least . . . not with her?

"There's not much else to share, Shay. I'm no one special."

She held his gaze, realizing the shame of his PTSD was making him think that way about himself. "I don't buy that, Reese. My father respected you the moment you walked into his room. He rarely gives anyone that kind of deference. Charlie looks up to you, too. I saw it. And the vets here all look up to you." Her fingers tightened for a moment on his arm. "Stop thinking of yourself as a failure, Reese. Because you're not. Not to me." She touched her heart. "Not to the vets or anyone else who meets you here in Wind River Valley."

Reese gave her a wry look. "Shay, I've had two years of being shunned, ignored, cursed, and kicked around."

Her voice broke. "That's changing now, Reese. You are changing." Never had she wanted to hold a man more than him. In Reese's expression Shay saw the devastation, the fall from grace, that he had experienced. She knew if she held him, loved him, it would help put the torn pieces of him back together again. It was a knowing so deep in her heart that it drove tears into her eyes. Removing her hand from his arm, she added in a trembling tone, "You don't see yourself. But I see you. Everyone you come in contact with, Reese, admires and respects you. Surely, you've realized that?"

He winced and looked away from her. His hands tightened around the mug. Finally, he forced himself to turn and look into her moist eyes. "I have, but I'm afraid, Shay."

She stared at him, uncomprehending. "Afraid?" Of *what?* Shay knew PTSD had insidious, octopus-like tentacles that toxically moved into a person's head and emotions. It destroyed their self-confidence. It made them question themselves on every level. It beat them down. Reese was the last person she would ever think was afraid of anything. He'd had the courage to support her, and had reaped the respect of the other vets, which was not an easy task. Charlie doted on him, praised him to the rafters, bragging about his accounting abilities. Even her own father respected him! That had blown Shay away.

Reese gritted his teeth for a moment, trying to put what he felt into words. "I'm afraid to hope," he rasped.

Her heart tore open. His low, unsteady voice devastated her as nothing else had in a long time. Shay gripped his arm. "Because of that monster ripping you up inside?"

"Yeah . . . that. I'm afraid it will come back. That this miracle that's happened inside me, the anxiety gone, will return."

"No, it won't," Shay said. "Taylor treated me a year ago and it's never returned. I know what it's like to feel on tenterhooks, waiting for that horrible anxiety to come blasting through you again. But it won't." She struggled to control her own, unraveling emotions. But she would not let go of contact with Reese because Shay knew it helped him. His eyes were cloudy with self-doubt, recrimination, regret.

Oh, she knew all those feelings only too well. She had them herself.

"I know how tough it is to hope again," she whispered. "I've hoped so often, and every time, it's been crushed in front of my eyes. It made me feel so ashamed. I know what you're saying, Reese. Every time we try to get up, someone smashes us back down again. They look at us as either vermin from the street, or they see us as weaker than they are. They don't understand how we got there. You can't, unless it's happened to you. I get all of that."

Reese gave her a quick glance. "I'm half the man I used to be, Shay. Even if my anxiety stays away, I've lost two years of my life. I destroyed my marriage. I couldn't remain in the Corps."

Anger and desperation curled through her at his words. "I accept what happened to you, Reese. I didn't know you before, but that doesn't matter. What does matter is how you've conducted yourself here at the Bar C since you've arrived. You've worked hard and consistently. You're a team player and the vets have embraced you wholeheartedly as one of them. You're not what you were before. You're climbing out of that hole."

She swallowed. "You have to realize how much you've helped me, Reese." Shay wasn't prepared when he lifted his head, his eyes widening with shock as though he hadn't believed how much he'd helped her when she'd told him before. "When you arrived here, I saw a wounded man and a vet. From the moment you walked in that door"—she jabbed a finger toward it—"you have conducted yourself with honor, Reese. Never once have you let anyone down. You know the value of working in a team environment. You care about all of us. I see it every day in large and small ways. You never ask anything for yourself, but you're always willing to put yourself out for any of us." She saw his eyes glitter with what she thought were tears, his mouth a hard line, as if holding back so many, many unspoken feelings.

"I wish," he began hoarsely, "that you'd met me when I was healthy and whole, Shay."

Startled by his words, she sat paralyzed for a moment, only now beginning to realize the depth of damage done to Reese by the PTSD, by whatever event he'd managed to survive. It haunted him like a demon: the horror of what had happened, of how he handled it, of how he'd survived whatever the event was. Unconsciously, she moved her fingers across his shoulder and down his arm.

"There is no one who doesn't respect you, Reese. No one." She stared into his moist eyes, watching him fight back tears. There was such devastation in his expression, hope buried in the carnage of his PTSD. Shay wasn't sure who would win that battle within Reese. And that's when she realized that only time . . . time . . . would decide the outcome of that war that he carried within him. Every day was a battle for a PTSD-ridden vet.

Every muscle in his body was rigid. She could feel the tension around him, how badly he wanted to dump all those feelings into words and share them with her. But he couldn't. It was heartbreaking to watch him use his internal strength and resolve to shove it all down deep into himself once again. Shay wanted to scream out to him to release it, but she knew it would do no good. Reese had years of experience pushing away his emotions in order to survive. Her heart twisted in anguish.

Leaning forward, she caressed his upper arm, forcing him to look directly into her eyes. "I *trust* you, Reese. Since you came to the ranch, you've been helping me to reach out and trust again. It's you. You've done that for me whether you realized it or not. You don't see yourself and how you help all of us in different ways. I know that. But you need to be made aware because you think you're less than us." She swallowed convulsively. "And you aren't. You never have been. You need to start seeing the people around you who love and care for you. That's how to rebuild your confidence and self-esteem. No one says it's easy, Reese. God knows, I wrestle with it every day myself, but I have made healthy steps forward. And so can you."

Shay watched her words envelop Reese. He sat up, blinking at her, his mouth softening. When she'd said she trusted him, everything changed in a heartbeat. The shock was followed by hope, as he stared at her with an intensity that stirred her on every level. Shay realized she was getting a peek at the hardened Marine captain who had been in the thick of combat. She knew that look. Knew it well.

And then that hardened warrior mask he wore was replaced with something so beautiful, so heart-opening, that her breath hitched in reaction. *Trust.* That was the key to Reese, Shay suddenly realized. A key to his climbing out of that hellish world living inside of him. Trust meant something so powerful to this beleaguered warrior that she could use it like a helping hand to pull him out of that dark internal prison he lived in.

Her fingers grew firmer around his biceps and she felt him respond, his muscles tightening beneath her fingertips. "I don't care if you think you're half the man you used to be or not. I see a whole man in front of me. Not half of one. What hasn't changed in you, Reese, is that people trust you. And you don't let them down . . ."

Chapter Fifteen

Shay tried to quell her nervousness as they walked into her father's room at the nursing home. To her shock, her father had called her yesterday, four days before the arena roof-raising was to take place. She didn't know of a time when she'd been busier at the ranch, setting up to receive seventy-five volunteers for the coming weekend to get the roof on the arena, not to mention, get four houses built.

Glancing up at Reese, who walked casually at her side, he carried his briefcase in hand. Some of her anxiety dissolved beneath his quiet demeanor. Neither of them knew why Ray wanted to see them.

She knocked on the door to her father's room. The mid-afternoon sun slanted into his room and Shay saw he'd had someone open up his window to allow fresh summer air to circulate. She knew how much her father missed being on the ranch, and being out in the elements.

"There you are," Ray grouched, waving them in.

"Hi, Father," Shay said, leaning over the bed and giving him a peck on the cheek. Today, he looked almost happy, and it shocked her. He was sitting on top of his bed and dressed in jeans and a dark blue cowboy shirt. Swallowing her surprise, she eased away as Reese came up and extended his hand to her father.

"Good afternoon, Mr. Crawford."

"Come in," Ray said, gripping Reese's hand with his left hand. "Sit down. Shay. Close the door?"

"Sure," she said, giving her father a confused look. What was going on? Normally he was angry and growly. Maybe it was because Reese was with her and Ray respected him?

She quietly closed the door and saw that Reese had pulled out two chairs beside her father's bed. Her heart warmed. Ever since their intense, emotional talk last week, things had quieted down between them. Shay knew what she'd said had affected Reese deeply, although he'd never said anything more about it. Instead, she saw a little more confidence in him afterward, as if he'd needed to hear someone else's view of him—someone whom he trusted.

Shay realized as the days went forward, Reese *had* believed her. He even walked with more confidence. Her heart swelled fiercely for this man, this warrior who was struggling daily like all of them, to make a life for himself that would give him back the self-respect he'd lost along the way.

"Sit down, Shay. I got some questions for Reese here."

Shay smiled a little. Her father had shaved. Over the past year he'd learned to do it with his left hand instead of his right one, which was now useless. Ray had refused physical therapy shortly after the stroke. And because of it, his right hand was shaky and weak.

"You look good today, Father," she said, as she sat down next to Reese.

Ray stared at them. "I just heard gossip that I want

confirmed, Shay. Are you really going to have four houses built on my ranch?"

"Yes, but it's more than that." She launched into the explanation of what would take place shortly. When she was finished, he glared at her.

"Why didn't you tell me about this before?"

Wincing inwardly, Shay tried to protect herself from his sudden anger. "I tried, Father. Several times. But when I started to tell you, you shut me off. You didn't want to hear what I had to say."

Ray scowled. "Well, maybe I shouldn't have."

That was as close to an apology as Shay was ever going to get from him.

Crawford focused on Reese. "Mr. Lockhart, I heard that you're headin' up this effort?"

"Well," Reese said, giving Shay a glance, "it's under your daughter's direction. She's the one who has asked Steve and Maud Whitcomb, plus myself and our wranglers at the Bar C, to coordinate the raising. If it wasn't for Shay, none of this would be happening. Plus, the vets at the Bar C are all involved in the details of coordinating this huge two-pronged effort. We couldn't do it without them."

Shay's stomach knotted. Her father had forgotten that Reese was a vet out at the Bar C. Sooner or later, Ray would find out, and then what? Would he hate Reese as much as he disrespected the other three vets who lived on the ranch? Her hands became damp in her lap as she gripped them, waiting and hoping the subject would not come up.

Snorting, Crawford said, "I'm surprised. They're worthless."

"Father—" Shay pleaded.

Reese sat a little straighter in the chair, his gaze on Crawford. "Sir, with all due respect, I'm one of those vets you're referring to."

Shay winced and gritted her teeth, watching her father's eyes suddenly widen in shock.

"You are? How could that be? You're smart and you helped me protect my savings."

Shay dragged in a ragged breath, feeling Reese's anger, although he hadn't changed his expression at all. What was going to happen now? Would Ray fly into a rage as he always did? Her father's face went from shock to grudging contemplation as he stared hard at Reese, the silence becoming heavy in the room.

"Your daughter was kind enough to take me in," Reese told him quietly, keeping his voice neutral. "She gave me a roof over my head, food, and something that money can't buy, a chance to pull myself up by my bootstraps."

"I see," Crawford grumbled, rubbing his chin, staring at Reese. And then he looked at Shay. "Maybe you didn't do half bad on this one," he grumped. "At least"—he waved his left hand toward Reese—"he has some redeeming qualities."

"All the vets do," Shay said firmly.

Reese reached out, placing his hand on her lower arm. "Let me handle this, Shay?"

Gulping, Shay felt the steadying strength of Reese's calloused hand. She gave him a swift glance and then settled her gaze on her scowling father. "Okay," she whispered.

Reese released her arm and focused on Crawford. "The other three vets that Shay has hired for the Bar C are good men, sir. Every one of them. Each of them works and brings money into the ranch, helping Shay meet that monthly mortgage payment so the Bar C doesn't slide into foreclosure." His voice lowered to a growl. "If it wasn't for them, you wouldn't have a ranch anymore. It's time to take stock of how you see these men who have sacrificed so much for their country, and give them the respect they deserve."

Shay's breath jammed in her throat. Oh, God, no one had ever spoken to her father like that before! She saw his eyes widen and then shrink to slits as he glared at Reese. It felt like two alpha wolves circling one another before they lunged at one another's throats. Her fingers were icy cold as she sat rigid, her heart pounding with dread as the two men faced off. Reese looked relaxed, but Shay knew differently. She could feel the fine tension running through him.

"I don't believe in what my daughter's done," Crawford growled defensively.

"They're saving the ranch, sir. They deserve your respect."

Cursing under his breath, Ray looked away, staring at Shay. "You never told me this. What's the matter with you?"

"I tried to," Shay said, defensiveness in her tone. "But you always shut me down, Father. You don't think anything I have to say has any importance." Her breath was coming out ragged, her voice tight and accusing. With Reese beside her, Shay had decided to fight back, to tell her father the truth. And she saw his eyes grow angry and then, to her surprise, thoughtful looking. His anger was gone. She waited, feeling like a dog that was going to get kicked by its owner sooner or later. Because that's how Ray handled everything in his life.

"Your daughter has a lot of good ideas, Mr. Crawford. She's single-handedly kept the ranch from going into foreclosure. For that, you should be grateful. What you don't know is she is working sixteen hours a day to get the place back on its feet."

Shay felt such relief when Reese spoke up for her, his voice low and firm, his gaze locked on her father. Mouth dry, she added, "Without these four vets, I could not have done it, Father. They are assets, wranglers who work from dawn to dusk every day. Even on weekends."

Ray stared at them, his mouth working. He rubbed his jaw and looked out the window at the sunny day.

The silence deepened.

Shay felt Reese's carefully controlled anger, felt his protection of her even though he hadn't made a move to touch her again. It was so good to have someone stand up for her against her angry father. Only now, as she watched Crawford's drawn face, he seemed mollified; there was not the usual amount of anger that was always on the surface. Another part of her felt sorry for her father. He was a strong man who had worked tirelessly on the ranch. It had been his drinking and gambling that had been not only the downfall but the near loss of the family ranch, as well.

Now, Reese was confronting him. Crawford would never take those words from her, and Shay knew it. He'd probably have started throwing anything he could get his hands on at her if she'd tried it. But for whatever reason, her father still respected Reese and it showed in his attitude and expression. Grateful, Shay felt her tightened stomach loosen by degrees as the silence continued.

Finally, Crawford turned his head, glaring at Reese. "Okay, so you're a vet. I can accept that because you're smart and you did something important for me. You protected my savings. I don't know those other three vets."

Shay felt her insides relax suddenly from her father's almost apologetic-sounding words. Ray had never said he was sorry for anything in his life, for what he'd done or the decisions he'd made. Shay didn't expect an apology from him, but she could see the respect for Reese in her father's eyes, and that made her draw a deep breath. The tension in the room began to dissolve. She gathered her courage and said softly, "Then maybe you should meet them. They're good men, Father."

Ray regarded his daughter, his mouth tightening. "That's why I called you in here, Shay."

Startled, she blinked. "What do you mean?" *Now what?* She didn't understand his change of behavior. Could Reese's one visit have influenced him that much? That quickly? Because every time her father looked at Reese, she saw his eyes change, the hardness and anger gone. What kind of magic had Reese worked on her father? Shay didn't understand, but that didn't matter, either. What did matter was that her father was less angry with her, less verbally abusive, with Reese in the room. For that, Shay was more than grateful.

"I want to know about those houses you're building." He looked at Reese. "You tell me about them."

"No, sir, that's Shay's department." He turned his head, giving Shay a firm look. "She's the owner of the Bar C. Everything that happens on that ranch is because of her insight, her business sense and decisions. She should be the one to tell you, not me. All I'm doing is helping her to organize it."

Shay wanted to cry with relief. Reese was giving her back the respect her father had long ago taken away from her. How badly she wanted to throw her arms around Reese's strong, broad shoulders right now. But she couldn't. She saw her father's gaze move grudgingly to her.

"Well?" he demanded. "Tell me about this plan of yours."

Swallowing against a forming lump, Shay told him. Little by little, as she spoke, she saw that gleaming hardness that was always in her father's eyes, begin to soften. By the time she was done with the explanation, the extent of her vision for the wranglers having a home of their own, she watched her father become pensive. He moved his left hand across the bed covers. She knew how hard he'd worked all his life on the ranch. If he hadn't been an alcoholic and a gambler, Shay knew the Bar C would not be in the shape it was in presently. And surely, her father, who was always in denial about his drinking and gambling, never taking responsibility for his actions, had to know that. Didn't he?

"Are they gonna be paying rent?" Ray demanded.

Shay looked to Reese and then to her father. "They will send the monthly mortgage payment directly to the Whitcombs."

"Then what are you getting out of this?"

His voice was like a whip and Shay tensed. "Because they are already giving fifteen percent of the money they earn to the ranch, that's what."

Ray studied her. "You never told me that."

"I tried to. Many times, Father."

He snorted. "What the hell is fifteen percent of nothing?"

"It's not nothing," Shay argued tightly. "Harper and Noah have bimonthly checks coming in from their jobs. Garret runs big construction equipment and he hires himself out to the ranches in the valley to get work. It's not as steady, but it's getting better. And Reese has a part-time accounting job with Charlie at his hay and feed store. They are all working, and you have to realize it's *their* fifteen percent that makes the mortgage payment, Father."

"What's this Garret doing with his free time?" Ray muttered darkly.

"He cooks three meals a day for all of us," Shay said. "It frees me up to do a lot of other things that need to be attended to around the ranch."

"Then you're giving them these houses for free?"

Her hands knotted in her lap. "I already told you they are giving me fifteen percent of their income each month."

"It's a damned handout! Who the hell gets a free house?"

"Maybe you see it like that," Shay shot back, "but I don't! People need to help one another, Father. I know you don't believe in that, but I do. The land they are being built upon is my donation to each of them. They've earned the help I can give them." Her breathing was becoming chaotic as she locked in with her father's escalating rage.

"You don't ask for help, girl. You *know* that!"

Reese stirred. "Sir, I'm only going to say this once to you. Your daughter deserves the same respect you give me. She's not a girl. She's a woman. She's your blood and she's saving the Bar C. I think you need to reassess how you're treating her. Don't you?"

Shay heard the steel in Reese's low, hard voice. She'd never heard him speak like that to anyone. Now, she was seeing the Marine Corps officer coming out in him; a man in charge, a man who was going to have it his way or else.

"She's my daughter, dammit. I'll treat her any way I like, Lockhart! You butt out."

Reese slowly got up and looked down at Shay. He held his hand out to her. "This conversation is over," he told her quietly. "Come on, we have better things to do with our time."

"Now you hold on a minute!" Ray snarled, sitting up tensely on his bed.

Reese held the older man's glare. "No sir, we won't. No one deserves this kind of abuse, Mr. Crawford. Your daughter should *never* be treated as you're treating her right now. And until you can talk respectfully to her, she's not coming back here to see you again. Instead, I'll drop by when I can, to check in on you. Are we clear?"

Shay gripped Reese's dry, strong hand and stood. Her knees felt shaky. It felt like a bomb had just gone off in the room. Her father turned red in the face, his expression one of shock. He was speechless. She felt Reese's fingers move gently around her own. He placed her in front of him.

As they reached the door, Reese released her hand and turned toward her father.

"Mr. Crawford, you owe your daughter an apology. She's done nothing in this last year but help you as much as she could. She doesn't deserve to be treated like a dog. If you need anything, you call the ranch and you ask for me. As of right now, Shay is out of the mix. Understand?"

Stunned, Shay numbly opened the door, hearing her father gasp. Reese placed his hand on her shoulder, guiding her out into the hall. He turned, closing the door, looking down at her, assessing her.

"I'm sorry," he told her, sliding his hand across her slumped shoulder. "Are you all right?"

Hot tears jammed into her eyes and Shay gave a jerky nod. Turning, she walked quickly down the hall toward the entrance area. Pressing her hand against her eyes, the tears falling, she knew the people at the desk could see her crying. It wouldn't be the first time.

Reese guided her to the front doors and then halted. "Listen, I'll be at the truck in a minute. You go ahead. I need to talk to the manager of this nursing home for a moment."

She twisted a look up into Reese's hard-looking face. His green eyes were dark and filled with anger. "But—"

"No," he rasped, giving her a gentle look. "Let me handle this. Your father needs to learn a lesson and I intend to enforce it. We'll talk later." He opened the door for her.

Hesitating, Shay whispered, "Yes . . . I trust you, Reese."

Reese turned, moving with purpose toward the desk, where two women and a male nurse stood warily watching them. He was sure they'd probably heard Crawford's voice down the hall, even though the door had been closed. It wasn't lost on them that the bastard had been verbally abusing Shay every week. Now that he had seen it happen,

Reese wasn't about to let it go on. Halting at the desk, he said, "Who is the manager here?"

"Mrs. Dodge," the blond-haired girl said. She turned and pointed to the office behind the desk. "She's in there if you'd like to speak to her."

"Yes, I'd like to. Thanks."

Shay waited out in the truck, the window rolled down, allowing the warmth of the summer day to flow through the cab. In about ten minutes, she saw Reese walking out the door of the nursing home. There was determination in his expression. Her stomach was tight and raw from her father's attack. It was always like that when she left his room. And right now, Shay was in mild shock. Reese had stood up and put himself between her and her cranky father. Wiping the last of her tears off her cheeks with trembling fingers, she watched him open the door and slide into the truck. He placed the briefcase on the seat between them and turned to her.

"How are you doing?"

"Better," she croaked.

Reese reached out, cupping her chin, forcing her to hold his gaze. "Why didn't you tell me just how badly he was treating you, Shay?"

More tears blurred her vision. Just the roughened touch of his palm against her jaw made her start unraveling. "Well, I-I . . . there was nothing to be done about it. He's my father. It's my job . . . my responsibility . . . not yours . . . or any of the other guys'." She melted beneath his soft gaze, watching his tension diminish.

"Shay, you never have to take that kind of abuse from anyone. Not ever."

She sniffed. "I grew up with it."

"Well," Reese said thickly, "that's done and finished. Crawford is never going to treat you like that again." He reluctantly released her and sat up, sliding the key into the ignition, the engine turning over.

"Wh-what did you do in there?"

"I talked to Marcy, the manager. I told her that I'd be the one coming in to see your father from now on. That you had other things to do out at the ranch."

Gasping, her eyes rounded. "But—"

"You can't go on like this," Reese said, resting his hand on the wheel. "Do you know that the guys have seen how beaten down you are every time you return from a visit with your father?"

"N-no . . ."

"They see how shaken you are. You're pale. And you don't eat well that night at the dinner table. They aren't dumb, Shay. They see the outcome of those visits. Garret had originally warned me about it, and I told him I'd see what was happening."

His mouth compressed and he held her tearful look. "Your father's an alcoholic. He's not just cranky, he's abusive, that's clear. And there's too much going on with your ranch, now and in the future, for you to keep putting yourself in his gunsights, Shay. All he does is hurt you. The guys are worried about you, too. They *care* about you. And they want you out of the line of fire with your father. They see you going down and they're worried that if this doesn't stop, your father will destroy you, like he nearly destroyed the ranch."

"Oh, God," she whispered brokenly, pressing her hands to her face, shame rolling through her. "I-I didn't know they knew . . ."

Gently, Reese moved his hand across her hunched, tense shoulders. "It's okay, Shay. The guys told me, and I wanted to protect you if your father was hurting you. Seeing it firsthand, I'm sorry I didn't get involved a lot sooner."

Sniffing, she shakily wiped the tears from her eyes. "I-I didn't want any of you to come here with me. I knew how my father felt about vets . . . and I didn't want them hurt any more than they already were."

"I know," Reese whispered, continuing to gently move his hand across her shoulders. "You were protecting them. I understand that." And he drilled a look into her damp blue eyes. "You put yourself in the line of fire instead."

Weakly, she whispered, "There was no one to help me with this issue, Reese."

Nodding, he said, "Well, there is now. From now on, I'll be the one to visit your father. And it won't be three times a week, either. He's going to have to learn to be a team player and that the world no longer revolves around him. He's going to have to understand that he can't continue to abuse you, Shay. Ms. Dodge knows that your father is probably going to be angry, and she's okay with it. She agreed with me that you need to back off and stop seeing him for a while. The employees at the nursing home knew he was verbally abusing you, Shay, every time you visited him. But their hands were tied." Reese lifted his chin and stared out the window for a moment. "Until now."

Gratitude flowed through Shay and she took a tissue from her purse and blotted her eyes. "I-I tried to get him to change. Tell him he couldn't keep hurting me like this, but he just got angrier when I tried to defend myself."

"Because," Reese said gently, holding her unsure gaze, "he'd always used you as his whipping post from the time you were a little girl up to this moment."

Jerkily nodding, Shay blew her nose and wiped it. "I never realized that . . ."

"He's got some serious attitude adjustments to make,"

Reese warned her. "And I'm not letting you anywhere near him. If he wants to see you, I'll be with you. And if he calls the ranch, you're to tell him to talk to me. Don't talk to him, Shay. You can't break his pattern if you keep playing back into it. You're going to have to be strong enough to tell him that I'll return his call when I get back to the house. All right?" Reese held her anguished gaze. His hand tightened for a moment on her shoulder to emphasize his words. "You are through being the person he hurts all the time."

Shay barely nodded. "O-okay . . . I just didn't expect any help." She shared a soft look in Reese's direction. The steely expression in his eyes, the way his mouth was set, she could feel him in warrior mode. There was no other way to describe it and Shay felt an incredible amount of care radiating off Reese toward her.

"One of our problems," Reese told her, removing his hand from her shoulder, "is that we forget we can ask for help, Shay. This is one of those times for you. The guys at the ranch saw how hard it was on you to visit your father. They've been watching you go down a little more with each visit. They love you, Shay. They care. And so do I. We don't like to see women, animals, or children hurt. Their hands were tied because you never spoke up about it, you never confided in or trusted any of them enough to let them help you. Because they would have. That's what you have to learn out of this experience. Okay?"

"This feels like an intervention," Shay whispered. "Mine. And I deserve it. You're right, Reese. I should have spoken up. And I *do* trust all of them. But"—she sobbed once—"I didn't want to put one more brick on their load. They're all hurting. This ranch is supposed to be a place where they can heal, not come running to protect me from my father."

Reese groaned and twisted around. He put the brief-case up on the dashboard and growled, "Come here, Shay."

He eased his arms around her, drawing her against him, holding her.

Shay sobbed against his shoulder, tears dampening the blue plaid shirt he wore. She felt his arms come around her, holding her tightly against him, as if to shield her. It was an incredible feeling of safety. Her heart opened wide and Shay felt all those carefully closeted feelings for him, come to bright, burning life within her breast.

Tears flooded her eyes even more when his trembling hand grazed her hair, as if to try to soothe her, take away all the pain she'd carried for so long by herself. Her cries were strangled and she couldn't hear anything except her own sobs. Reese held her a little more tightly, as if wanting to silently absorb them, love and protect her. And never had anything felt so right, so wonderful to Shay as she wept ceaselessly, decades of hurt pouring out of her.

Chapter Sixteen

Garret, Noah, and Harper stood with Reese in the barn the next morning as they saddled their horses to ride the fence. In as few words as possible, Reese told them what had happened. When he finished, he saw relief on all the men's faces, nods of agreement and grimness in their expressions.

"You did the right thing," Garret said, praising him and slapping Reese on the back. "That old bastard needed to be put in his place. My teeth have hurt, gritting them, not saying anything to Shay about him being an abuser."

Noah grinned as he tightened the cinch on his horse, who stood quietly in cross-ties. "Shay needs our protection until she can get on her own two feet. And I know she can do it with a little support from us at the right time."

Harper, who had finished saddling his horse, Socks, walked up, reins in his gloved hands. "Yeah, but we all know that at some point, Shay has to talk it out with her father. Reese gave her breathing room, but the old man isn't going to change unless she confronts him and tells him, herself, to knock it off."

Reese double-checked the cinch on Smoke, his horse.

"You're right, Harper. I'm just a bandage to the larger abuse pattern she's dealing with."

"Well," Garret said, unsnapping his horse, Jak, from the cross-ties, "right now, you're stepping in on Shay's behalf. That's all right. In time, Shay will see on her own what she has to do to fix it permanently. She just needed a leader to show her how to do it." He gave Reese a proud look of "well done."

Reese couldn't disagree. "She's got a lot to think about," he said, leading Smoke down the concrete aisle toward the barn door. Dawn was barely on the horizon, grayness tipping the tops of the evergreen forest on the eastern slope of the Salt River Mountains. "And with this arena-raising coming up, she's pressured from another direction."

Garret walked out of the barn at Reese's shoulder. He glanced toward the ranch house to make sure Shay wasn't nearby. "Give her time to absorb this, Reese. Don't push her too far, too soon."

Glancing over at the wrangler, Reese said, "Right now, I think we need to be there for her in whatever capacity she wants us to be. We're all going to be busy this coming weekend."

"Hey," Harper said, sliding his foot into the stirrup and mounting, "maybe it's good this arena-raising is soon. Shay can focus on something positive. Her old man can sit and rot in his room for all I care."

Reese mounted, the chill in the air near freezing. There was a thick coat of frost on the green grass in the nearby pasture. "I have no idea what he's going to do."

"For sure," Noah said, riding up, "one thing he can't do is come out here. He's refused to use a wheelchair, so he's stuck in that bed of his. That's probably good, because Shay doesn't have to be around him 24/7."

Reese grimaced and turned Smoke toward the south

pasture they were all working to repair. "None of us knows Crawford that well. I have no idea what he'll do."

They would spend two hours working, ride back to the barn, and then get ready for their day jobs. Garret would go in and fix them all a hearty breakfast before the four of them scattered in all directions. Shay was going to drive down with Reese to the Wind River Ranch to have a final planning session with Steve regarding the activities for the weekend.

Shay had a burgeoning headache when she and Reese returned from the Wind River Ranch. Her head swam with the hundreds of details it would take to make the arena-raising a success this coming weekend. She had dropped the keys to the truck into a carnival bowl on the foyer desk when the phone in the kitchen rang. It had been ringing constantly that morning; many of the vendors who were coming with supplies for the weekend were making final calls to check in with Shay.

Groaning, she said to Reese, "Another one . . . I'll get it." She hurried into the kitchen, grabbing the phone.

"Hello?"

"Shay?"

Her father's voice was grating. Instantly, she froze, her fingers tightening around the phone. Reese stopped at the entrance, his eyes changing, as if realizing it was her father on the line. Her mouth went dry. She forced out, "Hold on, Reese is right here—"

"No! I want to talk to you."

Reese drew closer, concern on his face.

Shay was torn. She didn't want to talk to her father. But she'd lain awake last night knowing that while Reese had protected her, in the end, she had to deal with this herself.

Right now, Reese stood, his hands relaxed at his sides, his eyes reflecting concern. Holding up her hand, silently asking him to wait, she managed to ask in a low tone, "What is it you want, Father?"

"I need to see you. Alone."

"That isn't going to happen, Father."

"I promise, I'll try to respect you, Shay."

Her heart dropped. She heard a new, emotional tone in her father's gruff voice. "I don't know if I can trust you or not," she whispered, her heart pounding.

"Then come with Lockhart, but he keeps his mouth shut! This is between you and me. All right?"

Shay heard an almost pleading tone in her father's voice. Glancing up at Reese, who had moved closer, as if to shield her from the call, she met his dark green eyes. She felt his care surround her. "Reese and I will come tomorrow morning, then. I have the arena-raising and—"

"No, come now!" And then Crawford added, "Please?"

Shutting her eyes for a moment, Shay heard the desperation in her father's voice. She'd never heard him plead like this before. Looking up at the clock above the stove, she saw it was 4:00 P.M. "Hold on," she whispered, placing her hand over the phone.

"It's my father. He wants to talk with me in person, right now."

Reese nodded. "Okay, we'll drive over if you want."

Moistening her lips, Shay gave him a long look. "Are you sure? It's been a busy day."

"I'm sure. We'll be back in time for dinner at six."

"Right." She felt relief tunnel through her. She wasn't going to have to do this alone. Reese would be at her side, a silent partner of sorts. She'd fill him in on the rest of the conversation on the drive up to the nursing home.

* * *

Shay tried to gird herself for another angry session with her father. The staff at the nursing home, when they saw her come through the door, gave her a pitying look.

Reese was at her side as they walked down the hall to her father's open door. Taking a deep breath, she felt Reese's hand on her shoulder for a moment. He would never realize how grateful she was for his company. He fed her strength when she had no energy left. Whatever her father wanted, Shay knew she had to confront him herself. It wasn't something Reese could do for her. They'd discussed it on the drive. He was in agreement. His hand briefly touching her shoulder, supporting her, meant so much to her.

She met her father's eyes as she entered the room. He was sitting in the wheelchair. Surprised, she halted.

He glared up at her and then tried to hide his reaction. "Thought I'd finally try it out," he grumped. He waved his hand toward two chairs sitting near his bed. "Sit down."

Gulping, Shay gave Reese a panicked look. He knew that her father had angrily vowed to never use a wheelchair. The steadying look Reese shared with her, helped.

She sat down, gripping her purse on her lap. He sat down next to her, his attention focused on Crawford. She could feel tension in Reese, as if he were getting ready to defend her, should it become necessary. Above all, Shay scrambled to find some safe words to use with her father. He was dressed in jeans, cowboy boots, and a bright red cowboy shirt. Shock rolled through her over the change in him.

"Does it feel good to be able to get around?" she asked him in a low voice.

Ray shrugged, his left hand on the wheel. "It's different . . . not something I ever saw myself doin', that's for sure."

Hearing the vulnerability in her father's voice, Shay

nodded and swallowed hard. "I know it's difficult, Father. I don't think any of us ever see ourselves in this kind of situation."

His mouth worked and he looked toward the open door. "I decided it was time to move on. I hate stayin' in that bed all the time. I miss being outdoors, the sun on my face. I miss it all."

Her heart broke for him. "You were outside all the time," Shay said. She saw something other than anger in her father's eyes. And she saw him trying to be nice to her. The change was as shocking as seeing him sitting in the wheelchair.

Reese said nothing, looking casual and relaxed next to her, but underneath, Shay sensed he was ready to move into combat if her father's demeanor changed. He'd warned her in the cab that if Crawford thought he could savage her again, it wasn't going to happen. Reese had promised to give her the opportunity to defend herself, but if she couldn't, he would. He had no idea how much strength that gave her. Shay knew this was her battle, her war. Not Reese's.

"I've been getting Troy, the physical therapist, to help me to start using this useless right hand of mine," he said, jabbing down at it sitting in his lap. "I asked him if there was a chance I could get this right arm to work again."

"And?"

"He said in time, I could strengthen it and get back maybe seventy percent of it." Ray shrugged. "That's good."

Shay blinked, not believing her ears. For a year, she'd tried to persuade her father to get the advanced therapy he needed to strengthen the right side of his paralyzed body. "That's great news. You'll feel a lot happier if you could get out of this room when you wanted."

Ray nodded and muttered, "I want a favor from you, Shay."

Shay's stomach tightened. He'd never asked anything of

her. Just ordered her around. "Okay," she said, her tone tentative. Reese tensed subtly at her side.

"I want to be out there for the arena-raising. I want to see it happen. It's my ranch. I want to see what's going on out there since you took over."

Shay could see her father wrestling with every word, to remain respectful of her. It was not his ranch. He knew that legally she owned it now. But he never faced her with that fact, still calling the Bar C his property. She wasn't going to battle him on that point right now, though. Swallowing, she stared at him, her mind blanking out for a second over his unexpected request. "Well . . . sure . . ." She glanced apprehensively at Reese. He had his game face on, his gaze never leaving Crawford. She opened her hands. "We're going to be really, really busy, Father. I won't have time to take care of you—"

"Dammit! I'll take care of myself!" He scowled and added grumpily, "I've already asked Troy to be with me for the day. He'll drive me in their special van out to the ranch. He'll take care of me. I won't be underfoot."

"Oh," she whispered, her fingers against her throat. "That would be helpful."

"I know you're gonna be busy. But I'd like to see the plans, be a part of it."

Her mind kept blanking out. Her emotions were up and down. This was the first time her father had asked to come back to the ranch. Shay knew how important a moment this was for him. For her. But the timing was bad.

"It's going to be crazy busy, Father. I can't promise you anything at this point because we've got so many vendors arriving with trucks and supplies. And seventy-five volunteers are coming at the same time. I'm going to be out in the field most of the day. Reese and the other vets are the frontline bosses coordinating all this."

"I understand," he growled. "Troy will take care of me. I won't be a burden to you."

Biting her lower lip, she cast another glance at Reese. There was a thawing in his eyes. "Okay," she managed in a strained tone, "you're more than welcome." Instantly, she saw the relief in her father's face. And it shocked her again to realize just how important this was to him.

"Good," he said gruffly. "I'll stay outta the way. I won't make things harder on you. I understand what a barn-raisin' is. I've attended enough of 'em myself when I was younger. You were too young to remember them."

Shay managed a softer look at her father. "No . . . I don't remember any, but that's okay." Her hands were cold and damp. Part of her was in anxiety mode because now, her father would be there. Would he start trying to tell her what to do? Would he start tearing her apart in front of other people? So much could go wrong. But one look in Ray Crawford's face and Shay knew how important this was to him.

"I'll talk with Troy," Shay said. "We'll work out details, time of arrival and things like that."

"Good," Ray said, giving a sharp nod of his head, his eyes on Reese Lockhart. "I just want to see it . . ."

"Wow," Shay said in the cab of the truck as Reese drove them to the ranch. "I didn't see that coming. Did you?" She looked over at his rugged profile.

"No. But I think it's a good thing. Don't you?" Reese gave her a quick glance before returning his attention to the busy four-lane highway out of Jackson Hole.

Shay pushed some hair away from her cheek. "I don't know, Reese. Truthfully? I'm ambivalent about it. On the one hand, he's finally decided to get into the wheelchair, which will give him much more freedom."

"You're worried he's going to take you apart at the ranch?"

She smiled a little and gave him a warm look. "You always know what I'm really feeling, don't you?"

He reached out, curving his hand around hers on the seat. He squeezed it for a moment and then released it. "Sometimes I know what's bothering you," he admitted. "Not all the time, though."

"Well"—she managed a short laugh—"you do a pretty good job." Her heart swelled with love for Reese. Shay no longer tried to hide from what she felt about this man, part cowboy, part Marine Corps officer. He was a mix of the two, molded by hard work over the years. One would never be separated from the other. "Yes, I'm concerned. I saw my father struggling for all he was worth to be nice to me in there."

"Or," Reese said, "as nice as he could be. There's plenty of room for improvement on his end."

"I know," she said wearily, leaning back on the seat, closing her eyes. "In one way, I'm thrilled he's finally going to get physical therapy and start using the wheelchair. I don't know how he managed to stay a year in that bed. If I'd been in his place, I'd have gone stark raving mad." She opened her eyes, watching the passing scenery of the evergreens down below the road, the wide, green meadows dotted with horses and cattle here and there.

"Do you think it's a good sign he wants to come out to the ranch?"

Shay rubbed her head. "If I'm being unselfish, the answer is yes."

"But you're worried he'll want to stay at the ranch? Not be willing to go back to the nursing home?"

Her lips thinned. "Yes. But as I told him from the beginning, I couldn't take care of him *and* the ranch."

"I think he got that," Reese said. "He's hired Troy to take care of him while he's with us on Saturday. It's a good thing, because no one else has time. We will all be too busy."

Shay sat there, a mixture of so many emotions. "I don't know what his end game is, Reese. This sounds awful of me to say, but I've been in therapy weekly since I got home. Taylor Douglas had recommended a good psychotherapist, Libby Hilbert, in Jackson Hole. She's helped me see the games an alcoholic plays on the family around him. I feel like my father's manipulating me for his own reasons and he isn't about to tell me what they are." She rubbed her arm slowly, frowning and thinking.

"I had a couple of young Marines who came out of alcoholic families," he told her. "That's the game the alcoholic plays. He or she manipulates the family to get what they want. For whatever it's worth, I felt like your father was genuinely trying to respect you. But I felt he also had a goal in mind that he wasn't divulging to either of us. At least, not yet."

"Thanks, I needed to hear that," Shay whispered, giving him a grateful glance. "He struggled so hard to try to be nice to me, not angry."

"Yeah, he was definitely trying to change that about himself." Reese's voice grew deep. "And he should."

"But what does he really want? I hate myself for thinking badly of him, Reese. I know in the first three months after I got home, I pleaded with him to get into the wheelchair, that I'd bring him out to the ranch. I knew getting back here would help him so much."

"But he refused?"

"Brother, did he ever. He was so damned angry. He was screaming and yelling at everyone. My therapist counseled me to stop trying to get him to the ranch, that he was in shock over his stroke and taking it out on those around him. Especially me. So, I finally stopped asking him to visit."

Reese reached out, gripping her hand for a moment. "You've done more to help him than he ever did for you, Shay."

She wanted to keep the connection with Reese but allowed him to remove his hand from around her fingers. "Now I'm questioning his motives, Reese. I feel bad about that."

"You shouldn't. Not yet, and maybe never."

Blowing out a puff of air, Shay muttered, "I hope I can see what his game plan is, and keep one step ahead of him. I'm going to be so distracted on Saturday . . ." She felt a new sense of helplessness invading her. "I made it over one hurdle with my father, but then there's another larger, taller one right in front of me, staring me in the face. I always feel I'm in a war with him. It just never stops."

"Because you were in a war for eighteen years, Shay."

"Yes, and this change in him is coming at the wrong time. I'll be torn between the schedule, keeping things organized for the arena-raising—"

"I'll be there to help," he promised. "Garret, Noah, and Harper know about this too, Shay. They are there to support you. If your father starts to grate on you or disrespect you, come and find one of us."

"That's the problem. I don't want to take anyone's attention off the arena-raising. There's just so much that will be going on, Reese."

"Then stay out of the main house as much as you can," he counseled. "We've got the HQ set up in the aisle of the horse barn. Your father has no way to get that wheelchair out there because it's all dirt or gravel pathways. There's no concrete sidewalk. I'm sure Troy will keep him in the house or out on the front or back porch, where he can watch what's going on. I don't think he'll be anywhere near you for the most part."

"Yes, but I can't ignore him either. He's my father."

Reese heard the conflicting emotions in her low voice. Saw it in her face. "Look," he rasped, "you focus on the arena-raising. If you get a chance to drop by the house and see your father, fine. If not, he has to understand, and that's all there is to it. He knows he's coming out at a busy time. He shouldn't expect you to hover around him."

Shaking her head, she said unsteadily, "This is so damned hard, Reese."

His hand fell over hers. "Let's take baby steps on this, Shay. You know what your job is on Saturday and Sunday. Stick to that schedule. Troy is there to take care of your father. That's not your job. You have a greater responsibility to the ranch than to your father on that day."

Her fingers curled around his. "Thanks, I needed to hear that."

He gave her a tender look, squeezing her hand. "You already knew. I'm just telling you what you were already thinking, Shay."

She wanted to keep holding his hand. Reese had to drive, though, and he was coming up to the turnoff for the ranch. Releasing his hand, she said, "Well, we'll have a lot to tell the guys at supper tonight, won't we?"

Reese grimaced as he made the turn. "Yes. Don't expect any of them to be overjoyed about this, Shay. They know that your father isn't exactly Miss Manners. They may expect him to interfere or start ripping off people's heads. We need to sit down with them at dinner and really hash this out. We can't have them confronting your father or mixing it up with him." And then he added more gently, "They're protective of you, Shay."

Rubbing her face as he pulled into the parking space near the ranch house, Shay muttered, "You're right. We need to talk to them." And she felt like her stomach was tied in so many knots from all the worries she had, it only added to her stress.

Chapter Seventeen

Garret gave Shay a concerned look as they sat at the dinner table and she finished the story. He pushed the massive amount of mashed potatoes and gravy around on his plate. "My old man is an alcoholic," he admitted grudgingly.

Everyone at the table looked up at Garret, surprise in all their expressions.

Shay raised her brows because he had never spoken about his family. In their weekly group sessions, the therapist leading the group, Libby Hilbert, would ask, but he always avoided answering her. "So you know what I'm going through?"

His mouth quirked. "Yeah, just a little, Shay." He cut up a thick slice of pork. "And Reese is right that alcoholics can be world-class manipulators."

"But you have to give him a chance," Noah said.

"I'm going to," Shay said.

"It's bad timing, if you ask me," Harper muttered, taking a thick crust of bread and mopping up the gravy left on his plate.

"That," Shay said, "we can agree on."

"So," Garret growled, "he's gonna be out here with Troy

from the nursing home. Someone needs to give Troy boundaries for your father, Shay." He waved his fork toward the barn. "Your father can't be underfoot out in the barn. That's HQ. That's where we're coordinating everything. We'll be in touch with one another by radio, but we do *not* need him there. Does he know he has to stay at the house?"

"No," Shay admitted, "but I'll make it clear to Troy." She saw worry on Garret's face. And she felt Reese's discomfort, but he said nothing.

"My advice, based upon my old man, the former Marine sergeant," Garret said, "is the moment Troy brings Ray in here, you tell him, in front of your father, the lay of the land. That he's to keep him here." Garret jabbed his finger down at the floor.

"Okay," she said, "I'll do that."

"He's got something up his sleeve," Garret grumbled, scowling as he ate the last of his meal. "My old man always kept the family off balance. We never knew from one moment to the next what the hell he was up to. It was like playing whack-a-mole, but you never knew where or when that next mole would pop up."

Shay gave Garret a sympathetic look. This was the first time Garret had opened up. "I wish I'd known about this before. You could probably have helped me with my father. Sometimes I feel like I'm in a minefield with him, never sure what to say or do. Always afraid I'll set him off."

Nodding, Garret slid her a worried glance. "Maybe I should have, Shay. It's just hard to talk about."

Shay understood better than anyone. "Well," she said, giving him a gentle look, "do you mind if I come to you every once in a while to get your take on a situation? You've had it just as rough or rougher than I did growing up. At least my father wasn't a Marine Corps sergeant and DI like yours was."

Garret grimaced and pushed his empty plate away from himself. "Sure. I'll do anything I can to help you, Shay."

That was such a huge step for Garret, and Shay knew it better than anyone at the table. Garret was closed up like most vets, but she'd always seen him as even more armored than anyone else here at the table. Now, she was beginning to understand why he was that way. "Thanks. If nothing else," she joked sadly, "misery loves company. Right?" She saw one corner of Garret's mouth pull into a half smile of sorts. More pain than smile. He was carrying a lot of baggage within him.

"Yeah, birds of a feather and all that," Garret muttered. He got up, starting to clear the table of all the empty plates.

Harper looked over at Shay. "How can we help you, Shay? You're at the center of the bullseye with your father suddenly showing up here."

"Just do your jobs on the weekend. That is all the help I need," she reassured him.

"Yes," Noah murmured, "but you don't know what kind of wrenches your father might throw into this weekend plan."

"I don't," Shay admitted. "But I'm hoping the physical space separating us from him will be enough."

"I have an idea," Reese said, giving them all a studied look. "Shay? What do you think of asking one of the ranch women to be the person who comes in here every once in a while to check up on your father? She'll be a stranger to Ray. And once he knows that she's your lieutenant, who is responsible to see how he is, if he needs anything, it will give you the space you need. That way, he doesn't become a distraction to you."

Garret came over with a chocolate cake with chocolate frosting, setting it in the center of the table. "That is a damned good idea. It protects Shay and keeps her out of the line of fire with her old man." He went back to the kitchen to retrieve dessert plates.

"Plus," Noah offered, "whoever you choose has to have really good boundaries, Shay. She can't take any crap from your father."

"You're right about that," Shay slowly admitted. "Diana Adson, the wife of Chuck, who runs the local gas station at the edge of town, is supposed to help coordinate the food for breakfast, lunch, and dinner."

"She still can," Garret said, sitting down and beginning to cut thick slices of the cake and place them on the individual plates. "But along with those duties, Diana can become your spokesperson of sorts. And I seriously doubt your old man is going to go ballistic on her. She's a tall, big gal physically, an ex-cop, so she's used to handling heated situations and nasty people."

"I'll call her," Shay promised. "It's a good idea."

"Diana knows your situation," Reese pointed out, thanking Garret for the slice of cake. "She doesn't have to be brought up to speed. All she needs to do is drop by the house once every couple of hours and check in on your father."

"That way," Garret said, passing a plate to Shay, "your old man gets attention, but it leaves you free to coordinate things without getting trapped in any drama he might have in mind."

"I'll ask Diana if she wants to do it. If she doesn't, I'll deal with it."

Noah gave her a long look. "Well, if Diana can't do it, then you still need an intercessor of sorts. What you don't want is to get caught in his craziness."

"Yeah," Garret warned, digging into the cake he made, "he's gonna have questions. He's gonna be upset or disagree with something we've planned. You can count on it, Shay. You need to figure out who your messenger is so he can't reach you. That's just the way it has to be so we can get this arena-raising done in two days."

Hearing the grimness in Garret's tone, Shay nodded. "Okay, I'll do whatever has to be done." She saw all the vets' faces lose some of their worry. Shay had never felt so protected as now. She'd made a terrible error in not confiding in them sooner . . .

When she looked over at Reese, she saw warmth in his eyes, pride for her, if she was reading him correctly. And she did feel good about sharing the situation with the vets. These men were intelligent and quick to catch on. And they brought good ideas to the table as well . . .

"If things go to hell in a handbasket," Garret said to her, "what's your backup plan? What if your old man throws a temper tantrum? Or maybe he knows where there's liquor kept in the house? A thousand things can go wrong, Shay. You have to have a plan. My old man was real good at sabotaging me. He made it an art form."

Shay felt her heart break for Garret. She saw the pain in his hazel eyes, the way his mouth drew inward, as if to blunt what he was feeling. Even more, she realized he was being vulnerable in front of all of them for the first time ever. If nothing else came out of this discussion, it was a healing moment for him . . . and for all of them. "You're right, Garret."

Reese gave her a glance. "Do you have alcohol here?"

She shook her head. "No. I hate the stuff. I won't touch it. I remember him having stashes of bottles all over the place. There's no alcohol in this house now."

"He could talk Troy into stopping at a liquor store for him," Garret warned.

Wrinkling her nose, Shay muttered, "I need to call Troy about that."

"Yep," Garret said, "cover your bases, Shay."

Rubbing her brow, she muttered, "This is like learning all over again with him. I left at eighteen. I didn't know what he was doing while I was in the Corps. I didn't want to know."

"Is your old man clean now?" Garret demanded.

Shrugging, Shay said, "I honestly don't know. They don't allow alcohol in the nursing home, yet on one visit I thought I smelled it on his breath."

"Yeah, but someone could be going out to buy your old man a bottle," Garret said.

"Shay, let me handle Troy," Reese suggested. "I'll talk to the manager about this, too. I think we can find out if your father is still drinking or if he's sober."

"He'd be crazy to do it," Shay said, shaking her head. "The doctors have already told him he's got cirrhosis. That if he doesn't stop drinking, he'll die. That should stop him cold."

Snickering, Garret said, "Sorry, sweetheart, but alcoholics don't care. All they want is that next drink, even if it kills them."

She gave him a long look and felt the burden falling on her shoulders all over again. "You're right," she whispered, pushing the cake around on her plate with her fork. "There's a lot I don't know about his habits because I was gone so long and he refused to come back to the ranch after his stroke. I'm out of the loop."

"Let me handle this," Reese repeated. "If he's still drinking, someone at the nursing home will know."

"They'd smell it on his breath," Garret promised.

"Right," Reese said with a nod. "Tomorrow is Friday. I'll drive over and talk to the nursing home staff and see what I can find out. I'll buttonhole Troy and get plans set in regards to your father coming here."

It felt good to have help. "And I'll call Diana tomorrow

morning. See if she wants to help us this Saturday," Shay said.

"You need to set a time for him to leave here, too," Garret warned heavily. "We're working sixteen hours straight, Shay. We have lights to set up so the people building the houses can keep on going after nightfall. You don't need your old man around that long. Make it a short visit."

"You're right about that, too," she said. Feeling overwhelmed, Shay realized having her father here on Saturday was like an unraveling ball of yarn, and she couldn't quite get her hands around it to stop it.

"I'll talk to the manager," Reese told her. "She'll have suggestions on how long your father should be here. Let me get back to you on that?"

"Yes . . . thank you."

Harper gave Shay a kind look. "Listen, your focus is the arena-raising, Shay. Let us help you. You stay clear of your father except when and if you want to come in and check on him yourself. All right?"

"And let Diana Adson deal with him," Garret warned her darkly. "The more you come in to see him, the more he's going to expect it. So don't go there."

Shay sat at the trestle table, a cup of chamomile tea in her hands. It was 3:00 A.M. When she heard a door open and close down the hall, she knew Reese was getting up. Relieved, she saw him amble down the hall in a white T-shirt and blue pajama bottoms, feet bare. His hair was tousled and his eyes sleep ridden. Max got up, going to greet him. Reese leaned down, ruffling the dog's fur.

"How long you been up?" he mumbled, going to the cupboard for a mug.

"An hour," Shay admitted quietly.

"Did you get any sleep at all?"

Mouth quirking, she said, "Not really. Just going over everything that needs to be done here today. They're going to be bringing in the tents this afternoon to set up where we'll have the food and drinks. That has to be done first." She pushed her hair behind her shoulder as Reese came over and sat in his chair at her elbow. Her heart blossomed with such need of this man, who was like a quiet oasis in the storm of her life. And that's what it felt like right now: a hurricane shrieking around her.

"It's stressful, but we've got everything organized, Shay. Noah, Harper, and Garret are good men. They're leaders in their own right and they'll all be out there as your lieutenants. You're the general. Everyone will come to you and then you'll defer to one of them. Whoever has that area of responsibility, will take it, and then you're freed up again. It will work fine."

She absorbed his tender look and hungrily soaked in his low, deep voice still laden with sleep. "What woke you up?"

"Dunno," he said, sipping the tea. "Just woke up. Figured you'd be out here, so I got up." His eyes crinkled as he held her gaze. Max laid down between them.

"I just want this to go well, Reese. I'm so worried . . ."

He reached out, sliding her hand into his. "It's going to go fine. Like clockwork. You have military-trained people here running it. We know how to organize and execute. You know that."

"You're always the voice of reason in my life," she offered weakly, giving him a grateful look, hungrily soaking up the strength of his long, warm fingers around hers. "Thank you, Reese . . . You'll never know how much I lean on you, rely on you. I don't know what I'd do right now if you weren't here with me."

"You'd soldier on," he told her. "You're stronger than you think, Shay. You don't have to do this alone. You have four of us, and we won't let you down."

Blowing out a breath, Shay closed her eyes for a moment and nodded. Opening them, she fell into his dark green gaze that told her he yearned for her. Her lower body felt like coals coming to life once more; she was a woman who desired Reese. "I know that, and it gives me the strength to get through this."

"Everyone coming on Saturday wants to help you, Shay. The only potential problem I see is your father. And that's an emotional pull on you that no one can shield you from."

"It's okay, Reese." She gave him a wry look. "And poor Garret. This was the first time he's *ever* spoken up about his family. I felt so sorry for him last night. I could see he hated admitting it to us."

"I'm sure he had it rough," Reese agreed. "But like you, he's stronger for it. Adversity always makes us stronger, whether we realize it or not." He squeezed her hand. "I was proud of you with your father today. You kept your boundaries with him. That's a huge step, Shay. Don't you think?"

She rolled her eyes. "It is, yes, but I have to maintain it. I have to do it every time with him. That's what is scary, because it means I have to have a secondary alertness. I get easily distracted. I've got to totally retrain myself to do this right, and I will. But then to have him ask to be out here on Saturday? His request blew me away. I wasn't prepared for it. I'm still not."

"But we'll have people in place to protect you from him tomorrow."

"Isn't it sad, Reese, that I have to have protection?" She searched his darkening eyes. "I feel like a wuss. Like I should have anticipated all the things we talked about at dinner tonight. But I hadn't."

"You're an ACOA, adult child of an alcoholic, Shay. There's patterns that are in play between you and your father that you don't even realize. Others see them, but you don't. Someday, you will. Garret gave you a lot of excellent advice. And you're acting upon it."

"Of all the days he wanted to come to the ranch," she whispered, shaking her head. "Why now?"

"Do you think it's because he misses the ranch? Misses the way of life he's known?"

Snorting softly, Shay said, "I think he wants to come out here and start telling me how to run the ranch. That's what I think."

"I thought the same."

Shay stared at him. She felt his hand tighten a little around hers. "I won't allow him to do that," she said firmly.

"Legally, you're in charge and the ranch belongs to you," Reese reminded her.

"I don't want a war with him over the ranch, Reese."

"Don't go there. At least, not yet."

She felt fear invade her. Felt as if the whole world that she was trying to build, based upon her vision, suddenly was unstable. Her father was a hard, willful man and she knew how brutal he could become when he wanted his way. "Do you think he's coming out here to see what's going on? See how he can plan on taking it back? Taking over?"

Shrugging, Reese said gently, "We don't know, Shay. Not yet. I think when you talk to Diana, and if she's in agreement to be your intercessor with your father, she'll keep her ears open. He might ply her with questions about the ranch."

Grimacing, Shay looked at him. "I hope you're wrong about this."

"I do too," he said. "Let's take this one step at a time. You're overwhelmed and I can see it in your eyes." He released her hand and gave her a sympathetic look. "Maybe your father is lonely. Maybe he just wants to be back home. That nursing facility can't be much fun to live in. And maybe that's behind his request to come out here. It could be that simple, Shay. So we can't afford to jump to conclusions. What we can do is be aware of possibilities, and that's it until he shows us otherwise."

Shay sat on the side of the house, on the porch swing, watching dawn light up the tips of the Wilson Mountain Range far to the west and across the valley. The birds were singing gaily, flitting around, and she saw a herd of elk skirting the fir trees in the distance. She enjoyed the fog that lay in soft, gauzy strands across the pasture. Everything was quiet right now and she hungrily absorbed it. Looking at her watch, she knew the vets would be up in a few minutes. There was a lot of preparation to be done today to get the arena-raising on track and working fluidly for Saturday.

Her heart turned to Reese. Last night she almost asked him to come and sleep with her. Intuitively, Shay knew Reese would hold her and she'd sleep deeply in his arms. He was a calm, safe harbor in her life. He always said the right thing to her at the right time. He never told her what to do, as her father had always done. He treated her as an equal and someone he respected. It felt so good, and she ached to be in his arms, to know what it would be like to fully love this man.

So much stood in their way. Shay found herself wanting Reese. She loved each time he would hold her hand or touch her. She always wanted to touch him. The conversation where he'd said that he felt he was half the man he used to be, ate at her. And she couldn't ignore how Reese saw himself. Shay understood better than most about the shame that always came to a vet who had hit bottom. It was so hard to be objective and see that even she had made progress. Reese didn't see it in himself, either. She wanted to remind him of his goodness, of the things he did well, the people he helped and supported. Reese saw none of it. Not yet. With her help she silently promised him, one day, he would.

She moved the swing slowly with the toe of her boot; she was wrapped in a warm nylon jacket to ward off the cool morning air. The quiet was going to be broken soon. Everything was changing. Shay prayed that she had the strength and flexibility to change with it. A part of her heart wanted her father at the ranch for the day. Her head did not. He could become contentious, a burr under the collective saddle of their efforts to make the arena-raising a success.

Rubbing her brow, a headache lingering, Shay wondered if Garret was right: that her father had his eye on running the ranch once more. There was a lot of darkness in Garret toward his own father. Was he projecting that onto her's? Shay didn't know.

Her heart ached for Reese. How she wanted an intimate relationship with him. Shay knew it would help her. And she knew she could support Reese emotionally and help him, as well. He was a bright spot in her life. But what part would her father play in her life? Like Reese, Shay wanted to believe he was missing the ranch. Who wouldn't? Garret had darker suspicions, and she squirmed inwardly, feeling tightness begin in her stomach once more. Was she going to have to fight Ray at some point for control of the ranch? Was that his real reason for his change of mind?

Shay felt as if she were at the edge of a proverbial cliff with nowhere to go. Was her father coming out to watch, and then savagely scream at her and tell her she was destroying the family legacy? He was capable of doing it. He'd done it to her so many times before.

Wishing that Ray could see the good she'd done, how hard everyone worked to get the ranch back on its feet, was what she hoped for instead. But her father was an alcoholic. And he never admitted he had the disease, nor did he think he had a problem with liquor to this day. He was still in denial.

If her father could be that blind to himself, what made her think he was any less blind about the ranch? The headache worsened and Shay closed her eyes, wrapping her arms about herself as she rocked. Inwardly, she sensed Garret was right; that Ray wanted the ranch back. Wanted to remove her from running it. And if that was so, Shay knew he'd drive off the four vets. And herself. God . . .

Chapter Eighteen

By 7:00 A.M. on Saturday, all the equipment, vendors, and supplies, along with seventy-five volunteers, had arrived. It was cold, in the forties, everyone huddled in a large semicircle in the barn, dealing with directions and instructions from the various team leaders who would work on the arena roof or start creating those four houses.

Steve Whitcomb, Reese, and Shay, were in the main barn, both doors open, sitting at a makeshift plywood desk, built Friday so they each had a spot to work from. Max, Shay's golden retriever, lay at her feet, only his eyes moving, watching the comings and goings of so many people.

There was joviality, excitement, and vitality in the air. The wives, girlfriends, sisters, and aunts, were staffing the food tents below the barns. Busy men and women lined up, waiting for a hearty breakfast to be served on paper plates. Hot, steaming coffee was being poured liberally into waiting paper cups. Reese divided his attention between his responsibilities and keeping tabs on Shay.

He saw the smudges beneath her eyes, knowing full well she hadn't slept at all last night. He had, thankfully. The other vet leaders—Garret, Harper, and Noah—were at their makeshift desks out in the aisleway, each having management responsibility for different phases of the house building.

As the men and women filed in after eating a quick breakfast at the picnic tables set up in neat rows near the food tents, they received their work assignments. The air was festive and laughter was often heard. He saw Shay's spirit being lifted by the good-hearted people arriving to help her. Many of them came over and gave her a hug. Reese began to see the worry in her expression diminish over the next two hours.

As things got organized—on Friday the vendors had already brought in the materials needed—and the crane was in place next to the arena, Reese wanted to pull Shay aside and give her a break. She was looking a little strained. He knew at 10:00 A.M. her father would arrive in the van driven by Troy. It was on her mind and he could feel it. Walking over to her, he slipped his hand beneath her elbow to get her attention.

"Hey, let's take a break," he urged her. "How about some hot coffee, get out in the sunlight and warm up? Steve will pinch-hit for us."

Shay straightened and turned. "But can Steve handle all this by himself?" She turned, worriedly looking over at him.

"Everything's under control," Reese assured her. "Come on. Walk with me?"

"Let's see if we can get Steve something before we leave. Maybe he wants a cup of coffee, too. It's cold out here this time of morning."

Releasing her elbow, Reese nodded and stepped aside. How like Shay to think of others first. A fierce emotion swept through him, gripping his heart, gripping him. Reese kept trying to avoid the word "love" when it came to Shay, but he was old enough, experienced enough, to realize he was falling in love with this wounded but stalwart woman. The glistening look in her eyes as she came back from giving Steve a cup of coffee, smiling up at him, stole his breath away for a moment. Shay's light brown hair was loose around her shoulders. Like everyone else, she wore a down nylon coat to keep warm, jeans, and boots. He read such hope in her eyes as he walked at her side down the aisle and out into the morning sunlight.

The ranch looked like a busy ant colony hard at work. The noise of the bulldozer, the crane, and a backhoe, filled the air. The sharp rap of nail guns shooting nails into wood, was nonstop. As Reese guided her down the gravel slope, his hand cupping her elbow, he saw the trenches being not only dug, but the necessary sewer piping already being installed above the concrete foundations poured last week.

There were four hardworking house crews preparing the plumbing, which was the first step above ground, to manifest a house. There were a number of women working with the men, equally handy and knowledgeable about building a house. Ranch women were just as skilled as any male wrangler on their ranch. They had to be.

"Well?" Reese asked, pointing Shay toward the food tents that sat between the main house and barn. "What do you think so far?"

Shay smiled. "It's all working. I'm amazed, Reese." She gave him a proud look. "You and Steve are a great team."

Warmth stole through Reese and it felt good to be admired by her. "It's about teamwork," he agreed, returning her winsome smile. Right now, Shay looked so young, relieved, and joyous. The people who were working knew what they were doing. And the camaraderie was the glue that bound the group together. As they approached the food tents, he slowed.

"Are you hungry?" Shay hadn't eaten anything this morning, too upset and nervous.

"Some eggs, maybe?"

"Toast?"

"Yes."

"Strawberry jam on the side?"

Shay laughed and slid her arm around his waist, giving him a hug. "You know me so well. Yes, that sounds great. Thank you."

Reese walked her over to one of the empty picnic tables, his whole body vibrating inwardly from her unexpected hug. Everyone who was around would have seen it. Did Shay realize the signal she was sending out to the world? To him? As he released her elbow and she sat down, there was no mistaking the joy shining in her eyes. He ached to always see her this happy and free of her dark past. "I'll be right back," he promised.

Shay sighed, resting her chin on her hands, watching the crane slowly lift up another roof joist to be put in place by the awaiting crew on the arena roof. Everything was going like clockwork! That stunned her and she felt her stomach starting to loosen up and relax. Rubbing her eyes, she felt a sudden tiredness, realizing it was because of not sleeping last night and worrying about today. She watched Reese move through the breakfast tent, a number of women behind the tables scooping up eggs, bacon, and biscuits onto the two paper plates he held in his large, capable hands. Her heart warmed and swelled with such love for Reese. When had she fallen in love with him? And Shay knew it was love; this wasn't some passing infatuation.

He'd been a center of calm for her from the beginning. He'd done so much to help her. Most of all, he'd handled all the details concerning her father coming out at 10:00 A.M. today. Ray would be allowed to stay until 3:00 P.M., and then Troy was to drive him back to the nursing home. She wavered between feeling guilt and feeling relief. Not only that, Diana Adson had eagerly agreed to be a shield, as she referred to herself, between father and daughter. Never was Shay more grateful to her friend. Diana knew about her childhood and had been such an important support to her throughout this past hardscrabble year.

She saw Reese coming her way with two plates full of food.

"Okay," he told her, sliding one paper plate in front of her and then sitting down opposite her, "time to get some fuel into your body. We're going for sixteen hours straight today, and you have to eat, Shay."

She smiled a little, taking the plastic knife, fork, and spoon, and a napkin he offered. "Thanks." On her plate was a huge dollop of scrambled eggs mixed with bacon, onion, and cheddar cheese, the delicious scent wafting into her nostrils. Her stomach growled in anticipation. Reese had sliced two homemade biscuits, slathered them with melted butter, and piled them high with homemade strawberry jam. There were five sausage links on her plate. When she looked at his plate, it was piled twice as high as hers with twice the amount of food. Men worked hard out here and ate accordingly. Suddenly, she was starved, digging into the steaming, fragrant fare.

The noise was constant around Shay, but she loved the sounds because it meant that the roof was going to cover the arena by Sunday night. She could see quickly moving teams framing up the walls around the concrete foundations that had been laid last week for the houses. There were twelve men and women assigned to each house. She knew from what Steve Whitcomb had told her, that the framing on each home would be complete in a matter of hours, the bones to each home, in place. Next came the electrical. There were so many steps and each had to be done in the correct order, he'd told her. It was exciting to see these houses being created out of nothing. Laughter was everywhere. There wasn't one unsmiling face among the volunteers that Shay could spot. It felt more like a festive carnival taking place on the ranch than a brutal sixteen-hour day of nonstop work. Moisture came to her eyes as she felt intense hope sweep through her.

Since Steve Whitcomb was an architect by trade, the Whitcombs had a lot of earth-moving equipment at their ranch, and all of those machines had been brought in by truck on Friday. Shay spotted Maud outside one of the houses, helping to erect a two-by-four wall with her team. She might be in her fifties, but she knew how to use a nail gun and build those wooden frames.

"This is all like a dream," she confided softly to Reese as she ate.

He sipped his hot, steaming coffee. "Not everything in our lives is always a nightmare, is it?"

She sobered and lost her smile. "You're right." Shay savored the hot biscuit, melting butter, and tart strawberry jam. Reese was right. There had been many good times in her life, too. But with PTSD, the symptoms threw a dark curtain over everything. Today, though, Shay felt nearly free of that darkness as she turned and watched another roof joist being lifted into place on the arena roof, with the help of the crane and crew. The men and women on top of the huge structure knew what they were doing and worked in concert with one another. She glanced at her watch. In an hour, her father would arrive.

"How are you feeling about your father?" Reese asked.

"Scared, if you want the truth."

"Troy knows he can't take your father off that back porch. And he knows that no matter what Ray orders him to do, Troy will follow your wishes, instead. Relax." Reese reached over, touching her hand for a moment.

"I don't know what I'd do without you here, Reese," Shay admitted. "You've helped me so much . . . so often . . ."

"It's not work, Shay." His mouth drew into a faint smile as he held her gaze.

An intense yearning went through Shay as she held Reese's warm gaze. He wanted her. All of her. And he didn't try to hide it from her. She was old enough to see when a man clearly wanted her. And she wanted Reese equally as much. Her hand tingled where he'd touched it. Would there ever be a quiet time for them? Less pressure and stress surrounding her? It looked hopeless to Shay for a moment. "I wish we had some alone time," she admitted, giving him a glance, finishing off her breakfast. Nothing was left on her paper plate. A glint came to Reese's eyes as he regarded her.

"We'll know it when it happens," he promised her in a low tone, almost a growl.

Feeling the promise of his words sent a riffle of pleasure through Shay, touching every part of her hungering body.

"It's not always going to be this crazy," Reese promised her, sipping his coffee, his plate empty. Looking up at the light blue sky, the temperature now comfortable in the sixties, he smiled over at her.

"I feel inundated," she confided. "Now my father is in the mix. I shouldn't say it like that. From the beginning, I'd wanted him out at the ranch recovering, getting therapy after he suffered that stroke . . ."

"Shay? You need to remember we each have a story."

Tilting her head, she studied him. "What do you mean?"

"We each have a story to tell. We live it out daily. Your

father has his story. You have yours. I have mine. The trick, as I see it, is not to be living part of our lives in another person's story. There's nothing we can do to change their story, so we need to keep to our own tale of life. That way, you won't feel so inundated." He searched her softening blue gaze, understanding that she got the drift of what he was sharing with her.

"So," Shay said, opening her hands, "my father's story is his to own? Not for me to have a meddling foot or hand in it?"

"Right. From what I've seen in my young Marines who came out of alcoholic families, they couldn't separate themselves from the toxic pattern they'd grown up with. It was my job to help them to see that. I stumbled upon the idea of every person having a story to live. And that all our stories are our own. No one else has one quite like ours. It means we don't judge another person, nor do we mix ourselves into their story. You have to respect the person's journey, in other words. Some people have happy stories. Others have very sad and tragic ones. But within the story, Shay, each of us has choices to make. And we're allowed to make them. Others might try to tell us what's best for us as we live our story, but in the end, we have to make that decision alone and for ourselves, whether others agree with it or not."

"Your Marines must have loved having you as their CO." She watched his cheeks turn ruddy and he avoided her gaze for a moment, his mouth working to hold back unknown emotions. She saw regret in his expression. Sadness at the loss of his career that he was obviously good at. Her heart aching for Reese, she reached out, her fingers on the back of his clasped hands. "You haven't lost your touch, Reese. Not at all. I get what you are saying. I really do. It's a brilliant way to view people and their issues. Thank you . . ."

She reluctantly pulled her hand away from his. She saw the shame in his expression, the loss of everything he once worked so hard to have—to live his story as a Marine commanding officer of a company. Shay realized the power Reese had as a CO, but knowing him in the last few months, he never abused the privilege of his power. Instead, the man continually empowered those around him. Including her. Gratefulness drenched her heart and it only made Reese that much more endearing. How badly she wanted to wrap her arms around him and show him that he'd lost nothing, really. That he was the same person, just in a different circumstance, was all.

"You know," she said tentatively, holding his gaze, "your story changed location, Reese, but you are still the man you always were. I hope you know that. Because I see it every day here at the ranch, I see it with how you work with the vets and more than anything, how you work with me. Telling me about your story idea gives me an insight into you that I didn't have before." She smiled gently and whispered, "Your story is filled with courage, heroism, and compassion, Reese. You've never told me what happened to you, how you got the PTSD, but you know what? You have not allowed the PTSD to define the essence of you . . . your story template. It's the same, it never changed. You're still an incredible leader and manager." Shay turned, gesturing around the busy, industrious place. "All I have to do is look around me and I see your stamp, your ideas, your ability to plan and execute, all around me."

Reese moved uncomfortably on the bench. "Shay, you're a dreamer. You'll always see people at their best and finest."

"Why not?" she challenged, her smile deepening. "I saw it in you the day we met. I sensed it. And you proved me right. I know I'm not a hundred percent on reading people accurately, but I've read you." Shay shook her head, her voice growing low with emotion. "Reese, stop seeing yourself as less than the man you were before you left the Corps with PTSD. You're the *same* man. Nothing has changed except for the uniform you wear now." She waggled a finger at him. "And I love your story idea for all of us. Your story is to be a leader of people. A darned good one. I'll always see those wonderful qualities in you."

He swallowed painfully, dodging her gaze. "I've got such a long way to go, Shay . . ."

"Don't we all? But that doesn't mean I can't see the whole of you, Reese Lockhart. In the past few days you've dazzled me with your intelligence, your compassion and understanding. Your ability to lead people through their own minefield and not get blown up in the process, is incredible." Shay saw his cheeks growing even ruddier as he barely held her warm, sincere gaze. "Somehow, I swear I'm going to get you to see yourself as I see you, Reese."

Shay braced herself as she made her way through the busy teams at ten o'clock to go meet her father. She saw Troy had wheeled him onto the back porch that overlooked the corrals, the arena, and the area where the four homes were being built. Earlier, Diana Adson had called her on the radio, announcing that Troy and Ray had arrived.

Shay wore a bright orange, cap-sleeved T, jeans, and boots. She had pulled her hair back into a ponytail and wore a tan baseball cap on her head. The buzz of saws, the grinding of pipe being cut, the chugging sounds of the crane, and the growls and roars of the other heavy equipment, filled the air like a construction symphony. She saw the women who were taking care of the food tents, starting to prepare for lunch, which would occur at noon. There were going to be hungry crews coming in after working from seven o'clock onward, without much rest.

Mounting the concrete stairs, her hand on the pipe rail, she leaped to the broad wooden deck. Shay had always loved the wraparound porch on their home. It was wide and linked the east and west porch, where there was a large wooden swing. She saw her father in his wheelchair being pushed by Troy to a spot along the stout wooden railing where he'd get the best view of the work taking place. Today, he wore a straw Stetson, a dark blue kerchief at his throat, a starched white cowboy shirt with pearl buttons, his jeans, and boots. Ray looked so much like she'd always seen him growing up. Only, instead of a horse, he rode a wheelchair. Much to her surprise, he'd shaved, too. Usually, Ray wouldn't shave for days, reminding her of a grizzled gold miner in the Rockies. He sat straight in the wheelchair, his shoulders squared back with pride. Her heart twisted because she so desperately wanted him to love her and he never had. But even if Ray didn't have it in him, as Shay approached, she still leaned down and gave him a hello peck on the cheek.

"Welcome to the ranch, Father," she said, smiling and straightening. She nodded and smiled warmly over at Troy, who was dressed in black pants and a white shirt. He was six feet two inches tall, in his forties, and muscular. Shay knew some of the people in the nursing home needed a strong man to carry or move them around when necessary. And Troy, who was a gentle giant, was her father's favorite helper there.

"Looks busy," Troy said, gesturing toward the barn.

"Things have changed," Ray said, frowning.

Shay turned and stood near him. "For the better." She gestured to the many pipe corrals down below the house.

"I've gotten them cleaned up, the rust is off them, and we've replaced sections that couldn't be salvaged."

"Hmph."

Troy gave Shay an apologetic look. Shay smiled a little, used to her father's pessimistic attitude.

"That's a helluva crane," Ray said, pointing at it behind the large arena building.

"Isn't it?" Shay said. She saw interest in her father's eyes as he watched the slowly moving crane deposit another joist on top of the building.

"And you've painted the barn."

"Yes. It needed it." She saw her father turn and glare up at her. She had to be careful what she said. Ray had let that barn go for seven years and never painted it. Without paint, the wood wore and rotted away faster and had to be replaced much sooner. Wyoming winters were cruel to wood, and it had to be cared for yearly, or else.

"I didn't have time to get it done!" he snapped.

"Hmm," was all Shay said, nodding. She saw Diana Adson come out of the house. "Father? Diana Adson is going to be dropping in once an hour to see how you're doing and if you need anything."

Diana came around Shay and held out her hand. "Hi, Mr. Crawford. Call me Diana. I'm Chuck's wife. We own the gas station on the north end of town."

Ray grudgingly gave Diana's hand a tepid shake. "That old gas station? It was broken down and dying the last I heard."

Diana smiled at Shay and turned her attention to Ray. "Well, it was, Mr. Crawford. My husband and I rebuilt it two years ago, and we're just fine now."

Grumping under his breath, Ray turned his attention to the spectacle going on around him.

Diana gave Shay a merry look. "Why don't you take off? I know Steve and Reese need you out there. I'll take care of your father's requests."

"Thanks," Shay murmured. She leaned down, her hand on her father's shoulder. "I'll try to drop by later when I get a chance, Father. We'll have lunch together."

Ray turned, regarding her. "Why can't you stay?"

"Because," Shay told him firmly, "I'm part of a three-person team coordinating the building schedule. I can't do both. But, I am glad you came out to see what is going on."

"Hmph."

Okay, so much for being understanding, Shay thought. Diana gave her a sympathetic look, said nothing, but squeezed her hand as she turned to walk down the stairs. Shay hurried toward the path that led to the busy barn in the distance. *So far, so good.* She had been pleasant but firm with Ray. Reese and Garret would be proud of her.

And yet, her heart ached because she could see her father struggling to be "nice" to her. Why? Why was it so hard for him to be nice to people around him? Did he realize how hard and harsh he was on everyone? She felt very sorry for Troy, who had been his chief caretaker for a year now. But the big man, who was a physical therapist, too, seemed unaffected by Ray's outbursts, irritability, and anger. He was as placid and easygoing as Reese was, she decided, climbing the gravel slope up to the barn.

When she reached their table in the aisle, the place was crowded with people coming and going. Shay saw Reese look up the instant she entered the area. There was concern in his face, but she also felt the warmth of his gaze on her, too. Shay smiled at him. When she reached their desks, she saw Steve was busy with the four indoor house crews, who were now coming in to work. Reese had just gotten off the radio with the backhoe operator down below the barn. He turned.

"How did it go with your father?"

"Okay." She held out her arm. "No bites so far."

Reese grinned sourly. "Good to know. How did Ray like his new babysitter?"

"He tried to make me feel guilty and wanted me to stay instead of Diana," Shay said, picking up her sheaf of papers. "I told him I couldn't and why." She saw Reese beam at her. It felt good. "Honestly? I felt like I won that pitched battle with him."

Reese squeezed her shoulder. "You did, Shay. I'm proud of you."

She was proud of herself, her skin radiating heat where he'd laid his large hand briefly on her shoulder. It sent a river of heat to her breasts and her nipples hardened. That was how Reese affected her. A little shaken, she said, "Well, one battle. It's not the war."

Reese nodded, handing her the radio that blared to life. "Stick with the fact that you won one battle. That's as good as it gets." He winked at her.

There was such camaraderie between them. Despite the people milling around the different desks, the noise volume high, the air filled with the sounds of construction, Reese made her feel damned good about herself. He had the ability to lift her, help focus her, and point out the positives, not the negatives.

Chapter Nineteen

Shay tried to contain her emotional reaction as she and Reese had lunch with her father up on the porch. Troy had thoughtfully brought out a card table with a chair for each of them. Reese had told him to go to the food tent and grab a bite to eat. Troy smiled and thanked them, leaving Ray in their hands.

"Your favorite," Shay told Ray, giving him a paper plate that had barbecued beef ribs, macaroni salad, a huge mound of kernel corn with a slab of melting butter on top, and Texas garlic toast.

"Smells real good," Ray admitted gruffly, pulling the plate closer with his left hand.

Shay picked up his fork and knife. "Let me cut the meat from the bone for you?"

He gave his daughter a scowl. "I suppose . . ."

Paying no attention to him, Shay quickly separated the fragrant meat from the bone. "There. Do you need any other help, Father?" Shay placed the fork near his left hand.

"No, this'll do."

Reese said nothing, noting Ray couldn't even tell Shay thank-you for her thoughtfulness. He pulled out the chair for her. Then, he sat down next to her. There was nervousness in Shay's eyes, but Reese doubted Ray was aware of anything or anyone but himself.

Shay smiled at Reese as she picked up a large bone with meat and sauce on it. "I've been smelling this all morning. I'm starved."

"You've earned this meal," Reese told her. He raised his head, glancing at Ray, who sat opposite him. He was pretty good with his left hand, considering he was right-handed. He was making short work of that barbecued beef and the corn.

She looked over her shoulder. "Gosh, the place is suddenly quiet." Everyone was taking at least a forty-five minute break to eat and rest.

Ray looked up, his gaze on the crane. "You'll get that roof enclosed by tomorrow, sure."

"I'm hoping so," Shay agreed, wiping her mouth with the paper napkin. "It's a huge place, Father. Sometime, I'd like to get you down there so you can see the inside of the arena after its finished. It's really going to be amazing."

"How the hell do you think I'm gonna get down there?" Ray jabbed his finger toward the arena. "I'm stuck with these goddamned wheels, girl."

Reese opened his mouth to speak, but Shay beat him to it. Her voice was light.

"Father, if there's a will, there's a way. We already have plans to pour a concrete walk from our house up here, around the corral over there"—she pointed toward it—"and then on to the main entrance to the arena." She reached out, touching his shoulder. "And when it gets done, we'd love to have you come out and give it your blessing."

Reese ducked his head to cover his smile so Ray couldn't see it. The man just stared at his daughter, mouth open, nothing coming out of it. Pride moved in his heart for Shay. She'd handled that perfectly. Instead of getting snared within

Ray's anger and frustration and becoming trapped by it, she was detached, which in this case was a good thing. Shay had pointed out the positives and gave Ray something to look forward to in the future.

Reese glanced over at Ray. The man was looking at Shay like she was an alien from Mars who had just landed. He wanted to throw his arms around her and hug the hell out of her for breaking her old pattern of getting hooked into her father's anger. Glancing to his right, he saw Shay was composed and had resumed eating her meal as if nothing had happened. Her courage to try to change struck him profoundly.

"Well," Ray grumped, stabbing his fork into the mound of macaroni salad, "I'll think about that."

It took everything Reese had to swallow his smile.

"What do you think of the four homes we're building?" Shay asked him, waving her fork in that general direction.

"How big are they gonna be?"

"Twelve-hundred square feet. There will be two bedrooms and two full bathrooms."

Reese tensed, knowing that Ray didn't like vets in general. He saw his eyes narrow speculatively on his daughter.

"I just don't understand you, girl. You could not only hire real wranglers, but charge them rent for stayin' here, too. Instead, you're mollycoddling these guys."

Shrugging, Shay studied her father. "These vets are wranglers. And given that they're donating fifteen percent of their paycheck back to the ranch monthly, I think it's a just trade-off."

Reese heard the strain and tension in Shay's tone and saw hurt in her eyes. Her father didn't get it. His daughter was a military veteran. She had "another" family, the men and women with whom she'd served. But Ray didn't understand that dynamic in her life. He'd never been in the service.

"Instead, you could rent or lease those four houses out to anyone," he muttered angrily. "That could be a lot of money comin' in! Not a stupid fifteen percent!"

Shay winced and set her fork down next to her plate. "I've thought of that too, Father. But these men served with honor and they deserve our help. Our country has ignored them, but I refuse to. If I can offer them a hand up to get on steady ground once more, I'm going to do it."

The grit in Shay's voice made Reese's heart swell. He knew better than to try to stand between father and daughter. They had to hash this out on their own terms, but he was coming damn close to telling Ray to stop calling his daughter "girl." He held off, the tension turning brittle at the table.

Ray wrestled with himself. His thin lips pursed and he glared at Shay and then looked out toward the arena. Fingers never still on the fork, he kept tapping it on the card table. "You're bullheaded, girl."

"Father, stop calling me 'girl.' I'm not a girl anymore. I'm a grown woman. I passed that age and stage a long time ago, don't you think?" Shay burrowed a look into her father's squinty eyes.

"You *act* like one, Shaylene! You haven't earned the right to be called anything else."

Shay's nostrils flared. She avoided her father's glare and looked down at her plate for a moment. It hurt to swallow, her throat tight. Looking up, she met his glare. "I don't have to earn anything from you, Father. When I got home from the Marine Corps, this ranch was in deep trouble." Her voice grew strained. "I wasn't going to stand by and watch our family legacy be stolen out from beneath us by the bank. You don't have to like what I've done because this isn't about you. It's about our whole family, whether they're dead or alive. We have been on this land for 120 years, Father. Did you think I was going to come home and let it be taken from us? I grant I'm not a business person. I'm a truck driver, that's all. I knew vets were hardworking men and women. And I wanted to help those who were down-and-out. I know it's probably not the smartest business plan in the world, but you know what? It's working. We're making the monthly mortgage payments. We haven't missed one, thanks to those vets."

Reese saw Ray getting redder than a proverbial beet and he worried about him having another stroke. Rising, he said quietly to Shay, "I think it's time we head back to our offices in the barn." He saw the hurt and anger in her eyes. Reese wanted to shake the man, but he knew it would do no good to get physical with him. Ray had already paid a big price for his choices. He was the one in the wheelchair, not his stalwart, hardworking daughter.

Giving a jerky nod, Shay whispered, "Yes . . . let's go," and she stood, the chair scraping the floor. She gave her father, who refused to look at her, a softened look. "Troy will take you back to the nursing home at three o'clock, Father."

Reese came around and cupped her elbow, guiding her down the stairs. He wanted to keep his hand on Shay and transferred his palm to the small of her back as they left the stairs. She was walking stiff-legged. He could feel tension radiating from her and he checked his long-legged stride for her sake. The gravel crunched beneath her boots, her arms locked at her sides, hands in fists.

"Hey," he called, catching her hurt gaze, "you did fine back there, Shay."

"Dammit," she huffed, "I let him get to me, Reese! I swore I wouldn't!"

Reese knew they had at least twenty minutes before returning to the barn, so he angled her off around the corral, heading out toward the arena, where fewer people could hear them talking.

Her gait slowed, and finally she moved against his body, silently asking for his arm to come around her waist. Reese didn't disappoint her and he felt her surrender over to him as she rested her head against his shoulder. "I'm proud of you," he rasped. "You held your own, Shay. This isn't easy for you."

Shoving strands of hair away from her cheek, she muttered, "I blew it. I let him get to me, dammit! I was trying so hard to disengage from him. He kept calling me 'girl.' I hate that name! I hate it!" Shay jerked to a halt, turning toward Reese, her hands over her eyes, trying to hide from everyone. She refused to cry. *Dammit, anyway!*

Reese moved his hand gently across her tense shoulders, drawing Shay against him. He stifled a groan as she buried her face against his chest, her arms sliding around his waist, clinging to him. He felt her struggling to get ahold of her escaping emotions. Rubbing his hand gently up and down her back, he kissed her hair. "Just take this an hour at a time, Shay. Your father is a tough nut to crack and he's not likely to change. I was proud of you."

Slowly, Shay eased out of his arms. "He doesn't see me, Reese," she whispered brokenly. "The ranch has improved! We've all worked so hard to pull it back from the brink." She closed her eyes, her hand coming to rest on his upper arm. "It hurts so much . . ." The anguished words tore out of her mouth. In that moment, Shay looked like a ten-year-old little girl, confused and hurting, unable to sort out anything. Reese knew it was part PTSD, the other part of her trying to untangle herself from the dysfunction she'd grown up with.

"Listen to me," he told her, kissing her brow, sliding his hand against her cheek, holding her gaze. "You lean all you want on me while you're feeling like this. I'll hold you . . . do whatever you need, Shay. You aren't in this war alone with him. You have me now."

Gulping, she nodded and whispered, "Then hold me tonight, Reese? Be with me?"

Freezing momentarily, he searched her wide eyes intently. "Are you sure?" he demanded hoarsely. "Do you know what you're asking, Shay?" Shaken, Reese hadn't expected this. He saw the anguish and the need in her eyes.

"I need you, Reese."

Smoothing his fingers across her damp cheek, he swallowed hard. Now it was his turn to feel less than whole. He wasn't the man she thought he was. Reese felt old pain drifting up through him, memories of striking his ex-wife while caught in a flashback nightmare. This was the wrong place and time for this kind of deeply private conversation. "You'll have me," he promised her thickly. "But we have to talk first, Shay. You know that?"

Nodding, she eased away from him, as if realizing people were probably watching them. They were behaving like a couple who loved one another, unafraid to show their bond in public. Shay was sure many had seen them and she forced herself to push her feelings aside. "Yes . . . tonight?" She searched his eyes. "After everyone is gone and things are quiet. We'll talk." Her throat ached but the pain in her heart was twenty times worse.

She saw him waver, saw concern in his green eyes. Shay knew he was afraid of striking her at night while they were asleep. Moving her hand up his arm, she whispered, "We'll work through this together, Reese." Shay saw her low, husky words act like balm to him. It was clear he wanted her as much as she wanted him. Only the past stood in their way.

"We'll talk then," he promised her. "Come on, we need to

take our stations at our desks. We've got about five minutes before things start cranking up again . . ."

Diana went to find Shay at 3:00 P.M. She threaded her way through the gangs of volunteers milling in the barn at the various office stations, getting guidance or orders. She found Shay handing off some paper to one of the house crew.

"Hey," Diana called, gesturing to her. "Got a minute?"

Shay nodded and left the desk, walking over to Diana, who was leaning against one of the box stalls. Max slowly got up and walked after her, tail wagging at Diana. "What's up?" Shay asked.

"Your father," she said, giving Shay a worried look.

Max whined and looked up at Diana.

Diana laughed and petted Max's broad gold head. "Hi to you, too, good looking young man!"

Max wagged his tail, thumping it against Shay's leg.

"What now?" Shay groused, her hand on Max's head as the dog sat down next to her, panting.

"Always something with him, isn't it?" Diana asked, managing a twisted smile. "I went up to make sure everything was fine with Troy and your father. To say good-bye to them. You know? Be nice and all?"

Shay's mouth thinned. "What did Ray want?" He wasn't the type to not speak up. Automatically, she wrapped her arms around her chest, waiting for Diana to tell her.

"He wanted me to ask you if he could come back out tomorrow. Same times, same arrangements. Are you okay with that?"

Automatically, Shay wanted to say no. Her brows went down.

"Look," Diana said in a low voice, resting her hand on

Shay's shoulder, "he seemed pretty contrite. Did you two have a fight at lunch earlier?"

"You could say that," Shay muttered. Wiping her face, she whispered, "I don't want him out here tomorrow. Once is enough. There's so much going on. The pressure is going to be on all of us to get things finished by tomorrow night."

Nodding, Diana said, "I thought so, but I told Ray I'd come and ask you."

"Try to explain to him this isn't personal, it's about everyone being focused on finishing what we started here. He's a distraction, but don't tell him that."

"I got it," Diana reassured her gently. "You don't need to be tore up with him around and being cantankerous, either. He doesn't get how important this weekend is to your ranch. Or to you."

"I know," Shay said. She gave Diana a look of gratitude. "Thanks for having my back on this. I hope he doesn't blow up at you when you tell him I said no." She saw Diana grin.

"No worries. As a police officer I used to deal with really upset people all the time." Patting Shay's shoulder, she assured her, "I'll handle it. You go back to work."

Shay was glad that her father couldn't get out here except by wheelchair.

She patted Max, then the dog rose and ambled at her side as she walked back to the busy desk where Steve and Reese were. How did a person grow stronger with a parent like Ray? She wished there was an easy black-and-white answer to that question.

Reese felt his gut knot as he and Shay entered the house. It was 11:00 P.M. and everyone had finally left for the day. Exhaustion stalked him as he knew it did her. She walked into the kitchen, going to the cupboard to bring down the box of tea.

"Want some?" she asked.

"Sure," he murmured, joining her and taking two mugs down from another cupboard.

She felt calmed by Reese's quiet demeanor. In no time, they had their tea made and were sitting down near one another. "So much happened out there today, Reese."

He held her weary gaze. "All good. Tomorrow, by noon, that roof will be on the arena. The crew worked their butts off today. They're ahead of schedule."

She gave him a warm look, one corner of her mouth moving upward. "I loved the fact that Maud was urging the house crews to compete with one another."

Chuckling, Reese nodded. "She's a force of nature, no question. We're ahead of schedule on everything."

"And everyone's got to be feeling as bone weary as we do. Probably more so because we weren't doing the physical work. All we were doing was giving instructions." She looked at him with awe. "You're the one who put that schedule together, Reese. That was a lot of detailed planning, figuring out when a crew would finish one section of the work, and when to send them on to the next leg of it. That was amazing. I could never have done it."

"Bean-counter mind," he joked ruefully. "Steve, you, and me all worked well together. It happened because the three of us hammered out that schedule."

"Steve was amazing, too. He knows a lot about construction because he's an architect. The man saved our butt a couple of times today when we didn't have the right equipment for a particular job. He knew enough about bulldozers and end loaders to figure out a work-around to keep a job on schedule."

"He's built skyscrapers around the world," Reese told

her. "We all had our specialty that we brought to this dance, Shay. It was the right combination of people for a job of this size and complexity."

"You're all great leaders. Good people managers," Shay said, sipping her tea.

"You did your share, too," Reese reminded her. "You're no slouch when it comes to construction either, Shay. You grew up with it here on the ranch and you had the diplomacy to get those crews pointed in the right direction with the right tools."

"Compared to you two, I did very little."

He stared at her, the silence deepening. "You had extra pressures on you today, Shay. Don't discount what you did. Steve and I couldn't do what we did without your help and support. It was the three of us that defined the day for all the crews."

She managed a halfhearted smile. "You always make me feel important, Reese. You make me believe I can do it."

"Your parents should have imbued you with that same confidence, but they didn't, Shay. I want you to see who you really are, not who you think you are as defined by Ray."

"Oh," she muttered, shaking her head, "that family pattern?"

"Exactly."

"Well, I sure didn't do a stellar job today with my father, did I?"

He reached out, sliding his hand gently across hers. "You did fine. You went in and you won a battle."

"I lost one, too."

"There's always setbacks when you're riding a green horse. You know it's going to buck you off sooner or later," he teased. Reese didn't want to let go of her hand, but he forced himself to. He saw the defeat in Shay's eyes, knew she was thinking about how she had fallen into her father's trap when he started trashing the vets. She was so passionate, her heart on her sleeve, that she didn't know how to protect herself from people like him.

Reese knew how important a father was in a person's life. He had a good father and it was because of him that he kept fighting to reclaim his soul from the destructive PTSD symptoms. Shay had a father who fed her nothing but the lie that she wasn't lovable, that she wasn't to be respected and that she didn't count in Ray's universe. Those kinds of signals from a father to his child were devastating, and Reese was looking at the results of them in Shay.

"I really screwed up, Reese. I was so damned mad at myself afterward. I guess . . . I guess I got lulled when my father was half nice to me before that."

"You were both trying," Reese soothed, holding her sad gaze. "But you're both caught in that sick family pattern, Shay. I saw him struggling to be nice to you, to stop what he normally did or said to you. Both of you made a little progress today, and that's what you should expect and be focused on."

"But we snapped right back into our old pattern with one another later," she grumped.

Reese gave her a sympathetic smile. "It happened only once." He held her hand. "You're going to have to realize trying to change your behavior with Ray is going to be a lot of baby steps, forward and back. It's never easy. It's probably one of the toughest things you'll ever do in your life. And whether Ray ever decides to change isn't up to you. But you can change yourself. That's in your power and control. I'm damn proud of you and what you did out there today." He squeezed her fingers, seeing her eyes grow warm. Seeing the desire in their depths, he added gently, "And today, you asked me a very important question. We need to sit here and talk about it, if you're up to it." He searched her exhausted expression.

She slipped her fingers between his. "I was pretty upset out there earlier." She compressed her lips for a moment, holding his blue gaze. "Looking back on it now, and how tired I am and you must be, I think we need to not act on what I wanted."

"A wise decision," Reese said thickly, wanting nothing more than to bed this woman, love the hell out of her, let her know just how beautiful she was to him. Shay needed a man's love. A man who could reflect just how good a woman she really was. And that she came first in a man's life, not second or last. "I know you were upset. We all say things we don't mean."

She gave him a strange look. "I meant what I said, Reese. Do you think I didn't?" Her voice grew scratchy with disbelief.

His heart started a slow pound. "Shay, as much as I want you, you know what went on in my marriage. I struck my wife when I was caught up in a nightmare. Nothing has scared me as much, not even combat, compared to hitting Leslie like that." He hesitated, looking down at their hands. "I'm afraid I'll hurt you, too. I couldn't live with that. I really couldn't." He saw sympathy come to her eyes, saw the softening of the line of her mouth. "It's not that I don't want to be with you. That's not it at all."

"So you want a relationship with me and at the same time you're afraid you'll harm me?"

"That's it, Shay." He studied her luminous eyes, which reflected her desire for him. She didn't see the wall standing between them, as he did. "Look," he pleaded huskily, "we're both whipped. Let's table this conversation until another time."

"You're right," Shay whispered, easing her hand from

his. "Just the same," she said, standing, "thanks for being there for me today, Reese. Good night . . ."

Reese nodded and remained sitting, gripping his tea mug. The urge to stand, kiss her senseless, nearly overwhelmed him. "I'll see you at 0500," he said, strain in his tone . . .

Maybe learning to break old patterns with her father was having added benefits. She was trying to be realistic about their relationship, as well. He couldn't conceive of any woman wanting him in bed at night, possibly becoming his punching bag. Yet, the stubborn look in Shay's eyes served to put Reese on warning. She wasn't willing to let their own blossoming relationship be put aside. Judging from her expression, she wasn't going to wait long, either.

Watching Shay move, the way her hips swayed as she walked to the kitchen sink, made him feel hot and needy. As tired as he was, Shay turned him inside out by just the way she walked. And how many times had he dreamed of running his hands down that lush, strong body of hers?

Swallowing hard, Reese watched her disappear down the hall. He wanted to get up and follow her and take a shower with her. How many times had he imagined making love to Shay and hearing soft sounds of pleasure catch in her throat? Reese knew he could love Shay well.

His brows fell and he stared down into the empty cup cradled in his hands. He could love her. He could pleasure Shay. He knew he could help rebuild her fractured self if they were in a long-term relationship.

But what about afterward? What would happen when he fell asleep at her side? Would the nightmares and flashbacks return? Would he get ensnared within it and lash out, striking her? Maybe kill her by accident? He grimly studied his large hands, knowing the physical strength he possessed. Knowing that it could be inadvertently used against Shay. The last thing she needed was to be hurt by him. She'd been hurt enough by her father. He didn't want to be another man in her life doing it again.

Rubbing his mouth, Reese sat back, unsure what to do. His heart tugged powerfully in his chest, wanting Shay. Loving her. And yes, he bitterly admitted, he was falling in love with this brave woman vet. Her passion for wounded vets totaled him, in the best of ways. She was wounded herself, but that didn't stop her from pursuing her dream of helping vets like himself. And for that, he owed her. He wanted to give her his heart. But the baggage . . . the awful baggage gained in combat, came with him, too.

Could he love her, and protect her from himself at the same time?

Chapter Twenty

Shay battled back tears as a huge, triumphant cry went up when the arena was fully enclosed by its new roof. It was late Sunday afternoon, in the high seventies, all the work crews shouting, slapping one another on the back and congratulating one another. On the roof of the arena, the men and women of the crew stood, lifting their arms above their heads, yelling out in victory. Their job was completed!

She stood with Reese just outside the barn, glad for his closeness. He turned and smiled over at her. "You did it," he told her, satisfaction in his low voice.

Absorbing his pride, she managed a wobbly smile, trying not to cry. "This means so much . . . and it's not just for me, Reese. It's for all of us."

"Well," Reese said, touching her shoulder for a moment, "it was your vision. Your idea. All we did was follow up with the details of how to get it done."

Shay saw Maud and walked down to meet her. She hugged Maud, who was grinning broadly, her eyes dancing with happiness.

Maud turned, pointing toward the four enclosed houses. "Now, we gotta turn all our attention to those houses, Shay."

"That's the plan," Shay agreed, giving her a grateful smile.

"Have you seen the insides of the houses yet? Our teams have made a lot of headway."

Reese came down and hugged Maud as well. "Take the time to go look," he urged Shay. "Steve and I can hold things together down here."

Maud hooked her arm around Shay's. "Come on, let's check them out. See what you think."

Reese stood there, hands on hips, smiling as the women moved slowly down the gravel path toward the four new homes. A roofing crew had the roof on each of them. All the double-paned windows were installed. He knew all the details on the houses because he'd gone over them with Steve weeks earlier. The architect had wanted to spend the money to winterize them properly.

Turning, Reese headed up the slope, back to the barn, where weary crews who had finished their jobs on the arena were checking where they could be used on the next project. At 8:00 P.M., the work would stop. And all the people who had thrown their hearts and bodies into this two-day, intense project, would go home. Reese was sure there would be a lot of them soaking in bathtubs tonight, a lot of tired, aching muscles needing relief.

Steve met him at the lip of the barn. He gave him a weary grin. "Looks good, doesn't it?"

"Does it ever."

"Shay hasn't seen the inside of the houses yet, has she?"

Shaking his head, Reese said, "No, but Maud's taking her down there to look at them. I think she's going to be surprised at how much the crews have gotten done."

"Well," Steve said, lifting his gray Stetson off his head and running his fingers through his short, silver and black hair, "Maud wanted the drywall up and spackled today.

That's where they're working now. The plumbing and electric is already installed."

"The crews have gotten an unbelievable amount completed."

"Never say cowboys and cowgirls don't work hard," Steve agreed, pleased. He motioned toward the homes. "The detailed work that is left can be worked on in the coming week. Maud is bringing down one of her wrangler crews next weekend to get it finished. You and Shay up for that?"

"Let me ask Shay." Reese saw Steve give him a studied look. For a moment, he had a sense that Steve was going to say something, then decided not to. Off and on yesterday and today, Maud would come into the main headquarters area and tease the daylights out of him about being sweet on Shay. Did everyone around him see that he was falling in love with her? Feeling raw, needy, and unable to scale the wall that stared back at him from his past, Reese rubbed his jaw. "When she comes back from the house inspection, I'll ask her."

Steve nodded. "Sounds good. Let's get back to work. We've still got five hours, and we can do a lot with them."

Shay pulled off her boots in the mud room, putting them on a special mud rug. It was 9:00 P.M. and everyone had left the ranch. They were alone again. Moving her fingers between her aching toes covered with thick cotton socks, she saw the sky was darkened in the west over the Wilson Range. The ranch was quiet once more. Easing into a sitting position, she stared at the fully enclosed arena. Her heart swelled with joy. She owed so much to so many people in this valley for their kindness and hard work. Without them, this would never have been possible.

"Hey," Reese called from the hallway, "can I draw you a hot tub of water?"

She gave him a relieved look. "That sounds wonderful." She saw that Reese, who had come in to the ranch house half an hour earlier, had already taken a shower. His hair was damp. He'd also changed clothes, wearing a dark red polo shirt that showed off his powerful chest and broad shoulders. Instead of jeans, he wore ivory-colored chinos, and a pair of hiking boots rather than his usual cowboy boots. She almost told him that he looked like a civilian, and grinned to herself, thinking he'd probably not like her assessment. He was a military vet. A cowboy. Not a civilian.

"I'll get it started," he said, giving her a warm look.

Her heart beat a little harder in her chest as she straightened and stood. Padding down the hall in her sock feet, she could feel the grit and dust on her skin. Pushing her fingers through her hair, which she'd just taken out of a ponytail, Shay looked forward to washing it, too. The house was quiet except for some subtle instrumental music coming from the radio in the living room.

So many memories assailed her as she stood for a moment in that room. Some were of her mother cooking in the kitchen. Others, darker and unhappy, of her alcoholic father snapping and angry at her mother and herself. When she was alive, her mother was hardworking, kept the house, cooked, cleaned, and was constantly being verbally abused by her father. Shaking her head, Shay didn't know how her mother had tolerated it. And in some ways, she wondered if her mother had died early to escape it all because she saw no other way out. Shay's way out was to leave at eighteen and join the Marine Corps.

Walking quietly through the living room, she saw the bathroom door was open and heard the water running in the tub. Reese was crouched down by it, swirling fingers through the water to make sure it was the right temperature. Her heart swelled powerfully with love for him. Would her father ever have thought to draw water for his wife? No.

There was so much to like . . . love . . . about Reese. As she approached the bathroom, he lifted his head. She felt the tugging connection that was always between them, alive and yearning. And she saw appreciation for her in his narrowing green eyes. Beneath the light above, she saw his short hair gleam, still drying from his recent shower. Reese was continuing to gain back his lost weight. His face had filled out, and he was looking healthy, suntanned, and physically fit compared to when she met him months earlier. He didn't look like a down-and-out military vet caught in the snare of PTSD.

If Shay had any doubts about her efforts to help struggling vets, all she had to do was look at Reese. Longing flowed through her as he slowly unwound and rose to his full height. She offered him a smile of thanks.

"This is such a wonderful gift." She gestured to the tub. Already, the room was filling with warm humidity. Reese looked thoughtful. He had brought out a huge, fluffy yellow towel and set it nearby along with a washcloth and new bar of soap. There was so much to love about Reese. She might not have a world of experience in relationships, but Shay knew enough to appreciate the simple, important gestures between a man and woman.

"A well-deserved one," Reese said, moving past her. He halted at the door. "Are you hungry? I was going to fix some breakfast food for us."

Her stomach growled, reminding Shay that the last time she'd eaten was at lunch. She'd skipped dinner because she'd gotten caught up in last-minute instructions for the house crews. Everyone had worked right up to that eight o'clock deadline. "That sounds great."

He nodded. "Take your time. I won't start fixing it until you show up in the kitchen."

Reese had pancakes and scrambled eggs for their late evening dinner. Shay sat at the table enjoying every bite of the food he'd prepared for them. She had washed her hair and it hung damply around her shoulders. It had felt good to climb into her yellow granny gown, her feet bare. Reese was used to seeing her in it and as tired as she was tonight, it was the perfect outfit to wear. The look in his eyes told her he wanted her. It was almost palpable as they ate in companionable silence. Max was curled up on his bed in the corner, sleeping. He had remained with Shay throughout the two days, lying near her feet, beneath her makeshift desk, always watchful.

"You're as good a chef as Garret," she teased Reese.

"I'm okay in the kitchen. At least you won't die from what I cook." His mouth crooked as he lifted his head.

"You two will make great husbands someday." The words had slipped out before she could stop them. Instantly, she saw darkness come to Reese's eyes. *Damn!* When would she learn to think first before she spoke? "I mean," she stumbled, "you are both good men with so much to offer the right woman."

"Garret strikes me as coming along in his PTSD to the point where he's ready to re-engage with life," Reese said, swirling the last bite of sourdough pancake through the maple syrup on his plate.

She heard the edge in his voice and felt tension move through Reese. How was she going to get him to overcome his fear of hurting her as he had his ex-wife? Shay didn't know, but she was driven to do something that would break that log jam one way or another. Tonight, though, they were both exhausted and it wasn't a good time to have that kind of conversation. "Garret is almost there," she agreed, having cleaned her plate and pushed it aside. She picked up her cup of coffee. "I had a talk with him about it a week ago."

"And?"

Shrugging, Shay sipped her coffee. "I told him he was at a point where he could leave and make his way back into the world. He agreed, but he wanted to stay here."

"Because it's a family," Reese murmured, catching her gaze.

"Yes. We in the military are a funny lot in some ways. We're trained together as a unit. We're taught that the team, which in reality is our new family, is who we belong to now. It's our identity. Everything is done together, not apart or alone. We're taught to be responsible for the other person, to be there for them, to be part of a greater whole."

"Garret sees your ranch, this place, as his family now."

She pondered his words and held his green gaze. "I know."

"Is this what you'd planned? Or did you want us to leave the ranch at a certain time?"

"I didn't have a plan for that," she admitted, smiling a little. "I know each vet is different. And so much depends upon the individual and his or her dealing with their PTSD. For Garret, I think he needed continuity in his day and that helped him deal with the worst of his symptoms. They're not gone, but he's learned how to cope with them and normalize his life to a great extent."

"And he's willing to continue to give fifteen percent of his paycheck back to the ranch?"

"Yes. He feels it's more than a fair trade-off." She sighed

and felt her heart turn with such love for all the vets at the ranch. "He asked me if I wanted him to leave, and I told him no. That we need good wranglers. There's so much to do around here, to get this ranch functioning financially again."

"He's a good man."

Shay held his gaze. "So are you, Reese." How badly she wanted to reach over, slide her hand along his recently shaven jaw, and kiss him. She was coming to realize that fear had Reese captured, and it was up to her to break through it. She wasn't necessarily the aggressor when it came to letting a man know she was interested in him, but Shay was going to have to rethink the whole dynamic. And maybe after a good night's sleep, she would try to come up with a way to do it.

"I *was* a good man, Shay," he told her gently.

"You still are. You never lost those qualities within yourself, Reese. You never will. Look how you orchestrated the last two days. Everyone loves you, respects, and admires you. I saw time and again that if a team leader had a question, they'd go to you first. Not Steve. Not me. But you. That says something about your leadership abilities, Reese, whether you want to admit it or not. You're a good, quality person and people instinctively know it." She reached out, patting his forearm, giving him a tender look. "In time, you'll see that." Because one way or another, Shay was going to trap Reese, hold his heart in her hands, kiss this man senseless until he could forget his past and anchor himself firmly into the present. With her.

Shay sat with Diana Adson at Kassie's Café for lunch a week later. She'd asked Diana to meet her because she was in a quandary. They sat in a booth at the windows, watching the tourists along the main plaza.

"So," Diana said, "I get the feeling we're here for a reason. Want to spill the goods, Shay?" She took a bite of her juicy Reuben sandwich.

"Busted," Shay said, holding up her hands, grinning. She picked up her grilled tuna melt sandwich. "You're my good friend and I need some advice."

"Okay," Diana said, a sparkle in her eyes. She picked up a French fry. "Fire away."

"It's Reese. Well, actually, it's about us," Shay said in a low voice, not wanting to be overheard. "I really like him."

"Does he like you? Judging from the way I'd sometimes catch him looking at you the weekend we raised the arena roof, I'd say he's like a lovesick puppy over you."

"Really?"

"Love," Diana pronounced. "Very clear. You've fallen in love with him, haven't you?"

Grimacing, Shay nodded. "Busted again. Does everyone know except the two of us?"

Chuckling, Diana shrugged. "Maud has been predicting when Reese will ask you to marry him."

Groaning, Shay rolled her eyes. "No!"

"Hey, she's a wily player. Knows people. Can see right through them." Diana's smile increased. "Heck, she took one look at Chuck and me and started in on us. Neither of us realized how drawn we were to one another at first. But Maud sure saw the signs between us."

"She's something else," Shay admitted, shaking her head. "Scary."

"Only in the best of ways," Diana said, laughing.

"I hope she doesn't tell Reese this. He's jumpy enough."

"No, she wouldn't do that. This particular conversation is just between us in the immediate family. You know we get together with the Whitcombs for Sunday dinner? That's when we find out stuff like this."

"Phew," Shay whispered. "I can just see Maud catching Reese at Charlie Becker's store and telling him."

"Well," Diana said, giving her a wily look, "that might not be a bad idea. So, what's bothering you about Reese?"

"It's him. I can see it in his eyes that he wants a relationship with me, but he's afraid to move ahead on it."

"Why?"

"When he was married before to Leslie. He had PTSD and came home after a deployment and hit her one night when he was asleep in the bed with her. He'd had a flashback, Diana, and when Leslie woke up and tried to shake Reese awake, he turned and struck her with his fist. It horrified both of them."

Diana's face became somber. "I'm the right person to talk to about this. When Chuck and I started living together, he was afraid of that happening between us. He's an ex–Delta Force operator and his muscle memory goes into a defense posture if he's feeling threatened, whether awake or asleep. He worried about that. About hurting me by accident."

"What did you do? I need to know, because right now, Reese has dug his heels in. He's admitted he likes me, wants to explore what we have, but he won't budge. He's still caught up in the fact that he hit his ex-wife in his sleep."

Sighing, Diana gave her a sympathetic look. "You need to talk this out with him, Shay. Chuck told me if he ever got into a nightmare or flashback while asleep, to get out of bed and get away from him. He told me that if I rolled over, touched, or tried to shake him awake, he'd lash out and hurt me. Instead, we had this plan that I'd get out of bed, out of his reach. He wanted me to stand at the end of the bed and call out his name. Not scream it or anything, but just keep calling his name, telling him to come back to me, that he was safe."

"Did it work?"

"Has so far. He gets nightmares maybe once or twice a month. It wakes me up in a hurry, because we're so close and in tune with one another. I can feel him when he's stressed. I wake up instantly"—she snapped her fingers— "when he's trapped in a flashback. So, I ease out of bed as quietly as I can so that I don't disturb him. I then go to the end of the bed and call his name."

"Does he hear you?"

"Eventually. He's so tied up in the reality of his firefight, or whatever he's replaying, that it might take five or ten minutes of me calling him back. But it works. And that way," she said, sighing, "it keeps me safe."

"I didn't know that," Shay whispered, giving her friend a kind look. "War . . . it's so horrible."

"When you see what Reese goes through, it will tear you up, Shay. But you have an advantage because you were in the military, too. You understand the stressors. I wasn't in the military, so as a civilian, it's hard for me to understand that my husband gets trapped in dangerous nightmares where he's fighting to survive. Every human survival mechanism kicks in. And it can be dangerous for the wife or partner. The way we deal with it works for us. I think Leslie made her mistake when she tried to shake Reese out of it. And Reese, in his nightmare, thought it was probably the enemy grabbing him instead. He would strike out. It wasn't his fault."

"But he takes on the blame," Shay muttered unhappily. "And he's so horrified by what he did, he's afraid to approach me because of that one experience."

Diana looked sad. "This happens all the time to returning vets. And there's no easy answer, no one answer, that will help all of them. So much of it hinges on the partners talking to one another. Chuck sat me down and we had a no-holds-barred conversation about it. We have guns, but they are locked away. He doesn't want any weapon or even a knife, anywhere near that bedroom. The weapons safe is in our basement and he wants that kind of arrangement to keep us both safe. And he didn't leave anything out. It was pretty upsetting to me, and it upset him, too, because he doesn't like talking about what happened to him."

"I'm going to have to bring it up," Shay muttered. She wiped her hands on the paper napkin, gazing out over the busy plaza for a moment. "Every time I do, he backs off. I see the worry in his eyes. I hear it in his voice."

"But he loves you?"

"I think so. Maybe he won't call it love."

"Lust?" she teased.

"I sense it's more than that, but I'm not in his head, Diana. I wish I were . . ."

"But you love him, Shay?"

"What I feel for Reese is so deep and wide, it takes my breath away. And I discover more and more new feelings for him every day."

"That's love."

"I've just started admitting it to myself the past week," Shay admitted, shaking her head.

"He's a good man."

Shay gave Diana a sad look. "If only he would admit that about himself."

"But he'd fallen so far," Diana whispered, reaching out, touching Shay's hand to comfort her. "He only sees the fall and his failure. Not getting up and coming back to who he was before. Granted, he's not an officer in the Marine Corps anymore, but I saw him in action for two days during the arena-raising. He's a natural at leading others. Even

Steve Whitcomb, who's a lot like him, recognizes Reese's abilities. And Steve would know a good leader because he's one himself."

"Reese is rebuilding his confidence in himself. I see it growing and taking hold within him every day. It's working, and I'm so grateful that he's healing. His sticking point now is his emotions toward me."

Diana finished off her sandwich and wiped her mouth with the napkin. "I don't think either of you entered into this with the thought of falling in love with one another."

"For sure," Shay muttered darkly. "I guess I never saw myself in that way. After growing up with my alcoholic father, being married wasn't the starry-eyed dream I wanted out of life. I had eighteen years of suffering under my father. For sure, Diana, I did not entertain meeting a guy that I wanted to ever have live under my roof."

Giving her a kind look, Diana said, "Love often catches us off guard, Shay. Just when it's the last thing on our horizon, it plants itself in our heart. I know. It happened to me. Finding Chuck and then feeling this instant, invisible connection to him was a shock. I felt from the moment our eyes met, I was on some kind of slippery slide that I had absolutely no control over. My heart leaped. My body went hot. I was going crazy inside and resisting it with everything I had."

"That sounds like me and how I felt when I met Reese. It was instantaneous. Magic. But at the same time, I felt panic. I didn't want to be drawn to him at all."

"Yeah, I was scared witless too, and I carried a lot of baggage from my past," Diana admitted wryly. "But the heart doesn't care, you know? The heart wants what it sees as wonderful, beautiful, and joyous. But I hadn't had a wonderful life, so I felt overwhelmed with all these needy, wanting emotions where Chuck was concerned. I didn't know what to do with them. I was afraid to speak to him about it. I thought it was all one-sided because he didn't let me know for a long time how he felt."

"Well, at least Reese and I are a little further down that road. He admits he's drawn to me and vice versa. But he's told me more than once, he can't go there because of his past."

"You need to figure out ways to convince Reese that it's worth giving his heart to you, despite everything else."

Glumly, Shay looked at Diana. "I've never taken the lead on letting a man know how I feel about him."

"You need to in this case, Shay. I'm not saying it's easy."

Rubbing her brow, Shay said, "I'm not an assertive kind of person. I'm afraid if I try, he'll push me away . . ."

"Rejection? Yeah, I know that one," Diana commiserated. "Maybe small steps, Shay. Touching his hand? Letting him know you're interested? Moving closer to him? Letting him know you want him? That's more subtle, and it won't be lost on Reese."

Nodding, Shay whispered, "I was thinking in that direction, too. But I'm so afraid, Diana."

"That's the risk you have to take and there's no easy way around it. And you can't shield yourself from it, either, Shay. Maybe you need to listen more closely to your heart? What feels right to do at the time or moment if it comes up? Sometimes we overthink situations and then destroy the moment. But if we allow ourselves to switch to our hearts, our feelings, then often, it's a much clearer path to take. Not so filled with landmines."

"That feels better to me," Shay admitted. "I'm such a wilting lily of a woman. I've been beat down by my father, and I've been learning since eighteen to stand on my own and speak up for myself."

"And that's all good," Diana praised. "Now, you have to

take another step. If Reese isn't going to come to you on his own, you'll have to lure him to you."

Pursing her lips, Shay dragged in a ragged breath. "I just want Reese to give us a chance. To explore and see if what we feel for one another is real."

"Make it real for him," Diana said. "That doesn't mean you have to jump in his bed and insist on making love. That would probably blow him out of the water and you'd be back at square one. This has to be subtle, but constant— wear him down little by little, get him used to the fact you're around, that you want him and you're not taking no for an answer."

"Is there a book written on this?"

Diana laughed and shook her head. "No, this is Life 101, Shay."

"But I'm not some kind of femme fatale."

"Don't have to be. Use normal, daily situations to see where and if you can connect with Reese. Chuck had his hands full with me. I was the one running from a potential relationship with him. He knew it and set about rectifying that by the very things I've been discussing with you. He didn't come on strong and bullying. He came on subtle and gently. I got used to him being in my space, being with him. I let my guard down and began to enjoy him."

"I have to make Reese want me more than outrunning the fear that drives him?"

"Exactly. But subtly. Daily. Seize upon openings and just gently slip into his space."

"We've seen so much violence," Shay admitted wearily. "I mean, I couldn't be brazen. I think gentle is the only thing either of us can handle at this point in our lives."

"Subtle is underrated," Diana agreed. "And because you've both seen combat, being aggressive or in-your-face with him, just isn't going to work."

"Okay, I'm so glad we had this conversation. It does give me some ideas . . . some ways to maybe quietly lasso Reese and let him get used to the fact I want him in my life on a steady, everyday basis."

Grinning, Diana reached out, squeezing Shay's hand. "No one is more subtle than a woman when she wants something. I think at first, Reese won't know what's going on. I know I didn't when Chuck focused on me . . . on us, getting me used to the fact he was going to be in my life one way or another. He's an operator. He knows stealth like the back of his hand. And he used that on me. And it worked."

Shay gave her friend a warm look. "Stealth 101. That, I think I can do. Or at least, it doesn't seem as daunting as the other way."

"My bet's on you. Heck, Maud already has you two getting hitched." Diana laughed.

Chapter Twenty-One

Shay used the next two weeks to let Reese know she was clearly interested in him on an intimate level. Sometimes, he would call her into the office to show her financial information. Instead of standing across the desk from him, she would come around to where he was sitting and lean close enough to inhale his male scent, which made her body respond powerfully to his presence. Then she'd place her hand lightly on his shoulder and remain close with some physical contact.

At first, she felt his confusion. And then, the second week, he was finding small ways at different times to touch her hand or arm in return. Inwardly, Shay thanked Diana for her counsel. It was working. She could see it. And now, when they met late at night out in the kitchen for tea, she was very aware of him being sexually interested. It was tough to hide an erection in a pair of cotton pajamas. And it always happened after they sat down together to talk over their tea. Shay began to realize that those touches, looking and holding Reese's gaze, were turning him on.

She wasn't sure how long she could keep on doing it because Reese stirred her physically, too. One night, she had a torrid dream of Reese making love to her. She'd awakened, shaky, dampness between her thighs, her lower body heated. Being accessible to Reese was, it seemed, making her desire him more openly. She wanted to kiss this man. Feel his mouth across hers, have him take her to places she'd never been before. Shay knew Reese would be a tender lover. Her whole being ached whenever he was near her.

She wished that Diana had explained that letting Reese know she wanted him would make Shay, too, feel turned on and sexually vibrant. Never had she ached for a man like she did Reese.

Reese was out in the July heat in the main barn. The box stalls needed to be cleaned daily and he took turns doing it with the rest of the vets. Shay had just ridden in on Jak, the black quarter horse, from working on fence repair, dismounting at one end of the aisle when she spotted Reese at the other end, closing the last box-stall door.

The smell of fresh straw and hay that had been placed in each stall, filled the air like perfume. She took the reins, pulling them over her gelding's neck, and walked into the aisle, glad to get out of the hot sun. She saw that Reese had rolled up his sleeves to just below his elbows, and his face was glistening with sweat. His Stetson was hooked on a peg on the wall.

Her throat tightened as she saw him look up, his green eyes locking on hers for a long moment. Heat soared through her, and she felt her breasts tighten beneath his swift, fully assessing gaze. Tremors of heat flowed through her lower body, the coals of need flaring to life. Reese straightened, placed the pitchfork aside, and wiped his brow with the back of his forearm.

"You're a glutton for punishment," he told her with a

grin, walking casually toward her, his gloved hand ready to take Jak's reins from her. "Pretty hot out there, isn't it?"

It's hotter in here, Shay thought, watching how Reese moved with that feline masculine grace of his. No man had turned her on with just the way he walked before. But Reese did. "I'll take care of Jak," she told him. "You've been working hard. Take a break?"

Reese nodded. She stopped Jak, and Reese took the reins, removing the bridle and replacing it with a frayed green nylon halter. "Getting out of the office is a break," he told her wryly, pulling the panic snap over and hooking it to both sides of the horse's halter.

Shay nodded and began to loosen the girth on the saddle as he placed Jak into the cross-ties. "I love the sun. I like being out in it. I always come back re-energized."

Reese came around and slid the bridle up on his shoulder, lifting the loose saddle off her horse. "Your nose is red."

Shay grinned and touched it, feeling nearly giddy with his nearness. "Summer is such a short season that I'm trying to get out every chance I can to enjoy it. Small price to pay." There was a new openness between them. Reese had brushed near her shoulder to reach out to take the saddle. She followed him down the aisle and hurried ahead to open the large tack room for him so he could place the saddle on a rack. The fragrance of oiled and clean leather enveloped her as she stood aside and he walked in. The room was large and cool compared to the temperature outside. Shay pulled off her gloves, placing them in her back pocket.

Reese settled the saddle on the metal rack, meeting her smiling eyes. "On you, it looks good." He saw her eyes change, her lips part slightly as he turned toward her.

Shay sensed the charged air around them as he moved to his full height, his shoulders so broad, the fabric stretched tautly across his chest. Reese had gained back all the weight he'd lost. He was a terribly good-looking man, from the ropy muscles of his arms to his large, square hands. She moved toward him, holding his gaze. At first, she saw a question in his eyes, but then a burning, narrowed look replaced it as she drew within a foot of him. There was nothing she wanted to say, driven by the weeks of teasing torture that Reese had awakened in her.

He towered over her, so broad, powerful, and pure male as he searched her eyes, realizing that she was going to kiss him. Shay followed her heart this time, pushing away any fear of rejection. She laid her hand on his chest and instantly felt his skin grow taut, the muscles tightening beneath her fingertips. Shay cupped his jaw, closed her eyes, and lifted her mouth to his.

The first contact made her ache. His mouth was firm, male, and she felt his arm come around her, pulling her fully against him. If Shay had any question whether Reese wanted to kiss her as much as she wanted to kiss him, it was lost in the plundering heat of his mouth sliding hungrily across hers.

A moan vibrated in her throat as she opened up to him, pressing her breasts wantonly against his chest, the scent of man, the earth, and sweat all combined in her flaring nostrils. His fingers moved through her loose hair, her scalp leaping with tiny flames of pleasure as he kissed her more deeply.

The world ceased to exist. Just Reese, his mouth growing gentler after initially taking her fiercely, tasting her, asking her to meet and match his need for her. Shay's breasts grew taut, and she felt his other hand come around her waist, pulling her fully against him. She could feel his erection against her belly. He tasted so good to her! Their breathing was chaotic, their mouths hungry, as if they couldn't get enough of one another.

Drowning in the strength and tenderness of his mouth as he moved his lips against hers, she felt as if she were the most cherished woman in the world. Unable to get close enough, she slid her hands around his shoulders, needing every inch of physical contact she could get.

The pounding of his heartbeat was in time with hers. Their breath mingled, their lips clung to one another. Shay felt if she let go of Reese, he would be lost to her forever. It was such a sense of joy as she moved her hips suggestively against his. Instantly, Reese groaned, his arms tightening around her, his mouth taking hers hotly, more deeply.

Yes! Shay wanted all of this and more. Much more! No longer did she care what Reese might think of her boldness. Shay knew there was something more beautiful that existed between them and she wanted to give both of them a chance to explore it fully.

Slowly, reluctantly, Reese eased from her mouth, gently pulling her away just enough to stare darkly down into her half-closed eyes.

"Shay . . ." he rasped, his entire body taut with need.

"Come into the ranch house with me," she whispered unsteadily, searching his stormy green eyes. "I want you, Reese. I know you want me . . ." She saw such agony for a split second in his eyes. Her fingers tightened on his shoulders. "I'll take whatever you can give me, Reese. No strings. Just us. Please"—her voice broke—"I need you . . ."

She felt a quiver go deep within him. His gloved hands grew more firm around her. For a moment, she thought he might step away. *No!* A new urgency thrummed through her, and she whispered, "I'll take you just as you are, Reese. It's more than enough for me. Let's explore what's there? What we know is between us?" A lump formed in her throat, his possible rejection terrifying her. His eyes grew hooded, burning with white-hot desire for her.

Relief soared through Shay. She finally understood that to get Reese to acknowledge their connection, he needed to hear that he was enough man for her. He'd said he was half the man he used to be. It had been the right choice of words at the right time to push him over the edge and into her arms. And into her bed.

Reese looked up toward the open tack room door. His mouth worked and he looked down at Shay. "Are you sure?" he rasped, tangling his fingers through her hair, easing it across her shoulder.

Shay gave him a tremulous smile. "Never more sure, Reese. Come on. Come to my bed. I want to love you. I want you to love me."

Shay didn't think she could make it from the barn to the ranch house on her jellylike knees. Reese's heated, powerful kiss had begun melting her like red-hot lava inside. They agreed to go individually into the house, not together. She knew that Harper and Garret were gone. Noah was down working with his horses. Reese had concerns about their relationship being seen by the other vets, unwilling to let them know anything just yet. Shay had agreed.

She entered the house, the screen door creaking as it closed. She was sweaty and dirty from working all afternoon on the fence line. Entering the bathroom, she quickly shed her clothes to take a quick, cooling shower. She was shaking, literally, from anticipation as she made fast work of getting clean and washing her hair.

By the time she emerged from the bathroom, Reese had arrived. She had a towel wrapped around her, one hand holding it together between her breasts as he walked quietly down the hall toward her. The look in his eyes thrilled her. It was as if Reese had finally gotten around that block within himself. She met him halfway, holding his gaze.

"I need to wash up," he told her, halting, threading his fingers through her damp hair. "Shay. Are you still sure about this?"

Closing her eyes, she leaned into his cupped hand against her cheek. "Never more sure, Reese." Now, she had to be the strong one. Shay realized she was further along in her own, internal healing process than Reese was.

Nuzzling his palm, she placed a kiss in it and opened her eyes, staring up into his darkened green gaze. Reese wanted her. The hunger was stark. Stirring. Her whole lower body exploded with yearning for this brave warrior. "Meet me in my bedroom?"

"I won't be long," he promised her thickly, dropping his hand.

Shay nodded and opened the door, watching him disappear into the bathroom. Her heart beat with joy and anticipation as she allowed the towel to drop away. She'd never thought of herself as a bold person, but now she was being just that. And it seemed to give Reese the confidence he needed in order to take this step with her.

Smoothing the quilt across her queen-size bed, the light soft from the eastern window, the pink curtains lacy and feminine, she sat down on the edge of the bed and waited. Worried that Reese would back off if he got a chance to think about it, Shay was proven wrong.

She heard the bathroom door open fifteen minutes later. She straightened, her eyes on the open door to her bedroom. Reese walked in silently, a towel draped low over his narrow hips. His erection was clear to see even through it. She dragged her gaze upward across the expanse of dark hair on his chest, to his proud, broad shoulders, to his eyes. He closed the door, turned, and didn't hesitate as he walked over to her, his gaze raking her naked body, appreciation in his expression.

"You continually surprise me," he rasped, standing before her. He reached out, sliding his fingers through her drying hair.

"I like surprising you," she admitted, her voice becoming tremulous as his touch wreaked fire across her scalp.

Reese removed his hand and couldn't keep his eyes off her beautiful, lush body. "I wasn't expecting a kiss in the tack room," he told her wryly, sitting down, sliding his arms across her shoulders, drawing her against him so their thighs were pressed to one another.

"I couldn't help myself," she admitted, moving her hand across his chest, his hair damp and slightly curly beneath her fingertips. "I've wanted you ever since I met you."

Reese searched her face, memorizing her . . . memorizing this moment. "I never thought this would happen, Shay."

Resting her palm against his heavily thudding heart, she whispered, "I didn't either."

"So? What changed?"

"Me, I guess." She gave him a rueful smile, watching his mouth curve faintly upward. "There's something good between us, Reese. I want the chance to explore it with you." Her voice lowered with feeling. "You're more than enough for me just as you are right now." She saw her boldness tearing away all the damage Reese had undergone for the last two years. Shay turned and got up on her knees, pressing her breasts against his arm. "I see you so differently than you see yourself, Reese. I like the man who is here, now, with me. I've watched you reclaim yourself, you've regained all your lost weight and"—she smiled deeply into his eyes—"I like the way you look . . ." She leaned down, caressing his lips, hearing him groan, his hand gripping her shoulder, hauling her against him more securely.

Just getting to be intimate with Reese, to move her fingers across his damp skin, inhale his male scent, feel him ardently returning her kiss, set Shay on fire. He eased away just enough to break their kiss, their lips less than an inch apart, their breathing unsteady.

"I don't have a condom on me, Shay," he rasped. "I never thought I'd need one . . ."

Her heart winced with pain as she saw the regret in his eyes, the loss, the need for nurturing, needing her love and knowing he might not be able to consummate what they both wanted so badly.

"It doesn't matter," she whispered, her lips grazing the taut line of his mouth. She felt the tension he carried dissolve. "I'm on the pill." And then she broke their kiss, smiling into his hooded eyes. "I'm clean, no diseases. You?"

"Same," he answered in a guttural growl. And he took her as if she weighed nothing, positioning her onto the middle of the bed, on her back. Reese took the towel off, dropping it to the floor, laying his long body alongside hers. "It's been a long time for me, Shay. Two years . . ."

"Two years for me, too," she whispered, sliding her hand along his jaw.

"Sweetheart, I'm afraid I won't last for you . . ."

She shook her head. "Don't worry about it. We're both a little rusty at this. And I want you inside me, Reese. I don't care if you come sooner than you wanted. It has been two years . . ." She gave him a smile she hoped would ease his worry.

Moving his hand lightly down her arm, cupping her breast, he nodded. "I'll do my best to please you, Shay."

Her flesh tightened beneath his large hand teasing her flesh. "Then, we'll just have to wait and let you rest up a little bit and try it again, if it happens." She saw the relief in his eyes that she understood his concern that he might lose control. Reese wasn't selfish. By the way he was caressing the curve of her breast, he wanted to pleasure her first. Shay felt him relax and she saw it reflected in his eyes as well. All she wanted to do was love him. That knowledge gave Shay the courage she needed to move beyond her own realm of experience, to trust her heart, because she was falling in love with this man. She knew she wasn't any consummate lover, did not have the experience or skills, but it didn't matter. Shay could love him, regardless. Because love wasn't about experience, it was about sharing how she felt about him.

Reese was pleasantly surprised once again as Shay flowed like liquid fire into his arms and opening hands. There was an innocence about her that made him go hard and achy. Her lips caressed his at the same moment his thumb brushed across her tightened nipple. The sound that caught in her throat told him unequivocally that she enjoyed it, her hips insistent against his, her warmth against the steel of his erection trapped between them. More than anything, he wanted to please Shay, to give back to her first. He felt so close to exploding, he doubted he could stop it once he entered her. She deserved to be brought along with him, not left behind. Yet, the years without the warmth of a woman, the softness of Shay's arms surrounding him, her lips dismantling him because he was so starved for exactly this, left him vulnerable.

Fighting his own needs, he focused on Shay, drowning in her luminous blue eyes that radiated such love for him. Just that look alone stole his breath away. Every gliding touch of her fingertips across his shoulders, the movement of her mouth opening like a blossom beneath his, tore his resolve away like an ocean pulling sand from the shore. The velvet firmness of her warm skin was a perfume to his heightened senses. Her tongue shyly touched his and a low growl tremored all the way through him, causing an earthquake of starving need to plunge into his depths. Everything Shay did broke him down a little more. He was helpless to ignore the sweet touches of her fingers wrapping around his erection, squeezing him gently, reminding him he was a man with needs. And when she opened her thighs, welcoming him, guiding him to her slick, wet entrance, he gritted his teeth, straining to stop himself. But he couldn't. And Shay wouldn't allow him to as she wrapped her slender lower legs around his, arching her hips up to pull him deep into her welcoming body.

A low, guttural sound rolled out of him as he slid into her, drowning in her honeyed fluids, her tightness and the throbbing, rhythmic movement of her hips defying him to do anything but pump hungrily into her. She gave him no quarter, no time to do anything but thrust his hips powerfully, repeatedly against her own. And within moments, he felt the red-hot explosion ripping down through him. All Reese could do was clench his teeth, straining, his spine taut and frozen as the potent fire flowed powerfully into her. He crushed Shay to him, his jaw against her hair, groaning, sounding more like a wild animal in the throes of such pleasure nothing could compare to it. Nothing, nothing had ever felt so good as this, with Shay, with her arms around him, holding him tight against her. Holding him.

So many suppressed emotions, good and bad, flowed to the surface. He felt the last of his strength ebbing, felt her legs holding him so he could not ease out of her.

Understanding Shay wanted him in every possible way made his heart fly open. Her sweet kisses along the sweaty column of his neck, cool fingertips grazing his long back, caressing his hips, moving hers against his to prolong his ecstasy—he had never felt so lavishly loved as right now.

As he lay on top of her, realizing his weight was crushing her down into the mattress, Reese started to rise.

"No," Shay whispered. "Stay, Reese . . . I love how you feel on top of me . . ."

The words were so powerful, moving him almost to tears, he rested his brow lightly against hers, holding her tightly. Afraid he was going to suffocate her, he loosened his arms a little. Her soft, undulating body was still stroking him within her, and he felt the hot fluids caressing him, loving him. Reese didn't try to avoid the word any longer. Shay had unselfishly offered herself to him, understanding he'd never last more than a minute within her. It had been too long. *Years.*

His throat tightened. Shay had given herself, her heart, her trust to him without expecting anything in return. How could such a woman exist? Reese had never had an experience like this and it left him vulnerable, with a mounting desire to not only love Shay, but share his love for her in nonverbal ways. He was a skilled lover, and yet the years had taken a toll on him, on his ability to have ironclad control over his own sexual urges. Shay had boldly approached him, pulled him into her arms, trapped him with those long, strong legs of hers, and given herself to him.

Weakly, he lifted his head, turned and pressed a series of kisses along her hairline, moving to her closed eyes, her flushed cheek, and finally seeking out her lush lips. And she did not disappoint. A happy sound arose in her throat as he cherished her mouth, moving deep, stroking her tongue, emulating the rhythm of her hips still moving gently against his own. His strength was returning and Reese eased off her, despite her mewing protests. Already, he was starting to harden within her and he wanted to take advantage of the situation and please her until she screamed with satisfaction.

As her arms fell away from his back, Reese caught one wrist and then the other, moving them above her head, holding them against the pillows with one of his large hands. Now, she was trapped in the best of ways, unable to move, a feast to his eyes, body, and heart. Seeing the radiance in her half-closed eyes, the arousal burning in them, thrusting a little into her, watching her head tip back, a low sound of gratification spilling from her parted lips, he smiled.

"You're mine," he rasped, thrusting his hips against hers, watching her eyes widen with joy, her back arching to meet his sweet assault. Dipping his head, he settled his lips around one nipple that was begging for his attention. He slid his hand down the curve of her torso, across her hip, until it was beneath her cheeks. Lifting Shay just so, getting an angle he knew would engage the swollen pearl just inside her entrance, he felt her shudder and moan, head thrown back as he pumped swiftly into her. Reese knew it had been a long time for Shay as well. She was more than ready to orgasm, and he felt her walls contract around him. He held her firmly, pulsing into her. With each stroke, she whimpered and continued to strain against him.

"Look at me," he commanded roughly, staring down into her flushed face. Shay opened her eyes and he saw animal lust in them and he hummed inwardly, knowing he was satisfying her as much as she had him. Her lips parted and suddenly she cried out his name, her entire body nearly lifting off the mattress beneath him, the orgasm so powerful it took them both by surprise.

Shay's cries were ecstasy to his ears as Reese increased his thrusts, keeping that angle of her hips, milking her until all her sounds became little sobs and whimpers of utter satisfaction.

Finally, Shay sank weakly against the mattress, her eyes closing, her breath ragged, her lips curved. Only then, did he release her wrists and ease his hand from beneath her hips. Watching as her flesh grew rosy from her chest upward, and continuing to give slow, deep thrusts into her to maximize her enjoyment, he saw her smile and open her eyes, drowning in his gaze.

Nothing had ever felt so good, so profound, as loving Shay. Her brown hair lay mussed around her head, golden highlights here and there among the clean, strong strands. She looked wanton, wild, and she was his. Nothing in two years had ever made Reese feel as good as he did right now. He felt such incredible love for this brave woman who had dared breach his walls and call him out.

And no one was more grateful than he. For so long, he'd given up on himself. Shay had slowly brought him back to life, whether she knew it or not. Back home to who he was. As he moved strands of hair off her dampened brow, smiling deeply into her fulfilled gaze, Reese knew he'd taken the first step of many to come back to living life once more. Not allowing the fear to always rule him as it had for so long before she'd walked into Charlie Becker's store and offered him a job.

Chapter Twenty-Two

Shay slowly awoke and found herself wrapped in Reese's embrace. Her cheek lay against his upper arm and she lifted her lashes, meeting his calm green gaze. "I must have dozed off," she whispered, rubbing her eyes.

"You've been through a lot of late," he murmured, smiling a little. "Good loving does that to a person."

Nodding, she stretched languidly, savoring full contact with Reese's naked, warm body. Nothing had ever felt better. "Did you sleep?" Because she saw the light had changed and shifted. The clock on the dresser read 4:00 P.M. In another hour, the vets would be home and Garret would be in the kitchen down the hall. Shay didn't want the time to hurry by; she wanted to stay here with Reese, absorb him, love him.

"No," he said. His hand came to rest on her shoulder. "You dozed for about half an hour."

Frowning, she whispered, "But weren't you tired afterward, Reese?"

"Yes."

"Then—"

"I can't sleep with you, Shay."

The words came out sad.

Her heart tripped with anguish. Slowly, she sat up, pushing her hair behind her shoulders, facing him. Sliding her hand along his broad shoulder, she looked deep into his eyes. "I want to share a very important story with you." She proceeded to tell him about Chuck and Diana. His eyes narrowed and he listened intently to her. When she was done, she gave him a pleading look. "I want to sleep with you, Reese, unless you don't want that. Maybe I'm reading too much into what I feel we have."

Gently, he ran his hand down her left arm, engaging her fingers with his. "We need to give ourselves the time to explore one another, Shay. I'm not opposed to sleeping with you, but I'm not over that hurdle yet."

"Because you're afraid you'll lash out in your sleep and hit me?"

Reese nodded. "Very much so."

"Couldn't we try what Diana and Chuck do?"

Silence settled into the room as Reese thought about it. "I don't know . . ."

"Look," she said huskily, "I'm a vet with PTSD, too. Why aren't you afraid of me waking up and swinging?"

"You have a point," he conceded, and then tried a little teasing. "But if you hit me, you aren't going to cause much damage. If I hit you, I could break your nose . . . your cheek or jaw, Shay. That's the last thing in the world I want."

The worry in his eyes tore at her. "I want to try this method, Reese. Please, don't tell me no."

With a groan, he sat up, leaning against the headboard, drawing Shay into his arms, settling her against his body. He lightly rested his chin on her hair, holding her close. "What if it happens, Shay?"

Shrugging, she whispered, "I don't think it will. This time, it's different." She looked up at him. "We're different. Things aren't the same as they were when you hurt Leslie.

You can't lay that experience on us, Reese. We've both been in the military, we both have PTSD." She slid her fingers across his jaw, feeling the sandpapery quality of it. "You're at a different place with your PTSD than when you were married to her. You were trying to hide it. You're not doing that anymore. It's in the open. Everyone knows."

Nodding, he rasped, "I hope you're right, Shay." He leaned down, taking her mouth gently, kissing her for a long time, savoring her taste, her scent. Lifting from her warm lips, he met her worried look. "I would do anything for you, Shay. But I'm not in control of myself when I'm sleeping. That's why I tried to avoid you for so long. I've wanted to kiss you senseless from the moment I saw you. I've wanted you like I've never wanted anyone or anything in my life. I kept forcing myself from wanting you because I live in fear of harming you."

Giving him a stubborn look, Shay knew she was fighting for both of them, for the dream she knew they could reach together. "And I live in fear of hitting you in my sleep, too, but I'm not going to let fear rule me, Reese."

"Well, the last couple of weeks, you sure wore down my resistance," he said wryly, giving her a crooked smile. "Every time you got near me, I could barely keep my hands off you."

"You needed a gentle push," Shay said.

"You're a pretty gutsy lady."

"You were worth me becoming that way to get you to move toward me, Reese."

"I was digging in," he admitted somberly. "I didn't want to . . ."

"I knew that better than anyone," she whispered, sliding her hand across his shoulder, delighting in his tightening skin, the play of muscles leaping wherever she grazed his flesh. "Diana gave me the courage I needed to do it. I was at my wit's end trying to persuade you to let go and come to me."

Reese gave her a grateful look. "Okay," he said quietly, "we'll give this sleeping together a try. And we'll try out Diana and Chuck's method of dealing with it. Fair enough?"

Hope rose strong and fierce within Shay. "Thank you," she quavered, throwing her arms around his shoulders, hugging and kissing him for all he was worth.

Two weeks later, Shay called the vets together just before dinner. Garret was in his bright red-and-white checked apron at the kitchen counter when Noah and Harper ambled in. There was some curiosity on all their faces as Shay asked them to sit down, Reese beside her. Garret came over and sat down, giving them both a guarded look.

"Something's up," Garret drawled.

Shay grinned, unable to keep her happiness to herself any longer. She glanced to her left at Reese, who smiled, too. "Yes, and I'll bet this isn't going to be a surprise to any of you," she said.

Reese claimed Shay's hand and said, "We're in a relationship," he told the men.

Garret gave the other vets a wolfish I-told-you-so grin.

Harper smiled.

Noah laughed.

"None of us missed the signs," Garret informed them archly.

"Wouldn't expect otherwise," Reese told the men. "But Shay and I wanted to share the good news with you."

"That's what you get for letting this cowboy sleep in your house," Noah said, teasing Shay unmercifully.

Shay colored. "It just happened. I mean, I wasn't looking for anyone, Noah."

Garret raised his eyes to the ceiling. "Lord, let that happen to me. Please? I need a good woman to warm my bed at night instead of hearing these two hombres snoring." He gave Noah and Harper a black look.

Snickering, Harper said, "Hey, in another week, those four houses will be done. We'll each get one. You won't have to have your beauty sleep interrupted anymore, Garret."

The whole table laughed.

"Seriously," Noah said, holding out his hand toward Reese, "congratulations. We were all betting that it would happen."

Shay gawked at them. "You can't be serious?"

"Oh, honey," Garret soothed, "we're black ops. We see little teeny, tiny signs civilians never pick up on. Harper, Noah, and I made a bet that by this time, you two would be hitched."

Coloring, Shay gave Reese a nonplussed look. "Did you know about this?"

"Me? No. I lived under this roof, not with them."

Garret chuckled. "Have you proposed to her yet, Reese?"

Now it was Reese's turn to blush. "No . . . not yet. But . . . soon."

"What are you waiting on?" Noah asked, smiling.

"Figured we'd give it some time," Reese told them.

"Time?" Harper said. "Listen, we all know you no longer live your life in the future. And it's clear you two love one another, so why not make it official?"

Shay looked over at Reese. "I'm open to the possibility."

Reese nodded. "I'll get right on it."

The vets grinned widely, as if congratulating one another for pushing Reese into it sooner, not later.

Shay dug into her pocket. "Guys, I've got something for

you." She smiled and handed each of them a key. "The key to your new home." Her voice grew watery with feelings. "Thanks to Maud and her crew coming in last weekend, plus you guys working your tails off with them, the houses are going to be ready to move in to next week. You each picked the color scheme of your home and you only have to paint the rooms."

Garret looked at Shay, the key in his large palm. "Thanks, Shay. This means a lot to all of us. You know that."

Wiping tears from her eyes, she sniffed and said, "I love it when there's good news for everyone." She gave Reese a fond look. "I get this wrangler and you all get a new house to live in."

Noah got up, walked around the table, and hugged the hell out of Shay. His voice was deeper than usual, with feeling. "Thanks, Shay. It was your dream and now it's coming true for all of us."

Harper got up next, clearing his throat, and hugged Shay. "You're one of a kind, lady," he said, his voice muffled against her cheek. "Thank you." He released her and turned quickly away, wiping his eyes before sitting down at the table once more.

Garret reached out because he sat at her right elbow. Squeezing her hand, he said, "Now who is gonna cook for all of us? Are you kicking us out of your house?"

Shay clung to Garret's large, scarred hand. "Well, that's something we need to discuss as a group." She looked at Reese and said, "I do like the idea of having my kitchen back. Reese and I were thinking that maybe on Sundays, all of us would meet here for midafternoon dinner? Garret? You could cook for all of us then, if you felt like it. If not, I can do the cooking, no problem."

Garret gave Noah and Harper a look with his eyebrows

raised. "Oh, you two are in big trouble. You'll have to cook for yourselves. That is gonna be interesting to see. Neither of you can boil water." He snickered. He devoted his attention to Shay. "I'm fine with that. How about you vets?"

Noah said, "Sounds good to me." His lips lifted. "At least we'll get one good meal a week."

Harper groaned. "I'm in deep trouble. But yes, Shay, you deserve to have your house and your kitchen back. I like the idea of a family Sunday dinner together."

Shay snuggled into Reese's arms, their damp bodies against one another. Her lower body rippled with the glow of orgasm and she sank into the intense satisfaction he had given her. She sighed, nuzzling her face against the hard line of his jaw. Relishing his arms around her, drawing her against him, he pulled up the sheet to their waists. Their hearts were still pounding and she placed her palm over his. "I feel like I'm in a dream," she confided.

"I do too." He sighed. "At least," he said against her hair, caressing her nape and damp shoulder, "there's been no nightmares since we've started sleeping together."

Shay heard the amazement in Reese's low, gruff tone. It had been nearly a month since they'd started to test the waters with one another. "Well," she said, smiling against his neck, "we're making love nearly every night. That's enough to make anyone sleep like a baby afterward." Shay heard him chuckle, felt the rumble through his chest beneath her hand.

"Whatever magic we have together, it is working," he agreed, kissing her hair, caressing her cheek.

"Are you worried about it as much now, Reese?" she asked, lifting her lashes and moving back enough to engage his gaze.

The changes in him had been nothing short of stunning to Shay. The tension that was always around his eyes, was gone. Reese slept deep and hard every night. She knew because sometimes she'd awaken in the middle of the night, finding him snoring softly, dead to the world. Most of all, he was regaining his confidence in himself in large and small ways. Shay knew it was because they loved one another. Her heart swelled with quiet joy. She couldn't think of two people who deserved happiness more than they did. It wasn't a complete antidote to PTSD, but at least they had one another, and it helped them through the rugged moments they still had from time to time.

"No, my worry has been pretty much laid to rest," he admitted to her quietly, skimming her brow with his index finger. "I guess it's in my nature to worry a little."

She saw the love clearly in his eyes. "Good," she murmured, smoothing her hand across his chest. He was a tall man, built lean, and he'd muscled up, reminding Shay of a boxer in his prime.

Reese eased onto his elbow, settling Shay on her back so he could study her in the moonlight drifting through the lacy curtains at the window. "I want to marry you, Shay."

Her breath caught for a moment. Lifting her hand, she touched his chest, seeing how serious he'd become. "We've only known one another since May."

Shrugging, he traced her eyebrow with his thumb, continuing to caress her warm, velvet cheek. "It's long enough for me. What about you?" He gauged her suddenly very serious expression. "I'm okay with waiting, too. It's whatever you want, Shay. All I want is for you to be happy."

She sat up, her lips meeting and melding with his. Shay felt his hand fall lightly on her naked shoulder, drawing her toward him until her breasts grazed his skin. Moaning, she felt her nipples growing hard, tangling in the soft hair on his chest. His mouth took hers swiftly and heatedly, making her entire lower body spasm with need all over again. The man could kiss her into oblivion and she'd float in clouds of pure ecstasy as that mouth of his wreaked a special magic upon her. Never had she been so well loved. She had seen the gratification in his eyes so often after he'd pleased her. Shay never knew a woman could have so many orgasms in one night! But Reese brought out her love for him and her body thrummed in concert with her heart. He loved her. Fully. Completely. Forever.

Slowly, he eased from her lips, opening his eyes, cupping her cheeks, their mouths still touching one another. "Say yes," he rasped, sliding his fingers gently across her cheek. "Say you'll be my wife, my best friend, Shay."

She sank tighter against him, her breasts feeling electric shocks of pleasure. "Yes," she whispered, tasting him, tasting his maleness, the strength he held in check when he loved her. "I'm so happy, Reese . . . I don't want anything more in this world than you," she whispered against his mouth.

Sliding his hand more firmly against her jaw, he angled her to take her mouth fully, tasting her special sweetness, feeling the lushness of her opening to him, allowing his tongue entrance. Her breath snagged as his hand drifted downward, caressing her breast, teasing the nipple, making her gasp, and then flow against him even more.

In one motion, Reese eased her down upon the mattress, arm beneath her neck, his other hand curved around her breast. He broke their kiss, watching her in the shadowy darkness, his eyes gleaming, reminding Shay of a primal alpha wolf, and she was his wild mate. Reese made her feel wild. He'd shown her so much about her body, how to make it sing, how to hurl her into a universe where only intense ecstasy bubbled like an overflowing cauldron in her lower body.

"Marry me soon?"

She was taken aback by the seriousness in his eyes, feeling his thumb on her nipple, sending fiery sensations all over her body. How could she think when he was giving her such pleasure? And when he leaned over, his lips capturing her breast, she groaned, arching fully into his body, his erection tight against her belly. All her words fled. All she could do was feel the heat beginning to boil in her, dampness once more collecting between her thighs. A joyous sound caught in her throat as his hand moved between her thighs, caressing her wet, hot entrance.

"Soon?" Reese growled, his lips less than an inch from her nipple, his eyes trained on her.

Groaning, feeling his fingers begin to lavish her, Shay managed with a ragged gasp, "Yes . . ."

He smiled a very male smile and dipped his head, claiming her nipple once more, sending her into a wild, intense orgasm that undulated throughout her.

Shay lost track of time, her whole body glowing and satiated by Reese loving her one more time. She became helpless beneath his skilled hands, mouth, and body. The clock read 3:00 A.M. but she didn't care. Tomorrow was Saturday and the vets would all be around to paint their homes. She and Reese would be driving the truck out to the farthest point of the one pasture that they hoped to have finished by the time the snow began flying in mid-September. They would spend the day working the fence line, repairing it as they went. She had planned a picnic lunch.

Reese moved his hand down between her breasts, her flesh damp, as if to soothe her fractious, wildly satisfied body. His hand came to rest upon her belly. He leaned over her, gazing solemnly at her. "I want to marry you soon, Shay. I want to make this official."

She smiled and closed her eyes, her hand resting over his. "Because?"

"Because I love you. I don't want to spend one more night without a ring on your finger. You're mine. I'm yours."

She opened her eyes, drowning in his darkened, stormy-looking eyes. "You're such a male alpha wolf in disguise, Reese Lockhart." She watched him give her a heavy-lidded look. Her body clenched, knowing that heated stare.

"You wanted the old Reese Lockhart back. Right?"

"Uh-huh."

"Well, now you're meeting him."

"What?" she teased breathlessly, "that you're an alpha male beneath that calm exterior?"

He moved his hand lower, watching her breath halt for a moment as he slid his hand between her thighs, feeling her heat and wetness. "That was the part I lost," he told her, becoming serious. He moved his hand, engaging her folds, stroking her entrance, hearing her moan with pleasure, her hips automatically lifting, wanting more contact with him. "Are you okay with it?" He smiled a little, pride in his expression.

She sighed and moaned as he stroked her lightly, teasing her, and it felt delicious. "Oh, yes . . . I love your alpha male coming back. Don't . . . ever . . . stop . . ."

His smile grew deeper and he gently pulled his hand away, coming to rest once more across her belly. "If I don't stop, we're not going to get any sleep tonight, Shay. You know that."

"I think we're sex starved." She laughed breathily. "I love having you give me orgasms nearly every night."

Nodding, he moved his lips against her velvet cheek, nuzzling her. "And you'll get as many as you want," he said gruffly. Her hair tickled his face and nose as he kissed each corner of her smiling mouth. A mouth that made him go hot and hard every time his gaze settled on it. Shay had no idea of the sensual, sexual woman she was, but he was going to open those doors fully to her so she could appreciate what she brought to him. She was a feast in every sense of the word.

"Mmm, that's an offer I cannot refuse." She sighed, turning, meeting his mouth, opening to him, absorbing his male power against her lips. The moments turned molten, the silence cosseting them as he once more teased her nipple. Catching her off guard, a moan of satisfaction caught in her throat.

"You're like a finely tuned instrument," Reese rasped against her mouth. "So sensitive . . ."

Shay arched into his hand as he continued his campaign to make her swoon.

"You're so wild, so willful, and natural . . ."

He opened her and she willingly offered herself to him as he moved his warm, hard body over hers. Meeting his narrowed eyes, the eyes of a hunter wanting his woman, she thrilled to the predatory look he gave her. It was a promise of so many wonderful and intense sensations to come. Ever since their first time, when he couldn't control himself, Reese had made sure of her satisfaction before taking his. Never once would he come before he'd coaxed at least two or three orgasms out of her. Then, and only then, would he release himself within her. He was part wild animal, part male, and the tenderness with which he held her, loved her, had made her cry on more than one occasion. Shay had never known what real love was until Reese walked into her life. She knew they were both damaged. But their love was a potent unguent that was helping them to heal a little more each day.

"Reese"—she sighed brokenly, feeling him nudge her entrance—"we're not going to sleep tonight . . ."

"No, I guess not. You okay with that?"

She laughed softly, opening her arms to him, pulling him down upon her, opening fully to him, feeling him slip deeply into her. "Oh . . . yes . . ."

Chapter Twenty-Three

Reese waited until noon, when he stopped their Ford pickup beneath a large oak tree near the fence that was next on the list to be repaired. The warmth of the early September day felt good on his back. Off to the west he could see storm clouds churning and gathering over the Wilson Mountain Range, not sure if it was going to be rain or snow by the time it reached the valley sometime sooner, not later. He opened up a small cooler that was strapped in the back of the pickup, carrying it over to beneath the oak tree. The leaves were already turning bright colors or had turned brown after they twirled to the yellowing grass beneath the shade of the tree.

Today, Shay's hair was in a ponytail and she was wearing a blue baseball cap. She'd removed her leather chaps, laying them across the fender of the truck, placing her dark blue nylon jacket on top of them. Beneath the jacket she wore a tight-fitting red T with long sleeves. His body went on alert as his gaze swept her breasts, remembering the feel and weight of them in his hands, her pink nipples so tight and needy. He couldn't look at Shay without having a sexual reaction to her.

Reese smiled to himself, thinking how innocent she

really was to the world of lovemaking, but she caught on damn quick.

Earlier, Shay had brought out a worn green wool blanket from the cab. He quickly removed rocks and limbs from beneath the tree and then she laid it on the ground. Her cheeks were flushed, her blue eyes radiant. He'd never seen her happier. Hell, he was equally happy. Even his PTSD seemed to have diminished in volume and intensity. Maybe that's because they were heady in love with one another.

"All ready," Shay called, on her hands and knees, smoothing out the last of the wrinkles so he could set the red and white cooler down on it.

"Hungry?" he asked, placing it near her. He took off his Stetson and then got rid of his chaps, laying them along one edge of the blanket.

"Starved." She flashed him a wicked look as she opened the cooler. "I never realized how sexual I am until you walked into my life, Lockhart."

He grinned and lay on his side, propping himself up on one elbow. "Thanks, that's a compliment."

"Sure is." She handed him a beef sandwich slathered with mayonnaise. Unwrapping one for herself, she sat cross legged, facing him. "I don't know what it is about you, but when I look at you, watch you work, or walk, I get really, really turned on."

He took a bite out of the sandwich. "That's never happened to you before?"

"Never." She pushed a container of sweet pickles his way. "Maybe being monks for so long, we're catching up?" She laughed, a little shy.

Her innocence always totaled Reese. Just the uncertainty in her eyes now, melted his heart, made him burn with need for her all over again. "I think that's part of it," he said between bites. "But the other is you're just one

helluva beautiful, curvy woman who is sensual by nature."
He saw her give him a confused look.

"Did your mom teach you about being a woman?" he
wondered.

"My mom," Shay said, "was always under stress. My
father was verbally abusing her every day. She couldn't do
anything right. She didn't want me underfoot or in the same
room with him, if possible. I think because she was worried
my father would start picking on me, we didn't get the time
most mothers and daughters spend together. It was her way
of trying to protect me. At least, looking back on it, that's
what I think now."

"Did she teach you about makeup? Fixing your hair?"

"No . . ." Shay gave a sad shrug. "It wasn't a priority.
Surviving was, and she always wanted to keep me out of
my father's way. She was just too scared."

"You don't need makeup anyway, Shay. You're naturally
beautiful," Reese assured her in a low voice, watching her
expression melt.

"Being a ranch owner, I don't often think of myself
wearing a dress."

He nodded, watching her as memories seemed to hover
at the edge of her large blue eyes. Reese could not erase
her past, nor could he make Shay forget what she'd lived
through. "You know what I'm looking forward to?"

She perked up, finishing off her sandwich. She took a
damp cloth from a quart jar she'd packed and cleaned off
her fingers. "What?"

"Seeing what kind of wedding dress you choose for
when we get married."

"I'm going to need help," she confessed, opening her
hands. "I've never been into fashion."

"I'll bet Diana and Maud will be more than happy to help you."

She grinned. "Yeah, what a pair to be on my wedding-dress team! I'm sure they'll get me dressed right."

Sitting up, he rubbed his hands on his jeans and dug down deep into the cooler. "Come here." Reese held out his hand to her.

Shay scooted over next to him. "What?"

Placing his arm around her shoulders, nestling her close to him, Reese brought out a small red velvet box and placed it in her hand. "Let's make this official," he murmured, kissing her hair. "Open it. See if you like them." Reese worried that she wouldn't. Maud had helped him pick out the wedding ring set at the local jewelry store. He'd saved his money since starting to work as Charlie Becker's accountant, and was able to afford what he hoped was a set of wedding rings that Shay would love. He relied on Maud to know what Shay might like. He unconsciously held his breath as she eased open the top of the velvet box.

Shay gasped. "Oh!" she cried out, touching the set delicately with her finger. "Reese . . . these are beautiful! And so practical!" She picked up the engagement ring that had three channel-cut pink diamonds flush to the ring setting, ensuring that the stones would never be damaged or knocked loose as Shay worked on the ranch.

"You really like them?" A lump formed in his throat when he saw tears in her eyes as she turned, smiling radiantly into his gaze. His heart clenched in his chest. There was nothing on this earth he wouldn't do for this woman he loved. She was part wild child, part warrior, part innocent young woman. And his. Automatically, his arm tightened around her shoulders.

"I *love* them! Here, will you put this on me, Reese?" Shay held out the engagement ring.

His fingers were large and long in comparison to the small, delicate ring. Shay turned a bit, holding out her left hand. Reese was struck by the slender length of her fingers. Those fingers made him run hot, held him, loved him. They healed him.

He gently cradled her hand and slipped the ring onto her finger. To his everlasting relief, it slid on without much difficulty. It fit. "There," he managed in a croak, his voice emotional. "Looks nice. What do you think?"

She moved her hand, the diamonds glinting in the sunlight dancing through the leaves above them. "I love it, Reese. It's so beautiful. So different. And the wedding band"—she looked closely at it—"is gorgeous. I love the leaves that are etched into it. That's so different. And it's wonderful because I love nature so much."

"I have a confession," he murmured, watching her eyes widen. "I asked Maud to go with me and help me pick them out. I didn't feel very qualified, Shay. You don't mind, do you?"

She threw her arms around him, whispering his name, her mouth finding his, cherishing him, getting as close as she could to him. Her lips were warm, eager, and he eased himself down on the blanket with her on top of him. His body went to scalding as her hips fitted perfectly against his. Her breasts pressed into his chest and a groan started deep within him as she kissed him with a passion he'd not encountered before. There was no question Shay liked the rings! A mountain of relief flooded him.

As much as he wanted to love her, Reese knew they had more work to do. Besides, the rain clouds were skidding off the steep slopes of the Wilson Range and were quickly heading out across the valley in their general direction. Gently bringing Shay to his side, he languished in the joy shining in her eyes and in the curve of her ripe mouth.

"I love you, Reese," she whispered, sliding her hand across his jaw. "I've never been so happy."

He took her mouth tenderly, kissing her for a long time, savoring the feel, the taste, and sweetness of Shay. As he eased away, he drowned in her glistening blue eyes. "So?" he asked, moving his thumb near the corner of her eye as a tear leaked out. "When do you feel like marrying me?"

"What about in early October? It's such a beautiful month. I know it snows a little off and on, but the trees are so gorgeous in their fall colors. I love color. What do you think?"

"I think it's fine. It's going to take a bit of time to find the right dress."

"And invite our friends." Her voice lowered a little. "And family . . ."

Reese knew she was thinking about Ray. "I want you to invite whoever you want, Shay. If you're not comfortable with your father being there, he doesn't come." Protectiveness swirled strongly within him as he watched her consider the situation. Yes, a little progress had been made with Ray and her. But they had a long, rough road to go with one another, and Reese knew it. Ray was a constant reminder to Shay of her eighteen years of pain, and the loss of her beloved but abused mother. He knew she had a lot of anger toward Ray and rightfully so, but Shay was trying hard to repair the bridges between them. And Ray wasn't exactly eager to change his habits. The only reason he was trying was because Reese wasn't going to allow him to verbally abuse Shay anymore. And intuitively Reese felt Ray was after something, but he didn't know what. Reese felt Ray was setting Shay up. He'd sure as hell like to know what the man was planning. He didn't like how he manipulated Shay. So Reese watched, and waited, not trusting Ray one iota.

Reese eased her into a sitting position and he kept his arm around her as she thought deeply about the situation. Finally, Shay sighed and shook her head.

"I can't not invite him to our wedding, Reese." She looked into his eyes. "Will you be okay with it?"

"I'll be fine with it as long as he isn't abusive toward you, Shay. He already knows I won't stand for it." He saw pain and then relief in her eyes as he spoke to her in a low, thick tone.

"Okay, he'll be invited. I need to try to get on a better footing with him. I know it's up to me to do it."

He rubbed her shoulder in a protective gesture. "You did fine on the Saturday he came out while we were roofing the arena. There were some positive steps taken."

Grimacing, she shrugged. "Some forward, some back."

"It's not going to get better overnight. It will get better in stages, with a whole lot of effort on both your parts."

"I think he wants to try." She licked her lips, watching the storm clouds darken over the Wilson Range, starting to drift over the valley toward them. "He looked lonely. I think he misses the ranch so much. I know I would."

"The only one who put himself in his present situation is him," Reese told her gently, keeping his anger to himself. "Ray had a choice after he had that stroke. He could have gone into rehab right after it happened and probably gained back most of his physical mobility, but he didn't. Instead, he sat in that nursing home and sulked. It's his story. Not yours."

"I know," she whispered, holding out her hand, admiring the engagement ring. Lifting her chin, she gave him a warm smile. "I can't begin to tell you how nice it is to have you standing with me when I have to deal with him. I didn't have what it took to stand up for myself. I could for everyone else, but not for me." She grimaced, shaking her head, confusion in her expression.

"You don't have to do this by yourself anymore. There's work you have to accomplish, but Shay, I love you. I'm not going to stand by and let Ray take you apart with his anger. He's angry because he's made bad choices. And he's always blaming and taking it out on you." He kissed her wrinkled brow. "It's not going to happen again."

"To tell you the truth, it's nice not having to visit him three times a week. Once a week is enough."

"I'll always be there to protect you, Shay. And the minute he turns on you, starts making you feel bad, you tell me, okay?"

"Oh," she sighed, "I will. No worries there." She opened her hands. "And he's doing so well. I mean, you can see him getting stronger. He's working with Troy, the physical therapist, five days a week now. I've never seen him push himself like this. He keeps showing me his progress every time I go there. Last week, he was walking between the bars and doing really well, considering everything."

Nodding, Reese watched the roiling and churning black and gray clouds rolling off the mountains. As they flowed into the long, wide valley, they lost a lot of their cauliflower tops, smoothing out. He could see gray veils of rain beneath them, soaking the valley west of them. Within the next half hour, the rain would arrive in their vicinity.

"He's a man on a mission, no question." Reese wanted to share with Shay his gut feeling about Ray's sudden turn-around and getting physically fit again. But she had enough on her shoulders. From now on, he would have her back and be focused on her father. Shay was not going to be ambushed by Ray again if he could help it.

"Father keeps asking me if he can come and have

Sunday dinner with us." She chewed on her lip, stealing a glance up at Reese. "Has he been asking you that, too, when you talk to him on the phone?"

"No." His mouth thinned as he considered the information. The worry and guilt in Shay's eyes tore at him. "Look, he's always going to try to manipulate you, Shay. You're susceptible because he trained you for eighteen years to respond to him in a certain way." He gave her a look of pride. "But you're not falling for it. You haven't let him sit at our kitchen table."

"No, I haven't. I-I just couldn't handle it yet, Reese. I feel guilty because he *is* my father, but if he sat at our dinner table, I'd probably throw up."

He gave her a sharpened look. "Is that what happened to you as a child?" His gut knotted, unable to even begin to know her daily life as a child, growing up under Ray's toxic, abusive shadow.

"I used to hate coming to the dinner table to eat. I'd get nauseous . . . Sometimes, I'd run for the bathroom and throw up. It was pretty bad." She chewed on her lower lip, looking down at the blanket. "My father would get angry because I'd leave my meal uneaten. He'd yell at me because I was wasting good food."

Gently, Reese drew Shay into his arms and she came willingly, laying her head on his chest, wrapping her arms around him. "He might be your father," Reese growled, "but he has to earn the damned right to ever sit at our table." He looked down at her. "All right? Can we agree on that? If he can't conduct himself like a decent human being, I will not allow him to come anywhere near our home."

Nodding jerkily, Shay whispered, "That sounds wonderful, Reese. I-I'm just not there yet. He drove my mother to death when she was so young. I know he did. She saw no way out and wouldn't fight against the disease. She gave up and died. I watched it happen."

"It won't happen with you. I won't allow it, Shay." Reese saw the anguish deep in her eyes. He understood what she was wrestling with. Ray was blood. She owed him because he was her father. He saw those reasons so clearly in those large blue eyes of hers. And until she realized that she was as worthy a human being as her father, Reese knew he would always be her shield until she got on her own two feet.

"That's a good plan," she whispered unsteadily, giving him a grateful look. "Thanks for having my back. You have no idea how that helps me, Reese. I'll tell him we'll let him know about any invitation to have dinner with us."

He kissed her lips gently. "I love you, Shay. I'll always have your back. I want to be there for you."

She smiled gamely, rubbing her hand against his chest, the cotton cloth damp beneath it because they'd been working so hard on the fence line. "We can help support one another in so many different ways. Good ways. I know that."

"It's my turn to tell you how much you've helped me." He looked deep into her eyes. "We've been sleeping together for a month and never once has the nightmare come back. I've lived in a special hell, worried about hurting you by accident, Shay."

"I know you have."

"It hasn't happened yet."

"It may not," she whispered softly, caressing his cheek. "I believe you're at a different place this time around, Reese. Before, when you were married to Leslie, you weren't getting help. You were in denial. Now, you're not. That's a huge shift. I honestly believe you're past that stage, because you're working to heal yourself, not hide or run away from your symptoms. Diana said Chuck is having fewer and fewer episodes as time goes on, too."

Reese studied her upturned face, which held the hope of the world in it. "That's one of the many things I love about you, Shay. You hold out hope for the hopeless like us." He looked away, grappling to get ahold of his emotions. "Just like that storm approaching us." He gestured toward it. "I arrived here hurting, hungry, and I had no direction, just shame at how far I'd fallen. I was out of control. Nowhere to go. Just . . . screwed up."

She gave him a soft look. "But see where you are now, Reese? Look how far you've come in such a short time."

"It was because of you, Shay. You gave me a home. No one really understands how important that is until you don't have one." His voice deepened with raw feeling. "You opened up your home to me . . . to all the other vets. We're all getting better, we're healing instead of in free fall to a bottom we can't even see."

"And do you mind that after we get married, I'll continue my vision? To hire vets with PTSD? Who are down-and-out and need healing?"

Reese knew how important this was to her and he nodded. "All I want to do is support you, Shay. I fell in love with you just the way you are right now. I don't have a problem hiring men or women vets. Okay?" He saw relief in her eyes and realized that she hadn't been sure he would be all right with her pursuing her dream. That was her father she was reacting to, not him. "I would like Garret, Noah, and Harper invited to our wedding, too."

"Oh, no question," she breathed, happy once more.

"I want to call my folks," he told her. "You'll love them. I want them to come out here and meet you. I know they'll fall in love with you just as I did."

"I can hardly wait. I know how torn up they were when you left. They wanted to help you so badly."

Heaviness moved through his chest. "I know. I wasn't at a place where I could articulate everything that was going on inside me."

"I understand that. And I've seen so many vets walk away from a family who loves them but is helpless to know how to help and support them."

He heard the sadness in her tone and he squeezed her a little more tightly. "Looking back on my journey? I had to fall. I had to hit bottom." Looking down at her pensive face, he added, "When you met me, I had hit it, Shay. I was at a loss as to what to do. I didn't know how to help myself any longer. You picked me up. You dusted me off and took a chance on me."

"Yes, but you did all the work. I think that's why I fell so hard for you. I saw your struggles. I saw you fighting every hour to get better, to pick yourself up by your bootstraps. I saw your courage, your fearlessness."

"Well," he said wryly, staring into her luminous gaze that held so much love for him, "I had one hell of a cheerleader in you. You believed in me, Shay. You gave me back my hope."

She smiled, her lower lip trembling. "Sometimes, that's all a person needs, Reese."

Reese watched the dark, wide veil of rain beneath the clouds, spreading across the valley. "I like the idea of helping others, too. You've set your vision on the ground, Shay. We can hold that hope together for others who might come our way. And vets are the hardest working, most loyal group of people you'll ever meet. We know that. And it's easy to give them a chance to save themselves from falling any further."

Nodding, Shay snuggled into his arms, content as never before. "I'm going to love being your wife, your partner, Reese. We're really a great team. We've already proven that."

"I like having you as my best friend, my wife, my lover, at my side. It's a good feeling." He leaned over, kissed her tenderly. And Reese would spend the rest of his life loving this woman who held everyone else's heart with such gentleness and hope. Forever.

Chapter Twenty-Four

The rain started pelting down on the ranch just as they drove into the parking area. Shay made a quick run for the front porch and Reese drove the truck back to the barn.

She stomped her feet on the bristly mud rug on the porch. She saw the lights in the kitchen. Tonight, Garret was cooking for them while she was out working with Reese. She heard Noah and Harper talking in low tones in the kitchen, probably enjoying a well-earned cup of hot coffee. There was nothing to do, with rain coming, so they'd probably come in to grab a cup. Shay's heart swelled with such joy that she thought she'd burst as she double-checked her boots to make sure they were clean before proceeding to the kitchen.

"Hey," Garret greeted her, standing at the stove, spatula in hand, "thought you two lovebirds might be home soon. Big winter storm rollin' in, from what the weather woman on the radio station said."

She took off her baseball cap, hooking it on the wall peg, and took the rubber band out of her hair, allowing it to fall free around her shoulders. Grinning, she waved to Noah and Harper, who were sitting at the trestle table with cups in hand. "Yeah, it was a race to get here before it hit. Reese saw it starting to form over the Wilsons." Lifting her left hand, she said, "Look . . . Reese bought me a ring." She choked up a little as Garret stopped what he was doing and held her hand.

"Hey, that's some engagement ring," he said, nodding his approval. He released her hand and hugged her. "Couldn't happen to a better woman, Shay. Congratulations."

Noah and Harper got up and came over. Blushing, Shay showed them the ring just as Reese entered the kitchen. They smiled, each of them giving her a hug of congratulations.

Smiling over at Reese, who hooked his Stetson on a peg next to her cap, Garret turned and brought two cups down, pouring them coffee.

The vets went over to Reese, each shaking his hand.

"Finally did it," Garret teased him.

"Best thing I've done in my life," Reese said.

Garret returned to the stove, pushing around the meatballs frying in the skillet. "Hate to ruin your happy moment, Shay, but your old man called about half an hour ago."

Frowning, Shay felt her heart squeeze. She'd just seen her father Friday. What was he calling about?

"Anything urgent?" she asked, taking the cups to the table. She saw Reese frown with concern. They both sat down.

Garret shrugged. "Well, I hate spoiling this happy moment for you, Shay." He gave her a look of regret. "I was the one who picked up the phone and answered it. He said to tell you that he wants to move out here and live in one of those new homes we just got finished."

A bolt of shock plunged through Shay.

Reese reached out, gripping her hand. "He told you that?"

"Yeah," Garret said, taking the meatballs out of the

skillet and placing them in a bowl next to the stove. He put a dozen more into the frying pan. "I asked if he wanted to talk to you, because I know you gave us orders to always refer his calls to you, not Shay."

"Right," Reese said. "So he just came out with that demand?"

"He sounded like it was his right to come back here." Garret shrugged his thick shoulders. "Someone should tell that dude he needs to get socialized and vaccinated first. Either that or he can wear a permanent muzzle around his mouth so he stops biting and infecting everyone."

Noah grinned but quickly wiped it off his face as he looked over at Shay.

Harper cursed softly beneath his breath. "Shay, you don't need this right now."

Garret twisted a look across his shoulder at Shay. "Yeah, you're going to get married to a stand-up man. We want to see you happy. Not having to deal with your old man's shit."

Shay tried to gather her shattered emotions. She glanced at Reese, whose expression had gone into that warrior-mask mode, hard to read, and his mouth was tight. A flash of anger glinted in his narrowed eyes as he listened to what the other vets thought. Swallowing, she whispered unsteadily, "That fourth house was empty, and he knew it because I told him Friday that we are going to get married, Reese. He knew you'd be living here, in the main ranch house."

Reese puckered his lips, holding back a lot of emotions. "This is your call, Shay," he told her. "No one can do this for you."

She gave him a pained look. "I-I . . . God, Reese, when I first got home, I begged my father to come out here as soon as he went through rehab and got better."

"But he refused that," Garret reminded her darkly.

"Yes, he did." Moving her fingers through her loose hair, Shay closed her eyes, struggling to contain her guilt. How could she turn down her own father? Not allow him to come out to the ranch that he'd worked so hard to keep going? Although his drinking and gambling had brought the ranch down, too.

"If he came here," Reese told her quietly, "there would be some very firm rules in place. If he thinks he's coming back to reclaim this ranch, he can't. Legally, it's yours."

"Legal is one thing, but he's my father, Reese."

Nodding, Reese said, "I understand. And I'm fine with whatever way you want to go on this. If you do decide to allow him out here, there's a lot of things to consider. How mobile will he be? What are his needs? Can he cook for himself? Take care of himself? Can he keep his own house clean?"

"I know," she said, frowning. "That was why I told him no when he wanted to come and have me take care of him full time. I said I couldn't. I wanted to try to save the ranch, instead."

Reese squeezed her hand. "I think the first step is for both of us to go in, sit down, and talk with him. We need to understand what's really on his mind, what his expectations are of you, of us, and your ranch."

She dragged in a breath of air, grateful for his warm, calloused hand around hers. Reese gave her stability and that overriding sense of protection that she could literally feel around her right now. He was in guard-dog mode. And so were the other three vets. Reading their faces, none of them wanted Ray Crawford at the ranch. And she knew why. He'd bad-mouthed them, cursed them, called them weak, and accused them of so many untrue things. Word got around town, and Ray made no bones about telling the nurses and supervisor at the nursing home what he thought of her hiring vets who needed a hand up. What was she going to do?

Noah gave Shay a sad look. "Your father is sort of like a wounded dog. He's hurt, and you're not about to ignore that."

"You're right, Noah."

"But this dog bites," Reese grimly reminded them. His voice grew firm. "And under no circumstance will he come back here thinking he can either savage you or any of these men. I know you wouldn't allow it, Shay. And I'll back you up on that if Ray thinks he can do it and get away with it, because he can't."

His words were spoken with quiet authority, but Shay could feel the absolute power, the protectiveness, Reese was giving to all of them. She knew he was stronger than the other vets right now. He might have been down, but that officer/leader side to him had not been wounded. It was strong and worked just fine. Shay looked at the vets.

"Here's my promise to all of you," she said, her voice filled with resolve. "I need to see what my father wants. I need to hear him out. But he will not be allowed back on this ranch if he's going to continue acting as he has in the past. No one deserves to be abused, and my father, unfortunately, has made it into an art form. I love all of you and I want you to stay here and continue to heal and get strong. No one's leaving this ranch. And I won't let my father come back if he thinks he can destroy the vision I've had for this ranch, for all of you, and those who will come here seeking help and healing from us in the future."

Reese looked around, seeing the relief in the men's faces. Shay was right to let them know where she stood. He was so damned proud of her. It seemed when things went to hell in a handbasket, she was the staunchest, most reliable warrior in the thick of any battle. And this was one helluva battle coming up. Reese didn't try to kid himself about it.

"Look," Garret said, giving her a stern look and waving his spatula in her direction, "you have more happy things to think about. You just got engaged to this hombre. You have a wedding to plan. I'll bet a wedding dress to buy. Choosing the flowers you want for your bouquet. This is supposed to be your happy time."

Shay shook herself internally. Garret was right. "Well, one thing for sure," she told the vets, "you are all invited to the wedding." She traded a smile with Reese. "Want to tell them?"

Reese moved his shoulders, as if to rid them of the tension he was carrying. "Sure. Shay and I both agree that Garret, I'd like you to be my best man. And Noah and Harper, you'll be right behind him."

The vets hooted and grinned broadly, pride in their expressions.

Shay's heart spun with joy. She saw their eyes light up with happiness. They so desperately needed good news of any kind. Garret was preening. She knew he and Reese had grown close over the months. They reminded her of long lost brothers who had discovered one another after much time apart. "Hey, guys," she said, raising her voice above the laughter, "that means you have to wear a business suit. This is a dress-up wedding. And Garret? You have to wear a tux."

The room broke into guffaws, brutal teasing, and hooting.

Garret took it in stride, grinning like a wily wolf. "Then, I'll be almost as good-lookin' as that dude you're gonna marry. Maybe some beautiful single woman will see me and swoon?"

More hoots, jeers, hollers, and teasing.

Holding up her hands, Shay laughed. "Garret, I can

guarantee we're going to rent a tux for you, but we have nothing to do with how the ladies respond to you. Okay?"

For the next ten minutes, the kitchen was warm with friendship, shared happiness, and smiles. Shay watched Reese begin to relax. She loved these vets so much. They were the salt of the earth, working so hard, consistently, caring for what she cared about on this ranch. Yes, their wedding was going to be a highlight for all of them.

As she glanced over at Reese, she felt him pondering the problem regarding her father. She knew his mind well enough by now that she was aware he was not leaving one stone unturned. He was a man who studied details with critical analysis and delved far deeper than most people into the whys and what-fors of a situation, and that reassured her. Reese would not let her make a foolish mistake based upon guilt, because that is what her father used to manipulate her all her life. And her husband-to-be was well aware of the toxic pattern she had with Ray.

A little of the worry and shock dissolved as the men kidded and teased one another over the coming wedding, the bachelor party, and what they were going to do to Reese as part of that ancient celebration. These men were military vets; they played as hard as they worked. And judging from the expressions on their faces, they were enjoying the daylights out of it. It made Shay feel good despite the shocking news.

The rain on the roof sounded wonderful to Shay as she lay in Reese's arms, their naked bodies resting warmly against one another. Her lower body hummed with satisfaction, the rippling effect of orgasms still making her glow. Reese knew how to love her, what she enjoyed, and continued to show her more of what a man could do to please his woman. She moved her fingers through the damp hair across his chest, eyes closed, never happier than right now. His arm was curved around her shoulders, fingers draped over her shoulder, softly stroking her upper arm, sending delightful tingles through her. His leg was over hers, his other hand on her hip, keeping her as close to him as possible.

"This is the happiest day I can ever remember," she murmured against his chest, placing a kiss upon it. "You give me so much, Reese . . . so much . . ."

Reese smiled a little, nuzzling his jaw against her mussed hair. "You give equally to me, Shay. It's a two-way street."

"Well"—she laughed a little—"I'm not going to try to weigh, measure, or compare."

"Good," he grumbled with a smile. "Because I'm not keeping a list. A good relationship means a couple gives and takes. Sometimes it's more one way than the other, but in the end, it all evens out."

"I can't believe we're going to get married. I look at the last four-plus months and it's gone so fast. So much has happened."

"It has been a whirlwind," he agreed. "For both of us."

She eased away, looking into his half-opened eyes, seeing gratification in his darkened gaze. "I'm glad you called my father after supper and told him we'd drop by tomorrow to talk with him. Thank you."

"You don't have to deal with him by yourself ever again, Shay." He lifted his hand, smoothing down across her hair, searching her eyes. "No one protected you growing up. Well, that's over. You've got me now."

Nodding, she leaned upward, claiming the hard line of his mouth, feeling him in that guard-dog mode once more. Shay knew he didn't trust her father or his reasons for wanting to move out to the ranch. She didn't know what to think, strung between the past, as a child who had been thoroughly brainwashed and threatened, and the woman she was today.

Tasting Reese's mouth, feeling his lips soften beneath hers, his hand moving in a cherishing motion down the length of her back, she felt a sense of safety she'd never had before. Leaving his mouth, she whispered, "I love you, Reese Lockhart. I love your name, the fact that it contains the word 'heart' in it. You're all heart. You have been since I met you."

He gave her a slight smile, moving his thumb across her cheek. "I love you, Shay. We're two hearts who met and became one," he agreed in a roughened tone. "I like that we see through the eyes of our heart." He eased Shay up on top of him, their hips melding hotly against one another. He liked the way she flowed across his body, a warm, living blanket inciting him to want her all over again.

"Sometimes, that's easier than getting caught in the snare of our minds. It's a matrix of its own."

She smiled, resting her palms on his upper chest and then settling her chin against them, closing her eyes, absorbing his light, feathery touch across her back and hips. "Right now? I'm going to concentrate on us, Reese. Our wedding. Whatever is going on with my father? He's going to have to realize that his request will be dealt with after our wedding. I don't want to deal with it at the same time."

"My thoughts exactly. We'll listen to what he has to say, tell him we'll talk it over, and let him know our answer after our honeymoon."

"Honeymoon?" Frowning, Shay opened her eyes, peering up at him. "What honeymoon? We don't have money for that, Reese. I know we don't. And I'm fine that we don't have one."

Hearing the sudden stridency in her tone, he framed her face with his hands. "Maud."

Her brows moved up. "What do you know that I don't?"

"It's a gift," he admitted.

She pulled out of his hands and propped herself up on his chest. "Reese Lockhart, don't you keep secrets from me! What did Maud do?" She saw ruddiness come to his cheeks. *Serves him right for keeping a secret.* Grinning, she tugged gently on his short hair. "Come on. Out with it. No secrets ever between us. If she told you, then you have to tell me."

Reese gave a low chuckle. "Okay, you're right. But in all fairness to Maud, we bumped into one another at Charlie Becker's the other day. She'd already helped me choose the wedding rings for you and asked me where we were going on our honeymoon. I told her nowhere." His grin broadened as he held Shay's gaze. "I thought she was going to stroke out right there. Poor Charlie, he said he'd never seen her that upset in a long time. We finally got her settled down. Charlie brought her a glass of water and we just chatted."

"About what?"

"You," Reese said, running his fingers over her hair. "Maud wanted to know where you dreamed of traveling. I told her how you loved Hawaii." He saw Shay's eyes widen. "As a wedding gift, she's going to give us an envelope that contains reservations for a five-star resort on Kauai, near Princeville, and two first-class airline tickets, roundtrip, to Hawaii for seven days."

A gasp tore out of Shay. "No! Really?"

A chuckle rumbled through his chest. "Really."

"Oh, my God! That's—that's incredible, Reese!"

"Don't you dare let on that I told you," he said. "Maud had wanted it to be a surprise for you, and you'd better look surprised in order to save my hide."

She gave a giddy laugh. "Oh, don't worry! I'll be as shocked as I am right now. I'm just glad you told me."

She sighed, her hand on his shoulder. "She's such a fairy godmother to so many in this valley."

Reese shrugged. "I think if I were in her shoes, at her age, with the money she has, I'd be doing pretty much the same thing. You can't take it with you. Might as well ease the burdens of so many others who are struggling daily to make ends meet."

"This is just mind-blowing," Shay whispered, touching her brow. "I mean . . . all my life . . . as a little kid, I used to go through the computer and google Hawaii, look at the pictures and dream. I dreamed so much about it!"

"Well, a dream came true, then." Reese smiled warmly.

Shay sobered immediately. She got on her knees and leaned over Reese, cupping his jaw, kissing him passionately. When she finally ended the long, hot kiss, she whispered unsteadily, her eyes growing moist, "No . . . *you* are my dream come true, Reese Lockhart. Just you . . ."

If you enjoyed WIND RIVER RANCHER,
be sure not to miss
Garret's romance
in

WIND RIVER COWBOY

by
Lindsay McKenna,
coming to readers in
April 2017!

Turn the page for a special sneak peek!

"Do you have any questions about what I just covered with you, Kira?"

Kira felt enveloped by the warmth and care of Shay Lockhart as they sat in the kitchen of the Bar C's main ranch house. She'd arrived shortly after lunch, and had met two of the military vets, Noah and Harper.

Shay had fixed her a late lunch, introducing her to her husband, Reese Lockhart, who went down the hall to his office afterward. That left Kira with Shay to go over the employment opportunity. "No questions. You've covered everything pretty well."

Shay smiled and said, "Are you interested in taking the job?"

"Absolutely." Kira's hope had climbed in the last two hours as Shay had outlined her job responsibilities. Earlier, they had bundled up in their coats on the cold but clear day, and Shay had taken her around the main buildings on the Bar C. Kira was impressed with what the vets had done to start the repairs on the broken-down ranch. They were slowly fixing, building, and bringing it back to life. Shay's father, Ray Crawford, had met her and shaken her hand. He was nothing like her father, but she felt she could certainly do weekly housecleaning and make him his meals. Shay was more than fair about financial compensation and Kira wanted to work for someone like her.

"Okay, then the only other thing left to do is assign you to a house," Shay said with a smile. She took a pen and wrote HOUSE A on the file.

Kira knew there were four new two-bedroom homes built on the ranch property not far from the main house. Shay assigned each vet a home. The fourth house was for Ray Crawford. Shay had designed the homes to hold two vets each. She had told Kira that she wanted to eventually hire a total of six wranglers, all military veterans. They would each put down small monthly payments to own it with or without the second vet who lived in it at the time. All the vets liked the idea and could afford the payment, thanks to her generosity. Kira would be wrangler number four, and the first woman vet.

"Okay," Kira said.

Shay frowned and looked across the trestle table at her. "Are you sure you're okay living with a strange guy underfoot?"

Kira smiled a little. "He's a military vet. I don't think I'll have an issue with him, Shay."

"Well, not everyone gets along with one another," she said. "I'm assigning you to Garret's house because he's been here the longest with us. In fact, he was the first vet I hired. I feel he can show you the ropes, be kind of a mentor in some ways, introduce you to the ranch rhythm and the duties around here. He's a good go-to guy and is very helpful. But if you feel it's not working, Kira? Just tell me and I'll move you to another house."

"Thanks, that's good to know. He's got PTSD, right?"

"Oh, yes. It's pretty bad." Shay shrugged. "But then,

what PTSD isn't bad? He has nightmares, insomnia, and anxiety just like the rest of us do."

"I'll fit right in." She found herself more than a little curious. "You said his name was Garret?"

"Yes. Why?"

The front door to the ranch house opened and closed. Both women stopped and looked toward the entrance.

"Oh," Shay said, "that's Garret coming back. He was up in Jackson Hole for the last couple weeks. He's in construction and he had projects for two ranches down there. Jackson Hole is fifty miles north of here, so he stayed in bunkhouses on those ranches. It snows a lot and he didn't want to risk driving on icy roads."

Nodding, Kira heard the vet stomping snow off his boots in the mudroom, then the sound of him coming down the hall toward the kitchen. "Makes good sense."

Shay smiled. "Well, you'll get to meet him in a few moments. He had to see Reese once he drove back from the work assignment. He'll be coming by the kitchen here any second and I'll introduce you to him."

Kira nodded. "Are you sure he won't mind a woman in his house?" Her mind snapped back to another Garret Fleming she knew for three years. The man she'd fallen helplessly and completely in love with, who had been part of her A team. Kira wasn't even sure Garret had loved her. He'd always treated her like his sister. But she had secretly fallen in love with him. Utterly. Rubbing the red sweater she wore, Kira felt her heart ache without relief. She'd never known what happened to him. Where was he now? How he was doing? That part of her life was a black hole.

"Garret is easygoing," Shay reassured her. "All the vets know that sooner or later they'll get another military vet living in the same house with them. And they're okay with it."

Kira heard the echo of heavy boots meeting the cedar hardwood floor out in the hall. "What military branch was he in?"

Shay was about to answer when Garret came around the corner, his black Stetson in his hand.

Kira froze. Her eyes widened as Garret Fleming stood in the doorway, staring at them. Her heart crashed in her chest. His hazel eyes moved to her and stopped. And then, he blinked slowly as he stared at her sitting at the table.

Shay felt a palpable shift of energy in the room, as if a bolt of lightning had suddenly slammed into it. Confused, she looked at Garret and then at Kira.

"Kira?"

Garret's low, deep voice, filled with disbelief, plunged through Kira's heart. Her lips parted as she wrestled with the shock bolting through her. "Garret?"

"Yeah," he rumbled, scowling. "What are you doing here?"

Kira gulped. "I—uh—" She choked, unable to speak, her hands against her heart as she stared up at his tall, powerful form. Garret Fleming was six foot two inches tall, two-hundred and twenty pounds of pure, rock hard male muscle. He no longer wore a beard, which all Special Forces men in the teams did when in a Muslim country. His face was shaved clean and she saw how ruggedly handsome he really was. A beard hid so much of a man's face. Her heart stuttered and she felt swept away on the giddy joy that overwhelmed her. Garret had a square face, large, wide-spaced intelligent eyes that glittered with green, brown, and gold colors as he stared in disbelief at her. She wanted to get up and hurl herself into his arms. To kiss him. To celebrate he was alive! To Kira, he looked so strong and healthy, his face darkly tanned, exuding the vitality she knew when she was in the team with him.

"What's going on here?" Shay asked, puzzled.

Garret shook his head and gave Shay a wry look. "Kira was a member in our Special Forces A team for three years."

"Oh," Shay whispered, her hand flying to her lips, her eyes suddenly huge as she stared over at Kira.

Kira managed a jerky nod, her gaze never leaving Garret's. "Y-you're okay? I tried to find you, Garret, but I never could . . ." Her voice died into an aching whisper of regret. She saw his eyes grow stormy, that well-shaped mouth of his thinning as he regarded her.

"It's okay," he rumbled. Pointing at his left temple, he said gruffly, "I had amnesia for six months after I was flown to Bethesda. I didn't even know my own name until my memory came back on its own, Kira." He gave her an apologetic look. "I tried to find you, but I never did. I'm sorry, too . . ."

His low, emotional explanation filtered through her shock. A lump formed in her throat and she couldn't speak for a moment. So much had happened to them that night during the ambush. "I-I understand," she said hoarsely. "You were shot in the head. I-I remember . . ." Kira remembered everything. Her weekly nightmares guaranteed that. She saw Garret's face crumple with pain for a moment before he put on his game face.

"Oh, my God," Shay said, looking at first one and then the other, "you worked together? You were on the same A team?"

"Yeah," Garret said, moving his shoulders as if to get rid of the tension. "Black ops, Shay. Top secret."

Shay stared at Kira. "I didn't know you knew Garret."

Kira managed an abject look at Shay. "I didn't know he was here. I lost track of him." She waved her hand in a helpless gesture. "We were both wounded in a firefight.

I was sent to Bethesda after being at Landstuhl, Germany, and I lost track of him." Swallowing hard, Kira held Garret's unfathomable look. She could feel the bombshell reaction around him, but it didn't transfer to his face, which remained unreadable. She honestly didn't know if he was glad to see her or not. A year had passed since they'd last been with one another. A year that felt like a lifetime of pain and anguish to her without his larger-than-life presence in it. Now, he was standing six feet away from her, incredibly handsome, confident, and the same man she knew from the team. His face had deeper lines around his mouth, not surprising given the terrible circumstances they'd barely survived. It told Kira of the suffering he'd undergone, too.

Reese Lockhart ambled out of his office and down the hall. He stopped at the kitchen entrance, nodding hello to Garret. "What's going on?" he asked his wife.

Shay quickly filled him in.

Reese gave Garret a long look and then his gaze drifted to Kira. "Looks like you two have a lot of catching up to do with one another, then," he said. "Kira, are you okay still being assigned to Garret's house? Or would you rather not be?"

Kira looked to Garret. He looked surprised as hell. But then, she saw an emotion in his eyes, a flash for a second that she couldn't translate. "Well . . . I don't know. It's up to Garret—"

"It's fine," Garret told them in no uncertain terms. "Kira is welcome to stay with me."

Relief poured through Kira. For a brief moment, she saw a thaw in Garret's hazel eyes. Her heart squeezed with powerful emotions and she felt suffused by joy.

They'd always been friends, as she was with all the men of the A team. Nothing more. And she'd held secret her love for this man who was so heroic, a warrior, and a good person, who had helped so many in those three years they'd worked together. It was still her secret. Even now. Probably forever. Some of Kira's joy dissolved. They had never talked personally about how they felt toward one another. Always friends. Never anything more intimate.

Reese touched Garret's broad shoulder. "You got the paperwork from those two jobs?"

"Yeah," he said, rummaging around in the pocket of his sheepskin coat. Garret handed them to Reese.

"Great," Reese said. "Let's get business out of the way and then you can take Kira home with you."

Giving a nod, Garret said, "Sounds good." And then he looked at Kira. "This won't take long. I'll be right back."

Kira didn't know whether to laugh or cry. She so badly wanted to hug the hell out of Garret, to welcome him back into her life. Shay was watching her with some confusion and she offered, "We were on an A team in Afghanistan for three years."

"I know Special Forces teams try to stay together for long periods." Shay searched her eyes. "But you're a woman. I didn't know they had women in A teams."

"It was a top secret operation," Kira hedged. She could not speak to anyone about it. Not ever. Garret knew because he, like the other eleven men on the team, had signed legal documents swearing to never speak of it in detail to anyone. Shay sat back, digesting the information.

"Okay," she said, "but is this going to be a stress or pressure on either of you? It looks like you lost track of one another?"

"Yes, we did. I didn't know he had amnesia. It would explain why he never tried to contact me," Kira said quietly. She clasped her damp, cool fingers in her lap beneath the table, all her emotions in play. For the last year she thought

Garret had chosen to remain out of her life. Now . . . she knew differently.

"You tried to locate him afterward?"

"Yes." Kira held on to tears that burned in the back of her eyes. She closed them, taking in a ragged breath. "Our team was so tight, Shay. We were family . . ."

"Garret only told us once, during a therapy session, that of the twelve men in his team, only two survived." Shay gave her an anguished look. "That's so tragic."

It hurt to breathe at that moment because it brought everything back to Kira. Avoiding Shay's compassionate look, she whispered brokenly, "Y-yes, all of the other guys . . . dead. It was—horrible—awful . . ."

"Garret never said the other survivor was a woman."

"He couldn't. Legally, Shay, I was part of a top secret operation. It couldn't be talked about. Not even here, not even with other military vets."

"God," Shay whispered, her hand against her throat, grief in her expression, "that had to be so terrible for both of you . . . to lose so many friends all at once that you'd known for so long."

Kira wrestled with all her grief, her loss. "It lives in me every day, Shay. Three years of my life were with those guys. Every one of them was a stand-up man. They were good men who did good things for the people of the village we lived in." She compressed her lips, hanging her head and closing her eyes, trying not to cry. Shay was so kind and caring that it made it easy for Kira to talk with her, to allow her feelings to surface. General Ward had been right: Shay Lockhart was a true, maternal, loving type of woman. And it was something she'd missed so much, no longer having her own mother in her life. At the same time, Kira knew her top secret life in the Army had to remain as such.

"Listen," Shay said softly, "I'm here for you, Kira. I

understand what top secret means, but it doesn't stop you from talking to me about your feelings. We all need someone to lean on when trauma happens in our lives. If you ever want to unload, come and see me."

Warmth cascaded through Kira as she lifted her head and met Shay's kind blue gaze. "Yes, maybe in time. I need to prove my worth around here, first."

"I'm sure you will. I'm here for you, Kira. Just remember that. Okay?"

Kira heard men's voices drifting down the hall, honing in on Garret's deep voice. She heard laughter between the men and then the heavy, thunking sound of Garret's boots striking the cedar floor, coming in their direction. Her stomach knotted. Her heart started a slow pound, adrenaline leaking into her bloodstream. What was she going to say to Garret once they were alone? What was he going to say to her? Or do? Her mouth became dry and Kira seesawed between heaven and hell. She felt so tentative, so unsure about Garret. How did he feel about her? She honestly didn't know except that he was always her friend on the team. But so was every other man.

Garret pulled a hard rein in on his emotions. He'd been Special Forces for a long time and knew that emotions, when uncontrolled, could lead to people getting killed. As he drove Kira in the truck over to the house, he felt trapped. He had nowhere to run and hide from the past, now. He'd fallen hopelessly in love with Kira from almost the moment she joined their team, and suppressed it, not allowing it to surface.

Now, he felt gut-punched. Kira was a brutal reminder of his past and that firefight that he'd buried so damn deep within himself. He'd struggled to make sure it never surfaced again. Now, with her beside him, going to be a part of his life twenty-four hours a day, he felt scared and unsure. Garret was shocked by how she looked. Kira used to be strong, vibrant, and darkly tanned. Her smile had been constant, her teasing not hurtful, but infectious. The children of the village adored her and called her "mother" in Pashtun. She was a hard worker, a team person, someone every man could count on. He'd helplessly fallen in love. And he thought he'd lost her. But she was sitting beside him. *Right now.* The violent need for her, to pull her into his arms, crush her against him, feel her woman's body and heat, savagely tore through Garret. He was wrestling with the fear of the past rising up to overwhelm him, along with his powerful yearning to hold, kiss, and love Kira until they melted into one another. What the hell was he going to do?

His mouth thinned as he drove slowly around the ranch house and down the newly created road that passed in front of all four houses, which sat about fifty feet apart from one another. Snow glittered like diamonds across the covered tops of the dark green, steeply sloped metal roofs. Already, last night's snowfall had slid off the roof, keeping the excessive weight from putting stress on the structure. His gloved hands opened and closed around the wheel as he tried to figure out how to handle this situation. What had led him to say it was all right that Kira could live under his roof? What the hell was wrong with him? She'd be a raw, constant reminder of everything he didn't want to remember or feel.

What kind of sick, twisted life was he living since nearly dying? Chaos seemed to be part and parcel of Garret's days since he awoke in Bethesda not even knowing his name. It took six months before everything suddenly downloaded and he had his complete memory back. Some of it, he wished fervently, hadn't returned. The deaths of his ten friends haunted him without relief.

Pulling up to the house, the snow on the ground, the bright winter sunlight glancing off the western side of the sprawling ranch house, Garret said gruffly, "Here's your new home, Kira. Let's go in."

He tried not to be affected by her thinness. Or the dark smudges beneath her glorious gray eyes that used to sparkle like soft diamonds when she was laughing. An ache settled deep in his heart as Garret walked to the cleared concrete sidewalk sprinkled with salt pellets, and took the four steps to the back porch. Opening the door, he gestured for her to go in first. The Kira he knew had been open, vulnerable, easily touched, and accessible in the team. Now, as she moved past him like a ghost from his lost past, he saw how closed up she'd become. PTSD did that to a person. It had done it to him. Noah and Harper were the same.

Mouth compressed, Garret hungrily watched her move onto the mud porch and stomp her boots to get the snow off them. Feeling like a starved wolf, he wanted her all over again. There wasn't a day that went by in Afghanistan when he hadn't hungered to take her, bury himself in her hot depths and share her returning fire and need. He looked at her long, thin hands that were so graceful it made his lower body suddenly throb. How many hundreds of times had Garret dreamed of those hands roaming his body? Exploring him, learning what made him feel good. Imagining what it would feel like as she glided her fingertips across his hardened flesh.

Groaning inwardly, he went inside and closed the door. He'd never let Kira know of his personal desire for her. It would have destroyed the team in so many bad ways, so he'd stuffed it. Just as he'd buried his horror over that firefight.

Out of sight, out of mind. Now, Kira was here and Garret could no longer forget any of it. Or his feelings for her.

Kira stood, hands shoved in the pockets of her parka to warm them, studying Garret. He saw sadness and grief in her expression and it kicked him in the gut. Dammit, he'd spent six months violently shoving down all his emotions since remembering that deadly ambush. There was no way he wanted to connect with any of those feelings. He tried not to remember any of his friends. Their laughter. Their personalities. Their wives . . . their children who he knew like his own family. His heart felt like it had a deep, unending ache within it and it was getting more painful by the moment. Scowling, he wanted to blame Kira for bringing up all the shit he had so desperately tried to avoid.

Garret strode past her and opened the door that led directly into the kitchen. He hated that she gave him that look of vulnerability, as if seeking his protection against something. What? Him? He knew he was growly and irritable. PTSD at work.

Kira looked down, hands jammed deep in her coat pockets, and slipped by him like a wraith. He could smell her feminine scent along with cold, clean winter air. It was like breathing life into his dead body; he couldn't get enough of her, wanting desperately to grip her shoulder, turn her around, and yank her into his arms. That's what she needed, Garret realized. Kira felt stripped and naked thanks to her PTSD, he would bet anything. The look in her eyes wasn't something he'd ever seen before. Once, she'd been such a strong, confident, outgoing young woman. Full of life. Vibrant. Full of promise.

And he'd never stopped loving her.

Garret took off his Stetson and dropped it on a wooden peg next to the kitchen door. He turned, seeing that Kira had stopped near the granite island in the middle of the large, bright kitchen. She was so damned pale. In Afghanistan, she was deeply tanned, her black hair short, blue highlights dancing through those thick, silky strands.

Kira had never worn makeup of any kind in the Army. The odor of the cosmetic products would, first of all, alert the enemy they were nearby if on a mission or patrol. Hell, she didn't need anything, her black lashes long and thick, a frame for those incredible dove-gray eyes that were truly a window into her soul, to her many emotions.

She could never hide anything from him. She cried when a newborn baby had died. She held the mother, who rocked the dead infant in her arms, crying with her. Kira was so easily touched. Now Garret could feel the wall around her. Trying to keep whatever she was feeling within those walls and keep the rest of the world out. That's how he felt every day with PTSD. It was an endless, tiring, and wearing exercise. And he could see how worn down she had become.

His heart twinged. "Come on," he said, softening his gruff tone, gesturing for her to follow him, "I'll show you your bedroom."

Walking down the oak hall, their boots echoing, Garret pushed open a door on the right, swinging it wide. He stepped aside and said, "This is yours . . ."

Kira hesitated. "Where is your room, Garret?"

Lifting his thumb across his shoulder he said, "Right across the hall." He saw her wrinkle her nose, her gray eyes darken. "Why?"

Giving him a shy look, unable to hold his penetrating stare, she whispered, "Sometimes . . . sometimes I wake up screaming at night." She pushed strands of her hair off her brow in a nervous gesture. "My own screams wake me. They woke my father every time. That's why I had to leave his house. I kept waking him up." Her lips quirked. "I don't want to wake you . . ."

Garret forced his hands to remain on his hips. He was a tall, broad man, filling up the hallway. Kira was half his size and looking so damned vulnerable. He wanted to slide his hand across her wan cheek, cup it, lean down and kiss her tenderly to reassure her that everything would be all right. Garret knew better. There was nothing right with either of them anymore. They were twisted, wounded, distorted human beings trying to act and behave normally when normal had been destroyed in that ambush a year ago.

He cleared his throat and rasped, "Don't worry about it. I do my fair share of screaming in nightmares, too. Let's look at the positive side of it. We can start a symphony." His teasing eased the tight line of her lips. She studied him, her soft eyes widening as she searched his face.

His heart beating to underscore the ache now centering in his lower body, Garret cursed to himself. He had no damned defense against Kira, he realized sharply. It unstrung him for a second. And then, Garret realized the awful truth of Kira: she was already facing the demons within her from that ambush. He saw it reflected in her sad-looking eyes, the soft parting of her lips that tempted him as nothing else ever had. Kira was not hiding from what happened.

That terrified Garret more than anything else. He had successfully hidden from his grief and pain for six months. What the *hell* was he going to do now?